Madness in Post-1945 British and
American Fiction

Madness in Post-1945 British and American Fiction

By

Charley Baker, Paul Crawford, B. J. Brown,
Maurice Lipsedge and Ronald Carter

First published 2010 by
PALGRAVE MACMILLAN

Palgrave Macmillan in the UK is an imprint of Macmillan Publishers Limited, registered in England, company number 785998, of Houndmills, Basingstoke, Hampshire RG21 6XS.

Palgrave Macmillan in the US is a division of St Martin's Press LLC, 175 Fifth Avenue, New York, NY 10010.

Palgrave Macmillan is the global academic imprint of the above companies and has companies and representatives throughout the world.

Palgrave® and Macmillan® are registered trademarks in the United States, the United Kingdom, Europe and other countries.

ISBN: 978-0-230-21975-5 hardback

This book is printed on paper suitable for recycling and made from fully managed and sustained forest sources. Logging, pulping and manufacturing processes are expected to conform to the environmental regulations of the country of origin.

A catalogue record for this book is available from the British Library.

Library of Congress Cataloging-in-Publication Data

Madness in post-1945 British and American fiction / Charley Baker... [et al.].
    p. cm.
Includes bibliographical references and index.
ISBN 978-0-230-21975-5
    1. English fiction – 20th century – History and criticism. 2. American fiction – 20th century – History and criticism. 3. Mental illness in literature. I. Baker, Charley, 1981–

PR830.M46.B735 2010
823'.91409—dc22   2010023747

10 9 8 7 6 5 4 3 2 1
19 18 17 16 15 14 13 12 11 10

Transferred to Digital Printing in 2014

For Dr Spilios Argyropoulos who has nurtured my passion for madness, helped to shape my views and supported my academic work at all stages of my career. A sincere and lasting thank you. CB

Contents

Acknowledgements   viii

Author Biographies   ix

1. Writing Madness, Analysing Madness   1

2. Mental States   18

3. Power and Institutions in Fiction   61

4. Diversity, Ethnicity, Madness and Fiction   99

5. Creativity, Madness and Fiction   130

6. Postmodern Madness   159

7. Literature and Clinical Education   184

Notes   195

Bibliography   196

Index   211

Acknowledgements

We gratefully acknowledge funding from the Leverhulme Trust for the project 'The representation of madness in postwar British and American fiction' that has enabled the writing of this book. Grant number: F/00 114/AN.

We would also like to acknowledge the Arts and Humanities Research Council for funding the development of the international Madness and Literature Network (www.madnessandliterature.org), a second project that has been developed from the Leverhulme project research, and that has helped to inform this book. Grant number: AH/G009686/1.

We would like to acknowledge and thank Jamie Orion Crawford for his work on designing the cover for this book. The jacket illustration reproduces 'Woman in Anguish' by Paul Crawford © 2005.

Charley Baker would like to thank her parents, husband Simon, family and friends for supporting her while she was writing this book, and for getting her to a stage in her career where she could. She would also like to extend warm thanks to her PhD supervisor, Professor Robert Eaglestone. She thanks Paul Crawford, Ronald Carter, Maurice Lipsdege and B. J. Brown for guiding her through the process of constructing a co-authored book, and for creating the madness and literature projects. Finally, she would like to personally thank the Leverhulme Trust for the generous funding they provided, which has enabled her to enjoy her first academic appointment.

Paul Crawford would like to thank Lisa Mooney-Smith, Paula Gurteen, Rosamund Aubrey, Laura Pearson and Phaedra Stentiford for all of their support.

Author Biographies

Charley Baker is a Research Associate at the University of Nottingham, working on a Leverhulme Trust funded project examining representations of madness in postwar UK and US fiction. She is also co-founder of the Arts and Humanities Research Council funded international Madness and Literature Network (www.madnessandliterature.org). She has a BA and MA in literature from Goldsmiths College, University of London, and is working towards the completion of her PhD in postmodern fiction and psychosis at Royal Holloway, University of London. Baker has worked for the NHS in both adult and adolescent mental health, providing her with direct clinical insight and knowledge that has shaped her literary interpretations. She has spoken and taught on representations of mental illness in literature, and also has research interests in trauma, self harm and suicide – both clinically and as represented in literature and culture. She was invited contributor and literary advisor for a psychiatry textbook, *Psychiatry PRN* (Oxford University Press 2009), has a chapter on rape in Angela Carter's fiction in the forthcoming volume *Ethics and Trauma in Contemporary British Fiction* (ed. Susana Onega and Jean-Michel Ganteau), and reviews regularly for journals such as *Journal of Psychiatric and Mental Health Nursing* and *Mental Health Practice*. She has also published on the use of literature in clinical education, and the representation of self harm and borderline personality disorder in fiction. Baker was made Fellow of the Institute of Mental Health in 2009. This is her first co-authored book.

B. J. Brown has written widely on social theory, health care and communication. Most notably his books have included *Evidence Based Health Communication* (with P. Crawford and R. Carter, Open University Press, 2006) and *Evidence Based Research: Dilemmas and Debates in Heath Care* (with P. Crawford and C. Hicks, Buckingham: Open University Press, 2003). The core of his work has focused on the interpretation of experiences in health care, exploring how this may be understood with a view to improving practice and with regard to theoretical development in the social sciences, particularly concerning notions of governmentality and habitus from Foucauldian and Bourdieusian sociology respectively. He is fascinated by the way in which the analysis of everyday experience can afford novel theoretical developments. He completed a BSc. in

Psychology at Aston University in 1983 and a PhD on communication at Leicester University in 1989.

Ronald Carter is Professor of Modern English Language at the University of Nottingham. He has written and edited more than 50 books and has published over 100 academic papers in the fields of literary-linguistics, language and education, applied linguistics and the teaching of English. He has taught, lectured and given consultancies to government agencies and ministries in the field of language education, mainly in conjunction with the British Council, in over thirty countries worldwide. In the UK, he has worked as linguistic advisor to the UK Ministry of Education and to QCA on English in the National Curriculum and the Adult ESOL Core Curriculum. Recent books include: *The Cambridge Guide to Teaching English to Speakers of Other Languages* (CUP) *Language and Creativity: The Art of Common Talk* (Routledge), *From Corpus to Classroom* (CUP), *The Language and Literature Reader,* (Routledge) and *Cambridge Grammar of English: A Comprehensive Guide to Spoken and Written Grammar and Usage* (with Michael McCarthy) (CUP) which won the 2007 British Council International English Language Innovation Award. Professor Carter is a fellow of the Royal Society of Arts, a fellow of the British Academy for Social Sciences and was chair of the British Association for Applied Linguistics (2003–2006).

Paul Crawford is Professor of Health Humanities at the University of Nottingham. He is a fellow of the Royal Society of Arts, Professor of the Institute of Mental Health, and Visiting Professor of Health Communication at both the Medical Faculty, National Cheng Kung University, Taiwan, and the Centre for Health Communication, University of Technology, Sydney, Australia. Crawford leads the Health Humanities programme and is Co-Founder and chair of the Health Language Research Group at the University of Nottingham. He is also Principal Investigator for both the Leverhulme funded project examining representations of madness in postwar UK and US fiction and the AHRC funded international Madness and Literature Network. Crawford has held grants from prestigious Research Councils and charitable organisations and written over 60 peer reviewed papers or chapters and 8 books. His major critical work, *Politics and History in William Golding* (2003) led to reprinted chapters in *Bloom's Guide to Lord of the Flies* (2004; 2008) and a commissioned entry on Golding in *The Oxford Encyclopaedia of British Literature* (Oxford University Press, 2006). The British film producer, Jack Emery (The Drama House, London / Florida), has optioned his acclaimed novel about mental illness, *Nothing Purple,*

Nothing Black. His second novel, *Hair of the Dog*, is represented by Bell, Lomax & Moreton, London. In 2008 he was awarded a Lord Dearing Award for Excellence in Teaching and Learning.

Maurice Lipsedge is Emeritus Consultant Psychiatrist with South London and Maudsley NHS Trust, and Visiting Senior Lecturer in the Department of Psychological Medicine within Guys, Kings and St Thomas's School of Medicine. He is the former visiting Professor Georgetown University, Washington DC; former member of the Nolan Review on Child Protection in the Roman Catholic Church in England and Wales; former member of the Home Office Parole Board. He is author, with Roland Littlewood, of *Aliens and Alienists: Ethnic Minorities and Psychiatry* (1982; 1997, 3rd edn Routledge), and author of papers and chapters on occupational psychiatry, medical ethics, risk assessment and medical anthropology. Maurice is co-author and editor of medical textbooks including *Textbook of Psychiatry* with Linford Rees and Christopher Ball (Arnold, 1997), *Medical Masterclass – Psychiatry* with Vincent Kirchner (Royal College of Physicians, 2008), and *Psychiatry PRN* with Sarah Stringer, Laurence Church and Susan Davidson (Oxford University Press, 2009).

1
Writing Madness, Analysing Madness

> Deviant behaviour has always both repelled and fascinated mankind. Interesting to observe are the non-conformists, the sinners or the rebels, who violate society's supposedly normal standards. Social scientists continually debate the definitions and labeling of what is deviant and what is not. But from what better source could one learn about madness, violence, murder, deceit, betrayal, lust, greed, loneliness and depression than in writers such as Sophocles, Aeschylus, Shakespeare, Dostoyevsky, Faulkner, Genet, Nabakov, Burroughs and Stephen King? (Rieger, 1994a, p. 3)

To writers, dramatists, health professionals, and the public at large madness has long been, and remains, a compelling preoccupation. Despite the attention madness has received in both medicine and in popular culture, it remains a diverse and enigmatic entity or experience, defying efforts to comprehensively and adequately comprehend, categorise and manage it. Madness naturally confronts practitioners and researchers in the health and social care disciplines, but it is also encountered by other professionals in, for example, education, the media, and public administration. Most importantly, madness confronts, affects, and afflicts sufferers themselves, alongside their friends, relatives, and carers. The problems caused by mental ill-health, or as we prefer *madness*, have a pervasive effect on how we lead our public and our private lives. Finding ways of understanding the multitude and variety of experiences of madness is as urgent a project as it has ever been.

This book explores one potential source of the understanding and interpreting of madness: fictions published in Britain and the US in the period since the end of World War Two. As Barbara Tepa Lupack suggests, 'postwar experimental fiction searches for ways to deal with the violence, brevity and rigidity of life and carries to great extremes the themes of combativeness, fragmentariness, coolness and meaninglessness that are the marks of much modern fiction' (1994, p. 169). Literature from Homer to contemporary fiction presents an archive of madness – of bizarre or inexplicable experiences, mental distress, behavioural disturbances, and interpersonal difficulties. Fiction also depicts elements of fantasy, resistance, resilience, tenacity, resourcefulness, and creativity that can be labelled, depending on context and circumstance, either as positive qualities or as deviant entities. Whether we are health and/or social care practitioners, or our private life brings us into contact with people who may be seen to be mad, or whether we will at some time be sufferers ourselves, the archive of individual stories and representations of madness in literature has a vital role to play in our comprehending, mapping, and negotiating of madness. Stories – whether written or verbally narrated – are the most ancient yet often the most effective way of representing experience. They help to make sense of bewildering, consuming, or overwhelming events and experiences. The humanities have a vital role to play in assisting understanding, ameliorating, and offering comfort in experiences of health and illness, and are increasingly being used in the education of doctors and other health care professionals.

We have written this book firstly because we believe that contemporary fiction can help us to understand madness, and secondly because literature that focuses on madness provides a fertile body of material for illuminating and interesting literary analysis. In this book, we explore some of the themes and tropes of madness that occur in postwar American and British fiction, using an eclectic mix of analytical approaches, examining literary style and theme but also attending to the contribution that can be made by theoretical approaches such as postmodernism and post-colonialism. We hope that our deployment of perspectives will help to provide an organising framework that will encourage the future exploration of stories of human experiences of health, illness, and madness.

Taking madness as our key theme, it is evident that many post-war British and American authors have provided incisive, and at times conflicting, insights into a variety of unique and highly individual experiences of madness, attitudes towards those deemed mad, their treatments, and the social networks and institutions within which such experiences unfold. Literature that focuses on madness – sometimes transformed into film and theatre, or serialised for television – plays a crucial role in shaping public perceptions of madness itself and of institutions and personnel who work to contain and treat madness, and furthermore in forming stereotypes of individuals deemed mad themselves. One of the most well-known examples of this is the enduringly popular film *One Flew over the Cuckoo's Nest* (dir. Milos Forman, 1975), based on Ken Kesey's 1962 novel and recently revived as a successful play (Garrick Theatre, 2004 and 2006). The impact of tales like this on public opinion and knowledge is considerable, yet there is comparatively little systematic scholarship on the meaning and potential value of this body of work as a whole for psychiatry. We adopt a diverse, critical, and non-biomedical perspective on the literary representation of madness in post-1945 British and American fiction throughout this book. We examine the interanimation between fictional narratives and a variety of clinical discourses, while scrutinising the relationship between the novels and their evolving historical and cultural contexts. A novel like Kesey's *One Flew over the Cuckoo's Nest* represents a number of particular preoccupations of its time and, furthermore, has affected images of mental health care, therapy, and policy over the decades since its publication. In situating madness literature in the historical, political, ethical, and social context of the post-war world order and the context of contemporary psychiatric practices, we hope to provide a text that is simultaneously of use to literary studies and to the Health Humanities.

The term madness is, throughout this text, employed deliberately. We believe that the word *madness* represents the social, personal, and cultural context of the term as signifying a number of different meanings for different people. Were we to specify *mental illness* or *mental disorder*, or to name certain illnesses such as schizophrenia, we would be narrowing our focus to one that is mediated through a medical viewpoint. This is not an idea that we are unique in using – Jim Geekie and John Read (2009) suggest that by 'using the term "madness" the experience is wrested from the grip of a select few experts on "schizophrenia" or "psychosis", and portrayed not as a medical condition with an obscure Greek or Latin derived title, but rather as an aspect of the human condition, about which we can all have our say' (p. 16). We follow Geekie and Read's viewpoint throughout this book. *Madness* is a term that actively defies, as do many of the novels we look at, formal diagnostic classification. Definitional precision, or labelling, encourages objectification. This is a trap most keenly felt by the mid-twentieth-century generation of post-colonial theorists and writers – Aimé Césaire, for example, wrote of 'thingification' (1972, p. 21) and similarly, Frantz Fanon was suspicious of a comparable tendency 'to objectify, to confine, to imprison, to harden' (1964, p. 34). Both of these suggestions have a great resonance with the processes at work in psychiatry, specifically the potential objectification of an individual into diagnostic labels, many of which are themselves contentious *within* the discipline of psychiatry itself.

Psychiatric diagnostics have been applied to perceived instability, disordering, or irrationality of personhood, culture, or society. The term madness has, furthermore, been appropriated or reconstituted to suit different approaches to knowledge and modes of being in the world. For example, madness can refer to particular serious mental illnesses or disorders that impair a person's capacity to function, but it can also be viewed as a social construction or myth (Szasz, 1974). Often it is used as a rhetorical device. We are casting the definition widely by using the term madness because authors of fiction are not necessarily bound by the kind of disorders identified in the latest editions of the *Diagnostic and Statistical Manual of Mental Disorders* (DSM-4TR) (American Psychiatric Association, 2000) or *The ICD-10 Classification of Mental and Behavioural Disorders* (World Health Organisation, 1992). We want to remain open to the possibility that madness might confer creative advantages and insights rather than being associated exclusively with distress and disability, as is often the case in the medical disciplines. Indeed, Peter K. Chadwick's book *Schizophrenia: The Positive Perspective* (2009), now in its second edition, convincingly suggests there may be some positive and life-enhancing aspects to the apparently most damaging of madness diagnoses, schizophrenia.

One of our tasks in this book is to try to gain a theoretical grasp of what depictions of madness in literature might actually mean, and what purposes they serve. Literary appropriations of madness are evident in a wide range of fictional productions. One way of gaining a rough sense of what is going on in these texts is to think about what the author might be doing stylistically *and* thematically with the depiction of madness. In some post-war fiction, the utilisation of madness as an experimental style is evident. For example, William Burroughs's development of the cut-up/fold-in technique produces novels that appear to be formally or textually 'mad' in the sense that the work can at first glance have little sense to it and thus appears to be, literally, the random scribbling of a lunatic (particularly evident in Burroughs, 1959, 1961, 1962, 1964). Yet the development of what we define here as *psychotic texts* is in itself a vital part of the post-war interrogation of both language and of the lack of definitive boundaries between madness and sanity. This becomes particularly apparent when viewed with reference to the questions raised by postmodernist thinkers – indeed, this is a notion that we return to briefly in Chapter 2 and more thoroughly in Chapter 6. A key focus of ours will be separating those novels that are not formally experimental but which, through their examination of madness, contain sections that appear to mimic madness in some way, and texts that utilise elements of clinically defined madness, such as the psychotic symptom of thought-disordering, in order to develop innovative literary styles.

Broadly, we see two main functions of madness in fiction. Firstly, there is the kind of story where madness is used as a kind of device, a rhetorical or dramatic motif – madness acting as a kind of vehicle for entertainment. Secondly, there are texts where the theme of madness may have been adopted with provocative, informative and/or politically minded motives. In this kind of work, the author actively seeks to engage with, and at times subvert, the dominant cultural, social, and media-perpetuated public construction of madness. We seek to distinguish fiction that can be seen as offering subversive and challenging accounts of mental illness from writing that perpetuates or validates stereotypical, media-generated images of the madman or madwoman. Indeed, a number of fictions demonstrate how madness can be deployed as a comforting projection of social ailments and psychopathologies onto particular individuals who can be easily marginalised or scapegoated. In designating the mad person as Other, a text has the potential to either leave aside, *or* actively engage with, troubling questions about the rather fluid boundaries between madness and sanity.

Another striking feature of the literature we will be drawing upon is the sheer variety of permutations of creative performance that authors may undertake. For example, stories may be written from the point of view of the clinician or therapist, the patient, or some other family member or caregiver. This complexity is compounded when we explore the background of the author and the kinds of experiences they may have had, or have been reported to have had. The author may, for example, be drawing upon their own experiences as a doctor, nurse, service user or carer, or drawing upon experiences of earlier texts that they have encountered. Add to this shifting social, cultural, and political ecologies in both Britain and the US, and the difficulty of making sense of stories of madness becomes apparent.

A further task we have set ourselves is to examine the writer's fictionalised use of madness in the context of his or her own known mental health or illness – this is examined in our chapter on creativity and madness. Furthermore, authors who belong to particular genres or who are identified as belonging to a particular grouping or movement – for example, the postmodernists – may have in common a shared style and thematic of madness, which their tales consistently portray. We will not be drawing any sharp distinctions between arbitrarily designated literary, 'highbrow' works and fiction that is more popular, drawing on a diverse range of authors from Thomas Pynchon to Kristen Waterfield Duisberg, from J. G. Ballard to Sebastian Barry, from Kurt Vonnegut to Clare Allan.

It would be an impossible task to provide a sustained and thorough literary analysis of *all* British and American fictional texts that address madness as a key theme. In our selecting of texts from the quantity that could have been included, we have chosen novels where madness is a main subject rather than a secondary theme. This is not to suggest that we will be focusing exclusively on, or excluding, texts that define madness through a clinical framework. We plan to include texts that do have a more traditional clinical perspective, such as Antonia White's *Beyond the Glass* (1954) or Lisa Carey's *Love in the Asylum* (2004), but also those texts that do not seek to confine madness within a clinical sphere, be it institutional or diagnostically definitional, for example Thomas Pynchon's *The Crying of Lot 49* (1965) or Kurt Vonnegut's *Slaughterhouse-Five* (1969). Our desire is to explore madness as a whole rather than a more narrowly defined and clinically constructed notion of mental illness. In other words, we will not partake in a game of symptom- or diagnosis-spotting – for example, this character has schizophrenia, that one depression, another has an eating disorder, and so forth. Neither will we concentrate on the application of psychoanalytic theory and criticism – this has been explored by many others, for example Timpanaro (1976), and Frosh (1991). Instead of using frameworks that have been devised to demarcate and classify psychopathology, we explore literary representations of madness in and on their own terms, rather than to see them *only* as versions or visions of the mental illnesses that have been described in clinical and scientific literature and practice. We aim to align ourselves with the fields of Health Humanities and literary studies, rather than producing a dictionary-like list of all post-war texts that mention madness.

Whilst literary authors on both sides of the Atlantic were busy creating fictional representations of madness, their colleagues in medicine were also hard at work. The post-war era saw successively larger editions of the American Psychiatric Association's *Diagnostic and Statistical Manual of Mental Disorders* come into being and, in 1992, *The ICD-10 Classification of Mental and Behavioural Disorders* was published. In these definitive psychiatric texts, mental disorders were progressively recorded, named, refined, and enumerated. Furthermore, in response to the challenge presented by the anti-psychiatry movements of the 1960s and 1970s, psychiatry had to reassert and re-establish itself to some extent as both a vital and a medical discipline (Roth and Kroll, 1986). Thus the post-war period has seen an increasingly biomedical focus on mental illness within the discipline of psychiatry. In interpolating relationships between literary texts and other contemporaneous material, this book explores the complex interactions between clinical definitions of mental disorder and the depiction of mental distress and mental disorder in fiction. Our approach is not restricted, however, to what could be seen as a potentially narrow account of diagnostic realism, where literary presentations are selected as exemplifying diagnostic categories. Furthermore, to rely too heavily on psychiatric classification or psychoanalytic interpretation would in our view restrict the interpretation of experience via a discourse that compresses human experiences into somewhat reductive, rigid frameworks that themselves have a long and contentious history. Occasionally, however, brief reference is made to diagnosis, psychiatric phenomenology, or epidemiology where it might offer relevant insights, and we critically interpret the use, and indeed lack, of diagnostic and symptomatological naming or specificity in Chapter 2, Mental States.

A further invaluable source of insight for this book comes from accounts of the history of psychiatry and its conceptualisation in both Britain and America, which we shall allude to throughout. In addition, with all the popular excitement and debate over drugs such as the antidepressant Prozac through the 1990s, the interpretation of human distress has often been recast in terms of pharmacology (Healy, 1997; Kramer, 1994). These pharmacological developments have created fascinating new opportunities for examining how people formulate and attempt to deal with unhappiness, grief, sadness, and common personality traits – many of which are now deemed medicinally treatable disorders, such as shyness or, as it is medically known, social phobia or social anxiety disorder (Lane, 2007).

Of course, we owe a debt to other scholars who have gone before us in examining representations of madness in literature. There are publications that address the theme of madness in literature generically, or that reference madness fictions (Ellestrom, 2002; Feder, 1980; Felman, 1985; MacLennan, 1992; Porter, 1991; Rieger, 1994a, 1994b; Thiher, 1999). Authors have also tackled madness literature in particular historical epochs, such as classical literature (Hershkowitz, 1998), medieval and

Middle English literature (Harper, 2003; Reed, 1974), and renaissance literature (Grasi and Lorch, 1986; Salkeld, 1993).

Another large genre of studies, several of which are feminist in orientation, focuses on eighteenth-, nineteenth-, and some twentieth-century literature, drama, and poetry; and on specific authors, sometimes alongside histories of madness (Appignanesi, 2008; Bigler, 1998; Byrd, 1974; Camfield, 1997; Cheng, 1999; Colley, 1983; DePorte, 1974; Duggan, 2000; Gilbert and Gubar, 1979; Ingram, 1991; Lange, 1998; Logan, 1997; Lupack, 1995; Martin, 1987; McCarthy, 1990; Metzger, 1989; O'Connor, 1997; Orlando, 2003; Platizky, 1989; Pratt, 1996; Reid, 2002; Sass, 1992; Senaha, 1996; Showalter, 1987; Small, 1996; Trotter, 2001; Wiesenthal, 1997). Scholars have also looked at the effects of madness novels on the reader (Keitel, 1989), and at specific types of madness in fiction (Furst, 2002; Rohrer, 2005). Finally, there are medical humanities books aimed at clinical *and* literary audiences which are beginning to emerge (Oyebode, 2009c). Our acknowledgement to those that have gone before us will be evident where we draw upon certain literary scholars through this work. We hope that our book will be situated within the growing body of literature that falls under the discipline of Health Humanities.

It has been suggested that particular changes in discoursal and linguistic strategies for representing character or characters evolve over time and may be shown to be connected with, and to some degree determined by, changing historical, social, and cultural contexts (Bex, Burke, and Stockwell, 2000; Bhaya Nair, 2003; Emmott, 2002; Simpson, 1993). Our commitment is to examine the cultural context, function, and literary-linguistic features of fictions that focus on madness – fictions in which period-specific concerns, hope, fears, and desires are played out textually. The work of fiction is, to us, embedded within specific contemporaneous issues, which the novel then reflects, refracts, and attempts to navigate. As part of our non-affiliated and eclectic literary criticism, we interpret how different factors – such as point of view, characterisation, and the construction of dialogue and interaction – are crucial in the literary representation of behavioural and psychological elements of madness.

In the course of our explorations into post-war madness fictions, five main areas of examination have evolved, and these thematic spheres form the chapters of the book. In Chapter 2, we aim to provide an overview of madness in fiction. We briefly explore some of the existing critical literature on madness and fiction; illuminate some broad thematic concerns via a review of relevant fictions; and excavate the relationship between mental symptoms – or rather, the behavioural and psychological reporting and appearance of signs of madness – and their literary representation. In this chapter we refer to novels such as Doris Lessing's *Briefing for a Descent into Hell* (1971), Patrick McGrath's *Spider* (1990), Paul Crawford's *Nothing Purple, Nothing Black* (2002), Marge Piercy's *Woman on the Edge of Time* (1976), Kurt Vonnegut's *Slaughterhouse-Five* (1969), and Theodore Dalrymple's *So Little Done: The Testament of a Serial Killer* (1995), among others. This chapter suggests that in fiction, the *content of experience* rather than the *form of a symptom* is of more importance to characters than the ability to name and diagnose their experiences within psychiatric diagnostic frameworks. This notion is of importance to clinical practice. If we explore the individual's *own* meaning of their experiences and the concomitantly individual social and personal connotations and implications of these experiences, this may yield alternative and more creative ways to bring relief, or methods of using such experiences in a creative or positive manner: this again is beginning to be focused on in clinical literature (Geekie and Read, 2009). Attending to the content of an individual's experience may well be more constructive in terms of their recovery from distressing or destructive experiences and impulses. Even where people have patterns of symptoms which *could* be diagnosed as mental disorders according to the American Psychiatric Association or World Health Organisation criteria, this does not have to be the only way to proceed in terms of the management – and indeed *self*-management – of these experiences. Novels are an important source of ideas for deconstructing supposedly pathological states of mind that can, we suggest, inform both clinicians and a more general readership, enabling and promoting more diverse and individualised approaches to management and/or treatment. This section encompasses a wide variety of authors who are not seeking to comment exclusively or explicitly on the thematic issues addressed in our other chapters. The writers on whom we focus here are largely concerned with the experiences of individuals; how unusual mental experiences manifest themselves; their relationship to past events in the individual's life; how encounters with madness are experienced; and how such occurrences are either resolved or managed.

In Chapter 3, we explore how literary representation as a social practice may promote the empowerment or disempowerment of people with mental illness by reflecting wider debates surrounding individual autonomy and the role of institutions. We know that psychiatry is a potent agency of social control (Zola, 1972). The broad and far-reaching power of psychiatry has, interestingly, led to a diagnostic hierarchy, which actively excludes certain psychiatric diagnoses such as personality disorders – despite UK policy suggestions to the contrary (National Institute for Mental Health in England, 2003) – from accessing certain treatments. This is one example of a power process in psychiatry that enables a form of double-discrimination, with an individual potentially excluded from and/or discriminated against both socially *and* within the very system that has designated them as personality disordered – indeed, personality disorders are one set of psychiatric diagnoses that, it has been suggested, psychiatry dislikes working with, partly due to issues of treatability (Adshead, 2001; Brown and Crawford, 2006; Lewis and Appleby, 1988). Some have argued that the psychiatric system is similar to the judicial system – sanctioned by, and sheltering under, the auspices of the state.

Both types of institution wield ultimate in power through their legitimised and legal abilities to remove the freedom of those who stray from the agreed norms of society, particularly when those straying are *doubly* Other in terms of madness *and* ethnic background, as we explore in Chapter 4 (Cochrane and Sashidharan, 1995; Lipsedge, 1994; Littlewood and Lipsedge, 1982). Notions of risk and dangerousness are further practical reasons for the incarceration of individuals and the sanctions that psychiatry can impose. The theme of dangerousness and mental illness is popular in fiction and features in the work of writers as diverse as John Fowles (1963), Ian McEwan (1997), Patrick McGrath (1996), and John Katzenbach (2004) to name but a few – not to mention the array of crime or thriller novels that use psychopathy, violence, murder, and often sexual deviance in a highly sensationalised form. Examining in detail the fictional representation of the relationship between mental illness and dangerousness would take another volume in itself, and hence is only briefly discussed in this book, but this interest in the interweaving of madness and dangerousness further brings together the interrelationship between psychiatric and judicial powers. When described in novels, the struggle against incarceration and purportedly therapeutic regimes – which may appear to the sufferer (and perhaps the reader) to be oppressive, unintelligible, and even damaging – can provide an illuminating way of making sense of conflict, concordance, coercion, and compliance in mental health settings.

We begin in this chapter by drawing upon fiction that examines the historical development of psychiatry as a discipline, and we build up a picture of how madness came to be constructed in the moral and medical sense, looking at Sebastian Barry's *The Secret Scripture* (2008), *Human Traces* (2005) by Sebastian Faulks, T. C. Boyle's *Riven Rock* (1998), and Pat Barker's *Regeneration* (1991). We then draw upon Erving Goffman's seminal work on institutions, *Asylums* (1961), in order to examine the functions, types, and abuses of power that occur within asylum settings through Ken Kesey's *One Flew over the Cuckoo's Nest* (1962). We also use Goffman to explore fictional representations of alternatives to asylum care following the closure and de-incarceration of psychiatric patients that has occurred in recent years, looking at Paul Sayer's *The Comforts of Madness* (1988), Bebe Moore Campbell's *72 Hour Hold* (2005), and Clare Allan's *Poppy Shakespeare* (2006), among others. We end this chapter by considering how other factors involving power, such as family structure and gendered expectations, impact upon madness, in particular in Antonia White's *Beyond the Glass* (1954).

Chapter 4 of the book concerns the literary representations of madness in terms of race or ethnicity. Just as there has been growing public recognition of injustices, inequalities, and prejudice in the law in relation to ethnicity and diversity, psychiatry has been accused of biases against various groups within the wider population. For example, concern has been expressed about the over-representation of ethnic minorities in psychiatric institutions, and inconsistencies in the processes of care and the treatments administered (Burke, 1984; Montsho, 1995). Thus, one of our concerns in composing this chapter was to examine whether there were any predominant forms of 'common sense' (as referred to by Gramsci, 1971) in fiction about, or written by, people from specific ethnic groups or with a non-Western cultural heritage. One reason for beginning with this as an opening question is that there is a long history of concern as to whether American and European definitions of 'good mental health' (Hinsie and Campbell, 1970) are suffused by the assumptions of powerful groups in society. The yardstick by which both professionals and popular culture measure mental health is imbued with these assumptions. Consequently, the experience of ethnic minorities, and more importantly, the way this experience is construed by mental health professionals, may mean that some individuals are more likely to be treated against their will, subject to more invasive and disabling treatments, and altogether alienated from the mental health care system. In the light of the over-representation of young black men in forensic mental health settings, and their disproportionate likelihood of compulsory detention, a number of scholars proposed that this was partly to do with the stereotypes held by workers in the health care and mental health systems (McGovern and Cope, 1987; Lipsedge, 1994). The sadly commonplace narrations of young black males seen as antisocial, dangerous, aggressive, lawbreakers, lazy, and so forth were argued to be crucial in their higher rates of confinement and their being subject to more compulsory and invasive treatments (Cochrane and Sashidharan, 1995; Lewis, Croft-Jefferys, and David, 1990; Littlewood and Lipsedge, 1982; Rack, 1982).

One of our initial research questions for this thematic area was whether the sense of injustice found in the protest novels of mid-twentieth-century Black American literature had informed black and ethnic minority authors' accounts of the mental health system too. However, our initial expectations were confounded by what we found in the novels we selected and read for this chapter. Instead of overt critique there was a remarkable degree of acceptance of both the institutional approaches and the intellectual frameworks of mental health care, psychiatry, and psychology. In Bebe Moore Campbell's *72 Hour Hold* (2005), we expected some critique of coercive tendencies in legal and mental health care systems. Instead, the message of the novel is that the legal, psychiatric use of 72-hour holds is insufficient for effective treatment, leading to the assertion that longer periods of compulsory detention and medication are needed, as if these are unproblematically beneficial. In Alice Walker's *Possessing the Secret of Joy* (1992), one might find the stage set for a critique of European and North American models of psychological understanding, along with the critique of female genital mutilation. Yet a post-colonial reading of this novel suggests a remarkable degree of accord with Jungian psychology – elsewhere criticised for its frank racism (Dalal, 1988; Howitt and Owusu-Bempah, 1994) – and a somewhat one-dimensional view of African peoples and cultures. Leslie Marmon Silko's most famous novel *Ceremony* (1977) is of particular interest in Chapter 4 because of its depiction of madness associated with the aftermath of warfare, and because of the ethnic variations in therapeutic treatment approaches to what we now term post-traumatic stress disorder. The brutality of mental health treatment and its infliction along ethnic lines is made much clearer in Marge Piercy's *Woman on the Edge of Time* (1976) where Connie Ramos, a woman of Hispanic heritage, is subject to increasingly invasive and bizarre treatments, set against the background of a grim, dehumanising hospital environment. The contribution of traumatic experiences of oppression to confusing and peculiar experiences, fragmentation, and dissociation is explored in Toni Morrison's *Beloved* (1987), taking as its backdrop the abolition of slavery. The difficulties of forming a sense of self and building supportive social relationships for people haunted by traumatic memories, both of what those who owned them subjected them to and what the experience of slavery made them do to one another, are explored. These two novels contain elements of the bizarre or fantastic, such as time-travel or paranormal activity, yet are equally nuanced and compelling when describing material inequalities and oppression. The persistent theme running through a number of the books explored here is the notion of cultural identity and how this may be impaired or enhanced within social networks. That theme provides the background for this chapter.

Chapter 5 presents an overview of the broader context of research into the relationship between mental illness and creativity, before investigating a selection of novels that focus on this theme. There is currently little on illnesses such as schizophrenia or depression and their relationship to creativity, and this chapter examines the less scrutinised world of contemporary fiction and pursues a fresh, up-to-date examination of creativity and madness. Briefly discussing relevant historical and contemporary perceptions of the 'mad genius', the chapter goes on to consider the dilemmas and contradictions that arise in terms of individual creative production in the context of periodically debilitating mental states, and asks whether there is anything more to be learned from examining creative genius and mental disorders. First, it looks at novels that explore creativity and madness in relation to notions of social, semiotic, and personal fragmentation. Here, we consider Doris Lessing's *The Golden Notebook* (1962), Jenny Diski's *Then Again* (1990), *The Quickening Maze* (2009) by Adam Foulds, and Sylvia Plath's fictionalised autobiography *The Bell Jar* (1963). Second, we consider how madness and creativity can be thought of as offering some kind of consolation for the author in light of tragic personal experiences such as living through the suicide of a partner, or experiencing psychosis. Here, we look at Melvyn Bragg's *Remember Me* (2009), Patrick Gale's *Notes from an Exhibition* (2007), and Clare Allan's *Poppy Shakespeare* (2006). Finally, we examine how the theme of creativity and madness can be interpreted as representing the writer and the literary critic as engaged in a 'mad' coupling or *furor scribendi* – a rage, frenzy, or madness of writing that, at times, borders on mortal combat. As well as re-presenting forms of clinically recognisable madness, Patricia Duncker's *Hallucinating Foucault* (1996), Susan Hill's *The Bird of Night* (1972), and William Golding's *The Paper Men* (1985) develop situational kinds of madness in critiquing the obsessive pursuits of critics against the defences of the creative writer.

Overall, Chapter 5 signals that the use of the madness and creativity tropes in contemporary fiction remains open and versatile. These tropes are part of a growing genre and take a number of perspectives, suggesting a rich trading route for future fiction and ensuring that exhaustion in this combined topic is still some way off. In the works selected for this chapter we gain a vision of how personal loss through mental illness extends outwards to the family, and the wider culture and society. We learn how the drive for creativity is often accompanied by a range of vulnerabilities, some of which form a dark legacy for future generations.

We are presented with an uneasy relationship between psychiatric institutions and practices, and the creative activity of writing. While contemporary practitioners such as art or drama therapists see creative activity as affording clinical benefits to individuals, some of the authors and works examined here note the stultifying impact of mental health practices on individual attempts to be creative. While the debilitating aspects of madness are carefully laid out, there is a pervasive sense of the transcendent power and merit of creativity and, for some of the authors themselves, access to consolation. Thus, creativity is marked as both a gift, and a curse or burden. We examine the redemptive notion of the experience of mental illness as an opportunity for enhanced insight and human development, lending credentials to the author through his or her own suffering.

In Chapter 6, we focus on a specific type of post-war fiction, characterised thematically and stylistically as postmodern. The term 'postmodern' has a number of differing connotations. A postmodern novel, as Baldick succinctly suggests, 'greets the absurd or meaningless confusion of contemporary existence with a certain numbness or flippant indifference, favouring self-consciously "depthless" works of fabulation, pastiche, bricolage, or aleatory disconnection' (1990, p. 175). Examples of this are predominantly American, with writers such as Thomas Pynchon, Philip K. Dick, Paul Auster, and Kathy Acker creating distinctively postmodern fictions, alongside J. G. Ballard in the UK. Baldick defines *cultural* postmodernism as being 'a culture of fragmentary sensations, eclectic nostalgia, disposable simulacra, and promiscuous superficiality, in which the traditionally valued qualities of depth, coherence, meaning, originality, and authenticity are evacuated or dissolved among the random swirl of empty signals' (1990, p. 174–175). Postmodern cultural theorists have at times utilised the language of madness to illuminate their theories, for example Jean Baudrillard's notion of 'schizophrenic vertigo' (1983, p. 152). In the context of emerging post-traditional societies, where the moorings of family, community, and vocation are increasingly hard to sustain, reflexive self-awareness provides the individual with the opportunity to construct self-identities without the shackles of tradition and culture that previously restricted the options for self-understanding. Moreover, reflexive selves are constantly revising and reforming themselves in the light of new information or circumstances (Giddens, 1990).

In this chapter, we identify and interrogate constructions of the madman and madwoman in light of postmodern notions of the unreliability of knowledge alongside social and cultural fragmentation, suggesting from this perspective that ascertaining what madness – or indeed sanity – actually *is* becomes a very difficult task. The hallmark of postmodernism is a questioning of claims about reality, and this encourages an atmosphere where hierarchies that privilege the dominance of rationality are tested and challenged. The chapter explores the way in which the representation of madness relates to the changing social and historical context of the postmodern era. This is depicted in postmodern fiction as corresponding to mental disordering related to uncertainty, and the difficulty of establishing coherent narratives of self, identity, and purpose. In this chapter, textual mechanisms through which coherence and intelligibility are sustained in the face of the challenges of representing madness – when such representation can itself be incoherent – are examined.

In this book there is little space to examine gender and madness in literature and history, and this has been amply examined elsewhere in some excellent critical works (Appignanesi, 2008; Gilbert and Gubar, 1979; Showalter, 1987). However, during the period of postmodernity, writers from a number of feminist movements began to realise the subversive potential of postmodernism and postmodern theory. Postmodern women writers such as Kathy Acker have both utilised madness as a subversive tool and examined how gender inequalities can become a major factor in the induction and treatment of female madness itself. Some of Acker's work is explored in Chapter 6.

In our concluding chapter, we briefly explore the representation of psychiatrists in fiction and draw upon the discipline of medical humanities or, as we prefer, Health Humanities, in order to look at how literature can be of use in clinical education. The discipline of Health Humanities represents a broadening of the more unidisciplinary medical humanities, to include the great majority of allied professionals, service users, carers, and self-carers who share an interest in the ways in which knowledge from the humanities may apply to them, their work, and their experience of well-being and illness (Crawford et al., 2010, under review). For professionals, this movement may in turn promote empathy, greater understanding, and heightened awareness of the kind of experiences that comprise madness by furnishing clinicians and non-clinicians with contemporary lived and literary analogues of experiences of madness, and by showing what is at stake through the manner in which madness is constructed and framed within literary productions.

In these ways, this book contributes to the body of resources for education while assisting in the development of new ways of familiarising clinical students with the experiential and social aspects of madness and historical change. We hope this book will address the concerns of some (Stempsey, 1999) who charge that education via the medical humanities may not in fact produce more humane clinicians, by demonstrating the relevance of literature to clinical practice. Literary research has become a resource for medical and allied health-professional education, and has begun to penetrate education for health care professionals by promoting an emotional receptivity and empathic climate for clinical practice. Study of the humanities by students and professionals concerned with the science of clinical psychiatry has included a scant but growing exploration of madness and literature (Crawford and Baker, 2009; Oyebode, 2009c). In *Consciousness and the Novel*, David Lodge suggests that literature is 'the richest and most comprehensive' body of material that we have as a record of different versions of consciousness, reinforcing this claim with the suggestion that literature can 'disguise in the guise of fiction the dense specificity of personal experience, which is always unique, because each of us has a slightly or very different personal history, modifying every new experience we have; and the creation of literary texts recapitulates this uniqueness' (2002, pp. 10–11). In this book, in agreement with Lodge's assertion, we use fiction to help us understand unusual or unfamiliar states of mind – note our careful avoidance of the value-laden term 'abnormal' here.

Our assertion that this book is concerned with madness rather than clinically defined mental illnesses should not be taken to mean that it would be of no use to those working in or studying medically focused psychiatry. We hope that the analysis in our concluding chapter, and throughout this book, will stimulate health professionals, and the clinicians of tomorrow, as one part of a Health Humanities programme. It seems important to acknowledge here that different parts of this book will appeal to different readerships – for example, our chapter on power and institutions may be of more relevance to clinicians and students wishing to explore representations of psychiatric power in order to provoke and promote critical thinking around their own practices. Similarly, the chapter concerning creativity, madness, and fiction, and Chapter 6 on postmodern madness, may be of more interest to those with a literary focus. Our overall aim with this book is to examine representations of madness in fiction. In doing this, we hope to appeal to an eclectic and diverse readership who will, at different levels and for different purposes, find our explorations both interesting and useful.

2
Mental States

> Society has built the walls of mental institutions to keep apart
> the inside and the outside of a culture, to separate between
> reason and unreason and to keep apart the other against whose
> apartness society asserts its sameness and redefines itself as
> sane. But every literary text, I argue, continues to communicate
> with madness – with what has been excluded, decreed abnor-
> mal, unacceptable, or senseless – by dramatizing a dynamically
> renewed, revitalized relation between sense and nonsense,
> between reason and unreason, between the readable and the
> unreadable. (Felman, 1985, p. 5)

Literature has always shared a special space with madness, forming
a synergetic relationship. Literature, very broadly speaking, focuses
almost exclusively on the human mind and behaviour in one form or
another. Felman suggests in the quote above that every literary text
communicates in some way with madness, when madness is taken to
mean much more than a narrow, clinically defined, psychopathological
state. Indeed, what is evident in much post-war British and American
fiction concentrating on madness is that it is not always the explicitly
psychopathological that forms the focus of the narrative. In fictional
texts, it is the individual's experiences, their accounting for and their
interpretation of mental processes and events that are of primary importance. The writers on which we focus throughout this book are largely
concerned with the experiences of individuals – how unusual or seemingly inexplicable mental phenomena manifest themselves to others;
their relationship to life events; and how encounters with madness are
experienced. This chapter starts with a broad overview of the 'why and
how' of madness in literature. We then draw on two clinical debates

that are both illuminated by and argued through fiction. Finally, we explore some of the broad thematic elements that are prominent in post-war UK and US fiction which focuses on madness.

Madness in literature

Why does so much post-war fiction focus on the huge and relatively multivalent theme of madness? As Felman asks: 'Why this massive investment in the phenomenon of madness? While everyone today meddles with "madness," no one is asking: Why is everyone today meddling with madness? What does it mean to talk about madness? How can madness thus become a *commonplace*?' (1985, p. 13). Madness is multifarious and comes in multiple forms, and *madness* has become a commonplace term to describe any number of idiosyncrasies in contemporary life and society. The main discourse that sets out to define, describe, and encapsulate madness is psychiatry and related psych-disciplines such as psychology. This discourse provides the primary classificatory construction of the broad term 'madness' to describe a number of clinical states and conditions – which, in themselves, lack collective agreement regarding aetiology, symptomatology, diagnosis, and treatment. Nevertheless, it is not the place of this text to examine the multiplicity of discourses on madness. Psychiatrist and poet Femi Oyebode suggests that it 'is likely that personal experience of psychopathology or close contact with individuals who have it make for a more true-to-life characterisation of mental illness' (Oyebode, 2009b, p. 45). Indeed, it can be argued that everyone at some point in their lives will experience a form of madness, either on a personal level via their own experience, or via an encounter with the madness of others. Madness is uniquely individual and thus a 'true-to-life' characterisation, as suggested by Oyebode, refers either to a clinically identifiable, 'realistic' representation of mental illness, or to the singularity of life itself. Fiction writers do not seek clinical precision or standardisation; instead, they describe and depict the experience of experiences.

Scholars have argued that the fundamental basis of madness is the essence of being human – to be human is to be able to experience madness. Geekie and Read have brought this notion directly into clinical practice in their recent book, writing: 'We believe that the experience of "madness" is a quintessentially human experience, found in all human societies, and as far as we know, across all times' (2009, p. 6). As Alastair Morgan states in his introduction to a collection of essays on the relationship between madness and *being human*, developed from the work of Karl Jaspers:

> Whereas medicine treats physical illness as a model that applies to animality as a whole, when we are dealing with mental distress we are interested in a phenomenon particular and peculiar to human animals. Even in her physical embodiment, the human animal has important differences from non-human animals through the expressive uses of her body. Therefore, first and foremost, mental distress should be related to the particular potentialities of human freedom. (Morgan, 2008, p. 4)

Morgan continues his assertion that madness is a particular *human* characteristic by suggesting that we 'can only truly understand what it means to be human, and correlatively, what it means to experience mental distress, if we understand the multiple ways of living different forms of life' (p. 5). Madness occurs differently for each human affected by it, and to appreciate the individuality of madness a simultaneous appreciation of the singularity of living is needed.

Lillian Feder, in her highly regarded text *Madness in Literature* (1980), eloquently reiterates this argument within a more tangible framework, suggesting:

> In literature, as in daily life, madness is the perpetual amorphous threat within and the extreme of the unknown in fellow human beings. In fact, recurrent literary representations of madness constitute a history of explorations of the mind in relation to itself, to other human beings, and to social and political institutions. The madman, like other people, does not exist alone. (Feder, 1980, p. 4)

Given that the basic level of humanity that distinguishes us from other mammals is our ability to think, conceptualise, interpret, analyse, and to be aware of our self, it follows that humans have the ability to experience a disrupted psychology. It can be suggested that there is a virtually universal human fear of going mad, of 'losing' our minds. It is unsurprising therefore that literature should focus so explicitly on what Feder refers to in the quotation above as the 'perpetual amorphous threat' of 'the extreme of the unknown' (p. 4). Similarly, Rieger suggests:

> Psychology and literature can be complementary disciplines. Each probes the complexities of human perception, emotion and behavior;

each assesses the impact of environment and personal relationships on an individual. Each contributes, in its own way, to an understanding of personality. [...] Literature often presents fierce emotions characters cannot control, or which are in tremendous conflict with each other. (1994b, p. 224)

As Rieger suggests, given that the majority of literature examines people, personality, and psychology, we once again stress our argument that it should be no surprise that a large proportion of this literature thus examines what we might term the *otherness* of these elements – that which psychiatry terms *psychopathology*, the clinical collective term for *madness*.

Representations of madness in literature can be viewed as existing along a continuum. Feder proposes that in 'imaginative writing from the late Romantic period to the present, the increasing sense of aloneness in an indifferent universe and an amoral society is symbolically transformed into assaults on the very notion of an autonomous self' (1980, p. 279). Furthermore, she writes, 'the conception of madness as a revelation of mind or an expansion of consciousness, sometimes regarded as peculiarly modern, actually has a long history' (p. 279). Here Feder identifies two opposing states of madness that can be seen in literary representations: madness as despair, fear, and horror, and madness as a mind-expanding, revealing, mystical experience. According to Feder, the portrayal in literature:

[...] of the diffusion of drives and loss of ego are extremely varied, but it more often portrays despair, chaos, pain, and emptiness than it does transcendental oneness. These, moreover, do not merely reflect social assumptions about insanity, for such feelings are described in many works that counter generally accepted attitudes toward madness. (p. 282)

A continuum model of madness and sanity, as proposed by Richard P. Bentall in his critically acclaimed text *Madness Explained: Psychosis and Human Nature* (2003) may be usefully employed here. His detailed exploration of madness in all its forms broadly suggests that madness and sanity exist on a continuum of experiences without a universal and clear point of binary oppositional division. Bentall writes: 'the line between sanity and madness must be drawn relative to the place at which we stand. Perhaps it is possible to be, at the same time, mad when viewed from one perspective and sane when viewed from another' (p. 117). Literary representations of madness also exist on a continuum – from the view that madness is a mind-expanding state or veritable celebration of madness, standing in opposition to the generally accepted view that madness is one of the worst things that can happen to any individual, through to representations that emphasise the abject terror of those experiencing the horror of madness. It is clear here that the continuum of literary representations of madness reflects the continuum of the lived human experience of madness proposed by Bentall in 2003.

Literature provides a complementary, alternative, and altogether more empathic view of madness than is available in clinical literature or in society generally, as Rieger also suggests:

> The literary attitudes towards madness often reflect a greater awareness and understanding, as well as sympathy for, the realities of the human mind than do historical medical attitudes, thereby contributing significantly to the attempt of unraveling mysteries of personality. The oversimplified dichotomy between madness and sanity is repeatedly disputed in both clinical and literary treatments of madness and, like Wallace Stevens, one sees there is more than one way to look at a blackbird. (1994a, p. 13)

In the same paper Rieger writes: 'labeling promoted by the mental health field contributes to preserving the ambiguity of the fluid, changing term, "medical madness." How can one differentiate between literary madness and medical madness?' (1994a, p. 5). We return to notions of literary madness when we discuss psychotic texts in Chapter 6, but this is an interesting question, and Rieger is right to point out the abundant and confusing ways of conceptualising clinical madness – or indeed, of clearly differentiating between madness and sanity. In a 2008 paper entitled 'Artaud's Madness: The Absence of Work' Patrick Callaghan outlines the five main ways in which madness is constructed in contemporary society, philosophy, and the psych-disciplines. The 'lay perspective', he suggests, refers to the manner in which the individual's experiences are constructed as abnormal by non-psych-trained people. The 'supernatural perspective' accounts for much pre-modern explanation of madness, and can be seen in a number of religious discourses. The 'medical perspective' is the dominant view and needs little elucidation here, as with the 'psychological perspective'. Finally, the 'postmodern perspective', following the work of Foucault and others, casts a critical light on the other four perspectives (2008, p. 142). Crucially,

Callaghan states, while these five perspectives 'seek to explain the nature, or causes of madness, *they tell us very little about what madness is*' (p. 142, emphasis added). Literature can provide further, alternative perspectives on the question of what madness actually *is*, though perhaps not a definitive answer to this question. More importantly, what fiction can and does demonstrate is how madness may be experienced and what it may signify or mean for a variety of individual characters.

Rieger thematises 'literary madness' and suggests that it has been 'used as a critical device in three ways: 1) the "mad" writer; 2) the "mad" characters of writers; and 3) the critical method by which psychological terms from the field of medical madness are applied to literary madness' (1994a, p. 5). The notion of the mad writer is explored in our chapter on creativity and mental health, while Rieger's third category involves a potentially unsophisticated – and not particularly useful for the purposes of literary analysis – game of symptom-spotting in fiction. Along similar lines, Felman suggests an elaborate typology of literary madness:

> There are many more stylistically sophisticated ways by which literature communicates with madness: through reliable and unreliable narrators; through a narrator who (reliably or unreliably) claims to be a madman (Nerval, Flaubert) or, conversely, a narrator who claims to be sane but whose narrative perhaps says otherwise (the governess in James); through a narrator who, like Oedipus, occupies the fatal place of the unwittingly self-implicating psychoanalytical interpreter (the governess in James); through a theme, a character who is mad (Balzac); through a figure, a stereotypical cliché of "folly" as a metaphor for social deviance and dissidence (Flaubert); through a romantic rhetoric (Nerval, Flaubert) [...]. In asking what it means to be mad, the literary texts destabilize the boundary line between this "inside" and this "outside," subvert the clear-cut opposition between the other and the same. (1985, p. 4)

It is clear that there are a number of ways in which madness is used as a critical device in fiction. But one broad thematic question arises time and time again – how can we reconcile the mad-as-philosopher position of some literary characters with the equally-represented disintegrated lives and psyches of other characters? And if these positions are irreconcilable, then can we be content with suggesting that they represent the broadness of human experiences of madness, in opposition to the medically accepted model that madness needs containing, assessing, and treating?

We can return to Felman for help in looking at this question. She suggests, in two seemingly contradictory statements, that 'if one turns now to literature in order to examine the role of madness there (in Shakespeare's works, for instance), one realises that the literary madman is most often a disguised philosopher: in literature, the role of madness, then, is eminently philosophical' (p. 37). Reflecting on the work of Foucault and Derrida, however, she later writes that the 'philosopher ends up getting his bearings, *orienting himself* in his fiction: he only enters it in order to abandon it. The madman, on the other hand, is engulfed by his own fiction' (p. 49). These two positions – mad as philosopher and mad as engulfed by his own fiction to the extent of inability to see reality or truth (as the opposite of fiction) – are two potentially opposing positions, irreconcilable at times but both, crucially, represented in a variety of fictions. Yet accepting this, how do we then account for the author, or rather the imaginative constructor, of the madman – the author who may or may not be engulfed by a madness of his or her own, but who is certainly and necessarily engulfed by the process of weaving a fiction that then forms their novel? This theme will be returned to in Chapter 5.

In *Reading Psychosis* (1989) Evelyne Keitel proposes a seductive model of madness and mad literature via the exploration of novels that she groups as *psychopathographic* texts. It is worth examining Keitel's work at length as an interesting and illuminating theory of both literature and madness. Central to Keitel's thesis is the response of the reader who, she suggests, will be necessarily unfamiliar with the psychotic process, as indeed will the author: 'the need to discover novel ways of communication which will be understood means that the authors of psychopathographies, or at least the authors of those texts which have unusual aesthetic effects, can hardly be psychotics themselves' (p. 5–6). This statement is open to criticism as it seems to be a rather sweeping generalisation, which disavows the inner world of individuals and simultaneously situates 'the psychotics' as completely Other – those who do not or cannot read, write, or indeed communicate in any 'novel' way. However, Keitel *does* eschew rigid clinical schemata when examining literary madness and her construction of this literary subgenre is interesting, detailed, and useful for our purpose here.

Keitel suggests there are three categories of 'mediating' texts that form three types of psychopathography: theoretical (example given: Frieda Fromm-Reichmann's case histories), literary (example given: Doris Lessing's *The Golden Notebook*), and imitative (example given: Hannah Green's *I Never Promised You A Rose Garden*) (1989, p. 20). Each relies on a different reading process for understanding – reflection, projection, and contemplation (p. 20). Psychopathographies can breach the three classifications Keitel proposes – Doris Lessing's *Briefing for a Descent into Hell*, for example, according to Keitel, is a *'literary'* text 'interacting with a *theoretical* system' for example (p. 90). On a basic level, Keitel suggests:

> Psychopathographies are about psychotic personality dissolutions, about material which erupts from realms beyond the margins of discourse. [...] it is important to distinguish between phenomena caused solely by the interaction of text and reader, such as certain feelings involved in reading literature, and phenomena which do exist independently of the reading process, but with which the reader is not familiar from personal experience. The latter type are those addressed in psychopathographies. (p. 28)

Here Keitel begins to illuminate the response of the reader of psychopathographies as having different effects than those caused by the process of reading generally. Keitel suggests that psychopathographies

> [...] deal with an area of experience which resists linguistic representation. Now, one of the most striking features of pathographical texts is that they are predominantly written in a highly conventional linguistic style which leaves the *capability* of language to represent "reality" unquestioned. The literary strategies whereby psychotic experience is communicated are not – or, at least, are not all – marked by the unfamiliarity and strangeness of the subject matter; inaccessible material cannot be communicated in an unknown code. Instead, psychopathographies rely for their effect on textual strategies which are in part taken over from their literary context, and on experiences with reading other contemporary texts. (p. 14)

Forming a unique genre, psychopathographies draw the reader directly into the psychopathology depicted, as opposed to *pathographies* (literally, texts about illness) which maintain a relative distance between reader and experience. Central to this genre lies a crucial question: 'how can a literary text overcome certain specific limits of verbalization, while at the same time allowing for a psychotic experience to be communicated?' (Keitel, 1989, p. 3). The answer, suggests Keitel, lies in the effect the text has on the reader, and thus reading 'about psychoses in the literary type of psychopathography opens up a way into those dimensions of experience which are situated in the deep levels of our unconscious and constantly repelled by conscious perception' (p. 113) – reading *about* psychosis 'becomes a *reading* psychosis' (p. 118, emphasis added).

In terms of reader response, Keitel suggests that psychopathographies provide the reader with 'a *primarily emotional* experience of the basic structure of psychotic phenomena through reading' (p. 16). In fact, in Chapter 6 we argue that some texts explore the basic structure of madness through their physical textual construction. To move forward from Keitel's work leads us towards questions of authenticity in representations of madness – to paraphrase Keitel (p. 16), to look at novelistic representations of psychosis for the reader. The representation of psychosis is potentially at odds with the need for madness novels, in order to be published and available to the reader, to balance coherence and readable representation. This is something that Patrick McGrath, author of several novels that focus on madness – *Asylum* (1996), *Spider* (1990), and *Trauma* (2008) – is acutely aware of:

> It seemed a formidable task – that of rendering psychotic experience from a first-person perspective: first, because I myself had never had schizophrenia; and second, because it seemed to me that fictional narrative and psychosis were mutually exclusive entities. The latter, I thought, is characterised by chaos, irrationality, delusions, non-sequiturs and paranoia, whereas the novel demands a sort of swelling narrative progress grounded in causality and finally yielding a clear design. So this was the nature of the problem, to render the chaos of psychotic illness within the ordered frame of the novel without misrepresenting or trivialising the experience of schizophrenia. (2002, pp. 140–141)

How can authors provide a lucid account of madness, that may be inherently chaotic or incoherent, while remaining faithful to the *experience* of madness, especially when the author may never have experienced madness, chaos, or incoherence? Here we can perhaps see the crux of the relationship between madness and literature – literature provides one way of saying the unsayable, presenting that which is not understandable, giving the reader a glimpse into the foreign, unknowable, highly individualistic experiences that form pluralities of madness.

But how can literature do this and still be readable – what of the need for coherency in narratives of incoherency? Oyebode rightly suggests that novels 'are not written as scientific studies of psychopathology', continuing:

> The novelist's interest in psychopathology is because of the intrinsic fascination that we all have for how the mind works, in either

health or illness. However, for a story to work it has to be coherent and plausible. Therefore, psychopathology has to be comprehensible within the total structure of the narrative. Thus, even in an account of a disintegrating mind, the account still has to cohere. This means that Jaspers' notion of 'un-understandability' as a criterion for psychosis is usually breached in literature. There are, of course, researchers such as Bentall (2003) who argue that psychotic experiences are understandable. On the face of it, fictional accounts seem to agree with him, but I suspect that this is because of the need for fictional narrative to be comprehensible and coherent. (2009b, p. 46)

In fact, not all literature that focuses on madness *is* coherent, as we suggest in Chapter 6 where we write on postmodern fiction and examine a subgenre of postmodern literature that we refer to as *psychotic texts*. A more useful way of approaching the notion of coherence in narrative is to examine *degrees* of coherency. For the literary scholar who is examining mad fictions, incoherence can be a valuable representation of the *inside* of madness. The psychiatrist, who by profession attempts to create an ordered, diagnosable schemata from presented disorder, may conversely desire a more structured narrative for the purposes of using fiction to reflect on clinical practice.

Furthermore, not all fictions breach the 'un-understandability' criterion for identifying psychosis as opposed to neurosis that Karl Jaspers suggested in his seminal works: in some fiction there is no sign of the 'abyss of difference' between the distorted psychic life of psychosis and the interpretable neurosis and normality that Jaspers suggested (1963, p. 219). An expansion of the coherency question involves examining, broadly, the multiplicity of narrative and mimetic levels which madness texts operate on – the difference between *showing* and *telling* madness and, furthermore, the levels upon which the *telling* occurs[1]. Parallels can be drawn by examining the differences between *mimesis* – the 'showing', often seen in drama or film – and *diegesis*, the narrative action or 'telling' of a tale. On a basic level, madness texts often employ both tactics, sometimes simultaneously – madness is both shown and told. For example, Kathy Acker's *The Childlike Life of the Black Tarantula by Black Tarantula* (1973) mimetically allows the reader access to the incoherent inside of florid psychosis through complete disintegration of linear narration, tangential thinking, dislocations in space and time, and elements of paranoia. In many of Acker's books, thought disorder is directly replicated via the text. Similarly, sections of William S. Burroughs's work employs mimesis through use of his cut-up/fold-in technique. Mimetic texts sometimes directly invoke what psychiatrist-philosopher Jaspers saw to be the hallmark of psychosis, that:

> [...] we find ununderstandable what strikes the patients as not at all so but on the contrary quite well founded and a matter of course. Why a patient starts to sing in the middle of the night, why he attempts suicide, begins to annoy his relatives, why a key on the table excites him so much, all this will seem the most natural thing in the world to the patient but he cannot make us understand it. (Jaspers, 1963, p. 581)

What this *un-understandability* can lead to are novels that are un-readable and un-interpretable as wholes, but which allow understanding through their individual parts – again, what we name in Chapter 6 as psychotic texts. Paul Sayer's *The Comforts of Madness* (1988) is a diegetic text, using intradiegetic narration to provide a *telling* of the inside of madness through a readable, traditional narrative. Extradiegetic texts include Marge Piercy's *Woman on the Edge of Time* (1976) and Antonia White's *Beyond the Glass* (1954). Furthermore, a number of texts employ multiple levels of narration – for example, Doris Lessing's *Briefing for a Descent into Hell* (1971) uses the intradiegetic perspective while Charles Watkins is consumed in his madness, the extradiegetic perspective through the doctor's opinions on 'what' Watkins is (depressed, psychotic, or catatonic), and finally epistolary narrative through letters and commentary on Charles by others. A key feature of madness texts is the use of the (allegedly) unreliable narrator – for example, McGrath's *Spider* is deliberately written to mislead the reader by pitting objective reality against Spider's own internal, highly subjective reality, which is narrated via the first person. A further parallel can be drawn here between the literary device of the unreliable narrator and the clinical interpretation of the psychotic individual detailing his/her experiences. Psychiatrists and other clinicians routinely use external sources and opinions, such as reports by relatives and caregivers or staff in a ward environment, in order to prove or disprove a patient's own reporting of events.

Symptomatology in fiction

Psychiatry relies on a relatively arbitrary but disciplinarily necessary division between real and unreal. It is this binary that designates individuals as sane or mad. Why arbitrary? Because each individual's reality is different – the same external occurrence will be experienced differently by each individual. As Robert de Beaugrande suggests, fiction writers are allowed to reinvent reality, and readers accept their versions as a way of experiencing alternatives (de Beaugrande, 1994, p. 24). Yet this situation is not always the case and nor is it a simple one, he continues:

> [...] the freedom to contemplate alternatives would be mistrusted by groups who hold an unreflective allegiance to a certain order of things and see everything else as 'madness'.

And by virtue of this very distrust, the problematics of "literariness" can never be fully disentangled from those of "madness." We cannot maintain a genuine concern with literariness and yet ignore the commonplace defence whereby people who question established reality or propose an alternative have doubt cast upon their sanity; authoritarian societies apply this principle by consigning literary dissidents to mental asylums. What for some is a healthy and insightful release from constricting givens is viewed by others as a pathological and self-deluded breaking out of reality. (p. 25)

Literature and art, according to de Beaugrande, 'offer the difficult experience of a reality that is not "real" in the everyday sense, since it belongs to and originates only through the work, and yet tells us more about reality, about its provisional and incomplete status, than any actual bit of the everyday world can' (p. 27). Furthering de Beaugrande's argument, we can add to the 'provisional and incomplete' status of reality the uniqueness of each person's experience of reality. Lupack consolidates this position, suggesting that modern-day concern with the ever-diminishing distinction between fantasy and reality 'presents a peculiar dilemma for the contemporary writer. It challenges him to shape the shapeless, define the undefinable, legitimize the bizarre and reconcile the paradoxical' (1994, p. 171). The modern novel, according to Lupack, must 'hold up a mirror to the current sociopolitical madness and allow the contemporary hero (and his reader), by confronting it, to begin to conquer it' (p. 172). Indeed, as we shall see, existence within the external or dominantly defined reality, which for many writers does consist of many elements of Lupack's 'sociopolitical madness', is not always safe or comfortable. Novelists write madness and document individual reality through their imaginative creations, and readers readily accept these versions of reality precisely because they are authorised as fiction.

One such individual reality that is particularly well exhibited is in McGrath's *Spider*. In this novel McGrath uses the literary device of the unreliable narrator, as we have noted, and according to Oyebode:

> He manages to describe the world through the eyes of the protagonist, Spider, and the reader is taken in by the account. Spider's conviction of the reality of his beliefs and psychotic experiences convinces the reader too. Authorial coherence authenticates the narrative and makes Spider's account believable. It is true that Spider's world is never entirely explicable but none the less it has the compelling force of reality. It is a study of the architecture of psychotic experience. The struts and girders on which illusions, hallucinations and delusions are built are exposed. (2009b, p. 44)

Notably, as Oyebode points out, Spider's belief in the reality of his experiences is absolute, which resonates with the assertions made by Jaspers about the mad individual being convinced by, rather than questioning, his beliefs or sensory experiences (Jaspers, 1963, p. 581). McGrath's dazzling portrayal of an individual locked inside a terrifying madness completely tricks the reader, drawing them into and through Spider's version of reality before revealing something very different. Through slowly unpacking the singular experiences that led to Spider's totally mad reality, McGrath suggests something that is of great importance in psychiatry: listening to the *whole* rather than the part; understanding both the structure *and* the content of madness.

Recognising the content of madness is often an overlooked part of the treatment of psychosis. In a powerful paper, Mary Boyle suggests that the dominant agenda of psychiatry – assessing, diagnosing, and treating – ignores the individual's reality, that is, the *content* of hallucinations and delusions (the two psychotic processes that dominate the construction of psychosis). Boyle suggests that the reasons for this are fourfold. Firstly, individual content is not seen as important within the medical model of psychiatric illness while, secondly, the study of form is more scientific and thus universally applicable (Boyle, 1996, p. 28). Thirdly, there is a perception that 'if psychiatrists pay too much attention to content it might come to look as if they are acting as social agents in the suppression of certain belief systems, rather than as disinterested scientists applying general rules to distinguish the normal from the abnormal' (p. 29). Finally, given that beliefs can be culturally distinctive, once a decision is taken that the belief is removed from both culture and context (i.e., it is Other to the dominant system of the psychiatrist) then 'it seems to be assumed that we can safely ignore it or, at least, see it as an epiphenomenon, an idiosyncratic consequence of a biological illness' (p. 29). This denial or ignoring of content is not necessarily a malignant process. Boyle suggests that it actually has two important defensive functions:

> The first function is apparent in our society's tendency to deny, or, at least to de-emphasize, our capacity for bizarre beliefs and experiences. [...] it is as if such beliefs and experiences are so threatening to our rational image of ourselves and our society that we deal with them by denying that their occurrence and content can be understood within rational, scientific and technologically sophisticated Western culture. So such experiences can only be made intelligible by seeing them as a product of brain dysfunction. (p. 30)

Secondly, Boyle suggests that 'to search for meaning in "psychotic" behaviour, in other words to make the behaviour intelligible in its social context, comes close to suggesting that we do not need to seek biological explanations or, at least, not within a simplistic reductionist model' (p. 30). Thus, attending to content, and to its meaning, has the potential to threaten the entire enterprise of biomedical psychiatry.

From this starting point, it can further be proposed that through the neglect and devalorisation of content – and by content, we mean the individual's own meanings inherent in so-called mad experiences and belief systems – psychiatry is at risk of ignoring the whole person, attending instead to classifiable bits or parts which are deemed to be more objective. Of course, there are many clinicians who share, along with the more visible Boyle (1996), Oyebode (2009c), Chadwick (2009), Bentall (2003), and Geekie and Read (2009), the belief that recognising and appreciating the importance of the individual's subjective experiences, rather than the mere form of their symptoms, is both more humane and leads to more favourable outcomes. As Oyebode suggests:

> All psychiatric disorders, perforce, are disorders of persons. The symptoms and signs of the conditions are played out in the lives of real people and it is impossible to separate out the locale of the condition as distinct from the person. What the arts and humanities can do for psychiatry is to reinforce the importance of the subjective. Our current diagnostic approaches emphasise the objectivity of symptoms and understate the importance of how these symptoms are experienced by persons, this despite the fact

that the roots of clinical psychopathology lie in phenomenology. (2009c, p. viii)

The roots of contemporary psychiatric practice lie in the practice of descriptive psychopathology. Andrew Sims points out in his highly acclaimed medical – and humane – introduction to this practice that the 'nature of the content [...] is irrelevant in coming to a diagnosis' (2003, p. 17). For the patient, according to Sims, 'the *content* is all important' and thus 'the doctor's absorption with form is incomprehensible and frustrating in the extreme' (p. 16). Descriptive psychopathology, the gold standard of psychiatric assessment, diagnosis, and classification, is precisely *not* rooted in the subjective content of experience, but in symptomological form.

This prioritisation is reversed in madness literature – the content of experience rather than the form that this experience takes is of far greater interest and importance, to writer, character, and reader alike. On a very basic level, a novel that focused exclusively on symptomalogical form would be dull indeed. Symptomatology within a social context is often epitomised in fictional texts – or example, paranoia may be taken to represent something important about postmodern society and culture rather than being an indicator of mental illness (Melley, 2000; O'Donnell, 2000). In terms of engagement with content and context, Feder suggests:

> Although it may not always be possible to discover efforts at restitution in the delusions and hallucinations of psychotics, it is certainly true that both autobiographical accounts and imaginative representations of madness provide evidence that such bizarre constructions cannot be viewed merely as signs of withdrawal from reality. The very contents of the delusions and hallucinations of both literary figures and actual persons express symbolically an inner transformation of the world experienced through the deprivation, anger, pain, and guilt that have become the only emotional means of engagement with it. (1980, p. 26)

The 'inner transformation' (as Feder phrases it in the above quotation) of both Charles Watkins in Lessing's *Briefing for a Descent into Hell* and the character of Peter in Sayer's *The Comforts of Madness* provide differing representations of this turning inwards, moving away from external engagement with or in any social reality (as Feder phrases this above, the 'inner transformation' of individuals). In both characters, to a greater or lesser degree, the reader witnesses their disengagement from the world around them, in part because, as Feder suggests, the external world is experienced as painful, frightening, or dangerous.

In the case of Charles Watkins, his inward turn seems to be a straightforward madness – yet his experiences are not interpreted or experienced as sickness by Charles himself. Through epistolary narrative, Lessing directly contrasts the richness of Watkins's inner psychotic experiences with the medical accounting that occurs beyond this in the external world. Passages where the reader inhabits Charles's inner world mirror his behaviour in the external world, so his observable and externally reported behaviour – for example, lying down and rocking – simultaneously mimic his personal journey in his inner landscape, where he is rocking on a ship. Charles's madness is dense and complete: it consumes him. In Lessing's novel, we see a richness of narration through the content of Watkins's inner world that is not available in either clinical literature or the clinical construction of symptoms. Charles is desperate to stay in his madness: 'I do not want to be made aware, of what I have done and what I am and what must be, no, no, no, no, no, no, no, around and around and around and around and around and around …' (p. 60). The following passage exemplifies the contrast between the dry clinical discord between competing doctors attempting to bring Charles out of his madness, and the disjunction between the doctor and Watkins with his different concerns:

> I must record my strong disagreement with this treatment. If it were the right one, patient should by now be showing signs of improvement. Nor do I agree that the fact he sleeps almost continuously is by itself proof that he is in need of sleep. I support the discontinuation of this treatment and discussion about alternatives.
>
> DOCTOR Y.

> DOCTOR Y. Well, and how are you today? You certainly do sleep a lot, don't you?
> PATIENT. I've never slept less in my life.
> DOCTOR Y. You ought to be well rested by now. I'd like you to try and be more awake, if you can. Sit up, talk to the other patients, that sort of thing.
> PATIENT. I have to keep it clean, I have to keep it ready.
> DOCTOR Y. No, no. We have people who keep everything clean. Your job is to get better.

PATIENT. I was better. I think. But now I'm worse. It's the moon, you see. That's a cold hard fact.

DOCTOR Y. Ah. Ah, well. You're going back to sleep, are you?

PATIENT. I'm not asleep, I keep telling you.

DOCTOR Y. Well, good night!

PATIENT. You're stupid! Nurse, make him go away. I don't want him here. He's stupid/he doesn't understand anything.

> On the contrary. Patient is obviously improving. He shows much less sign of disturbance. His colour and general appearance much better. I have had considerable experience with this drug. It is by no means the first time a patient has responded with somnolence. It can take as long as three weeks for total effect is to register. It is now one week since commencement of treatment. It is essential to continue.
>
> DOCTOR X.
>
> (Lessing, 1971, p. 60–62)

The assumption is clearly made by the doctors that Watkins wants to be 'made aware', treated, cured. They fail to meaningfully listen to his own descriptions of the content of his inner world. Nor do they have a unified view on how his treatment should proceed. Watkins is more ambivalent within his psychosis:

> I can feel myself struggling and fighting as if I were sunk a mile deep in thick dragging water but far above my head in the surface shallows I can see sun-laced waves where the glittering fishes dance and swim, oh, let me rise, let me come up to the surface like a cork or a leaping porpoise into the light. Let me fly like a flying fish, a fish of light.
>
> They hold me down, they cradle me down, they hush and they croon, SLEEP and you'll soon be well.
>
> I fight to rise, I struggle as if I were a mile under heavy sour black earth and above the earth slabs of stone, I fight so hard and I shout, No, no, no, no, don't, I won't, I don't want, let me wake, I must wake *up* but
>
> Shhhhhh, hush, SLEEP and in slides the needle deep and down I go into the cold black dark depth where the sea floor is an earth of minute skeletons, detritus from eroding continents, fishes' scales and dead plants, new earth for growing. But not me, I don't grow, I don't sprout, I loll like a corpse or a drowned kitten, my head rolling as I float and black washes over me, dark and heavy.
>
> He is sleeping well, Doctor, yes, he is resting well, yes. (pp. 30–31)

Rising to the surface – that is, back into the external world – is described both in terms of light, flight and freedom, but also as a genuine struggle through thick, dense madness to reach a surface: but in glimpses of what is occurring in the outer landscape, Watkins is held down, constrained. There is a disparity between the actual external reality that Watkins is fighting and what he perceives he is battling. Watkins's madness, his inner land, is at times horrific:

> Next morning the dead lay in heaps, and the whole city smelled of blood. And now these animals, whose food was fruit and water, were gathered around piles of corpses and were tearing off lumps of hairy flesh and eating it. As I came in close to look, I felt afraid for the first time of these beasts, apes and Rat-dogs. I was now, as they were to each other, potential meat. They ignored me, though I was standing not twenty yards away, until I saw three of them become conscious of my being there, and they turned their pointed muzzles to me, with their sharp teeth white and smeared red, and I saw the blood dripping down as I had off the faces of my women. I went back to the edge of the sea and fell into a despair. I gave up hope then. I knew that the fighting would go on. It would get worse. (p. 79)

Yet as Watkins is treated and begins to recover, his distress at times *increases*. In this respect, as well as providing a poignant and incisive glimpse into a madness, Lessing also suggests a paradoxical challenge to the ethical aims of psychiatric treatment.

In *The Comforts of Madness*, Sayer proposes a more explicit perspective on the notion of turning inward through madness. The narrative is told through the eyes of Peter, a man locked wholly in his internal world having no communication with or participation in the world around him. To observers, he is a shell; in his dying moments towards the close of the novel, he is completely objectified. The doctor treating him states to his colleague, '[...] Here we have a remarkable example of a soul, in there, somewhere in that rag doll of a man, a zest for life, a will to carry on [...] There is much to be learnt here, much for the philosophising mind to get its teeth into' (pp. 119–120). The doctor apparently sees Peter as an object, referring to him as 'this' rather than 'he'. For the clinician, Peter is an impenetrable 'rag doll', but useful nonetheless for education and in some senses inspiring, if only in terms of his physical body surviving. Yet the reader, given exclusive access to Peter's inner world, finds that there is a man with a rich and interesting mind inside the shell. Peter suffers from paranoia, expressed without a hint of the irony inherent in his comments:

> Could there be wires in the walls? I had contemplated often, with distressing inconclusiveness, that there might be no other earthly reason for their taking me to the toilet, as they did now and then, and leaving me there for hours, except for the purpose of spying on me in isolation. I know, I know, these are not the thoughts of a rational man. Indeed, if I had heard these theories expressed by anyone I should immediately have categorised them as brilliantly typical of a certain kind of person with whom I shared residence. (p. 22)

Elements of Peter's madness are described with phenomenal clarity and, as we have argued elsewhere (Crawford and Baker, 2009), Sayer provides insights into a particular type of madness with an emotive narrative patterning. Whilst we suggested in our opening chapter that we do not want to engage in symptom-spotting, here it is worth noting, because of the descriptive power used by Sayer, that Peter suffers from nihilistic delusions: 'You see, bits of me were breaking loose, shaking free inside, kidneys, heart, spleen, even my intestines, were all freeing themselves from their moorings, lifting their roots from the brittle shell of my body which seemed to want nothing to do with keeping its respective components in place' (p. 39). This belief is described as being frightening for Peter and as interlinked with his belief that the carers at the facility he is in are out to harm him in some way – which, under the guise of treatment, they actually do, as we will discuss further in Chapter 3.

Yet merely providing names for each of Peter's symptoms – paranoia, nihilistic delusions; in other words, symptom-spotting – both denies the beauty of the language that Sayer uses and reduces Peter's complex experiences to single labels. Peter's insight into how others perceive him leads to a stark and moving emotionally insightful reaction:

> I was beset by depression, it had laid siege to me, coming in waves day after day, a withering possession that had taken hold and would not let go. [...] What was in it for them? Where did they find the initiative, this animated desire to take me apart, build me up, reinvent me? I had no satisfactory answer, save the recurrent notion that somehow they were really attempting a reconstruction of their own selves, imposing on me an image of the way they thought they were, or should be. (p. 63–64)

Peter is neither unintelligent nor emotionally catatonic, despite other people's assumptions, and he questions what the medical professionals around him are trying to treat and, more importantly, why. Peter makes an important point here regarding his desire to be left alone, untreated. Peter does not want to be reconstructed into what the doctors around him believe he should be.

Peter only communicates with the reader, not those around him in the novel, lending his claims a sense of truth and honesty, and creating a sense of closeness with the reader. Notably, Sayer does not explicitly provide a diagnosis for Peter's condition: 'so what was my problem, then? Why should I get myself into such a state, make such a fuss because people were trying to help me? What made me the way I was in the first place? Illness? Paralysis? Trauma?' (p. 47). In a diagnosis-spotting manner, from the textual presentation we can propose that he could be suffering from a catatonic psychosis, autism, or a severe developmental disorder. Again, as with naming his symptoms, this is not only supposition but also it tells us little about the mind and experiences that form Sayer's novel. What is clear is that Peter is not *allowed* to exist purely within his inner world. He is, at times, comfortable with his existence, and becomes distressed at notions of change:

> I had, it seemed, come to take my stillness and the comfort I found there, too much for granted. Yes, that was it – I had become complacent, too happy with my lot, and now I was being made to account for it. I had no inalienable right to contentment, I knew that, but these people were taking great exception to me and it looked as if they were not going to rest until they had come up with some permanent arrest of my catatonic state. (p. 47)

Both Lessing and Sayer examine the urge of the psychiatric profession to diagnose and treat. They look beneath the rhetoric of "what happens if we don't treat", and confront notions of autonomy, the pathologisation of experiences, and whether abnormality of experience should be assumed to be inherently negative. In a number of post-war madness novels, we can see an active defiance of diagnostic specificity and contempt for the spotting and collecting of symptoms. What the reader becomes drawn to, what makes these novels fascinating and thought-provoking, is the urge to consider what it may feel like to live and experience madness.

From Peter's account, we as readers could conclude that he suffers from nihilistic delusions and paranoia. That would suffice for a discharge summary. But it dismisses what is at the core of these accounts. Such a diagnostic account tells us little about the human being aside from the symptoms. An analogy between reader/doctor and character/patient can tentatively be drawn here. The reader and doctor are both story interpreters via the hermeneutics of the clinical encounter. The doctor reads the patient; the reader reads the text. The emphasis of literature is twofold – drawing attention to the content and context of experience, and emphasising the need to see the whole condition rather than the listed segments of symptom and subsequent diagnosis.

In Clare Boylan's novel *Beloved Stranger* (1999), the forward-thinking doctor treating the mad character of Dick diagnoses bipolar affective disorder. During his discussion with Dick's family he uses a number of synonyms to define *what* Dick has, also referring to the time-specific nature of diagnosis and refuting the usefulness of naming illnesses:

> 'Bi-polar disorder. But that's only a guess [...] Your father's head has taken a wrong road. It might be a long road. Best look at the ancient signposts first.' He tore open the packet of biscuits and studied them with care before selecting a chocolate sandwich. 'Mad, senseless, deranged, mental, insane, confused, demented, crazy.' Crumbs sputtered as he expounded. 'Deranged might do. Have you a dictionary?' [...] With a glare, she got up and fetched the frayed old Webster's, friend of her homework days. The Walnut licked his fingers, pushed his spectacles back on and thumbed with a leisurely sort of enjoyment. 'Deranged ... Here we are!' He looked at his audience to make sure of their attention. 'Thrown into disorder. That's about right. We won't say he's mad any more.' He nodded agreeably at Ruth. 'We'll say deranged.' (p. 58)

Here the doctor focuses the attention of Dick's family, and the reader, away from the human and psychiatric compulsion to name and classify, towards a realisation of the actual relative unimportance of naming or labelling. There is a discrepancy between the doctor's external observation of Dick and what may or may not be occurring internally, given that the doctor has no access to the actuality of Dick's thoughts – only his external behaviour and speech, as the doctor comments: 'He's showing signs of severe paranoid delusion and he's very excitable. He's deluded, but at the same time he's mostly very lucid. And he's no fool. He's foxy, and I can't yet tell if he's foxing himself as well as the rest of us' (p. 59). In Boylan's text, Dick's experiences are given to the reader through extradiegetic narration, allowing the reader no direct access to his inner world.

The reader can assume that what the doctor conceptualises as 'severe paranoid delusion' (p. 59) might be frightening, but this is contrasted with his excitability, which is generally taken to mean exuberance or happiness. This contrast exemplifies the uniqueness of madness, whereby no mental occurrence or reaction is duplicated by an, or any, other person.

Thematising madness in fiction

Of course, the goals of psychiatry – assess, classify, consolidate, console, diagnose, treat – are not malignant ones. However, in thrall to the legacy of Emil Kraepelin's seminal works at the dawn of the age of psychiatry, the discipline retains an assumption that there is a fundamental divide between normal and abnormal, sane and mad; and sanity is assumed to be the preferable state of mind (Bentall, 2003). However, in literature we see that attaining and maintaining a rational, coherent self is not always a goal for characters – as Feder suggests, madness can have a spiritual and/or exposing political aim or effect (1980, p. 285–286). Thematic representations of madness exist on a continuum, as we suggested earlier in this chapter. At one pole stands the experience of madness as absolute terror, leading to horrific psychological events and potentially self-/other-destructive behaviours. At the other extreme, we see veritable celebrations of madness, particularly in literature which exalts the widening of perception through the use of hallucinogens, and literature which suggests that madness gives insights that are otherwise unavailable. Along this continuum are a range of representations that suggest that madness *may* be a preferable alternative to the social, external reality that characters experience.

Take, for example Sayer's novel. At certain points it appears that Peter has chosen his catatonic state, horrid and dehumanising though it appears to those observing him as a human shell. Peter's experiences as a child lead firstly to his mutism, and then to his complete withdrawal. He experiences this as 'the first wave of a warm, comforting stillness breaking over me, a quiet madness of my own making. In a funny sort of way it was how I imagined a homecoming might be' (p. 105). Peter is petrified of his 'comforting stillness' being removed – rightly so, given the torturous treatments employed to 'cure' him. Yet we can also see that Peter experiences terrifying nihilistic delusions, depressive episodes, and acute paranoia within his madness. Sayer's achievement in this text comes from the unanswerable question that he poses – is Peter's madness preferable to existence in what he perceives (rightly or wrongly) to be a frightening, painful world?

Narratives that explore madness as absolute terror include Patrick McGrath's *Spider* and Paul Crawford's *Nothing Purple, Nothing Black*. A simplistic reading of these two texts is that they present the social reality for many individuals who suffer from madness. We can see in both books, for example, the profound impact of the closure of the asylums upon long-term institutionalised patients – both Spider and Crystal live socially isolated, poverty-riddled existences in miserable accommodation. They experience their madness in terms of emotions such as fear, anxiety, and panic, which ultimately lead them to terror and horror. McGrath's Spider begins to deteriorate mentally following his release from long-term institutional care. In contrast to the lethargic, sluggish prose of Spider's reminiscent narration are the passages detailing his descent into madness, replete with a range of terrifying olfactory and auditory hallucinatory experiences. These madness passages are notably more fractured and hurried, suggesting linguistically the quickening of Spider's heartbeat as he attempts to cognitively process his mentally distorted experiences, in this case his conviction that his olfactory hallucination of gas is coming from his own body:

> There was a third possibility, though it took several minutes for it to dawn on me: that the smell was coming from *me*, from my own body.
>
> This was a shock. I straightened up and tried to smell myself. Nothing. I staggered upright, clutching the end of the bed, and opened my shirt and trousers, fumbling clumsily at the buttons in my haste. Was it there? Again that awful uncertainty – I would seem to have it, then it was gone. I sat hunched on the bed, clutching myself around the shins, my forehead on my knees. Did I have it? Was there gas? Was it seeping from my *groin*? I lifted my head and turned it helplessly from side to side. Gas from my *groin*? It was at that moment that I became aware of the noise in the attic overhead, quiet laughter followed by a sort of bump – then there was silence again.
>
> I had little sleep the rest of that night, and the light stayed on. I tried to put the whole thing out of my mind, but it wouldn't go away, a terrible nagging uncertainty persisted. I was particularly uneasy at breakfast, for I had the feeling that they could destroy me, any of them, with just a glance. (McGrath, 1990, p. 30)

The reader here is given insight into the fear aroused by unusual, unpredictable experiences; the questioning of *everything* that it induces; the quickening pulse and helplessness of being caught in a circle of paranoia, fear, and uncertainty.

Paul Crawford's novel employs a similar tactic. In comparison to the sensual precision of ex-priest Harvey's narrated history, Crystal's psychological deterioration is vividly portrayed and at times frenetically paced. His initial deterioration from quiescence into hallucinosis is presented with crescendo-building pace, and the terror induced by the experience of hearing abusive, threatening voices is acutely portrayed:

> Crystal's voices had never been so fierce and unrelenting. Filth, shocking filth filled his ears. He had never heard anything like it before. They were getting much worse. They bored down into his skull, screaming and shouting sometimes above the noise of the crowds and trains. The cup of coffee shook in his hands and now and then he had to close his eyes in desperation, let the coffee burn at his lips. Once or twice he shouted out loud to try to drown out the voices, to block them. But they came back worse than ever, louder than ever. Coffee splashed over his legs and down onto the platform. The voices ate his nerves, fed on his terror, his panic. (Crawford, 2002, p. 169)

Crystal's sheer terror at the novel's shocking climax is clear, leaving the reader with an understanding of the pathway that leads him to his final murderous act and therefore, one would hope, with a simultaneous sort of sympathy:

> Crystal punched and kicked the thing. He heard it cry out in pain. 'You're dead meat,' the voices raged on. 'Here come the teeth. Here come the teeth. Bite the bastard in half! Chew him up!' Crystal was kicking and lashing out for all he was worth. He saw white teeth blur in slow motion. He felt mad. He saw blood. He heard wings beating. He had the beast by the neck, squeezing it till his knuckles blanched. There was something golden hung around its neck. It was a thick elaborate chain and cross. Crystal wrapped it around his fist and jerked it tight, the beast sinking into the ground. (p. 190)

Inherent within Crystal's murderous dénouement is the terror of threatening voices, the consumption of his entire being by madness, combined with his desperate fight to live – a fight that ironically leads to the death of Harvey. As with McGrath's presentation of madness, the short, punchy sentences here propel the reader on, suggestive of the fast-beating heart of the mad character.

In Bernice Ruben's *The Elected Member* (1969), the experience of madness as terrifying is also presented, but with a curious twist. Protagonist

Norman experiences a madness associated with drug-taking. There is a strange paradox in Norman's madness that strikes at the heart of the real/unreal dichotomy. The unreal symbols of Norman's madness are, in his mind, the only real witnesses to what he perceives as evidence of his sanity. Furthermore, these witnesses – the mysterious 'they' – are both terrifying *and* comforting:

> He screwed his eyes tightly against the dark. He knew that his short sleep was over, but he was too terrified to acknowledge it. He should never have let himself doze off. God knows what they were doing while he was sleeping, and God knows what they were doing now, and where else they were, and how many. No, he would not open his eyes. If they were still there, he could rely on them to stay. He pulled the pillow over his ears. He didn't want to hear them either. Yet he wanted to check that they were still there. He dreaded their presence, but their sudden absence would have terrified him more. They were the only witnesses to his sanity. (p. 8)

There is a contradictory rationality to Norman's irrational experiences, depending on the point of view taken. No one else believes in his hallucinations, delusions, and paranoia, which are absolutely real for Norman, and thus to him the very existent 'they' are the only witnesses to his reality – a reality that everyone else denies. It is not only in the auditory realm that Norman seeks reassurance that his unreal experiences are real – he finds further comfort in and 'proof' of their reality through imaginary smells:

> He lifted his ear from the pillow and he heard them, the scratching teeth-gnashing grind of their crawl. And something new too. Their smell. At first, he held his breath, then he sniffed gratefully around him. A dewy smell, like biscuits left uncovered, to soften. It was further proof that they were there. They had a right after all, to make a noise and to emanate some kind of odour. But he was frightened too. Each further proof of their presence frightened him. The more overwhelming the evidence, the less credulous his family became. (p. 9)

Again, in this passage we can see the presence of both fright and comfort and, more interestingly, the levels of belief that Norman credits his *experiences* with, rather than what he is *told* is occurring. As we learn in the narrative, Norman appears to have a drug-induced psychosis – he has to be sedated after his supply of 'white' (the drug he is addicted to) on the ward is suddenly halted, and he experiences acute drug withdrawal (p. 140). During this period, he again becomes what would be defined clinically as acutely psychotic, hallucinating and spreading detergent all over the ward in order to kill imaginary bugs in a frenzied way. Notably, he experiences tactile hallucinations and the feeling that there are insects under his skin – common in cocaine-withdrawal. More important than clinical accuracy or labelling here is what Rubens does with her narrative, which is to draw the focus onto Norman's cognitive interpretation and lived experience of his madness, experienced in part through sensory abnormalities. We are once again reminded here of both the work of Jaspers (1963) on the individual beliefs inherent in madness, which we discussed earlier, and also the more recent work of Geekie and Read (2009), who suggest that the individual's *subjective* interpretation of and accounting for madness experiences should be the focus of therapeutic treatment. Rubens, through the character of Norman, provides a classic example of the subjective experiences of madness-as-terror, as do Crawford and McGrath.

Narratives such as *The Elected Member* emphasise the negative side of drug abuse, addiction, and sometimes-concomitant mental illness. This is in contrast to a number of texts produced during the late 1950s and 1960s that paradoxically emphasise the *benefits* of a drug-induced opening and widening of perception – texts which appear to celebrate certain elements of madness. William S. Burroughs, possibly the most well known of this group of authors, suggested in letters to Allen Ginsberg – then an unknown poet – that there may be more to consciousness than is available in collectively experienced reality. In *The Yage Letters* (1969), a collection of letters between the two (interestingly, published in the same year as Rubens's text), Ginsberg writes on his experience following ingestion of the hallucinogen Ayahuasca (*Banisteriopsis Caapi*), or Yage (*Prestonia Amazonica*): 'I suppose I will be able to protect myself by treating *that* consciousness as a temporary illusion and return to temporary normal consciousness when the effects wear off – (I begin to glimpse the Call of Haitian Voodoo) – but this almost schizophrenic alteration of consciousness is fearful' (p. 55). Ginsberg's use of the psychiatric diagnosis of schizophrenia to describe his drug-induced state is interesting here, suggesting a direct link between hallucinogens and the madness experiences inherent in schizophrenia. Burroughs responds to Ginsberg:

> There is no thing to fear. Vaya adelante. Look. Listen. Hear. Your AYUASKA consciousness is more valid than 'Normal Consciousness'? Whose 'Normal Consciousness'? Why return to? Why are you surprised

to see me? You are following in my steps. I know thee way. And yes know the area better than you think. Tried more than once to tell you to communicate what I know. You did not or could not listen. [...] And always remember. 'Nothing is True. Everything is Permitted.' (p. 59)

Yage has been used for centuries for its visionary and healing properties (Schultes and Von Reis, 1995), and both Burroughs and Ginsberg experimented extensively with the drug, describing the alternate consciousnesses and perceptions it induced. In the quotation from Burroughs above, he suggests that 'Normal Consciousness' is a questionable entity, but that the insights produced by hallucinogens may be more valid, leading to a plane of consciousness otherwise unavailable. Paradoxically, Richard Evans Schultes, one of the founders of ethnobotany and investigator of medicinal plants in South America, was unimpressed by the psychoactive properties of *banisteriopsis* and *prestonia*. On hearing Burroughs describe his experience of these drugs as inducing life-changing experiences, he commented dismissively, 'That's funny Bill. All I saw was colours' (Kandell, 2001, p. C11). One interpretation here is that that one man's psychosis is another man's insight into alternative realities and consciousnesses.

Burroughs, a drug addict for the majority of his life, writes concisely yet in his own inimitable style on the reasons for his use of hallucinogens, in his semi-fictionalised autobiography *Junky* (1953):

I am ready to move on south and look for the uncut kick that opens out instead of narrowing down like junk.

Kick is seeing things from a special angle. Kick is momentary freedom from the claims of the aging, cautious, nagging, frightened flesh. Maybe I will find in yage what I was looking for in junk and week and coke. Yage may be the final fix. (p. 152)

Junky ends on the note of literal and metaphorical journey – a journey which Burroughs undertook immediately after finishing the book – to find the missing element to his life, which may be Yage – a drug that opens and widens perception rather than inducing the stasis or narrowing caused by other drugs. Burroughs differentiates, throughout his work, between narcotic/opiate addition and the consciousness-raising properties of hallucinogens. As a recovering opiate addict, he writes in the opening pages of *Naked Lunch* (1959):

I awoke from The Sickness at the age of forty-five, calm and sane, and in reasonably good health except for a weakened liver and the look of borrowed flesh common to all who survive The Sickness. [...] Most survivors do not remember the delirium in detail. I apparently took detailed notes on sickness and delirium. I have no precise memory of writing the notes which have now been published under the title *Naked Lunch*. (p. 7)

Withdrawal, stasis, and sickness are key themes throughout his most infamous and visionary text. In *Naked Lunch*, Burroughs suggests that junk, his preferred term for opiates (of which heroin is one), 'yields a basic formula of "evil" virus: *The Algebra of Need*. The face of "evil" is always the face of total need' (1959, p. 8). Withdrawal from junk leaves individuals 'literally insane and paranoid' (1959, p. 10). Burroughs appears to differentiate between those elements of madness that lead to absolute terror – and here, those are induced by opiates and other similar drugs – and those elements of madness that consist of sensory and perceptual changes, induced by hallucinogens. Albeit through the use of drugs rather than through a non-chemically-induced madness, Burroughs replicates our notions of representations of madness as existing on a continuum.

Curiously, in the midst of the meanderings in *Naked Lunch* on the benefits and drawbacks of a drug-induced mental state, Burroughs creates the 'Freeland Republic', an elucidatory satire on, among other things, the psych-disciplines. Managed by the sinister Dr Benway, who believes in 'Total Demoralization' (p. 31) as an effective mode of social management, a range of psychological and psychiatric tortures are used in order to produce 'total obedience' (p. 35). Drugs are used to *induce* depression, psychosis, and addiction which impact upon a person's sense of coherent self, proving to be 'an essential tool of the interrogator in his assault on the subject's personal identity' (p. 34). On a simple level the purpose of Freeland, and Dr Benway's previous assignment Annexia, is to create compliant human automatons. In order to produce these robots, drugs, psychological treatments and sexual manipulation are used. Proper analysis of Burroughs' Freeland Republic and Dr Benway would produce a book in itself – suffice to say here, Burroughs can be seen as critiquing Western models of psychology and psychiatry whereby one predominantly white, heterosexual, male mode of existence is dominant, and each and all deviations from this are subject to incarceration and treatment. Throughout Burroughs's work, several tensions can be identified – between the desired mind-expanding form of madness induced by hallucinogens, the very real negative effects of addiction to other drugs, and the treatment of variations of consciousness, perception, and belief in the Western world.

An American-born author, Burroughs celebrates, actively seeks, *and* fears anarchy, annihilation, and alienation throughout his work. Similarly, British writer J. G. Ballard both relishes and reviles post-war society as inducing a certain kind of breakdown in ethics and morals, leading to a uniquely celebratory, truly free psychopathology. In Ballard's novel *High Rise* (1975), the inhabitants of the quintessentially postmodern high-rise tower block must 'surrender to a logic more powerful than reason' in order to effectively function and survive in such a pressured environment (p. 65). Ballard's view, demonstrated throughout his extensive body of work, is that living a technologically consumed life leads to a constrained and highly unnatural existence. In *High Rise*, the building becomes 'a model of all that technology had done to make possible the expression of a truly "free" psychopathology' (p. 37). Living in the high-rise removed 'the need to repress every kind of anti-social behaviour, and left them free to explore any deviant or wayward impulses', the inhabitants being now free to 'explore the darkest corners' (p. 37) of their psyches. For Ballard, indulgence in the otherwise socially and psychologically repressed deviance of psychopathology is the only remedy for supremely sane but ultimately futile life in the postmodern world. Ballard's psychopathology has one other key benefit – it is *only* in immersion in the (psychopathological) imagination that any notion of true freedom can be found. As he stated in an interview:

> [...] if you have a world like that, without any kind of real freedom of the spirit, the only freedom to be found is in *madness*. I mean, in a completely sane world, *madness* is the only freedom!
>
> That's what's coming. That's why the suburbs interest me – because you *see* threat coming. Where one's almost got to get up in the morning and make a *resolution* to perform some sort of deviant or antisocial act, some perverse act, even if it's just sort of *kicking the dog*, in order to establish one's own freedom [...] Suburbs are very sinister places, contrary to what most people imagine. (Juno and Vale, 1984, p. 15)

In Ballard's final novel *Kingdom Come* (2006), the sinister nature of suburban life is fully expounded. Having, in the post-millennium era, unlimited access to every conceivable pleasure and self-indulgence, and having pushed the boundaries of human experience through sex, drugs, and warfare, what is left, according to character Tony Maxted (who, like many of Ballard's characters, is a psychiatrist), is:

> A voluntary insanity, whatever you want to call it. As a psychiatrist I'd use the term elective psychopathy. Not the kind of madness we deal with here. I'm talking about a willed insanity, the sort that we higher primates thrive on. Watch a troupe of chimpanzees. They're bored with chewing twigs and picking the fleas out of each other's armpits. They want meat, the bloodier the better, they want to taste their enemies' fear in the flesh they grind. So they start beating their chests and shrieking at the sky. They work themselves into a frenzy, then set off in a hunting party. (p. 103–104)

According to Maxted, psychopathology is, to a degree, an evolutionary process: 'Elective insanity is waiting inside us, ready to come out when we need it' (p. 104). TV presenter David Cruise echoes this statement to protagonist Richard Pearson, who is investigating his father's dubious role in a shopping-plaza shooting. Cruise states that his viewers – the 'masses' of middle England – 'know that madness is the only freedom left to them', believing that 'psychopathy is close to sainthood' (p. 148). *Kingdom Come* is the fourth in a series of novels by Ballard exploring notions of excessive leisure, unlimited pleasure, and suburban life as inducing a form of madness – the other three are *Cocaine Nights* (1996), *Super-Cannes* (2000), and *Millennium People* (2003) – but these are themes that resonate throughout his work, and madness, it can be argued, is his key preoccupation. For Ballard, the journey into and existence within psychopathology is characterised by paradox. He implies that descending into this distinctively postmodern mental state is induced by the technological landscape of postmodernity. Insanity is not only necessary for survival but is our only route to freedom. He stated in interview: 'In a totally sane society the only freedom is madness' (Revell, 1984, p. 44). On the other hand, Ballard repeatedly creates situations where this descent is ultimately unsuccessful, and often leads to a complete deterioration in mental functioning, for example the character Wilder's florid and self-destructive psychosis at the end of *High Rise*. Elective or otherwise, madness seems to be both a goal *and* a nightmare for many of Ballard's characters. For Ballard's characters, psychopathology is inevitable and inescapable. This post-war paradox – the notion that and/or becomes both and neither – is evident in a number of madness narratives.

In contrast to Ballard's paradoxical psychopathology, Marge Piercy's 1976 novel *Woman on the Edge of Time* provides one of the starkest visions of madness as a preferable alternative to reality by using literary utopian exploration to represent Connie's madness while the 'real' world around Connie is bleak, discriminatory, and dangerous. Connie is admitted to hospital following a series of adverse life events – the loss of her young daughter into social care, poverty and social exclusion, her niece's prostitution and drug use. Her niece's life leads Connie to encounter some nefarious individuals, one of whom – Geraldo, her niece's pimp – she assaults physically. This attack – which is presented as justifiable in the novel – leads to her admission to a ward where the admitting doctor talks exclusively with Geraldo and Dolly, failing to speak to Connie (p. 17). With her life outside the hospital marred by loss, poverty, and violence, she finds herself restrained, medicated, and silenced on the ward, and told in unequivocal terms that her reluctance to be in hospital is *itself* a sign of her madness (p. 17). Paradoxes such as this are common in madness novels, exposing the very real psychiatric paradox whereby admitting to being psychologically unwell is a sign of wellness.

Connie is trapped in degradation and pessimism, and it is unsurprising that she prefers to exist psychologically in the future, portrayed through her travels with Luciente, who lives in the year 2137. Psychiatric care in the future is vastly different from Connie's experiences of tranquilisation, threatened psychosurgery, violence, oppression, and restraint, which we explore further in Chapter 3. As Luciente explains to Connie:

> Our madhouses are places where people retreat when they want to go down into themselves – to collapse, carry on, see visions, hear voices of prophecy, bang on the walls, relive infancy – getting in touch with the buried self and the inner mind. We all lose parts of ourselves. We all make choices that go bad [...] How can another person decide that it is time for me to disintegrate, to reintegrate myself? (p. 6).

In Connie's world, disintegration, deviation, and degeneracy (if you are female) are punished. The site where reintegration and recovery should occur only leads to further punitive dehumanisation, physically invasive experiments, and psychological abuse. Interestingly, the depiction of madhouses in the future does in some ways mirror the development of alternative commune-style places for the treatment of madness that have emerged in the post-war period, for example the Soteria project (Mosher and Hendrix, 2004).

Piercy's visionary novel is the epitomic examination of madness and otherworldliness. In literary representation, madness itself is at times experienced as either utopian or dystopian, and often simultaneously *and* ambivalently both (once again emphasising the contemporary movement from and/or to both/neither). As Robert de Beaugrande suggests, 'our search for the relation of madness and literature brings us to the ultimately utopian dialectic of literature: to understand our understanding of ourselves and of our world through the unending creation of alternative worlds' (1994, p. 29). The revealing changes in vision and perception through utopian and dystopian literary narratives provide an excellent tool for exposing prejudicial social realities.

Crucial to questions of otherworldliness, unreality, utopias, and dystopias are dislocations in space and time. This can sometimes be very literal – for example Connie's translocation to Mattapoisett (Piercy, 1976, p. 52), and, in Kurt Vonnegut's 1969 novel *Slaughterhouse-Five*, protagonist Billy Pilgrim's time-travelling between 'real' life and the otherworldliness of Tralfarmadore. We learn early on in the novel that 'Billy Pilgrim has come unstuck in time' (p. 23):

Billy has gone to sleep a senile widower and awakened on his wedding day. He has walked through a door in 1955 and come out through another one in 1941. He has gone back through that door to find himself in 1963. He has seen his birth and death many times, he says, and pays random visits to all the events in between.

He says:

> Billy is spastic in time, has no control over where he is going next, and the trips aren't necessarily fun. He is in a constant state of stage fright, he says, because he never knows what part of his life he is going to have to act in next. (p. 23)

The narrator's wry 'he says' leads to questioning of Billy's tale, as is common in the reception of the mad person's stories. He has survived a severe head injury, and the reader asks: is Billy psychotic, time travelling, abducted by aliens, or a philosopher and seer? In the novel, he is all of these things, often simultaneously. Like Sayer, Vonnegut suggests that the outward appearance of individuals tells us little about their inner landscape – after his brain trauma, for example, Vonnegut writes: 'Billy's outward listlessness was a screen. The listlessness concealed a mind which was fizzing and flashing thrillingly. It was preparing letters and lectures about the flying saucers, the negligibility of death, and the true nature of time' (p. 190). There is a gulf between the doctor's view of Billy's story and Billy's own beliefs. The doctors insist that Billy has echolalia due to cerebral damage because it is easier to make this assumption (p. 192). This leads to Billy 'having an adventure very common among people without power in time of war: He was trying to prove to a willfully deaf and blind enemy that he was interesting to hear and see' (p. 193). The medical staff is the 'enemy', 'willfully deaf and blind' to Billy's inner landscape. While this incident occurs post-head injury, it resonates with the experience of individuals who are designated as mad, and thus are often presented in madness novels as having nothing interesting or useful to contribute to discussions – particularly when these discussions relate to their care.

Billy Pilgrim is presented by Vonnegut as a philosopher, a man given life-affirming insights into time, existence, and emotions. Differing ways of interpreting mystical, spiritual, and psychotic experiences have of course been proposed by a number of researchers and theorists, such as Chadwick (2009), whose text examines individual interpretations – outside the psychiatric sphere – of schizoid, spiritual, and mystical experiences. Billy's own experiences, whichever discourse they are interpreted in, have benign effects. Lupack suggests:

> It is, after all, precisely his craziness – his getting unstuck in time – which allows Billy to come to terms with the far greater lunacy of the war and of his own postwar society, the slaughterhouse of the modern world. Not simply does *Slaughterhouse-Five* indict contemporary obsession with destructive technologies (e.g., the firebombing of Dresden, a symbol of all that is best in Western Culture); it provides Vonnegut the opportunity to comment on the insanity of war generally and, by comparing Americans to Nazis [...] and other butchers who operate in the slaughterhouse of contemporary society, the American insanity in Vietnam in particular. (1994, p. 177)

Thus, according to Lupack, the exposing side of Vonnegut's visionary narrative allows a view to be put forward – a view of the insanity of contemporary life – that may be difficult to fully discuss within the framework of realism. This is reinforced by Lawrence R. Broer, who states:

> The fact is that these escapist worlds warn against rather than affirm fatalist sophistries. Such mirror reflections of our own planet enforce Vonnegut's position that the insane world of soulless materialistic lusts for fame and money, of suicidal wars and self-serving religions, that we presently inhabit is a world of our own lunatic invention. (1994, p. 198)

Broer also suggests that a 'striking paradox of *Slaughterhouse-Five* is that it presents us with Vonnegut's most completely demoralized protagonist while making what is to this point the most affirmative statement of Vonnegut's career' (1994, p. 202). In Vonnegut's novel, Billy is not demoralised throughout the narrative – indeed, when time-travelling, he is at his *least* demoralised. With the paradoxical notion of 'memories of the future' (p. 150), Billy's loss of linear temporality is psychologically beneficial and allows him a cool acceptance of the universal existential challenges of life, and of death:

> The most important thing I learned on Tralfamadore was that when a person dies he only *appears* to die. He is still very much alive in the past, so it is very silly for people to cry at his funeral. All moments, past, present, and future, always have existed, always will exist. The Tralfamadorians can look at all the different moments just the way we can look at a stretch of the Rocky Mountains, for instance. They can see how permanent all the moments are, and they can look at any moment that interests them. It is just an illusion we have here on Earth that one moment follows another, like beads on a string, and that once a moment is gone it is gone forever. (pp. 26–27)

In contrast to his life-affirming time-travelling existence, it is the inescapable and very real (in a literal rather than mental sense) trauma of war, as Broer suggests (1994, p. 198), that plunges Billy into a state of exhaustion and demoralisation. When the difference between sleep and wakefulness is indistinct, it is easy to see how a literal dislocation of circadian rhythms can lead to a metaphoric and/or concomitant psychotic break in temporality (Vonnegut, 1969, p. 34). These temporal breaks are not merely travels back in memory. Dys/utopian novels often show an existential dimension to madness – it is life-saving rather than life-destroying. Following Billy Pilgrim's admission to a psychiatric unit after the Second World War, in comparison to another patient with a similar history, Vonnegut suggests through Billy that each mode of recovery requires a different form of renewal and reinvention: both patients had 'found life meaningless, partly because of what they had seen in war' and as a result 'they were trying to re-invent themselves and their universe. Science fiction was a big help' (p. 101). The science fiction Billy refers to in the novel also provides a comment on psychiatry: 'The book was *Maniacs in the Fourth Dimension*, by Kilgore Trout. It was about people whose mental diseases couldn't be treated because the causes of the diseases were all in the fourth dimension, and the three-dimensional Earthling doctors couldn't see those causes at all, or even imagine them' (p. 104). Furthermore, the patient that Billy is compared to, Rosewater, provides food for thought when Billy overhears him talking with the psychiatrist who is sent to help them recover from their traumas: 'I think you guys are going to have to come up with a lot of wonderful *new* lies, or people just aren't going to want to go on living' (p. 101). It seems that physical and mental traumas, psychoses, and other forms of madness can indeed give characters in post-war novels insight into the reality of the insanity of the world around them.

The relationship between existential crises, mainstream post-war novels, and the genre of science fiction – with its fantastical other-worldliness and dys/utopian world view – is clear. Both science fiction as a literal and literary entity, and the more ethereal psychotic reality and journey inward, provide preferable and desirable alternatives to the traumas of 'real' life. Billy Pilgrim goes one step further than daydreaming or entering into his imagination for escape by stepping directly into the alternative, existing within the utopian. We may define this as psychotic, but this is a preferable reality to the horror within which Billy exists and has existed. Indeed, Billy experiences *pleasurable* psychotic phenomena as an escape from the atrocities of, in this particular scenario, wartime trench existence, for example the 'delightful hallucination' of having dry, warm feet that he experiences as 'the craziness of a dying young man with his shoes full of snow' (p. 49). The experiences of Connie and Billy are vastly different from those of McGrath's Spider and Crawford's Crystal. This continuum of representation demonstrates the acute need to consider each *individual* range of experiences as precisely that – unique.

Mad or bad?

As neurosis (sadness) and psychosis, or madness, become increasingly explained through various branches of psychiatry and psychology, inexplicably savage, deviant, or even colloquially-named evil behaviours are being scrutinised through a psychiatric lens, as explored philosophically by Bavidge (1989). Extreme cruelty is equated in the mind of the public with madness – if they did this awful, incomprehensibly evil thing, then they *must* be mad. The language used to describe individuals in the media, for example, often includes bastardised colloquial phrases from psychiatry – psycho, psychopath, psychotic, schizo, and so forth. While a degree of sympathy is afforded to those well-behaved individuals who are seen as eccentric non-conformists, any level of understanding, sympathy, or empathy are completely absent in the media and in literature concerned with evilness: we can see this in the deluge of crime novels, particularly those involving serial killing in a highly sensationalised manner, available in any bookshop. Yet the volume of such novels and their bestseller status indicates that while we are repelled by badness, needing to situate it firmly as Other to ourselves, we are simultaneously fascinated by it. The lack of neutral, non-sensationalised and accurate widely accessible material on 'badness' not only increases the distance between notions of madness, sanity/difference, and otherness, but also serves to further stigmatise individuals labelled as, for example, psychotic. At times, in the mind of the public, psychosis, or schizophrenia, equals (potential) serial killer – the view perpetuated by many tabloid headlines.

Theodore Dalrymple's *So Little Done: The Testament of a Serial Killer* (1995) is quite different from the crime novels of, for example, the highly popular Tess Gerritsen or Ian Rankin. Dalrymple – the pseudonym used by psychiatrist Anthony Daniels – very cleverly uses philosophical, anthropological, logical, and moral arguments to make an extreme case of 'badness' uncomfortably explicable and familiar, and he does so in an unnervingly successful way. Dalrymple uses direct contact via appeals to the reader as a device to reduce the distance between reader and character. Serial killer Graham Underwood, the first-person narrator of the novel, is an astonishing comic creation, self-important and sanctimonious. In the opening pages of the novel, Underwood outrages and alienates his reader:

> You hypocrites! You pretend (not only to others but even to yourselves) that you're reading this for a higher purpose, such as understanding the mind of a so-called serial killer like me. But why are you interested in the mind of a serial killer in the first place, may I ask? And what good would your understanding do you, even supposing it were attainable from reading what I have written? Would it prevent the emergence of a single such killer in the future, or facilitate his detection? No, it's not enlightenment you're after, but salacious entertainment [...]. (p. 5)

A highly intelligent though largely self-educated individual, Underwood draws on a number of moral and theoretical arguments to justify his killings – as well as making clear his contempt for the psych-disciplines:

> I have mentioned already my disdain for psychiatrists, a mongrel
> breed if ever there was one, claiming to be scientists and yet human-
> ists at the same time, when in reality they are officially-licensed and
> highly-paid gossips. But one among them once wrote something true
> and important (though naturally he was despised for it by his profes-
> sional colleagues, who conspired to ruin his career by withdrawing
> his right to practice). I refer to R. D. Laing, who wrote:
> We are all murderers and prostitutes – no matter to what culture,
> society, class, nation one belongs, no matter how normal, moral or
> mature one takes oneself to be.
> The unvarnished truth, ladies and gentlemen, whether you like
> it or not. At the least I have tried, consistently and without fail, to
> escape his condition. Are you able to say the same? And if not, should
> we not be changing places? (p. 61)

Underwood suggests that he has made an active choice to be morally
superior to his reader by escaping his interpretation of Laing's description – he chose his route rather than blindly living it. Considering the
sentencing judge's description of his 'wickedness', Underwood suggests:

> I never wanted to do wrong, but on the contrary have always tried
> to do my public duty, at the same time as developing my own per-
> sonality to its full potential. You may, perhaps, disagree with what I
> considered right action, but what is incontestable is that I wished no
> harm. I am, after all, the final authority as to what my wishes were:
> and they were always honourable. (p. 135)

Underwood's apparently honourable 'public duty' consists of only
murdering those who he feels have no function or use in society – the
lower-than-lower-class substratum of society, the majority of whom
(in his mind) smoke cigarettes, thus draining the National Health
Service of resources, rely heavily on social security benefits, and – in
the case of women in particular – are promiscuous. In killing off this
substratum of society, Underwood suggests he not only saves them
(and society) the cost of dying painful self-inflicted deaths, but that
he ends their misery in a humane manner – drugging, then strangling
them (p. 38). By reflecting on the moral judgements and assumptions that we are all guilty of making, thus closing that narrative
distance between morally superior reader and abhorrent character,

Underwood leads the reader towards challenging their own judge-mental tendencies.

It is possible to some degree to reflect in a clinical manner on Underwood's psychopathology, to ascertain whether he is 'mad' or 'bad' through the presented tale. He veers perilously close to self-pity when reflecting on his perceived abuse in childhood and his torture of animals, both of which are early predictors of adult psychopathy according to the commonly used psychopathy checklist developed by Robert D. Hare (1993). Indeed the latter factor has been singled out by a variety of scholars as predictive of potential cruelty to people in later life (Macdonald, 1963; Gleyzer, Felthous, and Holzer, 2002). In *So Little Done*, Underwood suggests:

An ill-used or maltreated child dreams of his revenge upon the world, but his means are limited by his size and weakness. Friendless and alone, what could I have done to right the wrongs I suffered? It was at the age of eight that I discovered the joys of inflicting pain upon other living creatures. And who dare blame a child of that age for his cruelty, who not only lacks the capacity to understand the wellsprings of his actions, but has no one who cares about him sufficiently to correct him? (p. 15)

Indeed, psychopathy, antisocial personality disorder, sociopathy – all conditions relating to conscienceless behaviour – stand as distinct from other psychopathologies like schizophrenia, yet are managed by the same institution (psychiatry); though often the criminal justice system is also involved. Dalrymple, like many fiction writers, provides a satire on psychiatry through the character of Underwood:

It is well-known that psychiatrists are not the most balanced of people themselves, yet they presume to judge the sanity of others. And what a procession of the intellectually halt, limping and lame passed before me in the name of psychiatric science! One of them [...] spoke in exaggeratedly dulcet tones, as if to imply that he would understand anything I said to him, and that this understanding was a form of infallible absolution. I had the distinct impression that another of them, younger than the rest but already balding, was excited, and perhaps even honoured, to be called upon to examine a personage as notorious as I, whose conduct had preoccupied the newspapers for days on end. He looked at me as though he was searching for visible signs of wickedness upon my countenance, that he asked the same foolish questions as all the others, that I might fit into the procrustean psychiatric moral and diagnostic schemata. (p. 24)

What follows is an amusing passage in which Underwood discredits psychiatric assessment and symptoms such as paranoia: for example, when asked if he is worried about people being out to get him, he replies that according to a recent newspaper campaign, there are a large number of people who would quite like to see him hang (p. 25). The question that is left through Underwood's lack of willingness to be bracketed in inflexible and inaccurate (in his view) psychiatric 'schemata' is, therefore, why? Because of the sadistic or sexual elements common in serial murder? Not so, replies Underwood to the selection of reasons produced by most psychiatric literature. He asserts that the actual killing of his victims gave him no pleasure, but that 'my pleasure was an altogether subtler thing, richer, more intellectual and ethical in nature: the realisation that the world now contained one fewer unworthy person to consume its scarce resources to no other end or purpose than the very consumption itself' (p. 121). Finally closing the gap between reader and serial killer, Underwood asserts '*I have only done what you, in your heart of hearts, have always wanted to do*' (p. 73). In some respects, Dalrymple's novel reads almost like a first-person medical case study of psychopathy, an autobiography that if written by an actual psychopath would be unlikely to reach the shelves of bookshops.

It is common knowledge that the majority of serial killers are male, and men are three times more likely than women to attract a diagnosis of antisocial personality disorder (ASPD) (American Psychiatric Association, 2000, p. 704). Women who fit into neither the mad nor sad categories are generally placed into their own 'badness' category, borderline personality disorder (BPD). Indeed, epidemiologically BPD is diagnosed predominantly (about 75 per cent) in women (American Psychiatric Association, 2000, p. 708). Furthermore, it has been suggested that those patients (usually female) who do not fit into the 'mad' category and are therefore given the 'badness' category of personality disorder are not well-liked by psychiatry, due to issues of treatability and behaviours seen as difficult, such as self-harm or violence to others (Lewis and Appleby, 1988; Adshead, 2001). Borderline personality disorder can be seen as like a modern-day version of the now psychiatrically redundant diagnosis of hysteria (Appignanesi, 2008), though the symptoms and forms of hysteria as a diagnosis continue to be used in psychoanalytical practice, and eminent critics such as Elaine Showalter (1997) have explored contemporary manifestations and epidemics of hysteria.

BPD becomes manifest in distinctly gendered ways: men externalise anger through violence, while women are trained socially to internalise their emotion, so anger is acted out upon the self, often through self-harming or self-destructive behaviours (Motz, 2001). Notably, there is a growing body of contemporary research acknowledging and exploring the still-taboo phenomenon of women who inflict anger, pain, and abuse upon others as well as themselves, but even this literature comments on the violence women enact concomitantly on their own bodies, for example Motz (2001).

Kristen Waterfield Duisberg is one of the few post-war novelists who explicitly examines the phenomenon of BPD, although she does not name it, in *The Good Patient* (2003). By not naming the disorder, Waterfield Duisberg depathologises character Darien's complex and bewildering emotions and behaviours. Darien describes herself from the outset as jolting between self-perceived notions of her identity as either good or bad, demonstrating a high level of intrapsychic conflict with no middle ground to fall back upon:

> From the inside out, these are my layers: bad, good, bad, good, and now – new – again bad. They attach beneath my skin, nestled one inside the other like Matruschka dolls, anchored with a pin through each skull at the top. They ring like a bell, scream and peal, complain, when layers and outsides clash. Beneath the layers, there is nothing: unbounded emptiness like the equation of the universe inverted so that one equals zero. (p. 1)

Darien's 'madness' is presented as inexplicable urges to harm herself among an array of self-destructive behaviours and unstable interpersonal relationships. Like Underwood in *So Little Done*, she has a low opinion of the ability of the medical profession to pin down her problem and thus resolve it:

> 'Why do I *think* I'm here?' After five doctors, I have the first visit procedure down and can go through the routine on autopilot, laying out the relevant data points like setting the table for a five-course meal. Anorexia at age ten, bulimia at twelve, alcoholism and sexual promiscuity with the onset of puberty; lying, nightmares, and self-mutilation for as long as I can remember. Everything from the knife rest to the fingerbowl. 'I know why I'm here. I'm here because I broke my hand, and because that's really just emblematic of a whole host of other things that are wrong with me, or that at least have been

wrong with me in the past.' I throw the last out there, eager for her to ask what those other things might be. Starving, puking, binge drinking, sluttiness, pathological lying – did I mention those before? I don't mind talking about them. (p. 11)

Although offering a menu of problems and symptoms, Darien struggles to find one illness, or indeed one identity, than can help her to contain emotions and self-destructive behaviours that feature so damagingly in her life, whilst simultaneously finding them inexplicable. As we have argued elsewhere about Darien's adoption of whichever psychiatric label happens to be in vogue at the time:

It is, perhaps, a testament to the extraordinary current culture of medicalisation – in the past, we may have objected to the attribution of distress to mental illness, whereas Darien suggests that her distress is only authentic if it fits a diagnostic category. Dr Lindholm appears to have an interesting perspective on the cause of Darien's behaviours, telling her after hearing her self-diagnosis, ' you're not going to persuade me by pinning your argument on personality. Especially not on personality. I'm one of the original unbelievers. I barely passed that course in college' (77). In this respect, rightly or wrongly, Dr Lindholm's casting aside of the PD diagnoses allows her the therapeutic space to explore the meaning and reasons behind Darien's actions. And, ultimately, this method leads to a successful outcome for Darien. (Baker et al., 2008, p. 24)

In fact, Waterfield Duisberg's novel is notable for its empathy towards BPD, and as we have argued it could be of great benefit to clinicians seeking to understand these personality difficulties, the madness-which-is-not-madness (Baker et al., 2008). It is only towards the end of the novel, when Darien has abandoned her therapy with Dr Lindholm and is seeking psychiatric admission, that she is told by admitting doctor Mintzer: 'Mental illness is not a game.' She continues:

I'm not going to admit you because you're not sick. I couldn't be having this conversation with you if you were. The patients we treat here are very, very sick. Schizophrenics and catatonics, for the most part, talking ragtime when they come here. Half of them are in restraints and the other half are so heavily medicated they don't need them. And yet I still have to fight like hell to keep most of them hospitalized. (p. 279)

Once Darien begins to realise that, rather than having an illness *per se*, her personality is distorted or disrupted because of traumatic events – in other words, once she casts aside the crutch of psychiatry – she begins to fare much better in life, to heal and recover. Novels like Waterfield Duisberg's and Dalrymple's exemplify the problematics of definitive description and diagnosis of illnesses, madness, and sanity that we have explored in this chapter via the very *absence* of madness contained within them – the absence of madness that is at the same time diagnosed and contained by psychiatry, the madness medical discipline.

The impact of madness on others

To conclude this chapter, we turn our focus briefly towards fiction that examines the impact of caring for an individual who is experiencing madness. A number of texts take an extradiegetic perspective on the madness represented, mediating the narrative through those that surround the mad individual. The perspective of an involved other – as carer – is a crucial part of the utilisation of literary portrayals of madness as a clinical tools, particularly in the UK where the role and importance of informal carers is being given prominence (Askey et al., 2009; Gray et al., 2009). Boylan's *Beloved Stranger*, as we have mentioned, explores the caring role from the perspective of both Dick's wife – who is bereft at the loss of her long-term partner – and his daughter. Kinsley Amis presents the frustration of caring for a son with schizophrenia in *Stanley and the Women* (1984), for example. Percival Everett provides a timely narrative exploring the difficulties and issues – both practical and emotional – of caring for a parent with dementia in *Erasure* (2001), a novel that we discuss further in Chapter 4. Michael Ignatieff in the semi-autobiographical *Scar Tissue* (1992) also explores the caring responsibilities of a child towards a parent, and the emotive issues at this difficult time. Wally Lamb's towering achievement *I Know This Much Is True* (1998) demonstrates the frustration, responsibility, and guilt that many carers feel when overwhelmed by the combination of caring responsibilities and external events. Furthermore, as the twin brother of an individual with schizophrenia, protagonist Dominick struggles with the dual guilt of carer responsibility and being 'the *un*crazy twin – the guy who beat the biochemical rap' (p. 47). His guilt is unending:

> When you're the sane brother of a schizophrenic identical twin, the tricky thing about saving yourself is the blood it leaves on your

hands – the little inconvenience of the look-alike corpse at your feet. And if you're into both survival of the fittest *and* being your brother's keeper – if you've promised your dying mother – then say so long to sleep and hello to the middle of the night. Grab a book or a beer. Get used to Letterman's gap-toothed smile of the absurd, or the view of the bedroom ceiling, or the indifference of random selection. Take it from a godless insomniac. (p. 47)

Examining the carer role is a particular literary preoccupation of Lamb's. His most recent novel, *The Hour I First Believed* (2008), also explores the carer role, written from the perspective of a fictional husband whose wife suffers from post-traumatic stress disorder following the Columbine High School shootings that occurred in America in 1999.

Bebe Moore Campbell's 2005 novel *72 Hour Hold* strikingly examines the impact of mental illness on families. In conflict with her ex-husband and daughter Trina's father, Trina's mother Keri struggles endlessly with a system that disempowers her as a carer while simultaneously recycling Trina through severe manic episodes. As a mother, she finds that guilt is an unending emotion:

Nothing is as resilient as a mother's guilt [...] Months of reading books about mental illness, months of support group, of psychotherapy, of assiduously learning that Trina's problem was not of my making (all together now: 'I didn't cause it, and I can't cure it!') was flung right out of my consciousness against a bleak sky. The jazz of my present existence scatted only one refrain: *Whadididowrongwhadididowrongwhadididowrong*? (pp. 89–90)

The drastic steps taken by Trina's mother because of her frustration at the lack of effective and available care for her daughter are explored further and in a critical light in Chapter 4. Our point here is that the narration of madness from the eye of the external observer, as opposed to the narration of the madness from within, is useful from both a clinical and a literary perspective, not least because it presents the manner in which unusual and individual experiences are both conceptualised and objectified by others. Furthermore, the representation of a range of perspectives provides an important mode of understanding the far-reaching consequences of madness for sufferers, families, and carers – a vital element of clinical practice.

3
Power and Institutions in Fiction

> Years ago novels used to end in institutions – marriage (if it was a happy novel), an insane asylum (if it was touched by despair); but contemporary novels *begin* in the institution and aspire to go beyond. [...] often right in the actual asylum, which becomes an apt symbol for the organised madness of modern life, particularly for those absurd forces which attempt to deprive the hero of his identity and individuality – ironically, at one time the very measures of his sanity and worth. Madness is both a result of the startling reality and a way of commenting on it.
> (Lupack, 1994, p. 172)

This chapter explores how madness fictions present issues of power and individual autonomy by focusing their narratives in and around psychiatric institutions such as the asylum or the day-care facility. Drawing upon historical fictions we can begin to build up a picture of how madness historically has been constructed, structured, and restructured, and demonstrate how this process is related to powerful agencies and structures. In particular we look at Sebastian Barry's *The Secret Scripture* (2008), *Human Traces* (2005) by Sebastian Faulks, T. C. Boyle's *Riven Rock* (1998), and Pat Barker's *Regeneration* (1991). We then move from the historical construction of the incarceration of people in asylums, drawing on Goffman's *Asylums* (1961), towards examining fictional representations of asylum care, the closure of asylums, and the move towards alternatives to incarceration as presented in fiction. Goffman's work informs our readings of the manifestation of power – and abuse of power – within psychiatric institutions and community care through the fiction of writers such as Ken Kesey (1962), Paul Sayer (1988), Bebe Moore Campbell (2005), Marge Piercy (1976), and Clare Allan (2006).

Fiction can highlight the sometimes oppositional and often marginal-ised discourses of sufferers themselves, particularly via the representa-tion of the abuse of patients by those with power in the psychiatric systems. Notions of institutional *and* individual power are explored in terms of rebellion or rejection of institutions and the systems at work within them. We also look briefly at conceptions of stigma and risk in fiction. Finally, by exploring the immediate social context of the per-son deemed mad, in particular their family and social relationships, we look at smaller power structures and the impact these may have on individuals – here we look in particular at Antonia White's *Beyond The Glass* (1954).

Re-reading the history of psychiatry through fiction

Contemporary fiction provides one way of reviewing the troubled and troubling history of psychiatry – a history that has been examined, debated, and criticised over many years (Alexander and Selesnick, 1967; Appignanesi, 2008; Berrios, 1996; Berrios and Porter, 1995; Micale and Porter; 1994; Porter, 2002; Scull, 1979, 1984, 1989; 1999; Shorter, 1992, 1997). A good deal of literature on the historical development of the asylum, following Foucault and later extended by Scull and Rothman among others, explores the asylum as an institution of social con-trol (Foucault, 1965; Rothman, 1970; Scull, 1979, 1989, 1991, 1999). Balancing this view, Grob and others have described the development of asylums as a humanitarian response to the medical and psychoso-cial needs of those with mental illness (Grob, 1994). Yet even authors sympathetic to the intentions of the asylum movement's founders gen-erally concede that the hopes of reformers were stillborn, and despite therapeutic intentions, Victorian asylums rapidly lapsed into custodi-alism where control and discipline was paramount, and patients were 'not subjects to be treated but objects to be managed' (Digby, 1985, p. 56). Scull has recently revisited the humanitarian versus social control debate by describing asylums as a means for reinforcing social con-formity whilst acknowledging the needs of sufferers and their families attempting to cope with madness (Scull, 2006). Indeed, Garton (2009) maintains that it was systematic under-resourcing combined with loss of commitment on the part of the medical profession in the twentieth century that led to the custodial and inhumane conditions identified by reformers and anti-psychiatrists later.

These debates are replicated in fictional form in *Human Traces* by Sebastian Faulks. In this lengthy novel, Faulks intersperses his fiction with factual events and historical individuals in order to effectively map the transitions in Europe from 'care' within the domestic sphere to asylums as overcrowded dumping-grounds for troubled, difficult, or marginalised individuals, right through to the notion of the asylum as retreat, a place of safety, treatment, and support. *Human Traces* opens with protagonist Jacques reflecting on his brother Olivier's own psychiatric history. Olivier is kept in an outhouse and seen as dangerous and animal-like by his family, except for Jacques who, under the watchful mentorship of Abbe Henri, embarks on a lifelong mission to revolutionise psychiatric care. Abbe Henri remarks that the early practices of the confinement of mad individuals are insufficient and stigmatising, and demarcate mad people as animalistic Others. His view on confinement is made clear in the following discussion between Jacques and Abbe Henri, which opens with the religious man's view that 'These are places where you feel the absence of God', continuing:

'We must not despair, Father.'
The Curé smiled at the way the boy had assumed the priestly role. 'I do not despair, Jacques. But the only way I can keep from that sin is by never visiting one of those places again.'
'Surely there are doctors,' said Jacques.
'There are doctors, alienists, in charge of the attendants, but they are powerless. And do you know what the strangest thing is?'
'What?'
'You would think these places could only exist after death – in hell, or in another world. Yet when you leave them, you rejoin the ordinary life of the town with its streets. It doesn't seem right that you walk from one to the other. It doesn't feel like a short journey you make with your feet. It feels as though you've passed into a different existence.' (pp. 18–19)

Jacques is a young man during these discussions, and the notion of early madhouses as being akin to hell, whereby individuals are, and were, literally chained to the walls, is merely one part of the troubled history of psychiatry. Passages such as these – and there are many in this novel that could be quoted here – serve to remind readers who may be unfamiliar with the history of psychiatry that contemporary notions of care and psychiatric practice do in fact have a lengthy history – and one that is fraught with difficulty and debate.

The character of Thomas, who becomes Jacques' partner in psychiatric care reformation, experiences his own hallucinatory voices, giving him increased empathy with patients. Thomas initially works in an English asylum run by Faverill, a character who reminds us as readers of the treatment of 'lunatics' prior to the development of asylums and of the well-intentioned aims behind asylum development – '[...] families once looked after their lunatics at home, but the great men of our calling – I hesitate to call it a profession until it is recognised as such by our equals – have demonstrated beyond contradiction that a well-run asylum can offer restorative benefits unavailable even to the most well-meaning family' (p. 72). Indeed, Faulks is notable for the depth of research that is evident in his fictional production, summarising more than adequately the history of psychiatry:

> The history of the subject was shameful and brief. There had been the dark ages, when wandering idiots were mocked or pilloried; there had been superstitious centuries when people spoke of 'possession' and other devilish nonsense; then there had been the era of cruelty, of imprisonment and taunting, when the idle sane paid to make faces at the lunatics. This had turned into the era of 'restraint', earlier in the century, when the gathering of many mentally afflicted people in one place for the first time had necessitated the use of manacles, irons and straitwaistcoats. Even before such practices had become widespread, however, they were starting also to become obsolete under the influence of enlightened thinkers, some medical men and some, like the famous Mr Tuke of the York Retreat, laymen of humane and philanthropic vision. This was, in Thomas's view, the true beginning of his medical discipline. (p. 101)

Yet the sheer size of the asylum Thomas works in and its volume of inhabitants makes any notion of care, let alone treatment or recovery, impossible, reflecting in fictional form the concerns and critiques of the historians and critics referenced above.

Human Traces is set during the most crucial developmental period of psychiatry. The age-old problem of biology versus psychology, and developments in the search for an organic basis to madness, are depicted throughout the novel, as are evolutionary theories and anthropological research. Thomas reflects here on a debate which continues to this day – that of the status of psychiatry as a medical discipline:

> It was curious, he had to admit, that the first medicine was not a herbal preparation or a surgical procedure, but simple kindness; odd, because the struggle of the pioneering mad-doctors had always been

to establish that illness of the mind was organic, a physical malfunction, to be treated in the same way as an illness of the liver or the foot, the brain being just such an organ, entirely comparable to the others – if more complicated. Yet one did not treat cirrhosis or a broken metatarsal with kindness, so here was a paradox. (p. 101)

We may view this novel as purely historical, but many of the debates of the early years of the development of psychiatry remain true today. Ultimately, as we argued in Chapter 2, what Faulks' novel reminds us is that 'that which makes us mad is almost the same thing as that which makes us human' (Faulks, 2005, p. 171), the very historical insight which ultimately formed the basis of psych-disciplines as a unique discipline within medicine. Faulks's novel rewrites the history of psychiatry – not through the manipulation or misrepresentation of historical fact, but by providing interested readers with a gripping narrative, as accurately fact-filled as any textbook. Indeed, one particular remark in Faulks' novel – 'The word asylum, never let us forget, denotes safety" (Faulks, 2005, p. 72) – seems to reflect a much-forgotten motto in twenty-first-century community-based care, as we shall see later in this chapter.

·T. C. Boyle, in his well-researched novel *Riven Rock*, focuses in a similar manner to Faulks on emerging conceptualisations of madness, in particular the aetiology of *dementia praecox* (later renamed schizophrenia); the sexology of Kraft-Ebbing; the psychoanalytical theories of Freud; and the eclecticism of Adolf Meyer. Boyle explores this historical period while concurrently paying attention to the rise of the women's movement in the USA. Stanley McCormick, the sexually deviant lunatic around whom the novel revolves, is placed from the age of 31 into a world of men, such is his sexualised madness and risk towards women. In parallel with the portrayal of Stanley's extreme sexual guilt and his subsequently induced psychotic remorse is Eddie O'Kane, his head nurse, who has few sexual morals, fathering illegitimate children in the novel and drinking alcohol excessively. Boyle here provides an interesting comment on sexual guilt as inducing madness in a world with strict morality: O'Kane does not experience guilt, and remains sane as a result. Despite Stanley's abhorrent behaviour towards women – for example attacking a woman on a train (Boyle, 1998, p. 60) – Boyle develops empathy between the reader and Stanley through two main devices, firstly by depicting his waxing and waning symptoms – and the array of treatments offered, from talking therapy to restraint and force-feeding – within a framework of understandability and empathy:

> Stanley loved his mother, his wife, his sisters, he loved other people's
> mothers, wives, sisters and daughters, but he loved them too much,
> loved them with an incendiary passion that was like hate, that was
> indistinguishable from hate, and it was that loving and hating that
> fomented all his troubles and thrust him headlong into a world with-
> out women.
>
>   He was twenty-nine when he married Katherine Dexter, a woman
> of power, beauty, wealth and prestige, a woman as combative and
> fierce as his mother, with heartbreaking eyes and a voice so soft and
> pure it was like a drug, and he was thirty-one when he first felt the
> cold wolf's bite of the sheet restraints and entered the solitary world
> of men. He went blank then. He was blocked. He saw things that
> weren't there, desperate, ugly things, creatures of his innermost mind
> that shone with a life more vivid than any life he'd ever known, and
> he heard voices speaking without mouths, throats or tongues, and
> every time he looked up it was into the face of masculinity. (pp. 3–4)

Secondly, by directly setting the largely mute character of Stanley
against the vocal character of O'Kane, Boyle provides a framework in
which similar instinctual sexual drives lead to very different outcomes
for two men of similar ages. O'Kane is a vile character, as indicated by
his lack of humane and expected horror at the thought of alternative
'care' facilities available as possibilities for his charge, Stanley: O'Kane,
for example, sees 'progress' in inhumane treatments:

> And then it was the morning routine. Say goodnight to Nick and Pat,
> who were just coming off their shift, and hello to Mr. McCormick,
> bent up double like a pretzel in his bed; then it was strip off
> Mr. McCormick's nightgown and swab up the mess he'd left on
> the sheets, pack the whole business up for the laundress and give
> Mr. McCormick his shower bath, and all the while O'Kane think-
> ing about Robert Ogilvie, director of the Peachtree Asylum in Stone
> Mountain, Georgia, who suspended all his catatonics on a rack in
> a big metal tub, day and night, and just changed the water when it
> got mucked up. No stains, no smells, no laundry – just a plug and a
> faucet. Now that was progress. (p. 91)

Confirming our suggestion that O'Kane stands in this novel as a counterpoint to Stanley is O'Kane's own sexual behaviour, his lack of conscience

towards the women he uses, and vague hints at his sexual arousal when viewing the monkeys that are kept in the gardens of Stanley's stately home as an experiment into psychological and social notions of sexual ethnology in animals unrestrained by human social morality. Indeed, the behaviour of these monkeys mirrors the sexual urges that Stanley is unable to control, but appears to have little other relevance for psychiatric research in the view of O'Kane, for as far as he can ascertain 'the only thing Hamilton had established was that a monkey will fuck anything, and how that was supposed to be applied to Mr. McCormick and all the rest of the suffering schizophrenics of the world, he couldn't even pretend to guess' (p. 155). The representation of nurses and attendants as abusive, degrading, and violent towards their charges is not uncommon in fiction.

Through Katherine, Stanley's dedicated wife, Boyle plays out the public history and tensions of the rising women's movement alongside the private and personal stress of being a woman with an absent and ill husband. At the end of the novel, with her husband finally broken, without hope of recovery, and continuing to attempt to physically attack her, Katherine is finally able to let him go and set herself free, after a life of dedication to an absent man:

> That was when she retreated to the closet, the last place she could go, the key on the inside of the door and the door shut tight, and nothing but darkness now and fear, fear and hate, because he was what she was afraid of and that made her hate him beyond all forgiveness or consolation. Stanley. Stanley Robert McCormick, the madman, the lunatic, the nut, the sexual hypochondriacal neurasthenic. And that was what she was left with when they came and got him and they put him in the straitjacket and the sheet restraints and used all their outraged male muscle to hold him down. (p. 461)

The use of the phrase 'outraged male muscle' here perfectly sums up the tensions of the period. Katherine is caught between her roles as a wife and an activist and early feminist, unable to be a 'proper' wife but remaining faithful nonetheless. Furthermore her husband, treated exclusively by men, is demonised by the 'outraged' healers, who are both horrified and intrigued by his sexual outbursts, so Stanley is denied any feminised or gentler treatments, left restrained, dying 'a prisoner' (p. 465). Boyle's novel is ultimately the tragedy of Katherine rather than Stanley.

As well as covering the broad history of asylum development and culture, both Faulks and Boyle are notable for examining the chronology of diagnostics. A similar but more specifically focused exploration of this subject can be seen in Pat Barker's three Regeneration Trilogy novels, first published in 1991, 1993, and 1995, which examine the emergence, conceptualisation, and treatment of war neurosis during the Great War (later termed shell shock and now called post-traumatic stress disorder – see Shepherd, 2001). William H. R. Rivers (1864–1922), who was both an anthropologist and psychiatrist, is the hero of Barker's trilogy. The first novel, *Regeneration* (1991), is of most relevance here. It incorporates biographical information about both Rivers and his most famous patient at Craiglockhart War Hospital for Officers, Siegfried Sassoon (1886–1967) and, like Faulks and Boyle, uses factual historical and biographical material to inform the fiction. The emergence of shell shock as a phenomenon of war brought to the forefront of psychiatric research the interaction between psychological conditions and physical illness, leading to much research on psychosomatic conditions such as mutism, discussed here in the novel by Rivers:

> Mutism seems to spring from a conflict between *wanting* to say something, and knowing that if you *do* say it the consequences will be disastrous. So you resolve it by making it physically impossible for yourself to speak. And for the private soldier the consequences of speaking his mind are always going to be far worse than they would be for an officer. What you tend to get in officers is stammering. And it's not just mutism. All the physical symptoms: paralysis, blindness, deafness. They're all common in private soldiers and rare in officers. It's almost as if for the ... the labouring classes illness *has* to be physical. They can't take their condition seriously unless there's a physical symptom. (1991, p. 96)

Barker makes an important point in the quote above regarding psychiatric or psychological illness – it is a strange anomaly that a non-physical illness can have physical effects. There are also differences in the severity of psychosomatic symptoms according to the level of the soldier/officer, according to Rivers, which may indicate something significant about variations in levels of psychological insight necessary to lead soldiers or follow orders.

Rivers is portrayed as sensitive and humane, applying psychoanalytic insights to the rehabilitation of shell-shocked soldiers:

> Rivers's treatment sometimes consisted of simply encouraging the patient to abandon his hopeless attempt to forget, and advising him

instead to spend some part of every day remembering. Neither brooding on the experience, nor trying to pretend it had never happened. Usually, within a week or two of his patient's starting this treatment, the nightmares began to be less frequent and less terrifying.

Sassoon's determination to remember might well account for his early and rapid recovery, though in his case it was motivated less by a desire to save his own sanity than by a determination to convince civilians that the war was mad. (1991, p. 26)

His kindness to Sassoon and others is contrasted with the brutal methods applied by Dr Yealland, who uses a mixture of hectoring and electrodes attached to the affected organ to cure paralysis and mutism (1991, pp. 224–233). The outward manifestations of shell shock/war neurosis mimicked many of the symptoms that were previously defined as hysteria – a feminine and female disease (Showalter, 1987, 1997). When men – and not only men, but men of rank and dignity – began to display these symptoms, a new, more dignified title needed to be found. Yet Rivers's treatment *itself* causes a crisis of masculinity, and is paradoxically rebuffed by soldiers who return to war despite their psychological and physical injuries: war being the ultimate demonstration of masculinity, requiring bravery, strength, and an unemotional attitude to all experiences, however horrific:

They'd been trained to identify emotional repression as the essence of manliness. Men who broke down, or cried, or admitted to feeling fear, were sissies, weaklings, failures. Not *men*. [...]

The change he had demanded of them – and by implication of himself – was not trivial. Fear, tenderness – these emotions were so despised that they could be admitted into consciousness only at the cost of redefining what it meant to be a man. Not that Rivers's treatment involved any encouragement of weakness or effeminacy. His patients might be encouraged to acknowledge their fears, their horrors of the war – but they were still expected to do their duty and return to France. It was Rivers's conviction that those who had learned to know themselves, and to accept their emotions, were less likely to break down again. (Barker, 1991, p. 48)

Rivers is left in a contradictory role as a military psychiatrist, patching up his patients psychologically in order to return them to the front line, with its very high risk of psychological trauma, mutilation, and death. In effect he works within one power structure – psychiatry – and both within *and* against two others – that of the state or government that sent young men to war, and that of the judicial system which ruled homosexuality to be illegal. Rivers and his mentor, Head, not only treat patients with war neurosis, but also assist homosexuals who are at risk of two years' hard labour. These patients are afforded medical mitigation with the exonerating label of neurasthenia. Both Rivers and Sassoon are placed, by a variety of power structures, in no-win situations, and one can see that feigning madness (a tactic used to escape conscription) can in some senses be seen as a form of supreme rationality: a stay in a psychiatric hospital being preferable to the battleground of war or a prison environment. The 'catch-22' of proving sanity by faking madness is of course a key feature of Joseph Heller's 1961 novel *Catch-22*, though unfortunately there is not space to examine this more thoroughly here.

Like her contemporaries, who focus on the historical development of psychiatry as a medical discipline through creative use of factual and fictitious characters, Clare Dudman offers a fictionalised perspective on the meteoric rise in the number of individuals confined in madhouses in her 2004 novel *98 Reasons for Being*:

> The number of mad is growing, they say, and tease each other to provide reasons. [...] Madness is everywhere, and always has been. It used to be hidden away in the backs of houses. It used to be chained down in stables and sheds. It used to be caged in baskets hired out from the town council and placed in the living spaces of their slightly saner relatives. It used to be confused with poverty and criminality and dwelt in filth and terror in prisons and poorhouses. On rare occasions it has been revered as holiness, its victims deified or vilified as possessed. The mad were either visionaries or the familiars of Satan, supremely blessed or adamantly damned. (p. 50)

The parallels between this passage and those quoted earlier in this chapter, from Faulks in particular, are clear – novelists focusing on the history of psychiatry use their fictions to reflect the fact that it was not the number of individuals affected by madness *per se* that increased during the asylum era, but that madness became a more public and visible issue through the development of public and private madhouses.

Issues around the chronology and development of *gendered* diagnostics are also played out in Dudman's novel *98 Reasons for Being*, which focuses critically on the diagnosis of nymphomania through a woman, Hannah, who is morally 'fallen' through non-marital sexual relations. Although Hannah is diagnosed as a nymphomaniac precisely because of having sex prior to marriage, her actual clinical presentation – recognised by the doctor treating her, Hoffman – is in fact a very understandable melancholia (or, in contemporary terms, depression) following heartbreak caused by the breakdown of her romantic relationship. Dudman's novel comments on the powerful masculine and patriarchal use of psychiatry to constrain the threat of allegedly uncontrolled and uncontrollable female sexuality, through the labelling of Hannah as a nymphomaniac.

Sebastian Barry also examines the historical use of psychiatry to contain women – or rather, the use of psychiatric power as a response to overt demonstration of female sexuality – in *The Secret Scripture* (2008). Barry reflects, through his psychiatrist protagonist Grene, and with a degree of disillusionment, upon the retrogression of asylum care; the power that psychiatry has gradually assumed through its rise to the status of genuine medical discipline; and, finally, on the relatively recent challenge of emptying the asylums of patients because of the move towards community care (see Barham, 1992, and also Bartlett and Wright, 1999). Grene is the physician responsible for discharging his long-incarcerated 'inmates' (p. 14) from the asylum. As with Faulks and Boyle, we can see in Barry's novel elements of critical reflection on the history of psychiatry, when Grene reflects that despite the benevolent aims behind the growth in asylum care, 'it all got worse again afterwards, and no sensitive person would choose to be the historian of the Irish asylums in the first part of the last century, with its clitoridectomies, immersions, and injections' (p. 14). The main thrust of *The Secret Scripture*, however, is the *personal* rather than *institutional* history of psychiatry.

The struggle for the individual narrative to be heard rather than the collective tale, the need for subjectivity in examinations of madness rather than the dryly objectifying aims of diagnostics and classification, are common themes in madness novels, as we discussed in Chapter 2. Barry's novel focuses on the very human imperative for self-narration, that is, the need to construct and tell our own stories, and also on the equally important demand for these stories to be heard and acknowledged. The main character, Roseanne, writes her story in secret. Her memoir intersects with the agenda of Grene, in charge of declaring her well enough for release following her lengthy incarceration. For Roseanne, the telling of her testimony is her last task before dying. In the opening pages of the novel, she says: 'I am completely alone, there is no one in the world that knows me now outside of this place' (p. 4). Roseanne needs to commit her story to paper, for her memories to be revealed through her testimony: this is crucial both for preventing future injustices and, more importantly, for her sense of *being*, of having a place in the world, a lasting presence, when she has been denied a presence by those with power – men, priests, and then psychiatrists – for so long. She is left, after decades of incarceration, as a 'thing', a 'remnant woman' (p. 4).

Roseanne's ultimately tragic story – from traumatic childhood to illegitimate pregnancy and subsequent incarceration – unfolds into a meditation on memory: on who remembers, and how; on the accuracy of ageing memory, and whether such accuracy matters when the stories told belong to the individual remembering; and on loneliness and loss. Roseanne is exiled in the asylum largely for defying the sexual morals expected of women during the period the novel is set in. As Father Gaunt, who commits her to the asylum following her illegitimate pregnancy, comments:

> If you had followed my advice, Roseanne, some years ago, and put your faith in the true religion, if you had behaved with the beautiful decorum of a Catholic wife, you would not be facing these difficulties. But I do appreciate that you are not entirely responsible. Nymphomania is of course by definition a madness. An affliction possibly, but primarily a madness, with its roots possibly in a physical cause. (p. 223)

As Roseanne documents her life story, Dr Grene has to construct Roseanne and her experiences through the report of the priest who committed her and a few scant notes. Roseanne has not spoken her story for so long that when she comes to talk about her potential discharge from the asylum – necessitating reflection on her admission – she is frozen, silent, and bound by shame. Barry's novel is here comparable to Dudman's. There is certainly no evidence in Roseanne's memory of nymphomania, the diagnosis used to confine her to the asylum – only of love, and of the very human experience of passion. Barry's fiction documents not only *the* history of psychiatry but *her* history, her story, the story of thousands of women. Indeed, as Roseanne says, Barry's novel tells the history of asylums where 'sisters, mothers, grandmothers, spinsters, all forgotten lie' alongside the 'human town not so far off, sleeping and waking, sleeping and waking, forgetting its lost women there, in long rows' (p. 32).

With its reminders of these hidden and forgotten women, in many respects Barry's account resonates with a significant strand of feminist commentary on women and madness: it echoes Elaine Showalter's examinations of the nineteenth-century masculine management and control of women's reproductive biology, seen as having a dangerous impact on delicate feminine minds (Showalter, 1987). Madness was historically believed to be linked with the menarche, menstruation, pregnancy, and the climacteric. In a similar vein, Ussher (1991) argues that in the Victorian era women were seen as the *dangerous sex*, irrational and overly spontaneous, and their madness was linked to their sexuality and specifically their reproductive organs. Henderson (1994) also asserts that from the point of view of many nineteenth-century intellectuals, madness in women was considered to be more or less inevitable, given their weaker and more reproductively oriented constitutions. Sebastian Barry demonstrates in fictional form the very real and very human tragedies that occurred as a result of such gendered beliefs.

History provides its own problems for Roseanne, not least regarding the accuracy of memory, but also because history, in her view, is 'a fabulous arrangement of surmises and guesses held up as a banner against the assault of withering truth' (p. 55). She continues on this theme: 'My own story, anyone's own story, is always told against me, even what I myself am writing here, because I have no heroic history to offer' (p. 55). The reader, moved by Roseanne's testimony, takes her words, her describing of her own history, for truth – and it is in many senses, despite Roseanne's view, a heroic history fraught with interpersonal challenge and difficulty. Yet she simultaneously states that she is fearful of giving Dr Grene only her 'imaginings', which she suggests is a 'nice sort of word for catastrophe and delusion' (p. 219). Roseanne can be interpreted here as suggesting that all memory is in some senses delusional, marred by time and maturity, relationships and emotion – as she states, 'I must admit there are "memories" in my head that are curious even to me' (p. 201). Furthermore, Roseanne's ageing memory becomes problematic for her storytelling, not through any age-related degeneration but because of the traumas that led to her admission: 'It makes me a little dizzy to contemplate the possibility that everything I remember may not be – may not be *real*, I suppose. There was so much turmoil at that time that – that what? I took refuge in other impossible histories, in dreams, in fantasies? I don't know' (p. 201). As we suggested in Chapter 2, madness does at times provide a refuge. Certainly here, Roseanne finds a form of sanctuary, an intellectual asylum, in the act of un-remembering, of remaking memory.

The versions of Roseanne's story – her own, the committing report of the priest, and the constructed history that Dr Grene comes up with – are conflicting. At the closing of the novel Grene reflects upon his realisation that his reading and surmising may have led to inaccuracy:

> It is almost a disgusting thought to me that I might have intuited this detail out of the aether, and supplied it unconsciously, anticipating a story that I had not yet read [...] Nevertheless I must conclude that to a large degree, both Roseanne and Fr Gaunt were being as truthful as they could be, given the vagaries and tricks of the human mind. Roseanne's 'sins' as a self-historian are 'sins of omission'. (p. 280)

In this respect, Barry's novel can be reflected upon by clinicians as a mediation on storytelling and story-creating – on who we listen to, whose version of a particular event or narrative is given more credence, and whose interpretation is given primary importance.

Total institutions

Lupack suggests that in 'some of the most significant contemporary American novels [...] the asylum becomes the place in which the protagonist defines his relationship to the cruelly absurd reality of the "sane" world' (1994, p. 173). For Connie in Marge Piercy's *Woman on the Edge of Time*, the absurdity of the world outside the asylum is magnified through the total and absolute loss of all power and human rights she experiences once locked away: 'Everybody outside had freedom and power by contrast. The poorest most strung out fucked up worked over brought down junkie in Harlem had more freedom, more place, richer choices, sweeter dignity than the most privileged patient in the whole bughouse' (p. 170). Connie, once confined in the asylum, becomes the least powerful type of individual in society, and – as Lupack suggests in the quote above (p. 173) – she becomes acutely aware of how absurd this seems when she compares herself to the lowest-of-the-low outside the asylum.

In Ken Kesey's *One Flew Over The Cuckoo's Nest* (1962), madness is, for McMurphy, seen as one method of gaining a form of power over the judicial system. Like a malign version of Pat Barker's Siegfried Sassoon, chief character McMurphy uses the asylum as a method of escaping the real world of punishment and consequences by feigning madness, telling the other patients on the ward: '[...] the court ruled that I'm a psychopath. And do you think I'm gonna argue with the court? Shoo, you can bet your bottom dollar I don't. If it gets me outta those dammed pea fields I'll be whatever their little heart desires, be it psychopath or mad dog or werewolf, because I don't care if I never see another weedin' hoe to my dying day' (p. 13). McMurphy find, however, that he is mistaken in thinking that being admitted to an asylum is a way of avoiding punishment – furthermore, the staff are not blind to the idea that he may be feigning his symptoms to escape work-based penal punishment (p. 42).

Narrated by the selectively mute Chief Bromden, Kesey's novel explicitly portrays the asylum as a place of absolute power in which patients are ruled with an iron fist. Interestingly, the staff hierarchy in the novel is not portrayed on the familiar, traditional, patriarchal doctor/nurse/ patient structure, as another patient, Harding, explains: 'We are victims of a matriarchy here, my friend, and the doctor is just as helpless against it as we are' (p. 56). According to Bromden, Nurse Ratched, through a process of emasculation of both other male staff and the patients/ inmates she is in charge of, holds absolute power:

> The Big Nurse tends to get real put out if something keeps her outfit from running like a smooth, accurate, precision-made machine. The slightest thing messy or out of kilter or in the way ties her into a little white knot of tight-smiled fury. She walks around with that same doll smile crimped between her chin and her nose and that same calm whir coming from her eyes, but down inside of her she's tense as steel. I know, I can feel it. And she don't relax a hair till she gets the nuisance attended to – what she calls 'adjusted to surroundings'. (p. 25).

As Chief accurately and insightfully suggests – despite elements of the fantastical in his beliefs about the affects like the fog machine inflicted by the 'Combine' (p. 100) – the ward is a capitalistic processing plant which holds society and productivity in the highest regard, and has little time or space for humanity or humane care. Indeed, humans are 'products':

> This is what I know. The ward is a factory for the Combine. It's for fixing up mistakes made in the neighbourhoods and in the schools and in the churches, the hospital is. When a completed product goes back out into society, all fixed up good as new, *better* than new sometimes, it brings joy to the Big Nurse's heart; something that came in all twisted different is now a functioning, adjusted component, a credit to the whole outfit and a marvel to behold. [...] He's happy with it. He's adjusted to surroundings finally. (p. 36)

As discussed in Chapter 2, 'adjustment' to the 'real' world is not always a goal for characters – and as we will argue in our chapter on postmodern fiction and madness, there are difficulties in ascertaining exactly who decides what notions of sanity or adjustment actually mean.

Kesey's novel can be interpreted with the aid of the work of Erving Goffman, and notably Kesey's novel was published a year after Goffman's *Asylums*. Goffman claims, in an uncanny echo of Chief's description quoted above, that the 'total institution is a social hybrid, part residential community, part formal organization [...] In our society, they are the forcing houses for changing persons; each is a natural experiment on what can be done to the self' (1961, p. 22). For Goffman, the aim of the total institution is utter degradation, manipulation, and reformation. One type of total institution is the psychiatric facility or asylum. The patient, upon entering the asylum, begins 'a series of abasements, degradations, humiliations, and profanities of self. His self is systematically, if often unintentionally, mortified. He begins some radical shifts in his *moral career*, a career composed of the progressive changes that occur in the beliefs that he has concerning himself and others' (Goffman, 1961, p. 24). When McMurphy begins his rebellion against the attempted abasements and degradations inflicted upon inpatients by the Big Nurse and the system she upholds, there is initially great nervousness among the other patients. This can be interpreted as indicative of their complete subservience to the institutional system that contains them, and their fear of challenging both it and those who maintain its complex power structure. These patients have been systematically ground down to less-than-men:

> I thought for a minute there I saw her whipped. Maybe I did. But I see now that it don't make any difference. One by one the patients are sneaking looks at her to see how she's taking the way McMurphy is dominating the meeting, and they see the same thing. She's too big to be beaten. [...] She's lost a little battle here today, but it's a minor battle in a big war that she's been winning and she'll go on winning. We mustn't let McMurphy get our hopes up for any difference, lure us into making some kind of dumb play. She'll go on winning, just like the Combine, because she has all the power of the Combine behind her. She don't lose on her losses, but she wins on ours. (Kesey, 1962, p. 100)

What occurs in Kesey's novel is a replication of Goffman's 'fraternalization process', consisting firstly of humiliating staff and secondly a process of social bonding among patients (Goffman, 1961, p. 59). Inmates such as Harding come to realise that there is a paradoxical power in madness, if not in institutionalisation – after all, McMurphy is ultimately silenced and overpowered at the end of the novel. But as Harding suggests, after alarming a passer-by by mentioning that he and his group are from the local lunatic asylum, on the patients' fishing trip: 'Never before did I realise that mental illness could have the aspect of power, *power*. Think of it: perhaps the more insane a man is, the more powerful he could become. Hitler an example. Fair makes the old brain reel, doesn't it? Food for thought there' (p. 204). The fishing trip marks a breakthrough for the men on the ward – escaping the confines of the unit, the rules of Nurse Ratched, and discovering for the first time that there may be a paradoxical power in powerlessness, albeit in this particular case the power to ignite an outsider's fear and stigma.

The character of Chief can also be viewed through the work of Goffman. Like Sebastian Barry's Roseanne, Chief has a great urge to tell his story: 'It's gonna burn me just that way, finally telling about all this, about the hospital, and her, and the guys – and about McMurphy. I been silent so long now it's gonna roar out of me like floodwaters' (p. 8). Chief's fear of the unbelievability of his story, given the gross abuses of power detailed throughout, is understandable. The idea of the story being 'the truth even if it didn't happen' (p. 8), as suggested by Bromden, is again reminiscent of Roseanne's *personal* memories being more important than the official or sanctioned version of her life. In the case of Bromden and McMurphy, no doubt the sanitised version of the truth would be far from the reality, such is the power of the institution and its masters/mistresses. Who, after all, would believe the ravings of the previously mute Bromden, officially designated madman and, ultimately, mercy killer? Chief's desperate need to commit his story – which is also the story of the other inmates – stands in stark contrast to his mute silence on the ward. While McMurphy's rebellions are vocal and visible, Chief's are far more subtle. A victim of bullying and racial assumptions, such as the assumption that he is illiterate (p. 192), Chief paradoxically holds ultimate power through his silence:

> They laughed and then I hear them mumbling behind me, heads close together. Hum of black machinery, humming hate and death and other hospital secrets. They don't bother not talking out loud about their hate secrets when I'm nearby because they think I'm deaf and dumb. Everybody think so. I'm cagey enough to fool them that

much. If my being half Indian ever helped me in any way in this dirty life, it helped me being cagey, helped me all these years. (p. 4)

Chief's silence, and the assumptions that are made because of his silence, allow him exclusive access to institutional politics, gossip, stories, and knowledge of how individual patients' histories are misrepresented by the staff. As Goffman points out, there are various methods of personal protection, adaptation, and rebellion available to individuals within total institutions. Chief employs what Goffman calls the tactic of 'situational withdrawal' in which the inmate 'withdraws apparent attention from everything except events immediately around his body and sees these in a perspective not employed by others present' (Goffman, 1961, p. 61). McMurphy invokes Goffman's 'intransigent line', whereby the inmate 'intentionally challenges the institution by flagrantly refusing to cooperate with staff' (p. 62), in his blatant, yet ultimately less successful, defiance. What Goffman calls 'withdrawn muteness' can be a double-edged revolt or rebellion for the individual, however, who must submit to verbal and/or physical abuse without making a sound (Goffman, 1961, p. 229). For Chief, feigned mutism ultimately allows him knowledge, which is power and then freedom.

Psychiatric abuses of power

A prominent feature of post-war narratives is the gross abuse of power by psychiatric staff and the system that these staff maintain. Like representations of mental symptomatology, abuses of power range in severity from lack of adequate care that would be expected within a medical setting, through abuse of the body and mind under the guise of treatment, to overt and outright abuse of vulnerable individuals, such as physical violence and rape. In Piercy's novel, for example, Connie makes clear that her initial expectation of the mental hospital as a place embodying the original notion of the asylum – care, healing, restfulness – is woefully misguided: 'The mental hospital had always seemed like a bad joke; nothing got healed here' (p. 194). The patient on the ward must 'look away from graft and abuse. To keep quiet as you watched them beat other patients. To pretend that the rape in the linen room was a patient's fantasy' (p. 194). Sebastian Barry's Roseanne also refers to rape as a feature of the psychiatric ward, in the same almost resigned tone as Piercy's, when comparing Dr Grene's kindness to psychiatric attendant John Kane 'with all his sins, his supposed rapes and wrong doing in the asylum' (Barry, 2008, p. 99). Rape and physical violence on the wards is given little space in these two novels, and the resigned tone used by the two female narrators when it is mentioned suggests that it is seen almost as an *expected* part of the female patient's asylum experience.

Wally Lamb, who is known for working in female prisons as a creative writer (Lamb, 2003), is more explicit about the threat and the reality of rape on psychiatric wards. In *I Know This Much Is True* (1998), Dominick comes to learn that male rape has been occurring on the inpatient ward that his brother Thomas is incarcerated in, via the horror of the brother's contracting HIV due to rape (pp. 688–697). For Thomas, already acutely troubled by his madness, the assaults occurring on the ward mimic his childhood experiences of physical and verbal abuse, and ultimately contribute to his tragic and untimely suicide.

Much of the abuse of power represented in fiction is more covert, disguised as treatment and cure. Peter's treatment at the One World Rehabilitation Centre in Sayer's 1988 *The Comforts of Madness* is at times horrific by any standard of human rights, yet it is done in the cause of curing him. The One World Rehabilitation Centre appears to be a progressive, experimental type of treatment facility, one which has both critics and supporters (Sayer, 1988, p. 40). Warm baths and gentle muscle-exercising are seen by Peter as pleasant, tender activities (pp. 43–45), but the overall aims of his treatment seem more malignant:

> John and Anna were ambitious, apparently insatiable in their pursuit of 'improvement' in my 'condition'. There was no mention of my being sent back to the hospital. Where would it all end? More importantly, how could I escape? I could not, of course; I could only endure. I would eat, I would shit, feel the cold, but after all there was no other option for me but to endure. (p. 48)

The force-feeding of Peter, the wooden medieval rack-like contraption he is regularly strapped to for exercise, and the subliminal thought-insertion treatment via a tape-recorded abusive voice that he is forced to listen to, are all increasingly threatening to Peter's fantasised comfort. The most brutal treatment plunges Peter into paroxysms of flashbacks and nightmare – he is suspended upside down by his feet in pitch blackness, alone: 'I began to see old forgotten images, not so much visually as by inference, pictures so powerfully suggested that I felt I had already passed beyond the point of death and was now keeping company with ghosts who had joyfully come to claim me as one of their own' (p. 76). Peter's failure to respond to this torture eventually leads to outright frustrated aggression from his 'carers'. As we discussed in Chapter 2, given the real-life abuses that are inflicted upon Peter, it is understandable that his madness provides him, paradoxically, with safety, retreat, and comfort.

Electro Convulsive Therapy (ECT) and (now rarely used) psychosurgery are depicted as perceived punishments rather than treatments in a number of post-war novels. They are both used punitively at times in fiction. Both ECT and psychosurgery can be viewed as doubly displacing treatments, and indeed are presented as such in several such novels: not only is the body incarcerated in the asylum, causing restriction of free movement, but the brain and thus the mind become constrained – and, in the case of psychosurgery such as lobotomy, irreparably altered. When Goffman discusses the systems that result in cooperation from inmates of total institutions, he writes that the 'over-all consequence' of the privilege/punishment system is 'that cooperativeness is obtained from persons who often have cause to be uncooperative' (Goffman, 1961, p. 54). In many novels, ECT is paramount both as treatment and threat, used in order to control a large number of patients with a minimum of staff, and eliciting cooperation from individuals who have described their terror of being forced to undergo ECT.

Janet Frame's 1961 novel *Faces in the Water* provides the most eloquent elaboration of this idea, based on her experiences as a psychiatric patient in New Zealand. Frame's novel is mentioned in much existing critical work on literature and madness, and though she is neither British nor American, her depiction of ECT is worth mentioning here. Through the character of Istina, Frame quite beautifully illustrates the theme of neurological treatments (ECT and psychosurgery) as a terror-inducing method of control rather than cure. Madness is described by Istina as being in one sense a form of protest on the ward: '[...] the ripple of humanity may take the forms of protest, depression, exhilaration, violence' (p. 168). But ultimately, as Goffman asserts above about cooperation (1961, p. 54), from Istina's perspective 'it is easier to stun the beautiful fish with a dose of electricity than to handle it with care and transfer it to a pool where it will thrive' (p. 168). ECT – the 'dose of electricity' in this metaphor – is cheaper and faster-acting than providing space and an environment in which an individual can recover and flourish. Istina's absolute terror of the potential for the loss of her core sense of self through her planned lobotomy is also strikingly evident:

> The thought of the operation became a nightmare. Every morning when I woke I imagined, Today they will seize me, shave my head, dope me, send me to the hospital in the city, and when I open my eyes I will have a bandage over my head and a scar at each temple or a

curved one, like a halo, across the top of my head where the thieves, wearing gloves and with permission and delicacy, have entered and politely ransacked the storehouse and departed calm and unembarrassed like meter readers, furniture removers, or decorators sent to repaper an upstairs room.

And my 'old' self? Having had warning of its approaching death will it have crept away like an animal to die in privacy? Or will it be spilled somewhere like an invisible stain? Or, discarded, will it lie in wait for me in the future, seeking revenge? What is the essence of it, that the thieves are like meter readers who unknowingly bear away a blank card, and furniture removers trustfully sweating at the weight of imaginary furniture? (pp. 216–217)

Doctors are described as 'thieves' who will steal part of Istina's soul and selfhood – and the stolen part may die or lie in wait for Istina's 'new' self to recover, only to re-ravage her mind. Istina's thoughts are in many senses deeply philosophical here, pondering the nature of the 'essence' of the self – but one wonders how Istina can simultaneously be mad to a degree that apparently warrants invasive psychosurgery, yet capable of such philosophical insight and metaphorical description. It is not until Istina is finally provided with humane care, allowed access to intellectual stimulation through books, and space to *talk* through the kindness of her physician Dr Portman, that her recovery can begin.

The threat of ECT also evokes subservience in the patients in Kesey's novel. Lupack documents that Kesey not only voluntarily took part in drug trials as well as working as a ward attendant, but also underwent ECT himself to 'lend further veracity to Chief's vision of the asylum' (Lupack, 1994, p. 175). She continues by suggesting that this was in part due to Kesey being 'as rebellious and irreverent as his characters Bromden and McMurphy', expressing in those characters his own belief that 'authority is not always absolute' (p. 175). Lupack suggests that Kesey's overarching message in the novel is that the disempowered mad character can paradoxically triumph: '[...] so long as they attempt change (e.g., McMurphy's trying to lift the panel), even their failures are noble, precisely because they try' (p. 175). Kesey's depiction of the after-effects of ECT, via Bromden, is vivid. Bromden describes feeling dazed for 'as long as two weeks' after a treatment, 'living in that foggy, jumbled blur which is a whole lot like the ragged edge of sleep, that gray zone between light and dark, or between sleeping and waking or living and dying, where you know you're not unconscious any more but don't know yet what day it is or who you are or what's the use of coming back at all' (p. 249). ECT is described here as sedating and as fragmenting the edges of consciousness, dampening an individual's spirit to the point of existential nihilism. It is little wonder that the threat of ECT works as a method of control and containment when its effects are so soul-destroying.

As Goffman writes, the 'intransigent' patient (such as McMurphy) is one who must be 'broken', sometimes by 'electroshock' (Goffman, 1961, p. 62). ECT is not enough to break McMurphy, however, and his final scene, desperately fighting the nurses and attendants, is all the more poignant for his final noises, the 'sound of cornered-animal fear and hate and surrender and defiance [...] when he finally doesn't care any more about anything but himself and his dying' (Kesey, 1962, p. 275). McMurphy's rebellion seems to be over – the intransigent is finally overpowered. Yet the subsequent self-discharge of previously subordinate patients, the escape of Chief Bromden, and McMurphy's release in death through Bromden's gentle suffocation supports the view taken by Lupack (1994, p. 175) that the ultimate motif of the novel is that the seemingly powerless good can triumph over the seemingly powerful evil.

In Piercy's *Woman on the Edge of Time*, the notion of madness as a preferable alternative to the insanity of the real, violent world of the asylum is lent weight by the new form of psychosurgery that patients in the novel are selected for. The patients are prepared for experimentation with no explanation as to *what* they are actually going to undergo. Connie's fellow patient Skip suggests that this is not the first time he has been forced to receive such treatment, describing the doctors placing electrodes on his penis and showing him pornographic pictures as an 'experiment' (p. 165). This form of bodily manipulation for psychological change also forms the basis of the infamous novel *A Clockwork Orange* by Anthony Burgess (1962), where violent teenage deviant Alex is institutionalised and shown macabre and revolting pictures and videos, whilst simultaneously being given emetic drugs. On his release, having been 'cured', Alex is unable to witness or perform any acts of violence without being terribly sick.

The secrecy and lack of explanation that surrounds the proposed treatment of the inpatients on Connie's unit leads her to speculate about the new treatment. The proposals masquerade as benevolent care, arousing her suspicion after previous experiences of ECT and medication:

'Needles in the brain...' It sounded like a crazy fantasy [...]. Maybe they had given Alice shot in the head, a new drug injected directly in the brain? That too was crazy. Those new drugs they tried out made your kidneys turn to rock or caused your tongue to swell black in your mouth or your skin to crust in patches or your hair to fall in loose handfuls, like stuffing from an old couch. Perhaps a drug injected right in the brain could turn you into a zombie as quick as too much shock. (pp. 193–194)

Even modern medications have the potential to cause some very difficult side effects: it is therefore understandable that individual patients are unwilling to take medication, despite then risking being labelled non-compliant, and subject to further restrictions on their bodily and psychological freedom. Non-compliance with medically proposed treatment is only one of the excuses advanced to justify the horrific surgical operations inflicted on patients in *Woman on the Edge of Time*.

The treatment itself is described in highly medicalised language that again excludes the patients on the ward, adding another layer of power discourse, that of inability to understand the terms of reference. The treatment stands in line with the ambitions of neurosurgeons and electronics specialists in the 1970s to create a 'psychocivilized' society by means of brain implants (Delgado, 1969; Horgan, 2005). In the novel, the surgery consists of inserting a radio-controlled device under the skull, as the inventor explains: 'You see, we can electrically trigger almost every mood and emotion – the fight-or-flight reaction, euphoria, calm, pleasure, pain, terror! We can monitor and induce reactions through the microminiaturized radio under the skull [...]' (p. 204). Piercy portrays horrific and humiliating scenes as the research team, along with invited others, come to monitor the effects of the new treatment, reminiscent of the practice of paying customers witnessing asylum inmates in their chains, described in Henry Mackenzie's *Man of Feeling* (1771) and elaborated in Porter (2002). Cost-benefit analysis features highly in the use of this revolutionary treatment, with the ward described as a 'zoo', as the inventor/salesperson of the new treatment suggests:

You have to administer tranquillizers several times a day. But this way, eventually patients will be cleared out, back to their families, back to keeping house, back to work, out into nursing homes. The state's short of money and they put a lot of pressure on you to get them out through the revolving door. But then you get to that fuss in the papers about patients being turned loose. Here's your answer [...]. Instead of a warehouse for the socially dysfunctional, you'll be running a hospital. (p. 205)

Economics are presented as being of far greater importance than the well-being of inmates in the 'zoo' (p. 205). Yet when the treatment is rolled out and used on patient Skip, an individual who has already suffered humiliating treatments, what occurs is far from the outcome they hoped for. Skip's 'violence' is turned on his own body, rather than towards those who have abused him: 'When they came to play with Skip, the doctors were not satisfied. The violence-triggering electrodes did not cause him to try to attack them, as Alice had. Instead he turned from them and drove his fist into the wall' (p. 263). Here, patients become the doctor's playthings under the auspices of care and treatment.

Connie herself describes her fears as being akin to facing the executioner during the night 'before the electric chair' (p. 279). Connie (rightly) perceives the treatment in terms of physical violation, referring to the planned operation as a rape – 'Tomorrow they were going to stick a machine in her brain. She was the experiment. They would rape her body, her brain, her self' (p. 279) – with the treatment removing all vestiges of personal identity and autonomy, leaving her as an 'experimental monster', the doctor's 'plaything' (p. 279). She is angry at being forced to undergo this surgery – anger being one of the emotions that needs, according to the psychiatric team depicted in the novel, electronic control. Connie's 'treatment' is, finally, unsuccessful in the most ironic of ways. At the end of the novel, she poisons six people. Speaking to herself in the mirror, she says: 'I murdered them dead. Because *they* are the violence-prone. Theirs is the money and the power, theirs the poisons that slow the mind and dull the heart. Theirs are the powers of life and death. I killed them. Because it is war' She adds that at least she knows she fought back, and has no shame for having done so (p. 375). Connie's rebellions, her murderous acts, finally afford her peace and a sense of power – because, ultimately, she has slain the figures of power. Furthermore, the closing pages of the novel highlight an enduring irony of the continuing use of certain physical psychiatric treatments. Clinicians are, in these novels at least, lawfully able to use violence to treat violence.

Of course, not all psychiatric treatment in madness novels is presented as violent, dehumanising, or abusive. The ideal in therapeutic care is repeatedly portrayed as consisting of empathic staff willing to listen and, more importantly, hear individual stories and experiences; and therapeutic regimes that have the core aim of empowering patients. Sebastian Barry's Dr Grene and Clare Dudman's Dr Hoffmann both represent a newer wave of psychiatrists who provide a listening ear, rather than physical control and constraint as the mainstay of treatment. Sylvia Plath's *The Bell Jar* (1963) also demonstrates character Esther Greenwood's (the fictionalised Sylvia Plath) terror of ECT, directly contrasting with her recovery following her experiences of supportive and empathic talking care. Lisa Carey's *Love in the Asylum* (2004) demonstrates that the concomitant use of medication and respectful psychiatric care, which strives to provide patients with a degree of autonomy, can be a winning combination against psychological and psychiatric disintegration. Carey names symptoms and disorders in this novel and we remain faithful to her practice, using her terminology rather than 'madness'. Alba is a young girl with bipolar affective disorder who, although a successful children's author, is designated certain roles by those who wield power over her, and she is infantilised by her father throughout the novel – 'Her father considers her writing a time-eating hobby; Dr Miller believes it's therapeutic; her publisher, after a few initial disasters, decided to waive her book-tour duties, claiming she'd alarm her young readers. No one thinks she has the personality of a children's writer' (2004, p. 81). Ultimately, the only role she is allowed to take ownership of is that of psychiatric patient. But through Dr Miller's kindness and care, Alba does eventually leave the caring but stifling grip of her father and begin a life of serenity.

As with a number of narratives, medication as a main treatment is a double-edged sword for Alba. It stabilises to her moods and gives her periods outside the asylum, yet at the same time it dampens her creativity. This is a relatively common issue with bipolar affective disorder and medication, as commented upon by Professor Kay Redfield Jamison in her powerful and critically acclaimed autobiography *An Unquiet Mind: A Memoir of Moods and Madness* (1995). Alba demonstrates ambivalence towards the medication she is prescribed and which, at times, she is forced to take:

> Her plan is this: she will take her medication every day for the rest of her life; she will live mentally muzzled and stop wishing for something more exciting. Excitement, her father insists, lasts for about six weeks, in that hypomanic stage, where she is brilliant and creative – alive – anything seems possible. It is always, without fail, followed by chaos, and then darkness.
>
> Of course, none of this is what she wants. What she secretly hopes for is a miracle – mental health without the dependence on drugs that snuff out her soul. The drugs buffer so many sensations, flatten all but the most benign feelings, that she wonders if death would be

all that different. No one, not her doctor or her boyfriends or, when she's sick, even Alba herself, believes that it is possible for her to live without the drugs. (p. 9)

Ultimately, it is only the *dual* process of talking therapy with Dr Miller (regarding the excruciatingly traumatic and painful adoption of her son) *and* medication that allows Alba a life without the crippling mood-swings of bipolar affective disorder. The historical letters that Alba finds provide a historical and culture-specific exploration of attitudes towards madness in the Abenaki Indian tribe in *Love in the Asylum*. In fact the novel examines many dualisms – talking treatments versus medication and chemical treatment, historical versus contemporary constructions and treatments of illness, white American versus Abenaki treatments and, finally, the contrasting notions of choice over illness, seen through Oscar's drug addiction (presented as a life-choice at times in the novel) and Alba's (illness/inherited) bipolar affective disorder.

The closure of the asylums

The 1960s saw anti-psychiatry movements, led by R. D. Laing, Thomas Sazsz, and David Cooper among others, grow in power, and movements began towards empowerment and autonomy of patients with mental health problems and humanistic, holistic methods of care. In the UK, the post-war period saw the large-scale closure of the asylums in a process which has been described as 'decarceration' (Scull, 1984) and resettlement in the community (Barham and Hayward, 1991; Barham, 1992; Bartlett and Wright, 1999). Sebastian Barry's character Dr Grene eloquently documents the dilemma for psychiatrists during the lengthy period and process of eviction:

These people are perceived by the all-knowing public at large, or let us say public opinion as it is mirrored in the newspapers, as deserving of 'freedom' and 'release'. Which may be very true, but creatures so long kennelled and confined find freedom and release very problematic attainments, like those eastern European countries after communism. And similarly there is a weird reluctance in me to see anyone go. Why is that? The anxiety of the zoo keeper? Can my polar bears do as well at the pole? (2008, p. 16)

In contrast to the quote above, criticisms have been made that the policy of community-based care led many long-term institutionalised patients to go without care (Ramsay, 1990; Sullivan, 1998; Welshman, 2007). Indeed, in both McGrath's *Spider* (1990) and Crawford's *Nothing Purple, Nothing Black* (2002) there is a notable absence of adequate (let alone successful or therapeutic) community-based care for both Spider and Crystal. Both characters deteriorate mentally without supervision and live poverty-stricken, socially isolated existences in hostels run by money-grabbing, unscrupulous proprietors who demonstrate little compassion for their residents. This representation – and its concomitant public perception – is common following the eviction of long-confined patients.

Perhaps one of the most elaborate imaginary alternatives to the present system is depicted in Bebe Moore Campbell's *72 Hour Hold*, which we explore more thoroughly in Chapter 4. For our purposes at this point, however, Moore Campbell's novel demonstrates the difficulties faced by Keri in obtaining care for her daughter during the post-incarceration era. Within the traditional US care system, Trina's illness leaves her suspended in a perpetual childhood, yet the system meant to contain and treat this illness gives her the rights of an adult (p. 39). When Trina is admitted to the ward, she may be physically in a safe place but her treatment consists of little more than medication, and her compliance with mood-stabilising medication can only be ensured for the 72 hours she spends on the ward. While Keri desires that her daughter remain on the ward and recover, she also sees other patients as physically obese 'zombies, anesthetized by meds that slowed down their metabolism, [who] roamed the halls. [...] It had always angered me that none of the psych wards or residential treatment centres was proactive in keeping weight off their mentally ill patients. Their meals were a carb fest, their exercise programmes a joke' (p. 77). Nevertheless, being on the ward is preferable to the problems and anxieties that Keri encounters when Trina is at home:

> I stayed at home for a few days, babysitting Trina. Guard duty would be more accurate. Watching, waiting, trying to come up with a strategy. I called around to price private-duty nurses and security guards. Too expensive. [...]
>
> During the weeks when Trina was still living under my roof, I called SMART at least half a dozen times. Each time they arrived in a timely manner and were unfailingly polite. Somehow, Trina was able to pull herself together in front of them. 'Ma'am,' they'd say, 'your daughter doesn't meet the criteria.' (p. 133)

It is only through notions of risk and dangerousness – danger from Trina to herself or others – that admission can proceed: 'No slit wrists for her; no bullet wounds for me' (p. 133). Keri is left with an unwell daughter who, ironically, has to become *more* unwell, demonstrate *more* danger, before treatment can occur. Trina herself does not realise she is unwell, and therefore will not go to any interviews or appointments, will not willingly take the medication offered to her. Several cycles of 72-hour holds later, Keri is introduced to the idea of an illegal, underground treatment programme run by those who feel the American system fails people with mental illness. As we suggested towards the end of Chapter 2, Moore Campbell's novel is notable for its realistic portrayal of the frustration of carers who are as much at the mercy of the system as the patients themselves. Yet kidnapping and forcing an individual into underground treatment is not a solution either, and Moore Campbell provides a view of differing options which we will take a more critical look at in Chapter 4.

Clare Allan's *Poppy Shakespeare* (2006) provides a satirical but frighteningly accurate portrayal of the current UK mental health system – though her portrayal is rapidly becoming out-of-date as policy changes and economics dictate the closure of more and more day-care facilities in the UK. Allan's wry take on day-care within psychiatric units, narrated by a character known only as N who has been a patient (like her mother was) for most of her life, has much in common with Goffman's portrayal of asylum life some 50 years previously. For example, cigarettes are a crucial part of the barter system that forms an integral part of the microcommunity within total institutions (Goffman, 1961, pp. 242–248). In *Poppy Shakespeare*, this is presented humorously as an underground economy in which medication is exchanged for cigarette butts in a profitable recycling scheme (p. 112). Allan's semi-comic novel has darker overtones too. She examines the position of patients within the hierarchal mental health system – in particular how the system creates and maintains individuals in the dependant position of patient. The Abaddon hospital – which can be read as *a bad 'un*, a colloquialism for those individuals who go against the decreed norms of society (Allan's novel is full of gems such as this) – is a tower which mimics the hierarchy of illnesses themselves:

> The way it worked at the Abaddon was the madder you was, the higher you gone, then they move you down through the floors as you get better. And as you moved down you could do more things. On the seventh you couldn't do practically nothing, you couldn't even take a piss in private 'cause the toilets hadn't got no doors on them. On the fourth they'd let you have a bath though you had to

use your foot for a plug and they checked on you every three minutes
[...]. It was all meant to get you to lay off the mad stuff and start acting normal, like showing a dog a treat to make it sit. (p. 6)

Illnesses form entire identities for the individuals constrained
within the Abaddon: 'So you neurotic, psychotic or what?' I said, like
just making conversation. Ask most dribblers what's wrong, they's
that fucking grateful, they'll talk till their throats is raw' (p. 57).

While those 'dribblers' (patients) at the top of the tower are desperate to climb down, those at the day hospital are desperate to stay. The
upper-level patients become disruptive when confronted by the lower-
floor inhabitants: 'The flops said we eaten their cake or whatever, and
we didn't *want* to leave. Which was bollocks, and even if it *weren't*, if
we wanted to stay then that *proved* we was mad and if we was mad we
weren't ready to leave' (p. 8). The strange logic inherent in this statement mirrors the paradoxical and contradictory double-binds that
entrap the patients within the unit, evident for example in this wall-
notice on group rules:

1. If clients wish to attend, groups are voluntary.
2. If clients do NOT wish to attend, groups are NOT voluntary.
3. Voluntarily or otherwise, clients must attend all their groups.
4. Clients who do NOT attend groups will NOT remain clients.
   (p. 179)

Yet this same strange system provides a structure to N's life that, once
removed, causes her to become unwell and retreat into an isolated existence. When she is discharged from the day-care unit, N takes to her bed
and ceases to eat, smoke, take her medication, or communicate with the
outside world, even with Poppy, by then her friend (p. 316).

Paradoxically, Poppy is created as, or turned into, a patient by the
very system she tries to reject. From her initial meeting with N during
which, much to N's horror, she vehemently denied having or experiencing any form of madness, she gradually declines until eventually
needing admission to the upper floors of the Abaddon. Poppy's description of how she came to be required to attend the Dorothy Fish Day
Hospital is riddled with unlikely complexity, from going to a job interview to being diagnosed with a 'severely disordered personality' in one
easy step (pp. 145–156). Yet throughout the novel, Poppy protests her
sanity in a remarkably sane and reasonable manner. Eventually, however, the very system professing to treat her grinds Poppy down to a

dreadful point:

> By February Poppy was doing so good, it would of needed a very expert doctor to tell she was putting it on. She taken to boiling the skin off her arms, pouring the water straight out the kettle, dreamily moving the stream up and down, like watering plants, as the skin slid away in sheets. She was pulling her hair out by then as well, not just the odd strand, like huge fucking clumps. Parts of her scalp showing through totally bald like the coat of a mangy dog. (p. 297)

N sees Poppy's deterioration as a step forward, viewing Poppy finally becoming ill as achieving the goals of the Dorothy Fish attendees: to get MAD money, to remain a day patient. At the end of the novel Poppy has become an in-patient and, N is informed, has attracted 33 separate diagnoses (p. 339). The fantastical notions inherent within Allan's narrative both emphasise elements of N's own madness and serve to – much like many dys/utopian novels – accentuate the reality of situations she describes by paradoxically taking their depictions to literal extremes.

The mental health system Allan portrays is so riddled with paradoxes and idiosyncrasies that it both creates and maintains patients while simultaneously discharging those in actual need of care. Poppy's experience can be compared to Goffman's 'moral career' of the mental patient. In Goffman's pre-patient phase, for example, Poppy suffers 'embitterment', anger, and anxiety at her admission to the day hospital, starting with 'relationships and rights' and ending up admitted to hospital with 'hardly any of either' (Goffman, 1961, p. 125). During the 'in-patient' phase, Goffman notes in a footnote, 'once you come to the attention of the testers you either will automatically be labelled crazy or the process of testing itself will make you crazy' (Goffman, 1961, p. 143 fn), exactly as happens to Poppy. Her story, in terms of Goffman's notion of moral career, is interrupted by end of the book – yet the future looks bleak for Poppy, creating a dark ending to an uncomfortably comic novel. N's inimitable, almost magical realist style and exaggeration of situations both deadens and magnifies the reader's response to this mix of comedy and tragedy, in an illogical manner not unlike the very power systems she describes.

Multiple disempowerments

Allan's *Poppy Shakespeare* shows how psychiatric patients become enmeshed in multiple power systems – in this case, both the psychiatric system and the social benefits system, alongside a further power structure through the procedures for appealing medical decisions through specialist mental health solicitors. Allan's vision of the MAD money fiasco exposes and ridicules our bureaucratic UK welfare system. MAD money can be seen as a thinly veiled fictionalisation of the UK's system of welfare benefits – with multiple levels that are impossible to actually receive or understand: 'MAD money was like religion 'cept bigger. MAD money was every religion all added together and timesed by itself and bigger than that as well. Sniffs gone to college to study MAD money and come home knowing less than they did when they gone. People spent their whole lives studying just one single rate' (p. 140). When Poppy sees a solicitor to appeal against her compulsory admission to the day hospital, she finds herself caught in a further paradox. She needs to be in receipt of MAD money in order to see the solicitor, and in order to receive MAD money she must declare herself mad on the (endless) forms that have to be filled in, which then means she is *unable* to declare with any definitively unarguable certainty that she is *not* mad: 'I know it's crazy,' said Mr Leech. 'You have to declare yourself mentally ill in order to prove you're *not* mentally ill, but there you are; I don't make the laws, I just have to work within them' (p. 168).

Underlying and reinforcing multiple power networks ensnaring psychiatric patients lie notions of stigma. For Connie in *Woman on the Edge of Time*, the loss of her daughter is in part a direct consequence of her low economic and mental health status: 'The social worker was giving her human-to-cockroach look. Most people hit kids. But if you were on welfare and on probation and the whole social-pigeonholing establishment had the right to trek regularly through your kitchen looking in the closets and under the bed, counting the bedbugs and your shoes, you'd better not hit your kid once' (p. 26). Furthermore, Connie learns quickly that silence is her only defence, albeit a doubly ineffective one: 'They trapped you into saying something and then they'd bring out their interpretations that made your life over. To make your life into a pattern of disease' (p. 26). Similarly, Keri in *72 Hour Hold* tries accessing carer support groups but finds herself within a double minority – as a black mother of a mentally ill child (p. 49). Stigma, in both of these novels, extends far wider than an interactive personal process – it has far-reaching effects and invades every element of that person's life, laying bare all that the non-mad, or those untouched by the madness of others, wants to keep personal and private.

In Lamb's *I Know This Much Is True*, Dominick reflects on, and questions, the assumption that underlies stigmatising responses and misunderstandings about mental health. He refers to the very assumption that drives much mental health policy and care: the media-perpetuated assumption that madness equals risk, violence, uncontrollability:

> The maximum-security Hatch Forensic Institute, located at the rear of the Three Rivers State Hospital grounds, is a squat concrete-and-steel building surrounded by chain link and razor wire. Hatch houses most of the front-page boys: the vet from Mystic who mistook his family for the Viet Cong, the kid at Wesleyan who bought his .22-caliber semiautomatic to class. But Hatch is also the end of the line for a lot of less sexy psychos: drug fry-outs, shopping mall nuisances, manic-depressive alcoholics – your basic disturbing-the-peace wackos with no place else to go. Occasionally, someone actually gets better down at Hatch. Gets released. But that tends to happen *in spite of* things. For most of the patients there, the door swings only one way, which is just fine with the town of Three Rivers. Most people around here are less interested in rehabilitation than they are in warehousing the spooks and kooks – keeping the Boston Strangler and the Son of Sam off the streets, keeping Norman Bates locked up at the Hatch Hotel. (p. 68)

For several patients in fictional accounts of madness, the criminal justice system becomes intertwined with the mental health system, dispersing the individual through interrelated systems of health care, justice, and punishment – John Katzenbach's *The Madman's Tale* (2004) is a particularly good example of this. Dangerousness and risk are prominent features in the media generally and specifically in government policy on mental health, and this is naturally reflected in novels. Novels do, however, run the risk of sensationalising madness through their portrayals of the unrealistic and diagnostically absurd 'psycho-killer', evident in any number of crime fictions. But some novels do address issues of dangerousness in a more nuanced and sensitive manner. Ian McEwan's *Enduring Love* (1997), for example, examines De Clerambault's syndrome – a condition in which the sufferer becomes delusional and obsessed with another person – with finesse, acuity, and a large dose of realism. John Fowles's *The Collector* (1963) also examines notions of obsession and dangerousness in a humane manner.

Risks posed by mental illness and by others *to the sufferer themselves* are far more prominent in reality, but make less sensational fiction. Suicide, suicide attempts, and self-harm appear in several novels. In *I*

Know This Much Is True, Dominick's brother ultimately commits suicide after his discharge from hospital – discharge that follows an admission after the self-amputation of his hand. Darien in Waterfield Duisberg's *The Good Patient* repeatedly harms herself in response to her disturbing half-memories and traumatic history. Jeffrey Eugenides's 1993 novel *The Virgin Suicides* examines the catastrophic impact of another power structure on the lives of five sisters – the family. Growing up with the conflicting demands of peer pressure, burgeoning adolescent sexuality and a repressive, religious family life, all five daughters in this striking novel eventually commit suicide. Nonetheless, novels in which mad individuals are violent, dangerous, and criminal are produced in far greater numbers than novels in which sufferers of madness are more of a risk to themselves – or, even more realistically, of no risk whatever.

As in *The Virgin Suicides,* familial and societal expectations and demands placed on women appear in novels to induce various forms of madness, from lowering of mood to outright psychosis. One novel which explicitly links female madness with the repression of sexuality and oppressive familial expectations is Antonia White's *Beyond the Glass* (1954). In this novel, a clear implication is made by White – that repressed passion leads to mental breakdown. Main character Clara is caught in an unhappy, unconsummated marriage from which she is freed after a lengthy, religiously based process. Clara is unable to repress or satisfy her very human and normal sexual desires after falling passionately in love, which leads to her realistically portrayed breakdown, subtly played out by White from early signs through to full-blown psychosis. In many senses White's novel, like Barry's and Faulks', fits with a model of novel as history: treatments are historically rooted, and a period-specific sense of hopelessness about recovery is also clear. White's novel, aside from being an excellent example of feminist madness literature, reminds us of positive developments in psychiatry and attitudes towards the mad over the past 60 years.

Masculine and patriarchal expectations placed upon women during the period in which White wrote are highlighted as additional pressures on females during a crucial time in the development of women's history. Clara is infantilised to an extent by her father, who not only has high expectations of her but is also judgemental about her looks and behaviour, referring to her at one point as 'slatternly and unkempt' (p. 19). His well-intentioned judgements continue by focusing on what he perceives as 'defects' but which may now more reasonably be seen as a normal part of the process of growing away from the family during late adolescence and early adulthood:

> He had reason enough to be anxious about Clara. She had been mar-
> ried only a few months and it was obvious that things were not going
> well. Archie Hughes-Follett had begun to drink again and he sus-
> pected they were getting into debt. What troubled him far more was
> the swift and violent change in Clara herself. The last time he had
> seen her, there had been a defiance, even a coarseness in her looks
> and manner which had shocked him. Any real or fancied defect in
> his fiercely loved only child had always caused him such pain that
> his first reaction was to be angry with her. (pp. 9–10)

Clara's relationship with her mother is also difficult, and she becomes
caught between her father's desire to see her repress her natural instincts
and remain childlike in many ways – certainly, to avoid any appearance
of what he may perceive as coarseness or unfeminine behaviour – and
her mother's urging of her to feel emotion and release her instinctual
drives. In White's novel, this occurs in a manner reminiscent of Bateson's
'double bind' theory of madness (Bateson et al., 1956; Bateson, 1972):

> 'You hate admitting you have *any* feelings, don't you? At any rate
> to me.'
>   Clara flushed angrily. She could hardly tell her mother that she
> had a dread of being like her; emotional, impulsive, and greedy for
> praise and affection. The dread was all the more acute because, how-
> ever sternly she tried to repress or disown it, one side of her was con-
> stantly betraying her into behaving exactly like Isabel. At moments
> she could hear the echoes of her mother's high, straving tones in her
> own. (p. 55)

Clara's mother later makes a perceptive and prophetic response to
Clara's oblique admission of her sexual feelings by suggesting to her: 'I
wonder how much you *do* know ... No, there's something more frightening still. Discovering feelings in yourself ... violent feelings you never
even suspected you had ... Feelings that would make you throw up everything ... yes, even your religion ... just to be with a particular person ...'
(p. 63). Clara's mother goes on to refer to sexual passion and love as
being akin to a 'fever', an 'insanity' (p. 64). When Clara finally breaks
down, the doctor suggests that her mother stays away due to Clara's
'hysterical' ideas about her (p. 216). When Clara's mother suggests that
far from being hysterical, Clara has always been too controlled, their

family doctor responds by insightfully suggesting: 'Controls have a way of breaking down, you know. After all you told me earlier on about how she's been ever since that abnormal marriage of hers ... First the apathy and depression ... then this sudden emotional stimulus ... Perhaps this rather violent reaction isn't altogether surprising.' (p. 216). His hesitant tone here, indicated by the ellipses, mimics Clara's father's reluctance to acknowledge his daughter's status as an adult woman.

Clara's experience of acute psychosis is only described in fragments, snippets of memories. This has a dual purpose – firstly, it replicates textually Clara's heavily sedated state in hospital. Secondly, and more interestingly, it forms part of the metaphorical chain that begins prior to Clara's psychosis with a focus on (shattered) mirrors, glass, and reflection. Clara repeatedly finds herself unable to recognise her own face in the looking glass before her:

> [...] she found herself suddenly confronted with her image in one of the mirrors artfully disposed to make the room seem larger. She was startled as if she had discovered a stranger spying on her.
>
> Like herself, the other had fair, wildly disordered hair and wore a creased tussore dress but its face was almost unrecognisable. The eyes were dull and parched between the reddened lids; a pocket of shadow, dark as a bruise, lay under each. The features were rigid and distorted as if they had been melted down and reset in a coarser mould. (p. 33)

Interestingly, Clara sees her distorted features as though they have been remade in a 'coarser mould', mimicking her father's concerns about her 'coarseness' (p. 9). The early stages of Clara's psychosis are marked by wild mood swings and passionate outbursts. Yet she also experiences a suspension in time and a sense of increasing unreality, which resonates with themes of reflection:

> For the first time she realised, however dimly, that her standing there, staring at the dancing coins of light on the dark water, was part of a continuous stream of life. Since her marriage she had had an increasing sense of unreality, as if her existence had been broken off like the reel of a film. Nothing that had happened to her seemed to have had a connection with any past or to be leading to any future. Now she perceived, though she could not yet feel it, that her life could not, in the nature of things, remain in this state of tranced immobility. (p. 90)

Her temporal dislocation – note that she reflects (literally) upon this while walking by a river and watching the reflection of lights in the water, furthering the metaphorical chain or mirroring – as well as the unfamiliar and unwelcome passions stirred in her through meeting Richard lead her towards an inability to fix upon a stable sense of self or self-identity. Ultimately, her fragmentation in the mirror is replicated by the fragmentation not only of her image – an image held so dearly by her father – but of her entire being in madness.

A similar scenario is developed by Piercy. Due to varying economic, educational, ethnic, and gendered oppressions, Connie's identity is fractured into three parts. She says during a conversation in the future:

> Anyhow, in a way I've always had three names inside me. Consuelo, my given name. Consuelo's a Mexican woman, a servant of servants, silent as clay. The woman who suffers. Who bears and endures. Then I'm Connie, who managed to get two years of college – till Consuelo got pregnant. Connie got decent jobs from time to time and fought welfare for a little extra money for Angie. She got me on a bus when I had to leave Chicago. But it was her who married Eddie, she thought it was smart. Then I'm Conchita, the low-down drunken mean part of me who get by in jail, in the bughouse, who loves no good men, who hurt my daughter... (p. 122)

Notably, in the utopian future world, Connie is not judged, unlike her constant denotation as mad and/or bad in the outside real world. Connie in the world of the asylum, and in her real social world, suffers from multiple oppressions – as a Mexican woman who also suffers from mental health problems, is poor, and has few educational or employment opportunities – and fails, particularly in her socially expected role as a mother. Thus in Connie, as with Clara, we can see the impact of *masculine* power-driven, gendered, and socially constructed expectations on the individual's attempt to develop and maintain an honest, authentic or true, stable sense of self. These themes are also evident in Sylvia Plath's *The Bell Jar* (1963) and Jennifer Dawson's *The Ha-Ha* (1985).

Concluding remarks

In this chapter, we have looked at portrayals of power in fictional psychiatric institutions. We have not questioned the existence of madness itself, or whether madness is a productive way to conceptualise the human condition, or whether madness can confer advantages on its sufferers. The closest we come to investigating this is perhaps through *One Flew Over the Cuckoo's Nest*, where we acknowledge that characters such as Bromden and McMurphy are depicted as having individually valuable strengths and skills, but that these strengths are constrained by the universally powerful institution. Yet even in this novel, the depiction of the ward's chronic patients plays a counterpoint role, reinforcing the notion of a necessary medical model of madness. This model assumes that there is a universal human ambition for a stable self and sense of identity. This was something that we questioned in Chapter 2, and will again look at – though in a very different manner – in Chapter 6. Psychiatry is a powerful institution that does, in one sense, exist because of the suggestion that if only this stable self/identity could be achieved, enhanced, and/or consolidated, then better psychological health would ensue and more successful lives would be led. This thinking underlies a great many popular therapies and self-help approaches which have flourished in the post-war era. The fragmentation of identity in madness is enhanced by those oppressed through whichever power structure they fall victim to – be it psychiatric, gendered, familial, criminal, or economic – and leads, in the post-war novels explored in this chapter, to madness.

The themes of power, coercion, and confinement, outlined in literature long before our period of interest in this book through classics like Charlotte Perkins Gilman's *The Yellow Wallpaper* (1892), are amply reprised in more recent fictions. Connections between earlier concerns and those of the present period are explicitly referenced via the letters in Carey's *Love in the Asylum*. Common to the two periods, as well as various processes of medically sanctioned confinement, are experiences of being judged, evaluated, and assessed, often with a view to being further constrained should that judgement prove unfavourable. As we have seen, even systems of support can prove oppressive in their complexity – the satire in *Poppy Shakespeare* of the bewildering variety of benefits available to those suffering mental health problems provides one example of this.

Despite elements of abuse and inhumanity described in the selection of novels in this chapter, there is nevertheless in some cases a sense of optimism, with cure or improvement occurring. The institution of psychiatry and the power inherent within it is not universally represented or described in literature as essentially or completely negative. We see, through our examination of novels that look at the historical development of psychiatry, benevolent and caring aims in the creation of asylum care. We also see the problems, mistreatment, and at times overt cruelty that can occur when those placed in power abuse their charges. Treatments are seen (often rightly) to be malevolent processes by many of the characters in the novels explored here. As we suggested when looking at *Poppy Shakespeare*, the process of becoming a psychiatric patient can, paradoxically, be induced by or occur *because of* the very system and the treatments that are imposed to treat madness.

We have looked briefly in this chapter at more contemporary notions of community care as leading to neglect and, at times, the necessity for extreme risk to occur before care can be actually be attained. We have also exposed the paradoxical desire of some characters – as in *Poppy Shakespeare* – to stay *within* the psychiatric system compared to the desire for escape evinced by characters in, for example, *One Flew Over The Cuckoo's Nest*. Fiction provides no easy resolutions to the age-old and perhaps irresolvable problems of psychiatry and psychiatric power – but it can enable a critical reflection by clinicians which, at the very least, may lead to more empathic approaches within institutional settings.

4
Diversity, Ethnicity, Madness and Fiction

Here, [...] in this place, we flesh; Flesh that weeps, laughs; flesh
that dances on bare feet in grass. Love it, love it hard. Yonder
they do not love your flesh. They despise it. [...] Love your
hands! Love them. Raise them up and kiss them, touch others
with them, pat them together, stroke them on your face, 'cause
they don't love that either. You got to love it, You! And no, they
ain't in love with your mouth. [...] You got to love it. This is
flesh that I'm talking about here. Flesh that needs to be loved.
Feet that need to rest and to dance, backs that need support;
shoulders that need strong arms. [...] More than eyes and feet.
More than your life-holding womb and your life-giving private
parts, hear em now, love your heart. For this is the prize. (Lines
spoken by Baby Suggs in Toni Morrison, 1987, pp. 88–89)

In creating a single chapter on diversity issues in post-1945 literature,
we face a number of basic difficulties. There is little consensus on what
terms such as 'diversity' and 'ethnicity' mean. From the point of view of
scholars in the health care disciplines who address the practical manifestations of 'madness', these generic terms can have a deliberately wide
and inclusive frame of reference. In the inaugural issue of *Diversity in
Health and Social Care*, McGee and Johnson write that they 'adopt a very
broad view of the concept of "diversity". We see it as embracing all
aspects of difference, including, for example, culture, belief, disability,
gender, sexual orientation, race and ethnicity, as well as underserved
and marginalized populations' (2004, p. 1). In the latter part of the
twentieth century the racial categories promulgated by eugenicists
and physical anthropologists fell into disrepute and were increasingly
replaced by a more psychosocially nuanced, and often self-defined,

notion of 'ethnicity'. As sociologist Stuart Hall puts it, the term ethnicity 'acknowledges the place of history, language and culture in the construction of subjectivity and identity, as well as the fact that all discourse is placed, positioned, situated, and all knowledge is contextual' (1992, p. 257). As Fernando adds: 'In practical shorthand, ethnicity is taken to mean a mixture of cultural background and racial designation' (2005, p. 421). In the UK especially, the hospital system through which mental health care is administered has been viewed with some degree of suspicion by black and minority-ethnic clients (Fernando, 2005).

Despite the large volume of literature dealing with ethnic and racial experience, it is difficult to discover a distinctive black or minority-ethnic experience of madness in the fictional literature reviewed in this chapter. Notwithstanding the presence of a substantial literature by black authors from 1945 onwards, madness has not emerged as a prominent theme in this oeuvre, despite this being a period of time when Black American literature began to make inroads into the literary establishment, especially in the US.

A melding of advocacy, agitprop, and political analysis characterised a good deal of writing from authors of African descent in the twentieth century. Frantz Fanon's *Les Damnés de la Terre* (*The Wretched of the Earth*, 1961) was foundational in the movement towards decolonisation, especially in North Africa. Fanon developed and amended Marxism and psychoanalysis to understand the state of people in colonised nations and how their situation moulds their understanding of themselves and their ability to effect political change. The effects of colonial subjugation on colonised people were the subject of Fanon's *Peau Noire, Masques Blancs* (*Black Skin, White Masks*, 1952). As well as the physical privations of poverty and torture, there were, he argued, important colonising effects facilitated through language. Richard Wright's *White Man Listen!* (1957) explored the problems facing newly emerging nations in the post-World War Two period, their adaptation of European and North American models of government, and their appeal to people's pride in local cultural and religious traditions. This question of how to find a voice and a political programme is one which we shall return to several times throughout this chapter, as the authors position themselves in relation to patterns of inequality, frameworks of understanding, and, in some cases, in relation to other black writing.

In a domestic context within the US, the post-war surge of interest in African-American writing took to its heart the need to capture experiences and styles of expression, which were not at the time part of the mainstream literary canon. The popularisation of writing in dialect rather than literary English has been ascribed, among other possibilities, to the poet Paul Laurence Dunbar (1872–1906), who published a number of works in African-American style. Significantly, Dunbar lamented that whilst his dialect works were readily published, his more conventionally literary efforts were often rejected (Allen, 1938). But it was in the middle years of the twentieth century that such writing was popularised, and there were a number of publications by African-American writers which attempted to characterise the urban black experience in the US: for example, Richard Wright (*Native Son*, 1940), Robert Lee Maupin who wrote under the name of Iceberg Slim (*Pimp: The Story of My Life*, 1969), and Claude Brown (*Manchild in the Promised Land*, 1965) all attempted to explore themes of crime, violence, and poverty in fast-paced, dialect-rich narratives, yet they do not, by and large, reconnoitre themes of madness. An exception is Ralph Ellison in *Invisible Man* (1952). This signalled a breakthrough in that it was one of the first black novels in the post-war USA to attract the attention of a largely white literary establishment. It also contains some references to mental illness. Whilst at college, the unnamed protagonist is charged with showing around an important donor to college funds. On visiting a bar, they encounter a fight among war traumatised ex-servicemen. After this incident, his college career over, he is hospitalised as a result of a boiler explosion and discovers that during a period of unconsciousness and confusion he has been given electroconvulsive therapy without his consent.

Yet despite the focus on distressing experiences in the works referred to above, relatively little attention has been devoted to a specifically black or minority-ethnic experience of madness or psychiatry. At first glance, this might appear surprising. There has been over a century of reflection by black and minority-ethnic scholars on the nature of black consciousness and the relationship between this and experiences of inequality. For example, over a century ago African-American critic W. E. B. Du Bois wrote about the experience of the self for black Americans as a form of 'double-consciousness'. He spoke of 'this sense of always looking at one's self through the eyes of others, of measuring one's soul by the tape of a world that looks on in amused contempt and pity' (1903, p. 3). Double-consciousness posits that an African-American experiences the self as both an American and as an African American. These two selves are often in conflict, and only coalesce through personal will, he writes: '[...] two warring ideals in one dark body, whose dogged strength alone keeps it from being torn asunder' (1903, p. 5). Subsequently, black consciousness has unfolded in different geographical and political contexts, and authors and activists have deployed related concepts such as negritude and black power to formulate their situation and set agendas for change.

The relatively well-developed political agenda, which includes both personal accounts of picaresque adventures and more academically formulated analyses of broader patterns of disadvantage and inequality, contrasts oddly with the relatively scant attention devoted to themes relating to madness. This contrast is all the more marked when it is contrasted with the last half-century of work documenting black and minority ethnic issues in mental health care. There has been growing public recognition of injustices, inequalities, and prejudice in the law, and psychiatry has been accused of similar biases against various groups within the wider population. For example, concern has been expressed about the over-representation of ethnic minorities in institutions for the 'mentally ill', and inconsistencies in the processes of care and the treatments administered (Burke, 1984; Department of Heath, 2003; Keating, 2007; Montsho, 1995). North American and European definitions of 'good mental health' as defined by Hinsie and Campbell (1970) are suffused by the assumptions of powerful groups in society. Consequently, the experience of ethnic minorities, and more importantly, the way this experience is construed by mental health professionals, may mean that they are more likely to be treated against their will, subject to more invasive and disabling treatments, and altogether alienated from the mental health care system – for example, Western society's narrations of the figure of the black young male includes negative and socially negating terms such as antisocial, dangerous, aggressive, law-breaker, lazy, and so forth (Cochrane and Sashidharan, 1995; Lewis, Croft-Jefferys, and David, 1990; Lipsedge, 1994; Littlewood and Lipsedge, 1982; McGovern and Cope, 1987; Rack, 1982). Of particular interest is the stereotype of some ethnic minorities in Europe or North America, especially young black men, as dangerous or prone to deviant or aggressive behaviour (Lipsedge, 1994).

Yet the injustices which concerned scholars and activists have detected in mental health care have been balanced by a countervailing trend. As Bains (2005) documents, the period we are interested in concerning literature corresponds to the period in which transcultural psychiatry was founded and has flourished. Chief among its early protagonists was Eric Wittkower (e.g., Wittkower and Fried, 1958), who in 1956 originated the *Newsletter of Transcultural Research in Mental Health Problems*. This publication helped to create an alliance of psychiatrists and anthropologists with an interest in mental health issues, and how these might be manifested differently in varying cultural, ethnic, and national contexts. This group of professionals were interested in how the 'mental illness' which they encountered in individuals, communities, and nations was related to the wider sociocultural environment, and might yield to concerted multi-disciplinary action (Mead, 1959). Arthur Kleinman similarly encouraged psychiatry to 'learn from anthropology that culture does considerably more than shape illness as an experience; it shapes the very way we conceive illness' and to realise that 'a true comparative cross-cultural science of illness must begin with this powerful anthropological insight' (1977, p. 4). In present-day practical terms Bhugra sees the task of transcultural psychiatry with diverse clients as 'identifying not only their clinical needs but also developing culturally appropriate strategies to manage these needs' (2008, p. 402). Bhugra devotes particular attention to the lay explanatory models that clients may hold about their problems, as understanding these may help clinicians make sense of the client's actions. He also argues for the importance of experiences of migration and displacement, as well as careful and sensitive examination of a client's problems across all the languages they speak, for symptoms may not be apparent in their second languages, yet may be manifest or easily describable in their first language. Nevertheless, in spite of the efforts of many mental health practitioners to humanise the experience of mental health care for people from different ethnic or cultural backgrounds, the experience from the clients' or carers' point of view often involves a process of struggling to get the practitioners or institutions to fit the specifics of their situation or their distress. In fiction, this sometimes leads to elaborate fantasies concerning the kinds of care which might be possible or desirable, and a sense of adventure in the protagonists' efforts to resolve their own or their loved ones' problems.

Carers and coercion: *72 Hour Hold*

An example of this kind of journey of adventure consequent upon mental disorder is to be found in Bebe Moore Campbell's *72 Hour Hold* (2005), a title taken from Californian mental health legislation and a novel that we have briefly referred to in our preceding chapters. The author presents a vision of mental illness and its treatment which is partly a characterisation of bipolar disorder and which partly borrows from the thriller or action genre of writing. Moore Campbell, like a number of other African American writers in the last half-century, writes from the perspective of an aspirant black community seeking entry to the middle classes through business and professional advancement. The story revolves around a single mother, Keri Whitmore, a successful African American shop owner in Los Angeles, and her daughter Trina described as an attractive and intelligent daughter. She suffers from bipolar disorder and, having turned 18 and about to go to University, finds that drugs and alcohol exacerbate her problem. The story is possibly based on Moore Campbell's experience with her own daughter Maia, and her involvement with the pharmaceutical industry-funded National Alliance on Mental Illness (NAMI).

In Trina's descent into bipolar disorder there is a degree of antagonism between parent and child. Trina's actions, whilst they are deeply troubling to the protagonist and appear to be evidence of pathology, seem to Trina to be a kind of adventure. Even moments of closeness are contaminated by fear:

> My daughter's smile was bright and expectant, manipulative. Regardless of what it had taken away, mental illness had conveyed to her a kind of protracted childhood, a long pause filled with delusions of grandeur, and no responsibility, very few apologies, and endless adventure. And to me it should have bequeathed an elastic sense of gratitude for life's most miniscule concessions: My daughter was standing right in front of me; I didn't have to go looking for her. Instead, I felt anxious. *When is she going to get back to normal?* (p. 39)

Moore Campbell also depicts what she sees to be a great difficulty in admitting and talking about mental disorder in US black communities. Here she describes a support meeting and her reflections on the demographic composition of the attendees:

> People were already filling up the basement. I looked around. The meeting was on the west side of town, land of high real estate, fair-skinned people, and the coldest ice. Part of me resented having to trek all the way from Crenshaw to get help for my child's issues. But the truth was, a mental illness had a low priority on my side of the city, along with the color caste and the spread of HIV. Some things we just didn't talk about, even if it was killing us. So I had to come to the white people, who, although just as traumatized, were a lot less stigmatised by whatever went wrong in their communities. (2005, p. 49)

After a variety of tribulations over her daughter's problems she becomes increasingly frustrated with the degree of autonomy granted to patients. The '72 hour holds' permitted under state legislation are not long enough to permit stabilisation of her daughter's condition, leading to her growing impatience with anything that smacks of 'patients' rights'. Consequently, coercive treatment looks increasingly appealing. She finds a clandestine mental health intervention group that operates like the slavery-era Underground Railroad, capturing wayward patients and moving them from house to house across the country. They force Trina to stay on her medication and in therapy, and to desist from alcohol and recreational drugs. In the passage below we see how she first becomes aware of the group, and the secrecy that surrounds its activities:

> His voice was just above a whisper. 'We are a group of psychologists and psychiatrists who believe that the mental health system in this country is a sad joke,' Brad said. 'All the members of our group have worked in hospitals and in a variety of mental health institutions; we've experienced firsthand the wasted opportunities for people to recover.' He leaned in. 'Recovery is possible for people when the right conditions at present. We assist the relatives, mostly the parents, of people who need an intervention that are too sick to accept help. We forgo the nine-one-one, the SMART people, the conservatorship. We transport the ill person to a safe place: *our* safe place. Once the patient is there, the relative leaves and we take over.'
>
> 'What you do –'
>
> Brad held up his hand, his face suddenly stern.
>
> 'What we do is illegal. We can all go to jail. Kidnapping is involved at times. It's not for the faint of heart, and there are no guarantees.' (p. 166)

In a sense then, the novel speaks of the brutalising tendencies which emerge from continued frustration, and the way that these lead to increasingly coercive fantasies on the part of caregivers. It is as if the author is wondering what would happen if only we could keep them in hospital, or if only we could get them to take their medication. As another character in the book discloses:

> I believe in what they're trying to do. Early on, my wife and I encountered the kind of mindless bureaucracy that can frustrate anyone with a sick child. Don't get me wrong: There are good hospitals, good doctors, wonderful treatment facilities. Once we got the right information, I must say that the system worked very well first, up to a point: patients' rights. Patients' rights often clash with what's best for the mentally ill person. Once after we succeeded in getting our

daughter on a hold, she refused to see us, told the doctors not to speak to us, and so, of course, they couldn't.

I've gone through that. I felt like a beggar asking people for information about my child. I begged, and they still wouldn't tell me anything. (pp. 225–226)

Thus the central thesis of the book unfolds. The mental health system fails because it is *too* permissive – in contrast to the representations we have seen in Chapter 3 – and insufficiently constraining of people who, because of madness, do not know best for themselves. There is a kind of faith in the meaningfulness of diagnosis, the effectiveness of medication, and the virtue of austerity, at least as far as the patients are concerned. Whilst patients' 'illnesses' are attributed unproblematically to their disordered neurology, their pleasures and autonomies are seen as deeply problematic. Their weight problems are to do with their failure to curb their overeating, and their efforts at self-determination are profoundly suspicious, and may be merely manifestations of their inability to be well: '[...] mentally ill people relapse and go off their meds because they aren't ready for the responsibilities that come with being sane' (p. 57). The book ends with a reconciliation between Trina, Keri the protagonist, and Keri's own alcoholic mother. Moreover, the way forward for black people as a whole is depicted: 'Now the basement was filled with newly liberated black folks, free to seek help for and own up to loving people who had brain diseases' (p. 315). The solution, it is implied, is to swallow the agenda of the pharmaceutical industry wholesale and reformulate the problems experienced as 'brain diseases'. The degree of acceptance of the industry-dominated agenda is curious, given the way that, as we have seen, earlier African American writers' first-person narratives have so often offered trenchant critiques of the inequality in American society. Yet the layered experience of disadvantage is not in this case followed through into a narrative which offers an account of the relationship between mental ill-health, oppression, and commercial interests. Indeed Campbell, like NAMI itself, successfully disarticulates the experience of inequality and oppression from the purported 'brain disease' suffered by patients. In this case then, the voice achieved in the story resonates with that of other more economically powerful interests in society and culture, and appears to formulate salvation in terms of a largely pharmaceutical agenda. Now it may be that this is a particularly bleak and dystopian vision adopted for the purposes of the story itself. However, looked at in the

light of Moore Campbell's advocacy and media appearances, it suggests that her solution here is more than mere dramatic artifice, and
that her solution to mental health problems reflects her alignment
with an industry-sponsored agenda.

Post-colonialism and the novel

The suspicion that Campbell's tale is somehow colonised by interests
which are not necessarily the same as those of sufferers from mental ill-
health, and people who attempt to care for them, invites broader questions of how consciousness as well as countries can be colonised, and
how we can attempt to transcend this process of subtle colonisation.
With this in mind, let us now turn to a field of inquiry which might
be helpful, namely that of post-colonial studies, where the question
of how oppressed people can gain a genuinely independent voice has
been a central preoccupation. Post-colonial scholarship draws upon the
multidisciplinary contributions of anthropology, philosophy, political
science, sociology, and literary and cultural studies. It is an approach
which sees paradigms of inquiry as social constructions that do not necessarily yield a single unique 'truth' (hooks, 1990; Racine, 2009). World
views are seen as human constructions, so no paradigm can be said to
be inherently more truthful or trustworthy than another (Guba and
Lincoln, 1994).

Post-colonial inquiries involve both non-Western and Western
scholars seeking to analyse the colonial aftermath and challenge the
hegemony of Western scientific thought (Bhabha, 1994; Gandhi, 1998;
Quayson, 2000; Said, 1979;). Post-colonialism challenges accepted forms
of knowledge and instead seeks to go beyond them, to uncover inequi-
ties resulting from colonisation and neocolonisation (Racine, 2009).
This task is particularly important because 'all post-colonial societies
are still subject in one way or another to overt or subtle forms of neo-
colonial domination, and independence has not solved this problem'
(Ashcroft, Griffiths, and Tiffin, 1997, p. 2). Quayson adds:

> [...] it is necessary to disentangle the term, 'postcolonial', from its
> implicit dimension of chronological supersession, that aspect of its
> prefix, which suggests that the colonial stage has been surpassed and
> left behind. It is important to highlight instead a notion of the term
> as a process of coming-into-being and of struggle against colonialism
> and its aftereffects. In this respect the prefix would be fused with the
> sense invoked by 'anti'. (2000, p. 9)

Post-colonialism is intended to disclose the exclusionary effects of dominant ideologies in overwriting or marginalising other forms of knowledge. This marginalisation may be particularly acute for groups of people whose processes of knowledge and discovery are not rooted in the European and North American Enlightenment values of rationality and objectivity. With insights from history, economics, and politics, post-colonial studies aims to relate the experiences of marginalised groups to broader patterns of inequality. Bhabha elaborates: 'Post-coloniality, for its part, is a salutary reminder of the persistent "neo-colonial" relations within the "new" world order and the multinational division of labour. Such a perspective enables the authentication of histories of exploitation and the evolution of strategies of resistance' (1994, p. 6).

In analysing the experiences, storytelling, and relations of inequality that characterise the narratives told by and about members of oppressed groups, Gayatri Spivak used Gramsci's (1935/1971) term *subaltern* to refer to marginalised individuals who have been rendered voiceless by inequalities and oppressions based on sex, economics, and an interconnected web of global and local power configurations. In her widely cited essay 'Can the Subaltern Speak?' (1988), Spivak lamented the possibility of the subaltern ever being able to develop an autonomous voice. She contended that multiple, historically compounded oppressions had rendered the subaltern voiceless, so that there was 'no space from which the sexed subaltern subject can speak' (p. 307).

Given the role ascribed to the arts and humanities in increasing empathic and multi-vocal ethical reaches, and in illuminating experiences of suffering and healing, it is perhaps particularly apposite that we bring critical perspectives like Spivak's to bear on accounts of the suffering of underserved or marginalised populations. Michael Apple and Kristen Buras (2006) highlight the value of foregrounding voices emerging from conditions of subalternity. According to Apple and Buras, not only can subalterns speak, they are increasingly being heard. Perhaps the key question is to do with *how* the subaltern's voice can be most effectively heard. As Aronowitz (2006) argues, as well as foregrounding activity and agency on the part of the subaltern, equally importantly, emancipation of the subaltern requires 'a response from those privileged to acquire a global vision' (p. 177).

Accordingly, we now attempt to deploy a post-colonial perspective in formulating a critical response to two well-known novels depicting ethnically distinct, economically disadvantaged, and colonially oppressed peoples: Alice Walker's *Possessing the Secret of Joy* (1992) and Leslie Marmon Silko's *Ceremony* (1977). These books are presented here because of their wide-ranging popularity and the favourable critical notices they received. The focus on madness is pertinent because it is here that questions of meaning, empathy, and communication are most acute – they are frequently the only tools a practitioner may have to gauge what is troubling the client. Indeed, *Ceremony* and *Possessing the Secret of Joy* have been important novels in helping to formulate the experiences and sequelae of warfare and female genital mutilation respectively as simultaneously popular (in the case of the psychological impact of warfare) and under-acknowledged (in the case of female genital mutilation) clinical entities.

Ceremony: Tribes and tribulations

Let us deal first with the earlier novel, Silko's *Ceremony*. Leslie Marmon Silko is a Native American writer whose heritage derives partly from the Laguna Pueblo tribe of New Mexico, and is one of the key figures in what Kenneth Lincoln (1983) has called the *Native American Renaissance*. Her most famous novel, *Ceremony*, received laudatory reviews, and is highly regarded through to the present day. From our point of view it is of particular interest because of its depiction of madness associated with the aftermath of warfare, and was written at a time in the 1970s when the development of the concept of post-traumatic stress disorder was exercising the minds of clinicians and researchers working with combat veterans.

The story documents the troubles of Tayo, who like Silko herself is a mixed-heritage Laguna Indian. He is described struggling to cope after having served in the Second World War and having returned to the poverty-stricken Indian reservation at Laguna suffering from what in the 1940s was still called 'shell shock' or 'battle fatigue'. He is depicted as being troubled by memories of his cousin, who died in the conflict, and by his preoccupation with his deceased Uncle Josiah. Tayo's relationship with Pueblo Indian culture is troubled too, because he is regularly reminded that he was the product of an illicit liaison between a Native American mother and a white father. His mother could not care for him so he was looked after by her older sister, a character called 'Auntie'. Auntie sees Tayo as an embarrassment because of his illegitimacy and mixed heritage, and finds his care burdensome. By contrast, she has high hopes for her own son, Rocky. Tayo and Rocky enlist in the army, much to the consternation of Auntie, but Tayo assures her he can take care of Rocky and bring him safely home. As the army recruiter states in the novel: 'Anyone can fight for America, even you boys' (p. 64). Thus it is all the more poignant that Rocky perishes in the conflict, so that once he has returned, Tayo feels Auntie's disapprobation all the more keenly because he has survived and her beloved son has not. In addition, Tayo's own vulnerability is a constant presence. When he arrives at the railroad station on his way back to the reservation he is overcome with nausea, and when he sees a Japanese family in the street, he collapses. In the early stages of the novel he has curiously dreamlike experiences, involving his preoccupations with the deceased Rocky and Uncle Josiah.

The novel grapples with the different kinds of strategy employed by the World War Two veterans from the neighbourhood in their attempts to resolve and live with their experiences in the war. In his search for healing, Tayo first turns to drinking excessive alcohol with his old acquaintances Harley, Emo, and the other Indian veterans. But he has ambivalent feelings about this and attempts to spend time alone too, to think, and to avoid becoming part of a pattern of drinking and violence among Indian veterans. The treatment Tayo has received in the veterans' hospital does not seem to have been effective, nor to have addressed his trauma-related mental health problems. He and his family turn to traditional healing but this at first does not seem to be effective. There is an abortive visit to an old man called Ku'oosh who provides a bundle of Indian tea and a bag of cornmeal, but this does not bring relief:

> Old man Ku'oosh left that day, and as soon as he had closed the door Tayo rolled over on his belly and knocked the stalks of Indian tea on the floor. He pressed his face into the pillow and pushed his head hard against the bed frame. He cried, trying to release the great pressure that was swirling inside his chest, but he got no relief from crying any more. The pain was solid and constant as the beating of his own heart. (p. 38)

However, Tayo has a subsequent encounter with a traditional healer whom he is taken to see. At first he is sceptical, thinking that his family have merely tried to get him out of the way so he can be no further embarrassment. However, Tayo and this mysterious new healer, Betonie, strike up a sort of friendship, and he and Tayo talk of his experiences:

> They sent me to this place after the war. It was white. Everything in that place was white. Except for me. I was invisible. But I wasn't afraid there. I didn't feel things sneaking up behind me. I didn't

cry Rocky or Josiah. There were no voices and no dreams. Maybe I belong back in that place.

Betonie reached into his shirt pocket for the tobacco sack. He rolled a skinny little cigarette in a brown wheat paper and offered the sack to Tayo. He nodded slowly to indicate that he had been listening.

'That's true,' the old man said, 'you could go back to that white place.' He took a puff from the cigarette and stared down at the red sand floor. Then he looked up suddenly and his eyes were shining; he had a grin on his face. 'But if you are going to do that, you might as well go down there, with the rest of them, sleeping in the mud, vomiting cheap wine, rolling over women. Die that way and get it over with.' He shook his head and laughed. 'In that hospital they don't bury the dead, they keep them in rooms and talk to them.' (p. 123)

Through these conversations Tayo comes to see himself as a significant player in the broader scheme of human existence, and to achieve a more harmonious relationship with the natural and spiritual world. Tayo is reminded that his Native American heritage, with its stories, rituals, and practices, is important in his own recovery (Wilson, 2005, p. 75). Thus far, the story contains much that might seem to meet Charon et al.'s 1995 criteria in terms of its value for the medical humanities. This particular narrative, for example, has the potential to educate clinicians about the diversity of life history, belief systems, and perceptions of sickness and treatments that will be apparent in any inner-city mental health clinic and, furthermore, the need for clinicians to explore and educate *themselves* about ethno-specific issues in order to effectively help such individuals.

Betonie the healer is of mixed parentage too, and he has changed and modernised the healing rituals. As he says:

At one time, the ceremonies as they had been performed were enough for the way the world was then. But after the white people came, elements in this world began to shift; and it became necessary to create new ceremonies. I have made changes in the rituals. The people mistrust this greatly, but only the growth keeps the ceremonies strong. (p. 126)

Experiences with rituals and ceremonies such as this sow the seeds of Tayo's recovery. He embarks on a quest to retrieve some cattle which had originally belonged to Uncle Josiah. They appear to have strayed onto land belonging to a nearby (white) landowner. As he goes in search of them he meets a mountain lion who leads him to the cattle, but then he is accosted and detained by two men who accuse him of trespassing. However, they lose interest in him and move off in pursuit of the mountain lion. Tayo is eventually able to find the lost cattle again, and has a brief relationship with Montano, a mysterious woman who helps him by penning the cattle until they can be retrieved with a truck. Among other things, she leads Tayo to a cliff painting of a huge she-elk, which in Pueblo mythology is the carrier of all life. She also urges him to 'remember everything' (p. 235). Tayo then sees a vision of a sand painting at an abandoned uranium mine. He realises that the materials for the atom bombs for World War Two have come from his own sacred mountains, whereupon 'he had arrived at the point of convergence where the fate of all living things, and even the earth, had been laid' (p. 246). This convergence of stories is of particular significance in Pueblo mythology. His story has consilience with the stories of the Japanese, the Laguna, and the voices of the deceased Rocky and Josiah. He realises that what others think of as his being crazy – for example, his experiences of auditory hallucinations – in fact reflects a profound insight, in that he had seen the world for what it was.

This growing sense of empowerment is tested again when his fellow veterans come looking for him with the intention of doing him harm. They are unable to find him because he has hidden, but he watches while Emo and Pinkie take their frustrations out on Harley, whom they kill. All of these men had grown up together, and here Silko depicts the way that wartime experiences, alcoholism, and deprivation lead to people turning on one another. At the same time, Tayo appears to have escaped the 'witchery' that has entrapped the others. Even when Tayo has the chance to get revenge for the death of Harley by killing one of the others, he does not do so. Oandasan says: 'Nonetheless, Tayo denies himself this vengeance, and so he expands the love extended to him by Ts'eh' (1997, p. 243). Ts'eh is variously defined as being the feminine spirit or life force of the universe, or the feminine spirit of creation. Tayo chooses to fulfil his promise to Ts'eh to gather seeds and plant them so that the 'plants would grow there like the story' (Silko, 1977, p. 254). Now, Tayo has undertaken his own ceremony and can move from the status of an outsider to being initiated into full membership of the tribe. On recounting that he was assisted by the mountain lion and the she-elk, Tayo delights the old men who say 'You have seen her' and 'We will be blessed again' (p. 257). In retrieving the cattle and undertaking his own ritualistic healing journey away from alcoholism and posttraumatic stress disorder, Tayo is seen to have completed respectful acts for his family and the Pueblo community. No longer a ghost or outsider, he has become what Dozier calls the ideal Pueblo personality type – the man with a 'generous heart' (1983, p. 180).

In telling the story of how Tayo is guided to a more balanced and harmonious life – what the Navaho call 'walking in beauty' (Wilson, 1994) – Silko alludes to what she sees as a sense of identity and authenticity within the oral culture. One of the ways in which she does this is by invoking the concept of a story-within-a story. She tells the reader she is merely subordinate to Thought Woman/Spider Woman: 'I'm telling you the story she is thinking' writes Silko (p. 1) at the outset of the novel. Louis Owens, himself of mixed heritage, defines the central lessons of Tayo and Silko's stories: 'through the dynamism, adaptability, and syncretism inherent in Native American cultures, both individuals and the cultures within which individuals find significance and identity are able to survive, grow, and evade the deadly traps of stasis and sterility' (1994, p. 167). Rice says that in Silko's narrative there is a 'paradigm for the development of an inclusive self' (2004, online). The characters in the novel, she says, and the narrative itself, are created in such a way that they can stand in for many of us. In studying the means by which Tayo creates personal healing ceremonies to overcome despair, it might be possible for readers to fashion something similar for themselves, understanding and acknowledging personal responsibility for our actions, and facilitating deeper and more convivial relationships with families and communities. To do this, says Rice, we must 'feel' the stories of our communities. As Jahner asserts, this requires our new interpretive community to embrace the traditional while, at the same time, incorporating global, multicultural *ways* of knowing and understanding (1994, p. 509).

There is something appealing about the story in *Ceremony*. Tayo undertakes this journey which recollects earlier, more primordial rituals, and emerges as someone recovering, with an intact identity, a place within a community, someone who has turned his back on the alcoholism and violence which was at the time troubling young American males, particularly within Native American communities. As the novel demonstrates, the pressure of post-traumatic stress on war returnees is enhanced and intensified within already-troubled deprived ethnic communities. The motifs from Native American mythology are deemed to be so convincing that fellow Pueblo poet Paula Gunn Allen has criticised Silko, saying that she was disclosing tribal secrets that she did not have the right to reveal (1990). The traditional healing practices are depicted as affording a much deeper and lasting cure than anything the Veterans Administration, with its scientifically trained doctors and modern hospital, could achieve. In this sense it might appear the ideal 'diversity text' for the medical humanities. It addresses the criteria suggested by Charon et al. (1995), enabling the practitioner to appreciate the power and limitations of what they can do from within a Western scientific frame and the complementary powers of indigenous healing rituals, and it enables readers to appreciate new perspectives on healing practices.

Yet at the same time, despite the impeccable credentials of the author and the message of hope, there are aspects which are troubling in terms of the post-colonial concerns outlined earlier. The depiction of Native American people and cultures is worthy of comment. Significantly, it is those who can boast of a pure Laguna Pueblo heritage as the characters Emo, Harley, and Pinkie, or limited by their beliefs and rituals like Auntie or the healer Ku'oosh, who are locked into the cycle of drink and violence. It is those of mixed heritage, like Tayo and Betonie, those who integrate tradition with knowledge and practice from the newer European settlers, who are able to escape. The message of *Ceremony* is, then, an assimilationist one. Indeed, characters like Emo or Auntie act as if they are slaves to the culture in which they are embedded, and display comparatively little creative ability to negotiate new events or experiences, in contrast to those who are able to assimilate and adapt. Tayo's quest serves not as an alternative therapy, but more as a kind of incorporation stage to a process of recovery begun in the veterans' hospital. Indeed, the white healer, in the form of the doctor, acknowledges that Tayo's problem has to be addressed on his own home ground (p. 16). Psychiatry, and containment in the Veterans Administration hospital, can only go so far, and the psychiatrist, expansively, points the way to a different type of 'treatment'. Thus, the story reproduces and consolidates the notion of a biomedical core to the human potential for insanity, overlaid with the psychosocial and cultural therapeutic spheres. It is as if the 'ceremonies' in Silko's text are effective in the latter, existential domains rather than in relation to the biomedical, and hence purportedly foundational, problems of the human condition. Thus the 'ceremony' is a complementary therapy rather than a genuinely alternative medicine.

Possessing the Secret of Joy: Understanding and decolonising the African experience

The post-colonial concern about the representation of native or indigenous peoples in terms of Western or enlightenment moral and epistemological systems can also give some critical purchase on Alice Walker's *Possessing the Secret of Joy*. This novel is centrally concerned with the topic of female genital mutilation in African cultures. Though written in the form of a novel, it is formulated to expose the practice and enlist support for campaigns working towards its elimination. Briefly, the novel's plot involves a central character, Tashi, who is originally from an imaginary African nation called Olinka, undergoes the ritual of excision (or 'bath' as it is called) in order to show her allegiance to the causes of national identity, liberation, and cultural self-determination. She does so as an adult rather than a child, as is usual, because African American missionaries arrived in her village when she was a child and made the bath ritual impossible. As an adult seeking circumcision, her friends Olivia and Adam Johnson, both children of an African American missionary family, advise her against undergoing this ritual at the hands of a 'tsunga' or traditional circumciser. Yet from Tashi's point of view the operation seems increasingly valuable, especially in the face of the growing impoverishment of her people: 'We had been stripped of everything but our black skins. Here and there a defiant cheek bore the mark of our withered tribe. These marks gave me courage. I wanted such a mark for myself' (pp. 22–23). Complications resulting from the operation make her adult life very traumatic. Married later to her childhood friend Adam, she finds that she cannot enjoy sexual intercourse, and childbearing becomes an unbearably painful ordeal, yielding a child so injured by the birth that he has learning difficulties. This traumatic history leads to bouts of depression, and psychotic experiences. The story makes many explicit links between the experiences of the central character and psychotherapy, in particular Jungian archetypal analysis which discloses the roots of her suffering. Over the course of the story it becomes apparent that at an early age she lost her sister, who died of complications from a similar circumcision operation. Eventually, Tashi kills the old woman or 'tsunga' who had administered the operation to her older sister and her. The story ends with her facing execution for the murder.

Walker describes a three-way relationship between Tashi, her husband Adam, and a woman called Lisette. Unable to participate fully in sexual activity with Adam, Tashi looks on as Lisette and Adam have an affair, which makes her madness worse. Of Lisette's visits, she says: 'Often, while she is visiting, I have had to be sedated. On occasion I have voluntarily checked myself into the Waverly Psychiatric Hospital, in which, because it is run by a man affiliated with Adam's ministry, I am always given a room' (p. 47). The central character of Tashi is also known elsewhere in the book as Evelyn and Mrs Johnson – Tashi represents the African identity, whilst the acceptable and Westernised 'Evelyn' is never quite able to fully function in a Western context due to the ghosts of the past that are literally inscribed into and onto her physical being. Tashi has some problematic engagements with psychotherapy. However, her therapy with a character known variously as 'the Doctor', the old man, Mzee, and Uncle Carl is ultimately successful. This character is based on Carl Jung and borrows from aspects of his life and work, including his 'tower' in Switzerland, and the novel includes events in Tashi's therapy loosely related to the accounts of clients he gave in his 1935 Tavistock lectures (Jung, 1985).

Initially the psychoanalytic procedure with a 'white witch doctor' does not seem promising: 'I feel him, there behind my head, pen poised at last to capture on paper an African woman's psychosis for the first time' (Walker, 1992, p. 11):

> 'Negro women', the doctor says into my silence, 'can never be ana-lyzed effectively because they can never bring themselves to blame their mothers.'
> 'Blame them for what?' I asked.
> 'Blame them for anything' said he.
> It is quite a new thought. And surprisingly, sets off a kind of explo-sion in the soft dense cotton wool of my mind.
> But I do not say anything. Those bark hard ashen heels trudge before me on the path. The dress above them barely clothing, a piece of rag. The basket of groundnuts suspended from a strap that fits a groove that has been worn into in her forehead. When she lifts the basket down the groove in her forehead remains. On Sundays she will wear her scarf low in an attempt to conceal it. African women like my mother give harsh meaning to the expression 'furrowed brow'. (pp. 17–18).

The situation however is even more complicated when Tashi begins therapy with 'the Old Man'. Lisette, Tashi's husband's 'other woman', is the old man's niece. It is this family connection which means that he continues to see her despite being retired – 'I am an African woman and my case was recommended to him by his niece, my husband's friend and lover' (p. 47). Tashi also likes 'that he himself had at times a look of madness to match my own – though it was a benign look that seemed to observe a connection between whatever held his gaze and some grand, unimaginably spacious design [...]. In other words, he looked as if he would soon die', finding this 'comforting'. (pp. 47–48).

In Adam's interspersing narrative, there are some accounts of Tashi's distress which appear to recapitulate the experiences of slavery, though this is something Tashi herself and her immediate ancestors have not experienced:

> At first she merely spoke about the strange compulsion she some-times experienced of wanting to mutilate herself. Then one morning I woke to find the foot of our bed red with blood. Completely una-ware of what she was doing, she said, and feeling nothing, she had sliced rings, bloody bracelets, or chains, around her ankles. (p. 49)

The problems and symptoms Tashi/Evelyn experiences resonate with events in her more immediate circumstances. When her husband and Lisette's affair results in Lisette's becoming pregnant, this has a nega-tive effect on Tashi/Evelyn. Tashi's response to Lisette's pregnancy is perhaps particularly understandable given her own experience of child-birth subsequent to her genital mutilation, yet as narrated by Lisette her distress is reduced into a few mere statements with no acknowledge-ment of this fact: 'When Evelyn learned of my pregnancy with little Pierre [...] she flew into a rage that subsided into a year-long deteriora-tion and rancorous depression. She tried to kill herself. She spoke of murdering their son' (p. 119). Lisette's child is named Pierre and unlike Tashi/Evelyn's child, Pierre goes on to attend Harvard and becomes an anthropologist intent on empowering the people he studies.

Progressing through these and other difficulties, in the later stages of the book Tashi revisits her original village to find and kill the tsunga who performed the operation on her and many other girls in the village, who was also responsible for the procedure which killed Tashi's sister. In this sense, in a move anticipated by the tsunga herself, Tashi has bro-ken the cycle by liberating subsequent generations from the procedure, and the murder is to some commentators 'an act which gives life to all women' (Brown-Guillory, 1996, p. 51). Thus, one way of reading the novel is as 'a text that acts as a revolutionary manifesto for dismantling systems of domination' (Buckman, 1995, p. 93). The reader is invited to respond – presumably with outrage and revulsion – to scenes such as when the woman who has been sewn closed is cut open by her husband on their wedding night. Moreover, even talking or writing about female genital mutilation and facial scarification is revolutionary for, accord-ing to Adam in the novel: 'They've made the telling of the suffering itself taboo. Like visible signs of menstruation. Signs of women's mental power. Signs of the weakness and uncertainty of men' (p. 155).

Uncle Carl the psychoanalyst writes that Tashi and her husband 'are bringing me home to something in myself. I am finding myself in them. A self I have often felt was only halfway at home on the European continent. In my European skin. An ancient self that thirsts for knowledge of the experiences of its ancient kin. Needs this knowledge, and the feelings that come with it, to be whole' (Walker, 1992, 81). This character is revealed in an author's note to be Carl Jung himself. Walker thanks him, apparently without irony, 'for becoming so real in my own self-therapy (by reading) that I could imagine him as alive and active in Tashi's treatment. My gift to him' (p. 269). Jung's racism has been widely remarked upon (Dalal, 1988; Howitt and Owusu-Bempah, 1994), and his characterisation of Africans as primitive, childlike, and propelled by their 'unconscious' leaves us poorly equipped to discriminate between madness, genital mutilation, and the power imbalances in relations between the sexes, inequalities in levels of education and the low economic and social status of many women (George, 2001, p. 356).

The idea of African women 'possessing the secret of joy' despite their hardships comes not from Walker's novel but from a book called *African Saga* (Ricciardi, 1982) which has been criticised for being a somewhat colonialist text. That is, it is redolent of the world view and style of writing which adopts a European or North American point of view and describes travel to foreign lands and adventures with the usually exotic and colourful 'natives' who lead simple, happy lives despite their privations. Walker mentions this earlier book and describes Tashi's anger at this representation: 'These settler cannibals,' says Tashi, 'why don't they just steal our land, mine our gold, chop down our forests [...] devour our flesh and leave us alone? Why must they also write about how much joy we possess?' (p. 256). Yet Walker's novel itself is not immune from such charges. *Possessing the Secret of Joy* contains curious resonances with a much earlier genre of colonialist literature. The 'old man' based on Jung identifies himself with the suffering Tashi, an identification that echoes Marlow, Joseph Conrad's character in *Heart of Darkness* (1899), who travels to the 'dark interior' of Congo searching for Mr Kurtz. Likewise, the journey motif is characteristic of H. Rider Haggard's tales of exploration and adventure in Africa, and these were reputedly favourites of Carl Jung. Indeed, he is said to have derived his notion of the female principle or anima from the novel *She* (1887). In Walker's novel, Carl is said to see himself in Tashi and Adam, a self he has often 'felt was only halfway at home on the European continent' in his 'European knowledge of the experiences of its ancient kin' (pp. 83–84). For Carl, what has been done to Tashi has also been done to him via a 'truly universal self' which he calls 'the essence of healing' that he 'frequently lost' in his European, 'professional' life (pp. 80–81).

Further colonial themes emerge from the description of Tashi/Evelyn's therapy with the Western-trained therapist Raye, which is complicit with the notion that African women are somehow ignorant of, and lack control over, their own bodies and sexualities. Post-colonial critics caution us against this kind of presentation (Mohanty, 1996; Oyewumi, 2001). Tashi/Evelyn stands in as an 'average third world woman' leading 'an essentially truncated life based on her feminine gender (read: sexually constrained) and her being "third world" (read: ignorant, poor, un-educated, tradition-bound, domestic, family-oriented, victimized)' (Mohanty, 1996, p. 176). As implied by contrast with the characters of Raye the therapist, Lisette the sophisticated 'other woman', and Olivia her husband's sister, Tashi/Evelyn seems somehow naive and simple (Oyewumi, 2001) or a 'dolorous puppet' (Smith, 1992, p. 38). She contrasts with 'the (implicit) self-representation of Western women as educated, as modern, as having control over their own bodies and sexualities, and the freedom to make their own decisions' (Mohanty, 1996, p. 176). In *Possessing the Secret of Joy*, Raye, in stark contrast to the uneducated Tashi, is characterised as a woman who, though a descendant of slaves, has been educated (p. 125). Tashi describes what Raye does as 'an ageless magic, the foundation of which was the ritualization, or the acting out, of empathy', calling Raye 'a witch', a 'spiritual descendant of the ancient healers who taught' Olinka 'witch doctors' (Walker, 1992: p. 125).

The simplistic nature attributed to Tashi/Evelyn has activated concerns about the somewhat one-dimensional picture of the African people as a whole in Walker's novel (George, 2001), redolent of a broader meme in the representation of indigenous peoples which imposes a collective, static view of the world on traditional African peoples (Hountondji, 1983). Kanneh argues that when Western feminism characterises the 'Black Third World' woman as a victim of men's violence, 'The battle over the Black Third World woman's body is staged as a battle between First World feminists and Black Third World men' (1995, p. 348). In other words, the battle over Tashi's body becomes the battle between Alice Walker, Raye, Pierre, and Adam on the one hand, and patriarchy, personified by the Olinka man, on the other. For Mohanty this polarising discourse in which women are defined as 'archetypal victims', 'freezes them into "objects-who-defend-themselves", men into "subjects-who-perpetrate-violence" and (every) society into powerless (read: women) and powerful (read: men) groups of people' (1996, p. 179). From this perspective, Alice Walker and *Possessing the Secret of Joy* have fallen short of doing what Mohanty says is the best way to make sense of male violence: 'Male violence must be theorised and interpreted *within* specific societies, in order both to understand it better and to effectively organise to change it. Sisterhood cannot be assumed on the basis of gender; it must be forged in concrete historical and political practice and analysis' (1996, p. 178). Instead the explanation and analysis of Tashi's genital mutilation and its aftermath are not only woven into a colonialist narrative from books written by Europeans, but they also involve what Mohanty calls 'the privileged and explanatory potential of gender difference as the origin' of female body mutilation (1996, p. 179).

This means that Walker's novel is directed away from discussing how in Africa the actual cutting is only *part* of a rite that young people undergo as an initiation into adulthood. According to Diana Menya, writing in the *Lancet*, rites-of-passage ceremonies are not simply about abuse and mutilation: through them children learn about 'the secrets of their society' as well as being inculcated with knowledge about 'acceptable social and sexual behaviors' which affords some collective advantages (1993, p. 423). Menya suggests that Walker might have been afraid to lend 'a degree of respectability to the abhorrent practice of female genital mutilation' (p. 423). However, to critics such as Menya, Walker's 'silence' on these issues and her depiction of female circumcision 'out of its cultural context' resulted in the novel perpetuating the 'ethnocentric view of an outsider' (p. 423). Contemporary Western policies and attitudes, however, as represented in the 2008 World Health Organisation *Eliminating Female Genital Mutilation: An Interagency Statement* (2008), echo Walker and construe female genital mutilation as a violation of human rights, asserting that the practice should – and indeed in many countries has been – outlawed irrespective of local ethnic beliefs. On this view, the alleged collective advantages of this practice are far outweighed by its potentially fatal bodily effects.

Walker's and Silko's books therefore seem bound up with a view of indigenous people foregrounding notions of simplicity, traditionalism, and an inability to adapt to the experiences, mores, and politics of a world which is changing about them. In this it is complicit with the kind of anthropological vision criticised by Margaret Archer (1996), who takes early-twentieth-century anthropology to task for promoting a view of non-Western cultures as static, homogenous, and incapable of accommodating new knowledge, change, or dissent. This point is made also by Hountondji (1983) in his description of unanimism – the assumption that in 'primitive' societies all members will unanimously share the same beliefs. In this context, the local 'native' cultures in *Ceremony* and *Possessing the Secret of Joy* are depicted as somehow weak and in need of an infusion of change from more 'advanced' European or North American thinking.

There are common themes running through *Ceremony* and *Possessing the Secret of Joy* and the other literature we shall consider in the last part of this chapter. In common with Silko and Walker, a number of other authors have been concerned with the quest for understanding one's identity, and have evoked a profound ambivalence in the social relationships around the central character. The web of social relations supports the protagonist, but it also may entrap or restrict him or her. In the face of these limitations, and the assaults on the integrity of the body and the individual's network of social relationships, the resolution of a stable, satisfying sense of identity is elusive.

Fantastic fictions: *Woman on the Edge of Time* and *Beloved*

The next books we shall consider use the medium of the fantastic, fantasy, or paranormal to advance their storylines. Whilst attentive to the oppressions of race and of psychiatric treatment, they express these through imaginary scenarios in the future, the past, or via a fantasy landscape in a recognisable yet curiously surreal present, as discussed in Chapter 2. In the novels which we now discuss – Marge Piercy's *Woman on the Edge of Time* and Toni Morrison's *Beloved* – the fantastic or paranormal motifs abound and the reader is seldom far from scenarios depicting oppression. Yet these are far from simply protest novels. As James Baldwin noted as long ago as 1949, the 'protest novel' – and here he was thinking perhaps of the work of his friend Richard Wright – had 'failed': 'The failure of the protest novel lies in its rejection of life, the human being, the denial of his beauty, dread, power, in its insistence that it is his categorization alone which is real and which cannot be transcended' (Baldwin, 1949, p. 584).

Consequently, in the deployment of fantasy in a prominent role in these works, the oppressions of the mental health system or slavery are not so much challenged head-on as used as a starting point for speculative fictions. The inequalities that inform the historical and contemporary context of the events are described as if they coexist with a kind of fantasy. Piercy's story is of the hospitalisation of Consuela (Connie) Ramos, a 37-year-old Hispanic woman whose engagement with the psychiatric services is punctuated by elaborate and compelling visions of a future world, Mattaspoisett. As we described in previous chapters, Connie is introduced by one of its inhabitants, Luciente. Whether this future world is 'real' in a not-mad sense is left ambiguous, in contrast with the power differences between professionals and patients which are rendered in stark detail as we have seen. These are different from everyday differences of perspective – the judgements made have the power to alter the physical body and life course of the patient and those around them.

Yet in contrast to this, the future world to which Luciente introduces the protagonist in Mattapoisett seems remarkably calm and just: the ideals of the 1960s and 1970s countercultural movements have largely been achieved, and people live with a considerable degree of harmony. The new society has dispatched the problems associated with pollution, imperialism, totalitarianism, class subordination, racism, and homophobia. Whilst different cultural groups are apparent, these are not necessarily defined by their racial heritage, but by affinity. As Luciente explains:

> [...] we decided to hold onto separate cultural identities. But we broke the bond between genes and culture, broke it forever. We want there to be no chance of racism again. But we don't want the melting pot where everybody ends up with thin gruel. We want diversity, for strangeness breeds richness. (Piercy, 1976, p. 104)

Meanwhile, back in the twentieth century, the interventions to which Connie is subject become more invasive and disturbing. In line with the popular notion in the 1970s that behaviour could be controlled by means of electrical devices inserted into the brain, Connie sees the effects of some of these experiments on fellow patients and learns that such an operation will be performed on her too. The institutionalised violence of the mental health care system is described clearly and graphically, but in contrast to other tales such as Kesey's *One Flew Over the Cuckoo's Nest*, in Piercy's case it is embedded in a science-fiction narrative, where it is a counterpoint to the kinder, gentler world which might exist in the future.

There are fantastical themes in Toni Morrison's novel *Beloved* too, as she deals with the experience of slavery and its effects on people who are trying to adjust to life after they have been freed. The story is inspired by a historical account of an escaped slave, Margaret Garner, who in 1856 murdered her children in order, she said, to prevent them being recaptured into slavery. The novel *Beloved* attempts an account of the aftermath of such an event for the mother, her surviving children, and their companions. In this case the murdered child is called Beloved and the story is told largely from the point of view of her mother Sethe, who thinks of the events surrounding Beloved's death as 'the misery'. Following liberation Sethe and her daughter Denver, and sons Howard and Buglar, live at a house called 124 Bluestone Road. The house is troubled by a poltergeist – '124 was spiteful. Full of a baby's venom. The women in the house knew it and so did the children. For years each had put up with the spite in his own way, but by 1873 Sethe and her daughter Denver were its only victims' (p. 3). Howard and Buglar are forced to run away from home at the age of 13 by the poltergeist. Denver, Sethe's daughter, remains. But she is shy and has few friends, isolated perhaps by the poltergeist and perhaps also by the community's memory of what Sethe has done. Curiously, the spirit serves as company for Denver. A fellow-slave from the same plantation, Paul D, arrives and for a while the paranormal activity subsides. But then after they return from a carnival a young woman is sitting outside the house who introduces herself as Beloved and proceeds to involve herself in the family's life, eventually to the detriment of Sethe's welfare:

> The bigger Beloved got, the smaller Sethe became; the brighter Beloved's eyes, the more those eyes that used never to look away became slits of sleeplessness. Sethe no longer combed her hair or splashed her face with water. She sat in the chair licking her lips like a chastised child while Beloved ate up her life, took it, swelled up with it, grew taller on it. And the older woman yielded up without a murmur.
>
> Denver thought she understood the connection between her mother and Beloved: Sethe was trying to make up for the handsaw; Beloved was making her pay for it. But there would never be an entity that, and seeing her mother diminished shamed and infuriated her. Yet she knew Sethe's greatest fear was the same one Denver had in the beginning – that Beloved might leave. (pp. 294–295)

The revelation that Sethe has murdered her child Beloved turns out to be too much for Paul D who leaves, but eventually he returns so he can 'put his story next to hers' (p. 273). In one sense then, they are recreating the social solidarity, the sense of self and purpose, which were impossible under slavery. To varying extents, Sethe, Paul D, and Denver all experience this loss of self, which could only be remedied by the acceptance of the past and the memory of their original identities. In a way Beloved – as a poltergeist and as a physical presence – serves to open these characters up to their repressed memories, eventually facilitating the reintegration of their selves.

There are dissociative, depersonalised themes throughout the novel; Denver and Paul D frequently do not know if they are dreaming or awake. Is the young woman claiming to be Beloved real, or a ghost? *Beloved* is what Holloway has called a 'plurisignant' (Holloway, 1990, p. 618) text, one with 'the concurrent presence of multiple as well as ambiguous meanings' (p. 629). Whether the young woman claiming to be Beloved is really the long-lost daughter, or whether, as one of the other characters maintains, she is a servant from a nearby house who killed her master and absconded, is left deliberately ambiguous.

The question of identity, and how freed slaves and their descendants could develop a sense of integrated, core self of the kind which contemporary Europeans and North Americans take for granted, underlies a good deal of the narrative in *Beloved*. This is especially acute as relationships with others can be problematic for slaves and ex-slaves. As an economic asset one can be moved around, sold, or redeployed irrespective of family relationships and friendships. The harsh conditions mean that mortality and morbidity too may separate people. As the character Paul D puts it, thinking of Sethe: 'to love anything that much was dangerous, especially if it was her children she had settled on to love. The best thing, he knew, was to love just a little bit; everything, just a little bit, so when they broke its back, or shoved it in a croaker sack, well, maybe you'd have a little love left over for the next one' (p. 54). The notion of black people being forced to 'love small', which appears in this novel, was prefigured by Milkman's mother, Ruth, in *Song of Solomon*, Morrison's third novel; Morrison describes Ruth as a 'frail woman content to do tiny things; to grow and cultivate small life that would not hurt her if it died' (Morrison, 1977, p. 64). This lack of lasting social or familial relationships was compounded by mistreatment at the hands of slave owners, such that sometimes a slave's means of escape involved dissociation, a process of climbing out of one's own body to forget 'that anybody white could take your whole self for anything that came to mind. Not just work, kill, or maim you, but dirty you. Dirty you so bad you couldn't like yourself anymore. Dirty you so bad you forgot who you were and couldn't think it up' (Morrison, 1987, p. 251).

In the case of Denver, she eventually leaves the house and embarks upon a process of developing an identity, establishing a sense of self and, ultimately, womanhood. While this process takes place at an individual level, it also involves the bonds of social relationships and the encouragement of the community. The novel reminds us how the loss of maternal identity as a result of being separated from one's children involves not just a grieving process but a reconfiguration or disintegration of identity. As Koolish describes it, the apparent madness of characters such as Sethe, Denver, and Paul D, their engagement in what we might nowadays call the madness phenomenon of dissociation, represents a coping strategy (2001). In a sense it is a 'sane' response to a world gone mad, a strategy that a person invents in order to live in an unliveable situation. Morrison's view in this regard recollects Laing and Esterson's view that madness is not a sign of weakness or failure, but an act of sanity, resistance, and survival (Laing and Esterson, 1964).

Thus in Morrison's case the fantastical – the poltergeist, the dreamlike quality of life in 124 Bluestone Road – is used to deal with profoundly material and worldly difficulties. The separation from one's children, the beatings, the rapes, the experience of seeing violence inflicted on people you care about but being unable to do anything about it, and similar horrors, are aspects of a physically inflicted oppression. Morrison's novel is an exploration of what happens after that physical oppression ends and how people might gradually readjust. At the time it was written, North American popular and therapeutic cultures were replete with concern about post-traumatic stress disorder, and this particular lens has been popular in critical responses to *Beloved*, for example Koolish (2001). The characters in Morrison have 'a desolated centre, where the self that was no self made its home' (Morrison, 1987, p. 140). Morrison then draws on the ideas about the self that were current at the time when the novel was written. The idea of being able to 'like oneself', the experiences of dissociation so redolent of the discourses of the self which flourished in the 1970s, are perhaps anachronistic tools with which to reconstruct the experiences of people from a century previously. The 1970s are also known as a period when popular understanding of multiple personality was growing in the US, once again undergirded with a sense that this was often a consequence of traumatic experience. Hence, it is no coincidence that Morrison's characters speak a vernacularised version of the popular psychology of the time of writing, rather than the emotional lexicon of the nineteenth century that might be discerned through more meticulous presentation of social history.

The self under *Erasure*

This difficulty in finding a self, a voice, or a position from which to speak is also addressed in the final work we shall consider in this chapter, Percival Everett's *Erasure* (2001). In a narrative which embodies both tragedy and comedy, Everett revisits some of the themes with which we began this chapter, in particular the problem of positioning oneself within a culture which one does not control and within which one is bound to appear as a minority. Fiction is a particularly forgiving arena in which to reflect on matters of identity. Some of these dilemmas of life as an African American are rendered especially acutely in *Erasure*. This novel deals with different kinds and experiences of erasure, as the protagonist is subsumed by a white-defined notion of what a black literary voice should sound like, and as the protagonist's mother succumbs to Alzheimer's disease and becomes increasingly confused. The text is replete with references to other African American cultural phenomena – the choice of the protagonist's name, for example, Thelonious Ellison, references Thelonious Monk and Ralph Ellison. Frustrated that his attempts to publish his work are dismissed by publishers and members of the white establishment seeking what they think of as authentic black voices, Thelonious writes a grisly parody called *My Pafology* which is reproduced in the middle of *Erasure*. Written in a style which pokes fun at black urban dialects and whose storyline recollects Richard Wright's *Native Son* (1940), *My Pafology* draws on every grotesque stereotype of urban African Americans and chronicles the exploits of a young man with a prison record, homicidal tendencies, and four children by different mothers. Thelonious Ellison cannot bear to publish it in his own name and assumes the pseudonym Stagg R. Leigh (a pun on the blues song title *Stagger Lee*). It is bought by publisher Random House for $600,000 and is hailed by critics on a literary-prize committee. Ellison is serving on this committee, and the other judges do not realise he is Stagg R. Leigh. The other (white) judges insist on awarding it the prize despite Ellison's objections. The literary voice, then, is in this instance defined through the literary establishment's understanding of minority cultures, their languages, and their respective 'pathologies' – a modern twist on the constraints on expression lamented by the poet Paul Laurence Dunbar a century earlier.

Meanwhile, in *Erasure*, the protagonist's personal life is changed by a number of tragedies. His sister Lisa becomes increasingly concerned about their mother's confusion, which presages her descent into Alzheimer's disease. Lisa is working as a doctor and is shot and killed by an anti-abortion campaigner. Their mother appears not to understand the tragedy and mistakes Ellison for his long-deceased father. Ellison decides to take leave from his teaching post so that he can take care of his mother. Maintaining her functioning demands the most meticulous routine:

> Mother was down for one of the great battery of daily naps on which she had come to rely for a semblance of stability. Her most lucid moments seemed to occur when she first awoke and after that there were any number of cracks in the surface of her world through which to fall. There was no steering her toward solid ground; she stepped where she stepped. (p. 207)

The burden of care becomes increasingly onerous and the impending sense that he will need to place her in an institution – 'committing her' – becomes ever more urgent:

> I was exhausted, my eyes burning from having been open and staring at either Mother or the book in my lap all night. The backs of my legs had gone numb from sitting in the round-rimmed wooden chair. I was completely distrustful of any measure of stability the old woman exhibited that evening of Lorraine's wedding. I was terrified that I would wake and find her bed empty, then, after a brief search, her lifeless body floating in the creek or simply laid out at the bottom of the stairs. The business of committing her seemed so much more urgent now. I was desperate to know that she was safe and I was desperate to discontinue my feelings of desperation. (p. 224)

It is whilst caring for his increasingly disorientated and fragmented mother that he writes the novel *My Pafology,* on his deceased father's old manual typewriter. His credentials as a writer and his teaching experience mean that he can obtain some work at local colleges but it is part-time, poorly paid, and certainly not enough to live on. It is in this context that the commercial success of *My Pafology* (or as he later retitles it, *Fuck*) is desperately needed, despite the contempt he feels for that genre of writing. The loss of social supports, the death of family members, and the illness of others force one into awkward positions. Writing this kind of material, though not quite like the creation of the central characters in Wright's *Native Son* or *My Pafololgy,* means that part of one's sense of self or one's literary experience is subject to truncation – or as the title of the novel has it, *Erasure.*

Conclusions

Finally, it is apposite to reflect on some of the themes from the body of work we have reviewed in this chapter as a whole, and on what can be learned from these books. An overarching theme that cuts across all the volumes we have reviewed is that of the struggle for identity. Whether this concerns the blending of ceremonies and meanings from different traditions to overcome war trauma, the search for the self in psychoanalysis, the experience of oppression through ethnic disadvantage, psychiatry, slavery, or the limiting expectations of the publishing industry, these all occasion the need to reconstruct and re-evaluate identity.

A further theme in these books concerns the difficulties that arise from social networks and their disintegration. The disruption of social networks through betrayal in *Woman on the Edge of Time*, through the inhumanity of slavery in *Beloved*, or through neurodegenerative loss in *Erasure*, all lead to profound difficulties for the protagonists. Bereavements, losses, and displacements reconfigure our social and subjective worlds. Thelonious is left scrabbling for poorly paid part-time work, and struggling as a carer. Connie is in hospital struggling with increasingly invasive and disabling treatments, and Sethe is faced with the loss of a daughter and the difficulty of forming relationships that will sustain the self. In addition there are multiple strands of oppression for these characters: as psychiatric patients, as people who are racially disadvantaged, as people with histories of displacement, marginalisation, and exclusion from the cultural and literary world. Disintegration and the attempt to reclaim memory and identity proceed in similar ways for most of the central protagonists of these novels. For the sufferers, the memory of what has happened to them is pushed aside, repressed, externalised, and manifested through apparently unintelligible symptoms or drunkenness, or even given over to someone else via a pseudonym. Eventually, as matters are resolved, this dissociation gives way to the full reclaiming of that wounded self, and the reintegration of the previously denied parts of the self as a core aspect of one's being.

Yet the seductive ease with which authors and critics slip into these accounts of the protagonists is part of the problem. The reliance on psychological tropes of suffering and healing is one which flatters the sensibilities of the present. The values, the emotions, and the vocabularies of the self are those of currently modish therapeutic cultures, and draw the reader's attention away from the material inequalities that form a backdrop to the psychological distress suffered by the characters. The emphasis on psychological resolution is itself somewhat disturbing. As any critical study of psychiatry discloses, psychological interventions on offer in the Western world are not necessarily appropriate or kindly towards people who find themselves in minorities. This is not merely to do with the implementation of therapy. The concern is that at a more conceptual level it misconceives the situation, structure, and psychological make-up of humanity.

The challenge, then, is to identify ways of speaking and writing about human situations that do not entirely reduce material powers to psychological questions of pathology, distress, therapy, healing, and resolution. Everett's tale of how a writer can be encouraged to exhibit the 'pafologies' associated with black Americans, and be rewarded for doing so, suggests a growing self-awareness concerning some of these limitations. The conceptual limitations on how we conceive of the human condition are explored in Morrison's 'Unspeakable Things Unspoken', where she argues that the European intellectual canon has intentionally left out the contributions to the life of the mind which originated in Africa and Egypt, and that it remains for ethnic-minority writers to imagine life and reality for themselves, as opposed to life being imagined for them by someone else (Morrison, 1990, p. 20). These efforts offer the promise of liberating the subaltern from the legacy of colonialism, and of providing genuinely new and emancipatory positions from which to speak in fiction and in politics.

5
Creativity, Madness and Fiction

> For when he was writing, in full possession of all his wits, either before the madness touched him, or later, in the periods of calm and sanity between, he was above all a poet who believed passionately that content was inseparable from form. What he always tried to make were beautiful and meaningful structures. (Susan Hill, *The Bird of Night*, 1972, 11)

The theme of madness and creativity in fiction continues to inspire post-1945 writers who have been affected by mental illness or who want to comment on the link between mental distress and genius, for example Jenny Diski, Patrick Gale, Sylvia Plath, William Styron, and Susan Hill. Indeed, there is now a distinguished body of literature about the relationship between madness, eccentricity, and creativity (Barker, 1998; Becker, 1978; Gooch, 1980; Pickering, 1974; Sacks, 1984; Schildkraut and Otero, 1996; Saunders and Macnaughton, 2005). Similarly, various studies document a notable incidence of mental illness in creative people, and also in their immediate family (Andreasen, 1987; Dykes and McGhie, 1976; Eysenck, 1993; Jamison, 1989, 1993; O'Reilly, Dunbar, and Bentall, 2001; Richards et al., 1998). While some commentators object to such a link (e.g., Edel, 1959; Lindauer, 1994), there are convincing arguments to support the relationship between madness and creativity, as Richard Bentall indicates: 'Suffice it to say that, overall, the research is surprisingly consistent, and the long-held association between madness and creativity seems to be a real one' (2003, p. 114). Interest in the link between madness and creativity, of course, is not just a literary phenomenon and extends much more widely, for example to figures from art, science and philosophy such as Van Gogh, Einstein, and Socrates among others. To date, much of the literary analysis of this theme has concerned works produced before 1945, with a strong focus on eighteenth- and nineteenth-century writing. We know considerably less of contemporary literature that deals with madness and creativity, despite our living in an age of 'therapy culture' (Furedi, 2004). This chapter aims to rectify this to some degree, although the surfeit of material available from the US and the UK necessitates a brutal selectivity and a non-totalising approach.

From as far back as Aristotle, to whom is attributed by Cicero the statement *omnes ingeniosos melancholicos esse* (all men of genius are melancholy), the notion that creative writers or other creative individuals appear prone to depression, suicide, and other kinds of madness has provided a rich seam of compelling images down the ages. As Paul Sayer, author of *The Comforts of Madness*, notes in a recent email interview with Charley Baker, 'such writing is almost in a genre of its own' (Baker, 2007). As with the inmates of Bedlam being displayed to the paying public, there is something exotic about the figure of the 'mad genius'. In T. C. Boyle's *Riven Rock*, a historically congruent account of the psychiatric treatment in the US of wealthy Stanley McCormick at a family estate during the early twentieth century, Nettie McCormick explains away her son's 'nervous condition' as 'his extreme sensitivity, that's all, his artistic side coming out [...]' (p. 352).

This idea of an 'artistic side coming out' in madness has been a prominent, popular, and enduring conception: madness as a release of creative energy, something possessed by the 'mad genius', a figure with a rich Romantic and post-Romantic history. This figure is often stereotypically viewed as 'the lone artist suffering in isolation for his art or the individual (and often mad) scientist [...] persisting against all the odds with his singular vision in a remote laboratory' (Carter, 2004, p. 27; see also Pope, 2005). As Day and Smith (2009) note: 'There is a belief that creative people have a significant flaw in their character and that this is an integral part of their creativity' (p. 90). Yet the whole business of where madness or episodes of mental illness end, and where creativity begins, is a moot point. Are the best works of mad writers created in periods of madness or during periods of remission, as suggested by Rothenberg (1994)? Yet it would appear that at its most debilitating extreme, mental illness leaves little room for creative production of any kind, and its concomitant social exclusion or incarceration may further erode a creative life. The Romantic poet John Clare brilliantly juxtaposed the loss in mental illness and incarceration with the call to create. He is reported as complaining: 'Why they have cut off my head and picked out all the letters of the alphabet – all the vowels and consonants – and brought them out through the ears: and then they want me to write poetry! I can't do it' (Storey, 1986, p. 295).

Saunders' and Macnaughton's 2005 collection of essays *Madness and Creativity in Literature and Culture* provides a detailed and often contradictory map of the various links between madness, literature, and creativity across the centuries. In their book, the parameters of these tropes are clearly indicated. But we may wonder whether a saturation point has been reached in the play of these ideas in fiction and literary criticism. Is this field exhausted? It seems, as Alvarez (2005) suggests, that creativity and author destruction (in suicide) from the 1960s onwards has become a badge for celebrity, a facile dynamic exploited by publishers. We may ask, is there anything more to be learned from writing on creative genius and mental misery? Patricia Waugh (2005) is acute in her observations of a Dionysian counterculture against the deadening rise of biomedical and neuro-technical appropriation of the human mind – of creativity in and from madness as a bleeding into the unfeeling machine of science. But our question should not be whether madness in literature, the literature of the mad, or literature that welds creativity to psychic collapse and fragmentation, advances our knowledge of mental illness as disorder, for we sense repeatedly that it does. Instead, our question is, will it remain fresh and readable into the future, or will it become a depleted seam with diminishing returns? How much more scrutiny of these tropes and devices is required? They have been dutifully investigated by scholars such as Jamison (1993), and more recently by Berlin (2008) and Glazer (2009), demonstrating that there is indeed fresh research being done in this field. This chapter examines the less scrutinised world of contemporary fiction and pursues a fresh, up-to-date examination. As we hope to show, there is no need as yet to herald the near-exhaustion of this topic.

For the modest purposes of this book, we will focus on a small number of key texts across the post-war period rather than attempt a comprehensive survey. In particular, we will first look at a selection of novels that explore creativity and madness in relation to notions of social, semiotic, and personal fragmentation, touching briefly on Melvyn Bragg's *Remember Me* (2009) before considering Doris Lessing's *The Golden Notebook* (1962), Jenny Diski's *Then Again* (1990), Adam Foulds's *The Quickening Maze* (2009), and Sylvia Plath's *The Bell Jar* (1963). We move on to consider how madness and creativity can be thought of as offering a kind of consolation for the author. Here, we return to Bragg's *Remember Me* (2009) and also look at Patrick Gale's *Notes From An Exhibition* (2007) and Clare Allan's *Poppy Shakespeare* (2006). Finally, we explore the theme of creativity and madness used to present the writer and the literary critic as engaged in a 'mad' coupling or *furor scribendi* – a rage, frenzy, or madness of writing that, at times, borders on mortal combat. In addition to references to clinical madness *per se* in Patricia Duncker's *Hallucinating Foucault* (1996), Susan Hill's *The Bird of Night* (1972), and William Golding's *The Paper Men* (1985), these novels incorporate a situational kind of madness in critiquing the obsessive pursuits of literary critics against the defences of the creative writer.

Broken pieces

Our first theme of 'broken pieces' is perhaps rather predictable given post-war scepticism about unifying grand narratives and the rising influence of postmodernism across numerous academic disciplines – something we explore in detail in Chapter 6. Here we examine how the whole business of personal, social, and semiotic fragmentation plays out with madness and creativity. Indeed, Melvyn Bragg's *Remember Me* signals the direction here in being, at least in part, a disquisition on creativity and madness that remains inconclusive. In a key section of Bragg's novel, when protagonist Joe is producing a film, the artist Jessica states: 'If you are happy you can't be an artist. All artists have to be unhappy [...] Disturbed might be better [...] or depressed, flawed in some way, or wounded. Or all of them together, most likely. And the greater the flaws and the deeper the wounds the better the artist' (pp. 230–231). Joe objects to this generalisation, claiming that there are many prominent artists and writers not known for having mental difficulties, but Jessica retorts that trauma can always be found in their lives. Natasha signals the irresolution of this matter: 'I think [...] that the roots of all creativity are so tangled and dark that any attempt to identify them, using a single method, is bound to be unsatisfactory' (p. 231). And this is where the novel leaves us. As Joe puts it, despite the claims of a link between madness and creativity, 'the opposite is always just as true' (p. 232). This kind of complexity and inconclusiveness or, indeed, irresolution and fragmentation, in relation to creativity is evident in other post-war fiction, notably Lessing's *The Golden Notebook* and Diski's *Then Again*.

In Doris Lessing's *The Golden Notebook* we witness the disillusion and fragmentation of Anna Wulf, a young novelist and mother with writer's block. Fearing madness, Anna writes of her experiences in a series of notebooks. This whole creative process is clearly viewed by the character as something therapeutic, a counter to disintegration of personality and selfhood: 'I looked at this notebook, thinking that if I could write in it Anna would come back ...' (p. 522). Anna perceives her life to be falling apart and tropes of madness dominate – those of fragmentation, division, doubling, hysteria, chaos, vertigo, disintegration, or breakdown. Creativity here aligns with semantic dislocation, or what may be thought of as a process of excommunication:

> [...] words lose their meaning suddenly. I find myself listening to a sentence, a phrase, a group of words, as if they are in a foreign language – the gap between what they are supposed to mean, and what in fact they say seems unbridgeable. I have been thinking of the novels about the breakdown of language, like *Finnegan's Wake*. (p. 272)

Once again:

> I am increasingly afflicted by vertigo where words mean nothing [...] They have become, when I think, not the form into which experience is shaped, but a series of meaningless sounds, like nursery talk, and away to one side of experience. Or like the sound track of a film that has slipped its connection with the film [...] It occurs to me that what is happening is a breakdown of me, Anna, and this is how I am becoming aware of it. For words are form, and if I am at a pitch where shape, form, expression are nothing, then I am nothing, for it has become clear to me, reading the notebooks, that I remain Anna because of a certain kind of intelligence. This intelligence is dissolving and I am very frightened. (pp. 418–419)

In her preface to *The Golden Notebook*, Lessing acknowledges that different readings of her book are possible and that these might unhelpfully attempt to totalise the overall meaning of the work; that there will be some, for example, 'who can see nothing in it but the theme of mental illness' (p. 20). She writes: 'the book is alive and potent and fructifying and able to promote thought and discussion *only* when its plan and shape and intention are not understood, because that moment of seeing the shape and plan and intention is also the moment when there isn't anything more to be got out of it' (p. 21), continuing '[...] when a book's pattern and the shape of its inner life is as plain to the reader as it is to the author – then perhaps it is time to throw the book aside, as having had its day, and start again on something new' (p. 21). Here, Lessing seems to argue that it is in the surplus of meaning and meaning-making that the novel retains its richness and that there are clear deficits to drilling down through its patterns to totalise *what* the novel is and *how* the narrative works. Indeed, throughout the novel the attempt to find meaning through creativity and writing via patterns and patterning is undermined by an overwhelming sense that these will not cohere. As with Angus Wilson's *Hemlock and After* (1952), Lessing sets creativity against a backdrop of post-war disintegration and the apocalyptic light of nuclear annihilation. In both these novels, this very real threat and capacity for disintegrating human life and society mirrors the concerns with creativity and fragmentation that play out intracranially in the largely neurotic characters of Anna and Ella. Lessing, in particular, explores notions of creativity as restorative yet incapable of achieving resolution or coherence. She carefully problematises the whole creative business of making patterns, as in Anna's dream:

> I opened the box and forced them to look. But instead of a beautiful thing, which I thought would be there, there was a mass of fragments, and pieces. Not a whole thing, broken into fragments, but bits and pieces from everywhere, all over the world – I recognized a lump of red earth that I knew came from Africa, and then a bit of metal that came off a gun from Indo-China, and then everything was horrible, bits of flesh from people killed in the Korean War and a Communist Party badge off someone who died in a Soviet prison. (p. 230)

It is this focus on creativity, pattern-making, and mental fragmentation that is revisited in Jenny Diski's puzzling and multi-layered novel.

In *Then Again*, Diski explores madness and creativity as artist Esther battles her own mental fragmentation; the strange, intrusive dream-life identity of Esther/Elizabeth, a persecuted Jew living in the fourteenth century; and the total disintegration of her run-away psychotic daughter Katya who suffers from religious delusions and auditory hallucinations. The fourteenth-century Esther has a displaced identity as she is kidnapped after her parents are slaughtered for being Jewish and brought up as a Christian with the name Elizabeth. As she begins to discover her 'true' identity through asking existential questions to the priest Father Anselm she is unwittingly led to an altogether darker world of sexual exploitation by the priest, before being burned at the stake for heresy during the Inquisition. The modern-day Esther finds herself similarly exploited by her psychotherapist lover Ben, whose manipulative sexuality and seeming betrayal of trust around the care and treatment of Katya mirrors that of Anselm: Anselm supplied a letter to the Inquisition, and Ben sent one that resulted in her daughter being sent to a psychiatric institution. As much as the novel is about the fine line between sanity and madness, it is also about the need to question existence, to ask *What for?* In this, Esther, Esther/Elizabeth the Jewess, Katya who is raped by Kit, and her homeless soul-mate Sam, share an existential and ontological element in their personalities. Across the borderline between sanity and madness, and amidst the doubling of names and permeable identities, these characters engage in their own search for answers that seem to retreat as they are approached.

The attempt to find patterns in life, to bring some coherence to existence, is neatly captured in the creative effort of Esther, who begins painting plates with patchwork designs that have black lines separating different colours. These painted plates are both highly representative of her own state of mind and an attempt to manage fear, anxiety, and confusion through creative art. The plate design shifts to a purer form of fragmentation following the actual breakage of a plate and its reconstitution as a design of broken colours without the earlier black boundaries, which are now replaced by real lines of breakage. This brings the design to a new level in symbolising the drawing together with a non-totalisable existence, the tension between the reality represented in art and the external existent real, and the commitment to artefacts and patterns that might be unpopular (as with the figure of the mad person) falling out of favour with the buying public:

> Esther knew that the new design was disturbing. It was not comfortable and made no sense without the earlier designs in the series. But she also knew that this new plate must stand alone, without reference to the others [...] A cock-eyed pattern, a slippage between colour and design. It didn't matter what people thought, or what erroneous origin they gave it. [...] With each change of colour she had to wait for the adjacent colour to dry enough not to bleed when she applied the new one. It was getting towards dawn by the time she had finished. These plates would be expensive, if she priced them according to the time she took to make them. Then it struck her with absolute certainty that no one would buy them anyway. She could hear the ringing, confident voices of the women who owned the shops she sold her designs to. 'Well, it's just not – commercial. It's such a – mess. You know? I don't mean to be rude, but your fruit and flowers designs are much more, well, they sell. This just wouldn't look well on the table.' [...] Esther stared at the finished, but not quite dry, plate. She didn't mind. This pattern was hers, anyway. She wondered what to call it. *Then Again*, she thought, but

knew that she would not, in fact, give this particular pattern any name at all. (p. 211)

Here, Diski cleverly maximises the levels for interpretation and metafictional fallout in relation to her own creative act in writing the novel *Then Again*, and the possible reception and achievement of a literary 'mess' – a cock-eyed and labyrinthine story that takes us everywhere and nowhere all at once.

While not labyrinthine as such despite the evocative title, Adam Foulds's recent novel *The Quickening Maze*, which was shortlisted for the 2009 Booker prize, adopts the motifs of personal fragmentation or 'brokenness' and the disorientation of the 'maze' in his historical fiction about the madness of the pastoral or peasant poet John Clare and Alfred and Septimus Tennyson, among others, in a nineteenth-century asylum. Although not an obviously postmodern novel, it does deal with how madness disrupts and breaks down both identity and creativity. This is somewhat amplified by its admixture of fact and fiction. Indeed, as signalled in the title, it is a story about being lost and disoriented. Based closely on real events, this turn to historical fiction brings Foulds within a tradition of writing that includes British writers such as John Fowles, Lawrence Durrell, Julian Barnes, Graham Swift, Rose Tremain, A. S. Byatt, Jeanette Winterson, Peter Ackroyd, Salman Rushdie, and Jim Crace, as well as those writers that we discussed in Chapter 3.

At the heart of Foulds's novel lies the story of John Clare and his battle for creativity while subject to a mental illness that led to his incarceration, first at High Beach private asylum in Epping – where much of Foulds's novel is set – and then at St Andrew's asylum in Northampton. Foulds presents a vivid account of Clare's predicament and his struggle to remain connected to both those he loved *and* the countryside that had been transformed for the worse by the Enclosure Acts at the beginning the nineteenth century, when open fields and common agricultural land were fenced off for private gain and the labouring poor squeezed into ever deeper poverty and confinement. The characterisation of Clare is sensitively done, as the mad poet suffers delusions – believing himself to be Byron, Shakespeare, and the prize-fighter Jack Randall – and negotiates his freedom to leave the asylum and walk freely in the surrounding forest and countryside.

The description of asylum life is powerfully achieved by bringing together the reformist principles of Dr Matthew Allen, the asylum owner, and the inherent brutality realised in the figure of the chief attendant, William Stockdale. The forced evacuation of a patient's bowels will stay in the reader's mind much longer than the ordure Dr Allen wipes off his shoe, as will John Clare witnessing the rape by Stockdale of the ambiguated patient Mary/Margaret. But aside from the dramatic narrative exploration of levels of madness and abuses of power, much of the novel turns on the tension between creativity and madness which extends the more obvious cases of Clare and the Tennysons to include Matthew Allen himself who, for a second time, places himself in utter financial jeopardy with a ridiculous scheme to build a carving machine or pyroglyph. This is a very engaging novel that aligns the two tropes of madness and creativity in a way that retains an inherent respect for both the mentally afflicted and the transcendence of poetry. We also get a strong sense of variability in the levels of mental affliction that creative individuals endure, as in the following extract, when Dr Allen scrutinises Alfred Tennyson:

> The head was massive and handsome undeniably, with a dark burnish to the skin. Behind the dome of the forehead, strongly suggestive of intellectual power, very promising poems were being formed. He was very different in appearance to poor little Clare, but the forehead was reminiscent. The poet had been right about himself – he did seem deficient in animal spirits. The case was not nearly so morbid as his brother Septimus's, but Alfred Tennyson also moved slowly, as though through a viscous medium of thought, of doubt. (pp. 23–24)

Yet even with this more moderate affliction, his creativity is disrupted or blocked:

> Alfred Tennyson walked to loosen his blood. He had spent the day sunk in a low mood. The word 'sunk' was the right one, the mood soft, dark, silted, sluggish; it smelt of riverbed, of himself. He'd managed no new lines. Poems lay around half-formed and helpless, insects droned in the garden, a fly butted its hard little face against the window panes. (pp. 144–145)

But it is John Clare who is the chief funnel for the damaging and disorienting impact of madness on creativity in the novel. He is presented in a decline that robs him of his identity as a poet: 'But he wasn't a country man any more, or even a poet. What they saw, if they saw him at all, was one of the doctor's patients, a madman' (p. 86). His identity-based delusional madness is closely bound up with creativity, most prominently when he takes on the persona of Byron:

> Lord Byron awoke with a fearsome headache, in soiled garments
> [...] The pages he had written! There had been weeks of thousands
> of lines, his hand scurrying across the page hurrying to set them
> down, his lip fluttering, his head a butter churn of beating poetry
> [...] Poems had formed in his dreams, had become louder and clearer
> until they had formed a solid bridge into wakefulness. They would
> force him awake to serve them. Sometimes he would creep out of bed
> into his corner chair, find an unused scrap of paper and start scratch-
> ing them down before he realised that he'd written them already.
> Weeks of this frenzy. No wonder John Barleycorn was called upon to
> loosen the grip of words, to set him back on his arse and out of the
> violent machine of poetry. (pp. 219–220)

In a wonderful reversal towards the end of the novel we see John
Clare looking after his delirious doctor, telling him:

> 'Then rest. Lie down. Lie down on your sofa.' 'Yes, yes, I will.'
> Matthew accepted. Why not? Everyone pulling at him, requiring
> his decisions. Let them decide for a change. John stood over him as
> he subsided groaning down onto the cushions. John then took the
> blanket draped over the sofa's back rest and spread it as a coverlet
> over the doctor. Matthew Allen watched the broken poet's comfort-
> able fat face as he tucked the blanket under his side so that he was
> snugly wrapped, and remembered that the poor man was a father
> like himself. He had tended fevered children with presumably that
> same look of abstract, practical care in his eyes. It made the doctor
> helpless for a moment, wanting to weep. (p. 232)

Here again, it is the vision of the 'broken poet' that dominates.
Foulds's evocation of 'brokenness' is not random or casual. It lies at the
heart of this novel as clearly as it does in Foulds's long, prize-winning
poem, 'The Broken Word', where he 'adroitly mixed facts with imaginings' (Motion, 2009, p. 10). Throughout the novel, both the poetry of
Clare and his identity as poet are clear casualties of both mental affliction and asylum life. The novel appears to support a view of Clare as a
poet *in spite of* his suffering, rather than portraying mental illness as a
generative force behind creativity.

Perhaps the most iconic and stark novel dealing with the damaging
nature of madness on creativity and identity is Sylvia Plath's *The Bell Jar*.

Plath's fictionalised autobiography has become a touchstone for literature dealing with madness, creativity, and the ultimate fragmentation apparent in successful suicide. As William Styron writes in *Darkness Visible* (2001), his brief but powerful memoir of depression:

> Despite depression's eclectic reach, it has been demonstrated with fair convincingness that artistic types (especially poets) are particularly vulnerable to the disorder – which, in its graver, clinical manifestation takes upwards of twenty percent of its victims by way of suicide. Just a few of these fallen artists, all modern, make up a sad but scintillant roll call: Hart Crane, Vincent van Gogh, Virginia Woolf, Arshile Gorky, Cesare Pavese, Romain Gary, Vachel Lindsey, Sylvia Plath, Henry de Montherlant, Ernest Hemingway, William Inge, Diana Arbus, Tadeusz Borowski, Paul Celan, Anne Sexton, Sergei Esenin, Vladimir Mayakowvsky – the list goes on. [...] When one thinks of these doomed and splendidly creative men and women, one is drawn to contemplate their childhoods, where, to the best of anyone's knowledge, the seeds of the illness take strong root; could any of them have had a hint, then, of the psyche's perishability, its exquisite fragility? And why were they destroyed, while others – similarly stricken – struggled through? (p. 34)

Plath's semi-fictionalised novel charts via the character of Esther Greenwood her own descent into depressive illness, her suicide attempts, and her struggle to exist in a world constrained by conflicting familial, societal expectations of femininity, and the emergent women's movement. Her fragility of mental state comes through strongly, for example, in the following section:

> But when it came right down to it, the skin of my wrist looked so white and defenceless that I couldn't do it. It was as if what I wanted to kill wasn't in that skin or the thin blue pulse that jumped under my thumb, but somewhere else, deeper, more secret, and a whole lot harder to get at.
>
> It would take two motions. One wrist, then the other wrist. Three motions, if you counted changing the razor from hand to hand. Then I would step into the tub and lie down.
>
> I moved in front of the medicine cabinet. If I looked in the mirror while I did it, it would be like watching somebody else, in a book or a play.

That the person in the mirror was paralysed and too stupid to do a thing.

Then I thought, maybe I ought to spill a little blood for practice, so I sat on the edge of the tub and crossed my right ankle over my left knee. Then I lifted my right hand with the razor and let it drop of its own weight, like a guillotine, on to the calf of my leg.

I felt nothing. Then I felt a small, deep thrill, and a bright seam of red welled up at the lip of the slash. The blood gathered darkly, like fruit, and rolled down my ankle into the cup of my black patent leather shoe. (p. 142)

This psychological fragility and ensuing destructive actions are linked to a solitary and self-absorbed nature – something afflicting both the character Esther and, indeed, the creative author Plath:

I couldn't feel a thing. If Mrs Guinea had given me a ticket to Europe, or a round-the-world cruise, it wouldn't have made one scrap of difference to me, because wherever I sat – on the deck of a ship or at a street café in Paris or Bangkok – I would be sitting under the same glass bell jar, stewing in my own sour air. (p. 178)

In the novel we are presented with suicide attempts, a rich and sustained portrayal of private asylum life as contrasted with public provision, key professionals such as psychiatrists and nurses, and a range of treatments from medication and insulin to shock therapy. But the key dynamic in the novel is the co-occurrence of Esther's creativity as a minor but aspiring writer with depression, and the kind of psychological erosion and fragmentation that can, and did, lead to her suicide. The theme of creativity and madness incorporates Esther being assisted in her recovery by a more prominent writer, Philomena Guinea, and her own trajectory being marked against the brain-damaged character in a play. In the end, a more compassionate psychiatrist and a less punitive version of shock treatment lifts the 'bell jar' of depression and affords Esther some respite, but the reader is left suspecting – and has a final imprimatur on this in Plath's own suicide – that creativity and madness blend to damaging effects and ends.

In this section, then, we have seen how personal, social, and semiotic fragmentation plays out with madness and creativity in works by Lessing, Diski, Foulds, and Plath. There is a strong focus in these texts on the links between broken creative selves, broken or fragmented language, and fragmented literary forms and narrative. In the next section, we examine a number of recent novels that offer a 'dark consolation' in the midst of such psychic fragmentation or brokenness. Patrick Gale's *Notes from an Exhibition*, Melvyn Bragg's *Remember Me*, and Clare Allan's *Poppy Shakespeare* all deal with the topic of creativity and madness in such a way that we might consider them *consolation fictions*.

Dark consolation

In essence, Patrick Gale's novel is the story of the impact of bipolar affective disorder (BPAD) on an artist, Rachel Kelly, and her family. BPAD is a serious condition that is typically characterised by extreme shifts in mood from depression to elation or mania. It occurs in around one per cent of the population (Royal College of Psychiatrists, 2007). The narrative focuses on the ripple effect of bipolarity on those around Rachel, the genetic inheritance of mental health problems, and the inheritance-by-proxy of psychological issues caused by the strain of living with a close relative with this condition. Woven through several different perspectives, the novel provides insights into each character's own personal and psychological difficulties.

As Gale unfolds the relationship between Rachel and her family, we are presented with a kind of systemic case study of bipolarity and its admixture of creativity and despair, with oscillations between asylum admissions and home living. When Rachel, rather mundanely perhaps, dies of a heart attack in her attic studio, her husband Antony fills in some of the genealogical gaps in his wife's history and learns an uncomfortable truth. Rachel Kelly is really Joanie Ransome, a runaway from a Canadian asylum who, after escaping, emigrated to find a new life in Cornwall by assuming the name of a fellow inmate and escapee who killed herself by jumping into the path of a train. The representation of madness and its impact is detailed and extensive, yielding myriad views and perspectives on the nature of illness and the response of the family and wider society. Prominent themes in the novel are motherhood, the heady mix of creative genius and mental debilitation, the nature of the asylum versus community living, and chemical treatment of BPAD. In fact, Gale effectively conducts a 'grand tour' of madness, in particular BPAD, affording the reader an abridged version of a range of diagnostic or psychiatric perspectives, socio-cultural constructions, and more personal accounts of the lived experience of BPAD sufferers. Indeed, Gale's account owes much to those of Anne Sexton, Sylvia Plath's biographer, and the bipolar psychiatrist Kay Redfield Jamison, whom Gale acknowledges as influencing his knowledge and understanding of the condition and its link to creativity.

Creativity is presented as a flourish of chemical imbalance that affords high energy, elation, and mania. Such periods are appreciated and, indeed, welcomed by Rachel, but can be followed by crippling bouts of depression and poor social functioning. Withdrawing her medication suddenly in pregnancy results in a rich phase of creativity, followed by depression after the birth:

> Jack had made her brutally aware of the facts by now: that the only way to avoid the depression was to avoid the withdrawal from medication she insisted on during pregnancy. But – and this she had told nobody, not even Jack – the glorious ascent before the fall and the work she could achieve in climbing made it worthwhile. Perhaps. (p. 81)

The novel's treatment of creativity is strongly pharmacentric, presenting the creative impulse and activity as a playing out of a chemical imbalance, self-inflicted through medication compliance or otherwise, and often referring to the chemical management of BPAD and other illnesses. Indeed, the novel charts a shift from an early emphasis on ECT to a more contemporary medicinal reliance on achieving a 'chemical balance' as the treatment of choice. There are various references to overdoses of medication and its role in leaving the mentally ill person 'chemically manacled' (p. 348): 'They loosened the chemical straitjacket so that she could walk on her own. Well, shuffle' (p. 337). Indeed, post-war fiction on madness is often pharmacentric – we can see this, for example, in Hill's *The Bird of Night* and Carey's *Love in the Asylum*. This naturally reflects the rise in, and increased availability of, psychotropic medication from the 1950s onwards. But it is interesting that contemporary writers choose to give such emphasis to this aspect of mental health treatment. Indeed, the choice here highlights the dominant nature of pharmaceutics in the period, with the increased demand for evidence-based, biochemical solutions; and also as a replacement for the more obvious physical restraints applied in the asylums. This also shows an acute recognition of chemical influence in maintaining or closing down creativity.

In one very stark description in the novel, we find Rachel in postnatal despair, and looking for a chemical escape from life:

> And yet the darkness that stole upon her was like no darkness she had experienced before. It had no real cause and it came upon her with devastating speed, like a storm across bright waters. Quite suddenly,

in the space of little more than a day, whatever little gland provided hope or a sense of perspective ceased its merciful function and she woke from the afternoon nap that Truby King insisted mother and baby take in their separate rooms and Garfield was crying through the bedroom wall and softly, from the drawer where she kept the pills and Jack had weaned her off during pregnancy, a second, malign baby was whispering to her. She left Garfield to cry, fearing to look on him, and took the pill bottle from the drawer. It felt wrong to die in a house that was so good and where the good baby, the innocent one, was lying so she pulled a fisherman's smock over her jersey and her thickest coat over that and gathered up the pills and a bottle of sloe gin Fred had made for them and took herself out to the studio. There she swallowed the pills, in several painful fistfuls, washing their gritty bitterness away with great, greedy glugs of the sour-sweet liqueur. Then she lay back on the broken-down chaise longue with a blanket over her and waited for death. (p. 147)

Gale captures authentically and recognisably the life of the artist as mother, her breakdowns and creative breakthroughs, carefully charting the episodic nature of these breaks in part through a series of notes from a fictional exhibition that head each chapter:

By a cruel irony, she produced some of her greatest work in the periods of almost frenzied activity – and mental instability – in the weeks preceding the birth of each child. Unnamed Study (1967?) gains its putative date from the distinctly Op Art or Rileyesque ways in which the orange-coloured squares are made to vibrate or throb by the subtle application of contrasting greens between them. Another reason it is thought to have been executed in hospital is the lack of any finished, larger work produced from the study. (p. 283)

The changeable nature of creativity is dwelt on throughout the novel. When Hedley salvages his mother's drawings, which are of variable quality, he is struck by

not only her prodigious, careless talent but the maddening truth that art was the one thing that stilled and focused her impossibly restless personality; art won through where her family failed. There were no drawings from her depressions, only fleeting records of the periods of descent or recovery. She must have destroyed most of her hospital work before leaving hospital each time. (p. 183)

Often, this variability in productivity is set against a background of chemical treatments. Lithium carbonate, a mood-stabilising drug used in the treatment of BPAD, preserves Rachel's emotional stability, but it also demotes her art: 'Worse, she noticed a falling-off in her work and felt she now approached it coolly whereas her old turbulence had brought with it moments where she felt she was accessing a white heat of inspiration, something this new controlled safety had closed off to her' (p. 217).

In the novel, Gale extends the paradoxical gift and curse of mental illness in the figure of Rachel's daughter Morwenna, who is a writer. Here the chemical balancing-act continues as the 'genetic parcel' of both madness and creativity is passed on:

> It was a kind of curse, the obvious inheritance from her mother backed up by the gloomy genetic parcel from her father, whose mother had proved herself suicidal but had possibly been mildly unhinged as well. She had tried medication and rejected it. The personal reasons which her coolest, most rational moments showed her to be justified, she had chosen to surrender to her illness. [...] It drove her this way and that and was steadily wearing her out. She was like a plant rooted in too windy a spot. It would kill her sooner rather than later but death held no fears for her and suggested only the blank bliss of sleep. [...] When she was entering a high but was not yet in a dangerous, hypomanic state, she stored up messages for herself to help pull her through the dark times. She wrote stories, poetry [...] Through this process, much of it self-exploratory, she had become a writer. (p. 259–260)

It is perhaps unsurprising that Gale dwells on the genetic aspects of mental illness and creativity. The development of genetic science in the post-war period, especially towards the end of the twentieth and into the twenty-first centuries, may well be an influence here. At various points elsewhere in the novel, Gale presents the genetic inheritance and even 'genetic build-up' (p. 74) of both mood disorder and creativity as when Lizzy, the wife of Rachel's son, Garfield, speaks:

> 'Garfield and I have been trying to have a child for some time now,' she said and he clenched his fingers together in his lap. 'And I've been wondering whether one of the reasons it's taking us so long is fear that a child of ours might have the same mental health challenges as its grandmother. But – this sounds awful probably – but if a

child of ours did have those challenges but could produce a painting like that, we'd have nothing to fear. We'd be blessed.' (p. 68)

The novel is a complex treatment of the impact of bipolar affective disorder: its chemical treatment, genetic heritage, and creativity in family life.

In this novel Gale explores his own demons, not least the death of his younger brother in a car crash and the suicide of a former lover, the bipolar artist Graeme Craig-Smith, who jumped in front of a train. Gale achieves a codified mourning for these deaths in the novel and acknowledges the therapeutic benefits of this kind of writing in his short essay 'The Comforts of Fiction' (Gale, 2007a). Regarding Craig-Smith, he writes: 'Like most suicides, his death stirred up relentless cycles of guilt and anger in me which not even writing this novel has put to rest. But at least I got to weave my own sort of wreath for him. Much is said about the consolation fiction brings to readers but far less about what it can give its writer' (pp. 9–10). This consolation for the writer is also apparent in Melvyn Bragg's latest novel, where he weaves his own kind of wreath for his former wife, who committed suicide.

Bragg's *Remember Me* is clearly autobiographical in parts and, like Gale's novel, is a form of 'consolation fiction' that centres on the themes of creativity and madness. As Danuta Kean writes in her interview with the author:

> The line between Bragg's life and the plot of *Remember Me* [...] is so thin that at times it is hard to distinguish whether he is talk-ing about fact or fiction. Like Bragg, Joe graduates from Oxford, a grammar-school boy made good, works in the BBC and becomes a published author. Both work on acclaimed arts documentaries and films, marry their French girlfriends and leave for other women 10 years later. Both fail to return to their wives on the eve of their sui-cide, and the guilt they carry down the years is unbearable. For Bragg it unravelled into a second nervous breakdown – the first happened in his teens. (Kean, 2009, p. 22)

Furthermore, both women's suicides were preceded by the suicides of their therapists. The suicide of the therapist of Bragg's first wife, artist Lisa Roche, clearly infuriates him. He blames this for his wife's decline and tragic death. Roche's suicide lies at the very heart of the novel, with a confessional tone achieved through Joe's conversations with his daughter Marcelle – something that is mirrored in Bragg's anxiety for approval from his own daughter, Marie-Else. He comments in interview: 'She was glad for me, that I had faced up to it' (Kean 2009, p. 22). When questioned, Bragg sidesteps any notion of the book being cathartic, preferring and indeed labouring for a kind of redemption: 'Redemptive in the sense of a properly considered response and considered answer, but not in terms of absolution' (Kean, 2009, p. 22). Perhaps the redemption here is the gift he makes of telling the story for his daughter – as does Joe in the novel: 'Their daughter wanted to know precisely when they had fallen in love. Joe wanted to find a dramatic moment. Something wild and romantic, to smile over and cherish, a gift to one who had suffered so much, a light in the dark inheritance' (p. 29).

The novel deals with Joe Richardson's doomed relationship with a French poet, Natasha. Certainly, the novel works as a kind of memorial and, as with the title for the novel, memory and the act of remembering are signalled repeatedly. This is the case in the opening section of the novel, where the shadow of suicide is cast early in Joe's recounting his first meeting with Natasha:

> She was silhouetted against the log fire [...] He could not remember much of what they talked about but he always remembered not telling her, not then, that she looked like Shelley. Even many years later when it finally proved to be the time to tell her story, their story, to their daughter, to tell it in full as far as he could, it was this picture of her to which he returned, the silhouette, which made him want to cry out again for the violent death, the wounded life. (p. 3)

It is perhaps Bragg's sense of shame rather than guilt that stands out, as when later in the novel Joe confesses:

> The heart of it is shame. That is what he wanted to tell his daughter, but how could he convey it without running into an excess of self-reproach or falling into the arms of self-pity? [...] If he told her that since her mother's death shame had all but crushed him, had been the weight to be shifted before anything could be done, then what would that serve? What would it mean? That he was making excuses? That he was apologising yet again? [...] He would have had to say to her also that a life of sorts can be lived with that condition. There can be friendships, there can be work done, there can even be spans of happiness now and then, but any dwelling on the past summons up the shame and he could not leave the past alone. He could not pass this on to her just as he could not be at any peace

with her mother, not until he had served his time, the life sentence. (p. 64)

This sense of unending shame fits with Bragg's denial of absolution and suggests the limits of any comfort that he derives from the fiction. As much as *Remember Me* can be viewed as both autobiographical and confessional, it offers insight into the nature and extent of depression, and how this is inter-animated with the creative life in Joe and Natasha, and in Bragg and Lisa Roche.

In a very different way Clare Allan's wry, gritty, part-fantastical debut novel, *Poppy Shakespeare*, can be seen as affording the author consolation. The novel focuses on the lives of N, a long-term day patient and writer, and Poppy, newly admitted to 'Dorothy Fish', part of a rather odd mental health institution. The novel is narrated by N who is assigned by staff to induct Poppy onto the unit, where the sole aim of the day-patients or 'dribblers' is to avoid discharge. Their commitment to dependency annoys the inpatients or 'flops' who are held in Abaddon tower. Here, the worst cases are housed on the top floor, and only allowed to descend to lower floors as they improve and space becomes available. The 'dribblers' annoy the 'flops' because they are viewed as blocking the system and preventing such progress, as discussed in Chapter 3.

Aside from the novel's dark take on issues of dependency, power, and hierarchy in mental health systems, not least in terms of diagnosis and the social construction of madness, Allan crucially chooses to foreground the link between creativity and madness through N, who captures memories of her experiences with Poppy through writing:

> Unbefuckinglievable! I finally get there and look where I am with my chapters! Now I'm not being funny, but d'you know what I'm saying, that ain't coincidence. When I started writing about me and Poppy, I reckoned I'd do it all in one go. I made up a cafetiere of coffee, taken some Penguins from out the cupboard and sat myself down with an exercise book and an old copy of *Marie Claire* to lean on. But that weren't how it happened 'cause once I'd begun, it was like it just kept on coming. (p. 47)

In her instantiation of a creative 'mad' writer, N in the novel, we suspect Allan gains some consolation from this, even in a rather bitter sense, given her own experience as a writer and inpatient of mental health services. During her experience as a patient she considered that her creative writing was not taken at all seriously. Instead, it was considered a delusional feature of her mental illness:

> Before I broke down I had written two book length manuscripts. I
> had also published articles in the *Guardian*, and a number of maga-
> zines. I'd been working part-time to pay the rent but my 'job' as I saw
> it was writing. At the day hospital this was taken as so much delusion.
> I remember reading my notes upside down across the doctor's desk.
> 'Clare is a tall, slim young woman, well-kempt, who describes herself
> as a "writer"'. I was told that I had a major illness and I needed to
> adjust my expectations. When they started a creative writing group,
> I was forbidden from taking part. (Allan, 2006, online)

In *Poppy Shakespeare*, Allan appears to achieve some consolation by
marking the transcendence of the creative writer. Perhaps related to the
notions of author consolation or consolation fiction is the opportunity
that the tropes of madness and creativity offer in attacking literary critics, set in a broader context of interrogating the value of literature studies *per se*, as we explore in the final part of this chapter.

Furor Scribendi – A rage for writing

Our final theme concerns novels which bring together the tropes of
creativity and madness in presenting both the author and the critic
as a 'mad' coupling, caught up in a damageing *furor scribendi* – a rage,
frenzy, or madness for writing. This is demonstrated most clearly in
Patricia Duncker's *Hallucinating Foucault*, Susan Hill's *The Bird of Night*,
and William Golding's *The Paper Men*. In these texts, a situational
rather than explicitly clinical madness marks the critic or student of
literature as flawed and obsessive in their pursuit of knowledge about
also-mad writers and their work. A key dynamic here appears to be
an undermining of the role of the literary critic and therefore these
novels can be viewed as keeping company with other English fiction satirising the world of academia and literary criticism, such as
Malcolm Bradbury's *The History Man* (1975) or David Lodge's *Changing
Places* (1975) and *Small World* (1984). More broadly, they can be seen
as marking a tension between the creative act of writing fiction, its
critical reception, and a wider context of debate about the status of
literary criticism and, indeed, English literature studies. The issue of
what should constitute an English syllabus was contested through the
1960s and 1970s, reaching a crisis point in the 1980s (Widdowson,
1982), when the Colin MacCabe affair at Cambridge in 1981 sparked

heated and, at times, hysterical debate about what had happened to English literature (Jenkins, 1981; Williams, 1984a, 1984b). At the heart of this crisis was a 'growing debate amongst radical critics about the value of "Literature"; about the principles by which we evaluate different literary productions; and, indeed, about the validity of the category "Literature" itself' (Widdowson, 1982, p. 2). According to Widdowson, the 'Cambridge English debate' reiterated 'the centrality of the "canon" and the need ultimately to dispense with the distractions of history and theory in order to return to the unproblematic reality of the "literary works themselves"' (p. 4). In light of this, Widdowson predicted an uphill struggle between progressive, theoretical approaches and 'establishment' or 'conventional' criticism which advances 'common-sense' notions of literary 'value' (pp. 6–7).

In part, Patricia Duncker's multi-layered novel *Hallucinating Foucault*, about obsessive epistemological or explanative quests, love, and relationships, is an exploration of madness, literary creativity, and the limitations of critical reception. The narrator, an unnamed PhD student, finds in his academic quest to understand the work of the mad writer, Paul Michel, a similar psychological destabilisation: 'Writing a thesis is a lonely obsessive activity. You live inside your head, nowhere else. University libraries are like madhouses, full of people pursuing wraiths, hunches, obsessions' (pp. 4–5). It is an instability that segues into Foucaultian ideas on power and homosexuality as the novel explores the theme of Paul Michel's obsession with Foucault and the narrator-student's obsession with Paul Michel, something akin to *de Clerambault's syndrome* or erotomania, whereby an individual becomes deluded that another person is in love with them – a major theme of Ian McEwan's contemporaneous novel *Enduring Love* (1997). In *Hallucinating Foucault*, creativity and madness are frequently aligned with passion, destruction, or violence, as in Paul Michel's reference to 'the sheer creative joy of this ferocious destructiveness and the liberating wonders of violence' (p. 17), or the experience of extremity: 'You taught me to inhabit extremity. You taught me that the frontiers of living, thinking, were the only markets where knowledge could be bought, at a high price' (p. 72). But just as creativity might result from mental affliction and inhabiting extremity, it can also be its victim: 'He had a complete nervous breakdown of some kind in 1984. And he hasn't written anything since' (p. 22). In a ludic, postmodern, and perhaps predictable way, both the novel's focus on the link between madness and creativity, and the value of literary criticism, are undermined and critiqued by the question Paul Michel poses to the student-narrator:

> 'And have you come to describe me in your little doctoral disserta-
> tion on the link between madness and creativity?' He let out a hide-
> ous cackle and his expression became utterly grotesque. I shrank a
> little. He leered towards me suddenly, thrusting his nose into my
> face. Sensing hesitation and fear he at once pressed home his advan-
> tage. 'So you're another scrounging, whingeing, lying voyeur. You
> aren't the first, you know. I've fucked dozens of you.' (p. 97)

Later in the novel, Paul Michel further disrupts any simplistic or obvious link between madness, creativity, and literary production:

> 'Maybe madness is the excess of possibility, petit. And writing is
> about reducing possibility to one idea, one book, one sentence, one
> word. Madness is a form of self-expression. It is the opposite of crea-
> tivity. You cannot make anything that can be separated from your-
> self if you are mad. And yet, look at Rimbaud – and your wonderful
> Christopher Smart. But don't harbour any romantic ideas about what
> it means to be mad. My language was my protection, my guarantee
> against madness, and when there was no one to listen my language
> vanished along with my reader.' (p. 125)

In all, the novel traces the diverse and challenging 'monsters of the
mind' (p. 63) afflicting the writer/academic, and how rage and violence
reflect and refract human passion and homoeroticism in relation to
creativity and its reception, not least in suicide; it also, at a more modest level, considers various clinical and social responses to madness, in
particular the notion of 'asylum' and pharmaceutical treatments.

Susan Hill's *The Bird of Night* examines the relationship between bipolar affective disorder and creativity – the illness that is presented as both
creating genius and, sometimes simultaneously, destroying it. The novel
is partly carnivalesque, using the motifs of masks and painted faces to
create a sense of compromised personalities and identities: '"This isn't
my own face but it won't come off, don't you see what's wrong, *it isn't
my own face.*" And he began to tear at the skin with his fingers' (p. 30).
The text is narrated by Harvey from a first-person perspective, giving an
insight into the pressure on his abilities to care for and protect Francis,
who is seen as the greatest poet of his era but extremely unwell, with a
madness that is directly linked to his creativity. Less explicitly than in
Duncker's *Hallucinating Foucault*, the homoerotic elements of this novel

nonetheless lend a simmering edge of passion to the narrative, which reflects passions associated with madness, creativity, and genius. His illness is presented as the driving force for both his brilliant, tortured genius and for his decline and eventual suicide, something that features heavily in Duncker's text. Hill's novel is a compelling exploration of madness, almost completely removed from the medical system, in which madness is presented concomitantly as pathological and as a necessary part of the creative process:

> For when he was writing, in full possession of all his wits, either before the madness touched him, or later, in the periods of calm and sanity between, he was above all a poet who believed passionately that content was inseparable from form. What he always tried to make were beautiful and meaningful structures. (p. 11)

And again:

> Do you quite realize what an important poet Francis is? A great poet. That is what others have said, it is not only my judgment, it has been stated publicly by those whose opinions count in these things. [...] And if he is mad, it is because one man's brain cannot contain all the emotions and ideas and visions that are filling his without sometimes weakening and breaking down. (p. 141)

Hill's novel demonstrates a similarly disparaging view of obsessive literary critics or scholars pursuing the mad writer to that of Paul Michel in *Hallucinating Foucault* – Harvey chooses to live in a remote location to avoid such scholars, and is intent on destroying Francis' papers once he has written, rather ironically, his own tribute to the poet and his life:

> When I have written what I have to write I shall destroy all the papers. Perhaps I shall burn them, perhaps I shall walk for the last time down to the sea and sink them there. For I will not have the bones of them picked over, I will not have those arrogant, salacious young men sniffing about his books like vultures over carrion. (p. 50)

Elsewhere, scholar-critics are described as 'parasites' (p. 9) or 'wasps, asking, asking' (p. 56):

> 'Was he the greatest poet of this century?'
>   'Was he a genius?'

'Would he have been greater if he had been sane?' [...]
Francis would have screamed, he would have attacked them. But I
am silent. My brain spins. (p. 90)

This antinomy towards literary critics or students of literature is
further evidenced later in the novel through the view that Francis
expresses – that following the publication of his latest poem 'they will
all sharpen their knives and operate on me' (p. 168):

> I drop the final, crumpled sheet on to the flames and it is licked up
> and consumed at once. I wait until the fire dies down and then riddle
> the ashes through until they fall like dust down between the bars of
> the grate.
> Now I have finished. I have kept my promise.
> There are no papers. (p. 175)

By the end of the novel, Harvey has kept his promise to destroy the
poet's papers.

This kind of 'mad' coupling of the writer and the critic in a destructive
relationship, and the theme of unwelcome intrusion by the critic into
the madness of creativity, is also powerfully evoked in William Golding's
*The Paper Men*1. In this novel, a parody of Goethe's *Faust*, Rick L. Tucker,
an American assistant professor of English literature desperately pursues
the clownish novelist Wilfred Barclay in an attempt to become his official biographer, backed by Halliday, a mysterious, devilish businessman.
Tucker tempts Barclay to give up his 'life' to him, but Barclay goes on the
run. Damaging his brain with alcohol and becoming a 'dipso-schizo' (p.
116), he enters a mad, fantastical state which culminates in the merging of *delirium tremens*, volcanic tremors, and stroke-induced visions, not
least of a red-eyed Christ or Pluto figure. Throughout the novel, madness
is a key theme: 'Was I mad? Was Rick mad? There was an intensity at
times about his stare, white showing all round the pupils, as if he were
about to charge dangerously. A psychiatrist would find him interesting
[...] This was a mad house' (pp. 94–95). Barclay's madness is strongly
coupled with the obsessive, dog-like Tucker whose psyche, like that of
Hill's mad poet Francis, is fragmented. The motifs of doubling, division,
and masks come to the fore as Tucker appears to have 'two faces' that
'would slide apart' (p. 58) and a cleft chin which raises the question:
'Was it a sign of a divided nature?' (p. 84). Here, the stability of identity is interrogated in a way that mirrors R. D. Laing's *The Divided Self*
(1960), which presents the schizophrenic's estrangement from reality

and vulnerability to disintegration – something which can be applied to postmodern society as a whole perhaps.

This use of the split mind as emblematic of contemporary society also lies behind Theodore Roszak's *The Making of a Counter Culture*, in which he portrays a dominating and socially controlling technocracy which has estranged individuals from their true nature (Roszak, 1971). In its use of doubles and doubling, *The Paper Men* closely follows the representation of a schizoid, postmodern uncertainty in Golding's novel *Darkness Visible* (1980). Furthermore, Golding rather playfully creates Barclay as a doppelganger of himself, although as Crompton (1985) insists, biographical correspondence only occurs at a superficial level and as part of a metacritical discourse about autobiography.

This notion of Barclay as a double for Golding would include *The Paper Men* as part of that 'literature of duality' which Miller sees as providing 'a principled or accidental subversion of the author – of the kind of author who is deemed to create and control plot and character, to be separate from his characters, to be himself something of a character, and to hold, rather than administer or orchestrate, the opinions that go with a given work' (Miller, 1985, p. 99). This strategy is part of the short-circuiting that David Lodge diagnoses in postmodernist fiction: 'combining in one work violently contrasting modes – the obviously fictive and the apparently factual; introducing the author and the question of authorship into the text; and exposing conventions in the act of using them' (1977, pp. 239–240).

In *The Paper Men*, Golding seems particularly interested in representing the madness set against the totalising drive at the heart of creativity, and madly obsessive critical analysis. It is as if Golding, alongside writers like Duncker and Hill, find in the twinning of madness and creativity a vehicle to attack biography and critical scholarship as rather odious activities. Yet here, as with *Hallucinating Foucault*, but unlike *The Bird of Night*, the figure of the creative writer, Barclay, is as unpalatable as the critic Tucker – there is an attack on superficial pulp writers *and* critics against a backdrop of postmodern uncertainty and relativism. The creativity of Barclay and the critical drive of Tucker scrambling to secure his biography at all costs appear spent and entropic, bound up in shared, self-generated madness, moral decline, and shallow cultural productions. Whether Golding is conducting a serious analysis of the lines between creativity, critical reception, and the commodification of biography/autobiography, or simply indulging in a playful sending up of critics and raising their collective blood pressures, is a moot point. But what he *does* do is critique, in part through the theme of madness, the parlous state of some kinds of creative writing and literary scholarship that might as well be set down 'on lavatory paper' (p. 159). Between them Barclay and Tucker succeed in breaking the statue of Psyche which stands at Barclay's club, thus symbolising their combined mental deterioration and the fallout of their shared *furor scribendi*. This link is emphasised in the club secretary's comment: 'I simply don't know yet how much it'll cost to repair our Psyche' and in Barclay's response: 'Very aptly put, colonel, oh very apt' (p. 183).

Like Harvey in *The Bird of Night*, and indeed Golding himself (see Biles, 1970, p. 22), Barclay eventually decides to burn all his papers and deny Tucker the crucial material for his biography, resulting in the literary scholar shooting him dead. While some critics such as Dick view *The Paper Men* as 'misdirected revenge' (1987, p. 133) against the world of academia and literary critics, McCarron argues that Golding supports the notion that 'the author's traditional and previously unquestioned authority over the critic is finished' and therefore the novel 'celebrates the death of the author' (1995, pp. 45–46). This is a particularly poignant comment, considering the fates of the writers Francis in *The Bird of Night* and Paul Michel in *Hallucinating Foucault*.

Bradbury's *The History Man* is a possible intertext for *The Paper Men*, not simply because of its similar title, but in its satirical attack upon new radical academics who challenge liberal humanist traditions, and in its tragicomical view of contemporary history. Furthermore, both *The History Man* and *The Paper Men* are not merely antagonistic towards this new wave of theoretical enthusiasm but also question liberal humanist values and the authority of the creative writer. Bradbury declares that apart from the portrait of Howard Kirk, a Marxist sociology professor, as a loathsome character he also 'had it in for everybody else as well [...] including myself as novelist' (Haffenden, 1985, p. 36). *The Paper Men*, however, engages more clearly with the threat posed to the authority of the creative writer by new, radical literary criticism which, as Bryan Appleyard notes, took centre stage from the early 1960s onwards: 'The artist appeared to be losing the initiative. The ambitions and pretensions of the critical theorists suggested that analysis was taking over the task of art. Beneath the hard gaze of structuralism, to be an artist was of no more significance than to be a writer of advertising copy or a railway worker' (1989, p. 234).

The Paper Men is effectively a satire against *all* 'paper men' – all writers or critics who, perhaps, take themselves too seriously and share a damaging madness for writing, one that remains stubbornly self-focused and arrogant. As such the novel offers, as Crompton suggests, 'a passionate repudiation of a system that wants to elevate writers to a kind of priesthood, to find in their flawed gospels and the oracles of their interviews keys to the universe, or instructions for us all to live by', and a rejection of the 'whole Eng. Lit. industry, wastefully devoted to discussions of ludicrous or insignificant aspects of literature' (1985, pp. 164/169). In his essay 'Gradus ad Parnassum', Golding bemoans the academic influence on the literary world, particularly through creative writing courses and writer-in-residence schemes (Golding, 1970, pp. 152–153). He notes elsewhere that his fiction is 'the raw material of an academic light industry' and subject to its 'critical small-shot', and finds this activity, not least thesis-hunting, rather irritating (Golding 1982, pp. 169–170). Therefore Barclay almost speaks for Golding on the critical process of understanding 'wholeness by tearing it into separate pieces' (p. 25) and source-hunting as both limited and comparable to 'Vivisection' (p. 45).

Golding has frequently shown, if not distaste for literary criticism, then wariness about any conclusions it may draw. This is particularly so in terms of the newer, radical and theoretical criticism that came with structuralism and Marxism. Golding was very familiar with the world of the university and, at times, took delight in making jibes against literary critical approaches, not least structuralism: 'I was a structuralist at the age of seven, which is about the right age for it' (Golding, 1982, p. 160). This disdain of critics, particularly those engaged in structuralism, is reflected in *The Paper Men*, where Tucker's conference paper on Barclay's use of relative clauses is presented as deceitful and jaw-breakingly dull, and a female acquaintance is dismissed as a 'structuralist to boot' (p. 19). Barclay again seems to reflect something of Golding's antagonism towards critics when he celebrates the fact that despite 'being an ignorant sod with little Latin and less Greek, adept in several broken languages and far more deeply read in bad books than good ones, I have a knack. Academics had to admit that in the last analysis I was what they were about' (p. 21). Golding, then, was never entirely comfortable with the critical process, although he did make some adjustments to it in reversing his early rejection of the Lawrencian dictum, 'Never trust the artist, trust the tale' (Kermode and Golding, 1959, pp. 9–10), and giving some ground to the interpretations of critics and readers coming 'fresh' to his 'brainchildren' (Golding, 1970, p. 100). This might explain the contradiction or mixed message that McCarron alerts us to, that Golding both satirises literary criticism *and* incorporates its theory in *The Paper Men*.

Apart from its function of coupling the writer and critic in a shared *furor scribendi* and attacking the authority of the Eng. Lit. industry, *The Paper Men* as a whole develops a strong postmodern uncertainty and relativity that is central to what McCarron suggests is its 'cunningly buried commentary on the crumbling role of fictional authority' (1995, p. 46). In the following chapter, the links between madness, writing, and postmodernism are pursued more comprehensively.

Concluding remarks

It is clear from the selection of novels in this chapter that the use of the madness and creativity tropes in contemporary fiction remains open and versatile. The tropes are part of a growing genre and take a number of perspectives, suggesting a rich trading route for future fiction and ensuring that the exhaustion of this combined topic is still some way off. In some of these works we are presented with a sense of being hemmed in by disorder, and caught in a trajectory which unfolds independently of our individual volition, where breakdowns and vulnerability can be passed from generation to generation, as in *Notes from an Exhibition*. Sometimes it is the institutional context which is stultifying, as in *Poppy Shakespeare*. The focus on madness and creativity shows that authors are fully alive to the possibility that madness may be allied with creative output, artistic or literary talent, and a drive to produce creative work. In this chapter particularly the possible consolations of madness are demonstrated, in that no matter how dire characters' circumstances, their creativity can be seen flourishing – a *jouissance* which persists in breaking through both the medication and their prosaic and sometimes depressing circumstances. Thus madness can be seen as involving a kind of gift as well as a burden. Even in the case of people suffering a sense of fragmentation, as in *The Quickening Maze* or *The Bell Jar*, the processes of creation are threads that bind the fragments together. Moreover, creativity binds people together too, as with the mutual interest in writing which binds Esther Greenwood and her benefactress Philomena Guinea, or the relationships between John Clare, Alfred Tennyson, and Matthew Allen in *The Quickening Maze*. These examples provide a final and irresolvable dilemma in the relationship between madness and creativity: madness may be both creative *and* destructive, sometimes simultaneously. The contextual information we have about the writers in question, particularly Bragg, suggests that writing about madness can be a kind of dark consolation for the writer working through dilemmas, disappointments, and losses in his or her own situation. The theme of madness has also allowed authors such as Duncker, Hill, and Golding to examine critically the kind of relationships which develop between writers and critics, caught up in an unhelpful, if not unsavoury, *furor scribendi*.

6
Postmodern Madness

> If, as various takes on the subject suggest, fear and panic are the most evident somatic responses to the fragmentations and decenterings of the so-called postmodern condition, then paranoia can be viewed as the reaction-formation par excellence to the schizophrenias of postmodern identity, economy, and aesthetics. (O'Donnell, 2000, p. 11)

The post-war period of postmodernity provided a cultural and social milieu in which to discuss madness through a variety of discourses. Madness appeared, and continues to appear, to extend beyond occasional mental disruptions, through major mental illnesses and neuroses, to a base cultural condition. Both postmodernism and its literary outputs focus on madness to an unprecedented degree[1]. The postmodern novel is characterised stylistically and thematically by fragmentation of linear or coherent narrative, unreliable narration, and multiple and at times undifferentiated perspectives. Typically it is full of resonant themes of paranoia, conspiracy, and control, the individual's position within powerful networks controlled by external agencies, and his/her experiences of real and imaginary – no longer distinct – categories. A number of fiction writers articulated the pervasive mood of uncertainty as post-industrial society emerged. Genre demarcation lines began to fragment, leading to a blurring of boundaries between story, essay, fiction, criticism, and history. Plagiarism, parody, and reappropriation of now-suspect white, masculine grand narratives became a feature for some authors, not least Kathy Acker, who reviewed questions of feminine reality through her deconstruction and rewriting within a previously male-dominated literary canon. William S. Burroughs, like Acker, became notorious for his fragmented narratives, formed by jumbling cut-up/fold-in fragments, or as he termed them, 'routines', written while under the influence of a variety of illegal drugs. Indeed, drug misuse forms one of the themes interlinking madness and postmodernity in many post-war texts, for example Philip K. Dick's *A Scanner Darkly*. Other authors, such as J. G. Ballard, focused on madness as a collective, inevitable experience, while seminal postmodern writers like Thomas Pynchon and Paul Auster examined the impact of postmodern life on the individual's increasingly disordered psychology. Examining how psychiatry and the postmodern condition interact, their oppositions and similarities, is the focus of this chapter.

Defining and locating the 'Postmodern'

Defining the slippery term 'postmodern' is something that critics have attempted many times over. 'Postmodernism', the 'postmodern', and 'postmodernity' are generally thought to refer to the artistic, cultural, and social changes which followed the trauma and chaos of the Second World War. Following Adorno's dictum that after Auschwitz it was barbaric to write poetry – 'Nach Auschwitz noch ein Gedicht zu schreiben ist barbarisch' (Adorno, 1955, p. 26) – traditional notions of truth, reason, and definitive explanation were left in ruins, and this is amply reflected in the particular types of literary productions defined as postmodern. A paradoxically superficial *and* profoundly questioning mood invaded cultural, artistic, and social aspects of life ranging from art, architecture, literature, and film to concepts of the human condition and society's sense of itself. The quest for certainty, knowledge, and comprehension that defined the modern period revealed nothing more than that certainty was elusive. In many senses madness and postmodernism are synergetic entities. Indeed, as Louis Sass argues in *Madness and Modernism* (1992), there are broad affinities between madness, particularly schizophrenia, and modernism/postmodernism – he is elusive about the use of these terms at times – in their defiance of authority, relativism, distortions of time, and hyperreflexivity. This hyperreflexivity can be strange and unnerving, considering the sheer complexity of post-war experience. Because of its hyperreflexivity and complex, diverse nature, it is contradictory to even attempt to define 'postmodernism' as one specific entity. In pluralising the term to 'postmodernisms', we may gain a clearer understanding of the multifaceted nature and variety of cultural productions that are labelled with this controversial term.

Terry Eagleton defines postmodernism as 'a style of culture which reflects something of this epochal change, in a depthless, decentred, ungrounded, self-reflective, playful, derivative, eclectic, pluralistic art which blurs the boundaries between "high" and "popular" culture, as well as between art and everyday experience' (1996, p. vii). In terms of postmodern cultural production, he suggests,

> There is, perhaps, a degree of consensus that the typical post-modernist artefact is playful, self-ironizing and even schizoid; and that it reacts to the austere autonomy of high modernism by impudently embracing the language of commerce and the commodity. Its stance toward cultural tradition is one of irreverent pastiche, and its contrived depthlessness undermines all metaphysical solemnities, sometimes by a brutal aesthetics of squalor and shock. (1987, p. 194)

Note here Eagleton's adoption of a psychiatric term, 'schizoid', to describe the postmodern 'artefact'. Hans Bertens provides a deeper and more complex exploration of the development of postmodernism, writing that postmodernism 'is several things at once. It refers, first of all, to a complex of anti-modernist artistic strategies which emerged in the 1950s and developed momentum in the course of the 1960s' (1995, p. 3). It then became involved with the poststructuralist debate in the 1970s concerning 'representations that do not represent' (1995, p. 7). Furthermore, according to Bertens, it then grew more politicised in the 1980s, attempting 'to expose the politics that are at work in representations and to undo institutionalised hierarchies' and counter these by advocating 'difference, pluriformity, and multiplicity' (1995, p. 8). The key themes that emerge from descriptions of 'what postmodernity is' are ones that are simultaneously allied and aligned with madness: fragmentation, chaos, loss of coherency, randomness, fear, and loss of certainty.

Across various fictions, madness is deployed as a key device to represent the fragmentary nature of postmodernity. The uncertainty and scepticism that emerged within postmodern fiction came to define the post-war period: the culmination of a growing disillusion with the Enlightenment expectation that knowledge, science, technology, and reason would improve the human condition. The frustrated desire for evidence, explanation, and certainty about the world yielded an increasingly sceptical attitude. Grand narratives, in Jean-François Lyotard's terms (1984), which included the idea that psychoanalysis would explain the human condition, were deconstructed and shown to be empty and false premises. Postmodern theorists began to focus on the inadequacy of language to accurately define and explain the world, insisting that meanings are not defined by their correspondence with an external reality, but need to be seen and qualified within their social context. Because context is so variable, it became a difficult task to make any definite statements about the world in general. Gender, ethnicity, economics, and social status began to be questioned and shown to be discriminatory and exclusory constructs.

The insistent questioning of evidence and of the foundations of knowledge may indeed have led to the epistemological uncertainty which pervades postmodern fiction and creates the right psychological conditions for fragmentation. A key feature of both postmodernity and postmodern fiction concerns the lack of reliable and verifiable knowledge in a world where factual knowledge is claimed via scientifically based discoveries. A synergism can be seen between this idea and the presentation of psychiatry as a scientific discourse – seen in the ever-increasing biological, neurological, medical focus on models of mental illness. This is embodied by many postmodern fictions, which continually ask, can any individual and any individual's reality be pathologised as constituting symptoms of an illness – an illness that may not even exist as an entity? Postmodern fiction as a whole is characterised by this kind of question – and often follows by providing misleading or circulatory answers, typically ending without resolution.

Many theorists of postmodernity borrow, both conceptually and terminologically, from psychiatry in order to illuminate their theories. The postmodern lack of confidence and 'incredulity' towards metanarratives – of which psychiatry is one – was proposed by Jean-François Lyotard in his influential *The Postmodern Condition: A Report on Knowledge* (1984, p. xxiv). With the declaration of the end of grand narratives a move towards individualisation took place. Within postmodern fiction, experiences that are deemed mad by psychiatry are rarely named as pathological symptoms, but instead presented as highly individualised, but also very reasonable, responses to a fragmented and incomprehensible world. Here can be seen, in fiction, a move from the totalising grand narrative of psychiatry towards an exploration of the individual and their experiences. Similarly, Fredric Jameson identifies postmodernity as an era of schizophrenia, compared to the preceding age of neurosis (1991, p. 14). For Jameson, this move mirrors what he calls a 'crisis in historicity' which 'dictates a return, in a new way, to the question of temporal organization in general in the postmodern force field, and indeed, to the problem of the form that time, temporality, and the syntagmatic will be able to take in a culture increasingly dominated by space and spatial logic'

(1991, p. 25). With this move from temporality to spatiality, Jameson, borrowing from Lacanian formulations of schizophrenia, suggests that the individual in the postmodern world is schizophrenic in the sense of being unable to locate himself as a temporal being with a past, present, and future, reduced to 'an experience of pure material signifiers, or, in other words, a series of pure and unrelated presents in time' (1991, p. 27). The individual, for Jameson, is left in a schizophrenic perpetual present that lacks any sense of epistemological or ontological coherence or cogency, as we have argued elsewhere (Baker and Crawford, 2010, under review).

Jean Baudrillard is another theorist who has utilised psychiatry to illuminate his theories on simulation and simulacra, writing:

> Reality no longer has the time to take on the appearance of reality. It no longer even surpasses fiction: it captures every dream even before it takes on the appearance of a dream. Schizophrenic vertigo of these serial signs, for which no counterfeit, no sublimation is possible, immanent in their repetition – who could say what the reality is that these signs simulate? They no longer even repress anything (which is why, if you will, simulation pushes us close to the sphere of psychosis). (1983, p. 152)

Baudrillard's redefinition of the postmodern lack of definable, actual reality, leading to a dizzying 'schizophrenic vertigo', is one that recurs frequently in the postmodern fiction to be explored in this chapter.

This reappropriation of subject matter is circular – whilst theorists such as Baudrillard borrow from psychiatry, clinicians who focus on psychiatry also use postmodern theory to take a critical look at the psychiatric formulation, categorisation and treatment of individuals. Ian Parker et al. (1995) use Foucault's work on power and knowledge structures and Derrida's notions of deconstruction to examine current psychiatric practices, looking at both concrete, identifiable power structures and the more abstract question of 'how language accomplishes and reproduces the split between reason and unreason in the individual subject' (p. 17). Similarly, Dwight Fee, in the introduction to a collection of essays on postmodern psychopathology, argues that psychiatry as a discourse should use postmodern theory to address the 'pressing and often practical need for regarding mental disorder as entangled with social life and language, as well as a palpable, felt condition which damages mental functioning, interpersonal relationships, and other aspects of thought and behaviour' (2000, p. 3).

Furthering the philosophical turn in psychiatric theorisation, Patrick Bracken and Philip Thomas have pioneered the discourse of postpsychiatry (2005). They write, 'psychiatry is very much a modernist venture. Its *primary* discourse is scientific, mainly around biology and positivistic versions of psychology. Issues such as meanings, values and assumptions are not dismissed but they are relatively unimportant, *secondary* concerns' (p. 5). Bracken and Thomas believe 'Postmodern thought represents a struggle to free ourselves from the idea that there is only one path to truth, one way of using reason, one form that science and serious reflection should take' (p. 95). What this leads to, they convincingly argue, is a move towards a psychiatry that is '*primarily* about values, meanings and relationships and only *secondarily* about questions of treatment efficacy and outcomes' (p. 190). Throughout their text, Bracken and Thomas do not use traditional-style case studies to illuminate their work but instead form fictional, creative pieces – an effective and novel tactic. Postpsychiatry represents a break from the anti-psychiatry movement of the 1960s onwards, pioneered by clinicians such as R. D. Laing, David Cooper, and Thomas Szasz. Postpsychiatry is not 'anti' anything, but proposes a model of inclusive, non-value-laden clinical formulation and care based on some of the proposals of postmodern theorists. Here then, aligned with the synergism between postmodern fiction and notions of clinical madness, is a further synergism between the discourses of psychiatry and postmodern theory. Furthermore, we can see elements in postpsychiatry of the reflections that we made in Chapter 2 of this text regarding the need to look at subjective and individual experiences, rather than objective symptomatology or diagnostics.

Literature, in particular fiction, is one medium that gives madness a voice. When Felman suggests that literature communicates with 'madness – with what has been excluded, decreed abnormal, unacceptable, or senseless' (1985, p. 5) she is also describing those postmodern texts which are, and have been, descried at times as nonsensical, inane, and unreadable works of questionable value. In Chapter 2 we looked at Keitel's work on psychopathographic texts, where she suggests that psychopathographies provide the reader with 'a *primarily emotional* experience of the basic structure of psychotic phenomena through reading' (1989, p. 16). Similarly, aside from Keitel's convincing reader-response theory, the formal structure of postmodern fictions directly parallels the structure of madness. Multiple points of view are often given, at times in an undifferentiated manner. The fragmentation, derailment, fracturing, and incoherency of both the postmodern narrative form and of the characters within the texts mimics the clinical symptomatology of psychosis. Positive symptoms such as hallucinations, delusions of control, influence or passivity, and paranoia are all common features of postmodern narratives. The use of neologisms is also seen, for example in *A Clockwork Orange* by Anthony Burgess (1962). Symptoms of psychosis that are defined as 'negative symptoms' – for example blunting of affect, poverty of thought, lack of motivation, degeneration of social skills, and apathy – feature in Paul Auster's *The New York Trilogy* (1987). Characters' dominant experiences include acute alienation from the social and political realm, paranoia, and the alteration of temporal and spatial experience and perceptions. There is a manic quality to postmodern texts – the previously readable, linear form becomes a chaotic, polysemous swirl in which narration is fragmented and fractured. Postmodern fiction depathologises madness through the invocation of the inevitability of disintegration, fragmentation, and disorder, presenting characters in a state of culturally induced psychosis – indeed, Melley (2000) and O'Donnell (2000) have noted the cultural elements of paranoia in postmodernism.

Psychotic texts

There is a distinct subgenre of postmodern fiction which can be seen as *psychotic texts*. These are fictions of incoherence, dissolution, and irresolution. Their thematic concerns demonstrate that psychosis as described clinically is no longer a distinctly pathological event but more of a collective experience. Prevalent postmodern themes of paranoia induced by state and institutional power, thought insertion through the media and advertising, and the unreliability of abundantly available knowledge during the post-war period, all contribute to the development of this subgenre of postmodern fiction. In fact, reliable knowledge is made literally inaccessible through the destruction of linear narrative into fragments of text. The fragmented type of narrative is seen most clearly in the work of William S. Burroughs and Kathy Acker, as we mentioned in Chapter 2. In both of these authors' work the psychoticisation of the text emerges in three interrelated ways. Firstly, through structural devices which induce the uncomfortable and disquieting journey of psychosis in the reader, in a similar manner to that suggested by Keitel (1989); secondly, through direct narration of psychosis, usually in the first person, combined with the blurring of the use of the authorial 'I' and autobiographical material in the text; and finally, through thematic depictions of elements that induce or create madness. These very distinctive psychotic texts are narratives of *ideas* in which the fragment is more important than the whole. Psychotic texts are less novels *about* madness, and more novels that take the reader *inside* madness. On a textual level, examining these incoherent fictions through a framework of psychosis can illuminate this subgenre of postmodern literature.

Kathy Acker's psychotextual work is constantly in tension, leaving the reader with the struggle of situating events and meaning within temporal, external spatial, and internal psychological divisions. Her distinctive style is developed through the use of narrative fragments rather than a coherent story – as she states in interview with Sylvère Lotringer: 'There's a lot of power in narrative, not in story' (1991, p. 23). Acker was also heavily influenced by Burroughs. In an essay entitled 'William Burroughs's Realism' (1997), she writes:

> In terms of content and formally, William Burroughs's writings are those of discontinuity and dissolution. Both represented time and the books' temporal structures are fractured; time juts into and becomes space; humans melt into cartoonlike characteristics and parts of bodies gone haywire; the quality of humanity seems to be green mush or resolved into unheard-of mutations. Due to these psychotic realities, Burroughs, in his writing, was able to portray futures which are now our present. (p. 2)

The 'discontinuity and dissolution' that is present in Acker's work was influenced by Burroughs's cut-up/fold-in technique, best displayed in *Naked Lunch* (1959), *The Soft Machine* (1961), *The Ticket that Exploded* (1962), and *Nova Express* (1964). Burroughs portrays what Acker calls 'psychotic realities' precisely *because* of his use of fragment rather than whole, his re-presentation of singular images rather than linear story. Acker replicates this with an edge that deconstructs the male literary canon – the same canon which Burroughs also worked so hard to avoid.

In *Naked Lunch*, Burroughs suggests that the reader can cut into the text at any point, given that there is very little in the way of linear structure – a notion also expressed by J. G. Ballard in his own fragmented text, *The Atrocity Exhibition* (1993). Burroughs states, in his own inimitable tangential manner:

> You can cut into *Naked Lunch* at any intersection point. [...] I have written many prefaces. They atrophy and amputate spontaneous like the little toe amputates in a West African disease confined to the Negro race and the passing blonde shows her brass ankle as a

manicured toe bounces across the club terrace, retrieved and laid at her feet by her Afghan Hound. [...]

Naked Lunch is a blueprint, a How-To Book. [...] Black insect lusts open into vast, other plant landscapes [...]. Abstract concepts, bare as algebra, narrow down to a black turd or a pair of ageing cajones [...].

How-To extend levels of experience by opening the door at the end of a long hall. [...] Doors that only open in *Silence*. [...] *Naked Lunch* demands Silence from The Reader. Otherwise he is taking his own pulse. [...] (1959, pp. 176–177)

Burroughs's description of his writing practices – or, more appropriately perhaps, his description of the process by which he constructs his fragments into a novel – provides a further suggestion of how to read his texts. This description is actually found within the pages of the fictional *The Soft Machine* – as with most of Burroughs's work, separating fact from fiction, real from fantasised, requires much additional biographical reading:

I started my trip in the morgue with old newspapers, folding in today with yesterday and trying out composites – When you skip through a newspaper as most of us do you see a great deal more than you know – In fact you see it all on a subliminal level – Now when I fold today's paper in with yesterday's paper and arrange the pictures to form a time section montage, I am literally moving back to the time when I read yesterday's paper, that is traveling in time back to yesterday – I did this eight hours a day for three months – I went back as far as the papers went – I dug out old magazines and forgotten novels and letters – I made fold-ins and composites and I did the same with photos. (1961, p. 50)

Burroughs suggests that skimming the words, and thus seeing on a subliminal level rather than linear detailed reading, is how his texts should be read. In this respect, the experience of reading a Burroughs book is one of temporal disruption through lack of linearity, and the subliminal induction of ideas rather than story. Reading Burroughs becomes a reading of psychosis, a psychosis in itself – a literal evocation of Keitel's work (1989, p. 118). Burroughs's four cut-up/fold-in texts replicate the psychotic symptoms of thought disorder and tangential thinking through their loosening of associations and fragmentation of linear structure. Such a structure is mirrored in the un-readability of the psychotic text. There are elements of repetition in these four cut-up/fold-in texts – Burroughs used the same body of written and recorded material to form all four texts, and hence certain characters reappear at points in each novel and his thematic concerns remain similar throughout.

Indeed, repetition is a device which Acker utilises as part of her construction of a hallucinatory textual reality. *I Dreamt I Was a Nymphomaniac: Imagining* (1980), for example, has one section consisting of a scene repeated twice, and another comprising four repetitions of a specific dream sequence. This repetition forces the reader to re-read the four sections searching for differences and for meanings in the repeated image. The second segment includes autoscopy (a hallucination refer- ring to seeing oneself as another person) – 'I (outside the dream) look at myself (inside the dream)' (p. 102). The use of repetition has curious effects on both memory and reality rechecking for the reader, forcing re-reading and questioning of the reader's own intellect. More widely, repetition is a feature of Acker's entire corpus, occurring with two strik- ing tropes that are frequently re-presented – sex shows that often feature the figure of a psychiatrist, Santa or father, and the murderous/abor- tive/suicidal mother. In Acker's *The Childlike Life of the Black Tarantula by The Black Tarantula* (1973), she blurs pieces set in history and taken from various textual records of, for example, female murderesses, and autobiographical fragments. This blurs real and fictional identities and also effects a temporal disruption, with modern-day elements such as American 7-11 convenience stores placed alongside historical features, such as London's Newgate prison, with no demarcation between the time shifts (pp. 26–27).

In Burroughs, this temporal disorientation is caused through the lack of linear structure – or indeed spatial or geographical centring – and through the identity of the drug addict, who experiences time in a unique way: 'The addict runs on junk time. His body is his clock, and junk runs through it like an hour-glass. Time has meaning for him only with reference to his need' (1959, p. 170). What we can see with these stylistic devices – repetition, cut-up/fold-in incoherency, and the disruption of temporal stability in narrative – is the creation of literal and literary textual psychosis, taking the reader of the psychotic text directly inside the confusion and muddle of psychosis.

Selfhood/subjectivity/madness

Subjectivity has changed in postmodern fiction – identity, selfhood, and self-knowledge are no longer realistic, or particularly realist, attain- ments. With the loss of a stable sense of self, there is a paradoxical focus *on* the self in postmodern fiction. This self is increasingly isolated, fractured, and unreliable, as indeed the self becomes in madness. The fragmented structure of text, disrupted temporality, and loss of stable identity are interlinked in Acker's work – this example is taken from *I Dreamt I Was a Nymphomaniac: Imagining*:

> If I'm not an individual or if no individuals exist, no temporal relations exist. (In a world without individuals, any character can exemplify any other character. If temporal relations exist, a character could be simultaneously nose-picking and not-nose-picking. Contradiction.) By 'I,' I mean an unknown number of individuals. Each individual exists for a present duration and exemplifies one or more characters. These characters exist out of time. Example: 'I change.' 'I' exemplifies 'change'; 'change' exists, is timeless. (1980, p. 137)

Questions of identity, autobiography, and plagiarism are presented in a complicated fusion in Acker's work. This fusion is attributed by Acker to her interest in schizophrenia. She told Ellen G. Friedman in interview: 'I came to plagiarism from another point of view, from exploring schizophrenia and identity' (Friedman, 1989). For Acker, the most viable identity in the postmodern world is formed from a splitting, a hyperreal merging of false/true, constructed and reproduced. Within texts such as *The Childlike Life of the Black Tarantula by The Black Tarantula*, there is no stable I/dentity – the I's are multiple and undifferentiated. Acker suggests that in writing *Tarantula*, she wanted to explore '[t]he idea that you don't need to have a central identity, that a split identity was a more viable way in the world. I was splitting the I into false and true I's and I just wanted to see if this false I was more or less real than the true I; what are the reality levels between false and true and how it worked. And of course there's no difference' (1991, p. 7). The notion of an individual's inability to differentiate between a true or false 'I', or to find any stable 'I' at all, appears throughout Acker's corpus. The 'I' in Acker's work is frequently destabilised, and is often autoscopically displaced and externalised.

In Acker's novel *Empire of the Senseless* (1988), the key female character Abhor has to constantly question what is real, and what is hallucination or fantasy. Despite this novel's more linear construction, elements such as the fragmentation of sense of self and tangential thinking remain. Abhor and Thivai, the male voice of the novel, must search for a life-saving drug made by Dr Schreber, whom Abhor murders. In this dystopian world the quest is perilous and, in typical postmodern fashion, inconclusive. This key passage by Abhor on the difficulty of finding any stable and knowable 'I', and thus identity, summarises the identity fragmentation that she suffers as an individual while also commenting on feminine constructed identity in a patriarchal world:

> I thought all I could know about was human separation; all I couldn't know, naturally, was death. Moreover, since the I who desired and the eye who perceived had nothing to do with each other and at the same time existed in the same body – mine: I was not possible. I, in fact, was more than diseased. But Schreber had given me hope of a possible solution. A hope of eradicating disease. Schreber had the enzyme which could change all my blood.
>
> When all that's known is sick, the unknown has to look better. I, whoever I was, had no choice but to go along with Schreber. I, whoever I was, was going to be a construct. (p. 33)

Abhor has the final words in the text and has begun to establish her *self* – 'I didn't as yet know what I wanted. I now fully knew what I didn't want and what and whom I hated. That was something' (p. 227). In Abhor's world, outside of her madness, she faces rape, violence, and threat from every angle. Acker's work emphasises the fragmentation and confusion of previously unified identity within psychosis, but indicates that this is directly connected with the violent insanity of the external, 'real' postmodern world.

Another element which contributes to the fragmentation of self via text is the intermingling of fiction and autobiography in both Acker and Burroughs, with both authors appearing in their own texts as characters – in Acker, often under her own name. This is also a feature of Auster's *The New York Trilogy*. Furthermore, this merging calls into question notions of external and textual reality, authorial identity, and characterisation. An early fragment of work, *Politics* (1968), best exemplifies Acker's interweaving of autobiography and fiction – she was working in a sex show when she wrote the piece, which examines working in a sex show. In interview with Lotringer, commenting on *Politics*, she states that 'in the diary section I wasn't dealing with a fake I, with fake autobiography yet, I was cutting in tapes, cutting out tapes, using a lot of dream material, using other people's dreams, doing a lot of Burroughs experiments. It was all about the sex shows, with cut-in dreams, cut-in politics, cut-in everything' (1991, p. 5). Within Acker's work, autobiography and fiction, fantasy and the dreamlike unreality formed by her stream-of-consciousness style, all collapse inwards. The final line of *Politics* screams from the page: 'I say angelic I'm sick of fucking not knowing who I am' (1968, p. 35), which again echoes Acker's assertion in the interview with Lotringer that her early works, such as *Politics*, were formed from trying 'to figure out who I wasn't' and the idea that you 'create identity, you're not given identity per se' (1991, p. 7). In this respect, Acker's postmodern textual madness is a replication of her personal experience of existence within the postmodern world and her own lack of stable identity.

Characters in postmodern novels can be seen as reconstructing their own realities rather than exploring the objective, external world as seen in earlier literary styles such as realism. There is, at times, for postmodern characters a desire for chaos and individualism – hence a (sometimes comforting) retreat into madness. But there is also a paradoxical acute distress which occurs during the postmodern descent into madness, which can tentatively be attributed to two factors. Firstly, the distress can be seen as a socially programmed need for conformity, understanding, and explanation; secondly, our consciousnesses are unable to process and accept experiences that are different from 'the norm'. Postmodern theories characterise the postmodern experience in terms of subjectivity, the individual's relationship to the external world, to what is real or simulated externally, and how this impacts on the individual psyche – and, as Jean Baudrillard explores, the impossibility of separating the two categories of real and unreal (1983).

Although discourses on madness have seen many shifts in opinion over the past 50 years, the fundamental premise remains the same – that a person with abnormal (as deviating from a collective normality) mental experiences and emotions is psychiatrically unwell and thus in need of treatment. With critical theorists and philosophers characterising postmodern experience in terms of mental illness, is psychiatry pathologising a now-collective human experience? In postmodern literature, do psychiatric conditions exist as separable, treatable, abnormal entities, or are we all suffering with a degree of (postmodern-induced) psychosis? Whose reality is the right reality? Is reality individualistic, or can it be collectively defined? These are only a selection of the questions posed by postmodern authors. In postmodern fiction, we can see perhaps how everyday experiences of fragmentation, chaos, and paranoia may lead the individual to a familiarity with the traditional, clinically defined symptoms of psychotic illness, such as thought insertion and withdrawal, and delusions of passivity, of alien control, and of dissolution of ego-boundaries.

Fictional characters such as Pynchon's Oedipa Maas in *The Crying of Lot 49* (1965) are so bombarded with images of the real and with the assertions of the media that it becomes unclear whether their individual thoughts are their own or collectively inserted. We read how characters challenge their internal realities and the external landscape presented to them, and this raises questions of insight within postmodern unreliability, and the unknowability of knowledge itself. Within the postmodern landscape, characters are increasingly isolated, secularised, disenfranchised – immersion into an inner landscape is perhaps not only more likely but indeed at times inevitable. It is a seductive proposition – the turning away from an endless and restless searching within a no-longer-possible external, verifiable real towards a psychosis in which at least the symptoms are individually real. Illegal drug use, common in postmodern fiction, can be seen as illustrating the paradoxical desire to escape an uncertain and increasingly fragmented existence into a hallucinatory world. Hallucinations are an integral part of notions of reality and simulation, and they are common in postmodern fiction even without the accompanying use of psychotropic substances. Postmodern authors can be seen as commenting ironically here on the use of mind-altering psychiatric medicine to treat 'illnesses' which are denoted as distorted states of consciousness – they ask whether there is a 'correct' altered state of consciousness, and if so, who decides what is real and unreal?

Burroughs's *Naked Lunch* and the three texts which followed it comprise routines and fragments written while Burroughs was under the influence of heroin (as well as an array of other drugs). In this respect, Burroughs made a conscious choice to turn away from an externally presented reality into a hallucinatory alternative reality. As mentioned earlier in this book, his fiction literally comprises features of his own drug-induced psychosis as well as his imaginative, fantastical creations, events, and thematic concerns. In Burroughs, drug misuse leads to disturbing bodily mutations and hallucinations:

> The physical changes were slow at first, then jumped forward in black klunks, falling through his slack tissue, washing away the human lines. [...] In his place of total darkness mouth and eyes are one organ that leaps forward to snap with transparent teeth. [...] but no organ is constant as regards either function or position. [...] sex organs sprout anywhere [...] rectums open, defecate and close [...] the entire organism changes color and consistency in split-second adjustments. (1959, p. 22).

The defiance of external reality through descent into a hallucinatory drug-induced reality provides a frightening escape and ultimately fails to effect any social change – the change remains on an individual level in Burroughs's work.

Philip K. Dick's *A Scanner Darkly* (1977) is another text which uses psychotropic drugs in order to ask questions about notions of madness and identity in the postmodern era. Like a coherent version of Burroughs's *Naked Lunch*, *A Scanner Darkly* focuses on drug addiction, abuse, withdrawal, and neurological damage. 'Substance D', a highly addictive substance also known as Death, causes disequilibrium between the two hemispheres of the brain, leading to psychosis and eventually to irreversible cerebral damage. Bob Arctor, also known as Fred, is an undercover narcotics agent who must become a drug addict in order to do his job. Arctor/Fred uses a 'scramble suit' to mask his identity and remain covert. The 'scramble suit' is a device ironically developed by one S. A. Powers of Bell Laboratories after Powers injects himself with a mind-altering drug (p. 15). What this leads to is a fantastical futuristic creation:

> Basically, his design consisted of a multifaced quartz lens hooked up by a miniaturized computer whose memory banks held up to a million and a half physiognomic fraction-representations of various people: men and women, children, with every variant encoded and then projected outward in all directions equally on to a superthin shroudlike membrane large enough to fit around an average human.
>
> [...] In any case, the wearer of a scramble suit was Everyman and in every combination (up to combinations of a million and a half sub-bits) during the course of each hour. Hence, any description of him – or her – was meaningless. (p. 16)

Through the use of the scramble suit, agents are able to watch themselves on videotape (a futuristic form of autoscopic hallucination) while being completely unaware of who they actually are, visually and in terms of identity and selfhood. Self-identity and self-awareness are manipulated and fragmented throughout the text by Dick, and this confusion, combined with his drug abuse, leads Arctor into a curious madness whereby he loses his entire self:

> To himself, Bob Arctor thought, *How many Bob Arctors are there?* A weird and fucked-up thought. Two that I can think of, he thought. The one called Fred, who will be watching the other one, called Bob.

The same person. Or is it? Is Fred actually the same as Bob? Does anybody know? I would know, if anyone did, because I'm the only person in the world who knows that Fred is Bob Arctor. *But,* he thought,
who am I? Which one of them is me? (pp. 74–75)

Later in the novel, this extreme form of identity crisis becomes even
more acute:

When you get down to it, I'm Arctor, he thought. I'm the man on the
scanners, the suspect Barris was fucking over with his weird phone
call with the locksmith, and I was asking, What's Arctor been up to
to get Barris on him like that? I'm slushed; my brain is slushed. This
is not real. I'm not believing this, watching what is me, is Fred –
that was Fred down there without his scramble suit; that's how Fred
appears without the suit! (p. 132)

Ultimately, Arctor/Fred is completely destroyed and institutionalised,
where he is given a new, constructed identity as Bruce. The end of the
novel is bleak – 'There is little future [...] for someone who is dead. There
is, usually, only the past. And for Arctor-Fred-Bruce, there is not even
the past; there is only this' (p. 210). The parallel here between Jameson's
(1991) version of postmodern schizophrenia and Arctor/Fred's deterioration is clear: the novel ends with his suspension in a series of perpetual presences.

As we have argued in greater detail elsewhere (Baker and Crawford,
2010, under review), Auster's *The New York Trilogy*, composed of three
novellas, also explores the idea of existence in a series of perpetual
presents and notions of stasis induce madness. Like a literal version of
Jameson's schizophrenia, the characters in Auster's three novellas exist
in a series of moments in time with little sense of past or future. There
is a stagnation in the three texts, a freezing of time and space, and a
resultant reduction of individuals to the point of literal cessation of
existence – a ceasing to exist which goes far further than the psychiatric version of this seen in severe catatonia. Part of the madness that
Auster's characters experience is caused by ontological insecurity, a crucial element of R. D. Laing's explanation of schizophrenia illuminated
in *The Divided Self* (1960). According to Laing, individuals

[...] may feel more unreal then real; in the literal sense, more dead
than alive; precariously differentiated from the rest of the world, so
that his identity and autonomy are always in question. He lacks the

experience of his own temporal continuity. He may not possess an over-riding sense of personal consistency or cohesiveness. He may feel more insubstantial than substantial, and unable to assume that the stuff he is made of is genuine, good, valuable. And he may feel his self as partially divorced from his body. (p. 42)

Auster's characters, as read through Laing's work, suffer from onto-logical insecurity as a result of experiencing no sense of continuous self. In Auster's novellas, there is little in the way of ontological security and much in the way of madness. The characters in *The New York Trilogy* become literally and psychologically lost in their madness (Baker and Crawford, 2010, under review).

J. G. Ballard is a writer who focuses less on individual pathology and more on the contagion and breeding of madness in the postmodern landscape. His last four novels – *Cocaine Nights* (1996), *Super-Cannes* (2000), *Millennium People* (2003), and *Kingdom Come* (2006) – explore the impact on psychological health of modern phenomena such as expansive shopping malls, gated communities, and the paradoxical pressures of excessive leisure. Other themes in his work range from pathological sexual obsession, seen in *Crash* (1973), to one man's desire to escape the civilised world and challenge himself, and his sanity, to a battle against nature, seen most explicitly in *Concrete Island* (1974). Hysteria and collective, infectious madness are long-term interests of Ballard's, demonstrated most clearly in *High Rise* (1975), a prophetic and caution-ary tale about the psychological dangers of living in an exclusive high-rise tower block, which we briefly looked at in Chapter 2. The residents of the high-rise building become increasingly isolated from the world outside, and insidious psychological symptoms such as insomnia and excessive use of alcohol soon give way to chaos, degeneration, violence, and madness. Existence in the high-rise building requires 'a special type of behaviour, one that was acquiescent, restrained, perhaps even slightly mad. A psychotic would have a ball here' (p. 56). Yet these are the type of behaviours that are distinctly lacking as the high-rise build-ing – and, more importantly, its residents – deteriorate into violence, deviance, and madness. Ballard states in *High Rise*, 'the high rise was a model of all that technology had done to make possible the expression of a truly "free" psychopathology' (p. 37), directly mirroring his com-ments in interviews (Revell, 1984; Juno and Vale, 1984).

Ballard suggests in this novel that all individuals have the poten-tial for the behaviour exhibited in the high-rise – paranoia, violence, freely expressed sexuality – but that it is repressed. In the high-rise – a technological, postmodern space – repressed behaviour can be released and individual psyches are free to explore their deepest, darkest realms. Furthering this metaphoric use of the 'dark' side of humanity is the fact that, during daylight hours, the residents of the tower are mostly restrained, as the character Wilder reflects: 'only in the darkness could one become sufficiently obsessive, deliberately play on all one's repressed instincts. He welcomed this forced conscription of the deviant strains in his character. Happily, this free and degenerate behaviour became easier the higher he moved up the building, as if encouraged by the secret logic of the high-rise' (1975, p. 136). High-rise, postmodern living requires, according to Ballard, a unique and dangerous psychopathology.

Postmodern paranoia

Paranoia is one of the enduring characteristics of madness, and a frequently embodied theme in postmodern fiction (Melley, 2000; O'Donnell 2000). Postmodern paranoia is an integral part of an existence that is replete with agencies of control and manipulation, such as the government, the media, and electronic surveillance, rather than a diagnostic indicator of illness. The boundaries between paranoia – there *is* someone behind me, I *am* being followed, they *are* trying to harm me – a general sense of unease and distrust, and pathologically defined paranoia, are blurred in postmodern fiction. Paranoia is perhaps inevitable within the postmodern landscape when reality cannot be defined in tangible, discreet categories and knowledge is increasingly doubtable. Postmodern characters are at times paranoid about a vague and shadowy characters, rather than a specific individual, but there is an equal degree of paranoia, understandably, about agencies that wield an ever-increasing control over individual lives and thought. Technology and surveillance, and their effect on characters, can be compared in more tangible terms to the panoptical monitoring of patients with mental illnesses and the electronic tagging of criminals. Other key themes relating to paranoia in the postmodern narrative can be seen in the proliferation of detective and mapping tropes – the idea here being that some sense can be created from chaos and nonsense. This is evident, in particular, throughout Auster and Pynchon, and is explored in detail by Brian Jarvis in *Postmodern Cartographies: The Geographical Imagination in Contemporary American Culture* (1998). The postmodern world and society can be interpreted in literal terms as a breeding ground for paranoia and psychosis: through elements such as CCTV, financial institutions monitoring our spending and, of course, the Internet, we are indeed being watched, monitored, and calculated. This creates an environmental milieu which induces delusions and paranoia. The paranoia that features in so many postmodern texts leads to the question – who is controlling and defining the external real? In psychiatry, it is common to hear how a patient has 'lost control' and become unwell, and often patients can have 'command hallucinations' or feel controlled by external forces – but did they have control in the first place, or are we all, always, being controlled by external agencies? Such questions are taken to a literal extreme in postmodern fiction.

Oedipa Maas, the central character in Pynchon's *The Crying of Lot 49*, provides an epitomic literary example of postmodern paranoia, which Baker and Crawford have commented on (Baker and Crawford, 2010, under review). The novel opens with her discovering that she has been named the executrix of an ex-boyfriend's will. He has left property, shares in a company, and an extensive stamp collection. A series of apparently coincidental clues and a good deal of investigative work on her part suggest that there is a longstanding secret postal organisation in competition with the US mail, and clues are embedded in settings as diverse as public toilets, Jacobean revenge plays, and the stamps left by her ex-boyfriend. Set against the background of the burgeoning 1960s US counterculture, the story ends when her ex-partner's stamps are about to be auctioned as the eponymous 'lot 49', and Oedipa is hoping that a bidder might come forward to shed further light on the mystery. Like the reader, Oedipa is left with clues, trails that lead nowhere, and hints, but no resolution. During the initial stages of her quest, 'Oedipa wondered whether, at the end of this (if it were supposed to end), she too might not be left with only compiled memories of clues, announcements, intimations, but never the central truth itself' (p. 66) – truth being an element that is impossible to find in postmodernity. Furthermore, she ponders 'how far it might be possible to get lost in this' (p. 66) – and lost is what she does indeed get: lost in madness.

What Oedipa is left with as she tries to navigate her way through the 'metaphor of God knew how many parts; more than two, anyway' is a symbol and a word, Trystero (p. 75). During her night spent wandering through the slums of the city, the post horn symbol that has indicated a multiplicity of potential agencies and plots becomes 'muted' (p. 75): it loses its symbolic nature as it can no longer communicate meaning to Oedipa. By this point in the narrative, Oedipa may or may not be in the midst of a psychotic episode:

> Either Trystero did exist, in its own right, or it was being presumed,
> perhaps fantasied by Oedipa, so hung up on and interpenetrated
> with the dead man's estate. Here in San Francisco, away from all
> tangible assets of that estate, there might still be a chance of get-
> ting the whole thing to go away and disintegrate quietly. She had
> only to drift tonight, at random, and watch nothing happen, to be
> convinced it was purely nervous, a little something for her shrink
> to fix. (p. 75)

During her night of wandering, she feels 'she would have trouble
sorting the night into real and dreamed' (p. 81) once she has recovered
from the state of dreamlike unreality (during which she actively hal-
lucinates). During this madness episode, Oedipa feels that 'Nothing
of the night's could touch her; nothing did. The repetition of symbols
was to be enough, without trauma as well to perhaps attenuate it or
even jar it altogether loose from her memory. *She was meant to remember'* (p. 81). Yet all Oedipa has is a series of four possibilities, each
concerning the theme of plot and paranoia – note the unspecific use
of 'They' here:

> Either way they'll call it paranoia. They. Either you have stumbled
> indeed, without the aid of LSD or other indole alkaloids, onto a secret
> richness and concealed density of dream; onto a network by which X
> number of Americans are truly communicating while reserving their
> lies, recitations of routine, arid betrayals of spiritual poverty, for the
> official government delivery system; maybe even on to a real alterna-
> tive to the exitlessness, to the absence of surprise to life, that harrows
> the head of everybody American you know, and you too, sweetie. Or
> you are hallucinating it. Or a plot has been mounted against you, so
> expensive and elaborate, involving items like the forging of stamps
> and ancient books, constant surveillance of your movements [...]
> Or you are fantasying some such plot, in which case you are a nut
> Oedipa, out of your skull. (p. 117–118)

It is easier for Oedipa – and the reader – to interpret her experience as
the result of madness than to face the endless circular possibilities that
lead to no identifiable or definable absolute.

Bob Arctor/Fred in Dick's *A Scanner Darkly* also suffers from a
distressing descent into paranoia, caused in part by him mutating into

fluid identities and in part by his drug misuse:

> And for this shit there are no take-two's.
> What you get instead is wipeout. I mean, what *I* get. Not the people behind the scanners but me.
> What I ought to do, he thought, to get out of this, is sell the house; it's run down anyway. But [...] I love this house. No way!
> It's my house.
> Nobody can drive me out.
> For whatever reasons they would or do want to.
> Assuming there's a 'they' at all.
> Which may just be my imagination, the 'they' watching me. Paranoia. Or rather the 'it.' The depersonalized *it*.
> Whatever it is that's watching, it is not a human.
> Not by my standards, anyhow. Not what I'd recognize.
> As silly as this is, he thought, it's frightening. Something is being done to me and by a mere thing, here in my own house. Before my very eyes.
> Within *something's* very eyes; within the sight of some *thing*. Which, unlike little dark-eyed Donna, does not ever blink. What does a scanner see? he asked himself. I mean, really see? Into the head? Down into the heart? Does a passive infrared scanner like they used to use or a cube-type holo scanner like they use these days, the latest thing, see into me – into us – clearly or darkly? (p. 146)

Dick presents the loss of stable identity in the postmodern landscape – through both drugs and the range of technological creations in his science-fictional landscape – as being directly linked to survival 'in this fascist police state', a state in which 'you gotta always be able to come up with a name, your name. At all times. That's the first sign they look for that you're wired, not being able to figure out who the hell you are' (1977, p. 5). We have discussed how difficult 'figuring out' identity is, and in this context Dick presents a postmodern paradox: stable identity is an impossible achievement, yet without stable identity those with power can (and do) take action to remove and/or control individuals from society. Dick's novel uses the features of science fiction to present a psychotic reality.

A paranoid fear of state agencies of control is a prominent thematic concern in postmodern fiction. In Burroughs's *Naked Lunch* the commentary on social control is best illustrated through his creation of

Dr Benway and the ironically named Freeland Republic:

> Benway is a manipulator and co-ordinator of symbol systems, an expert on all phases of interrogation, brainwashing and control. I have not seen Benway since his precipitate departure from Annexia, where his assignment had been T. D. – Total Demoralization. Benway's first act was to abolish concentration camps, mass arrest and, except under certain limited circumstances, the use of torture. (p. 31)

In the present day there is a curious resonance with Burroughs's vision, as it becomes clear that sexualised torture was used against detainees during the US invasion of Iraq and may have been going on in Israel for several decades (Cockburn and St Clair, 2004; Menicucci, 2005; Taguba, 2004). In *Naked Lunch*, Freeland uses compulsory psycho-analysis, drug-induced psychosis, drug-induced depression, and sexual humiliation as forms of torture and as 'essential' methods 'of the inter-rogator in his assault on the subject's personal identity' (Burroughs, 1959, p. 34). In such ways, madness and psychiatric practices are delib-erately utilised by state agencies as a method of restricting individual freedom and reducing the individual to a state-defined, state-created, state-controlled identity. In Goffman's accounts of life in the psychiat-ric hospital, written shortly after Burroughs's signature work, inmates are subjected to numerous 'assaults on the self' which have a demoral-ising effect (Goffman, 1961; see also Quirk and Lelliott, 2001). Direct assaults which 'mortify' or 'curtail' the self include 'role dispossession'; the stripping of possessions; the loss of 'identity equipment', prevent-ing the individual from presenting his or her usual self to others, such as via clothes, make-up, or other personal symbols; the loss of sense of personal safety; and forced interpersonal contact and social relation-ships (Goffman, 1961, p. 24f.). Burroughs demonstrated these insights some years before Goffman.

The representation of psychiatrists in postmodern fiction is often hugely satirical, following a long literary tradition of representing mad doctors as mad. One example would be Will Self's creation of Dr Zack Busner and Dr Mukti who appear in several of his short stories and novels, not least 2004's *Dr Mukti and Other Tales of Woe*, in which the two doctors engage in a comical but dangerous bat-tle of clinical prowess by referring increasingly strange, annoying, or risky patients to one another. Burroughs's Dr Benway is also of questionable mental stability. One of the most fantastic creations of mad-doctor-as-mad is Dr Hilarious in *Crying of Lot 49*. Oedipa goes to see Dr Hilarious hoping that he can make some sense of her mental deterioration. However, following his participation in Nazi experiments, Dr Hilarious is suffering from his own array of guilt-induced paranoias, and other symptoms. He has been prescribing his patients LSD, as was common practice during the 1960s, but he says to Oedipa: 'There is me, there are the others. You know, with the LSD, we're finding, the distinction begins to vanish. Egos lose their sharp edges. But I never took the drug, I chose to remain in relative paranoia, where at least I know who I am and who the others are' (p. 94). Perhaps for Dr Hilarious the use of mind-altering drugs would, in fact, have saved him from the armed siege and florid madness he finds himself suffering from.

Yet these mad – medically and literally – doctors wield a phenomenal amount of power. This power is metaphorised in virtually all of Acker's work by using the fear and threat of, sometimes-literal, lobotomy. The fear of lobotomy has a synergetic relationship to the power that agencies of control – both macro (medical, government, police, and so on) and micro (families) – have over the individual's mind and freedom. In *Empire of the Senseless* Acker links this directly, though in a fictionalised manner, with the CIA experiments in the 1960s with LSD, while also commenting on the suppression and abuse of minority groups in society (pp. 142–146):

> By this time, since the CIA had tested chemicals on themselves to such an extent that they were now either lobotomy cases or insane, they needed new experimentees. Since the experimentees could know that they were such – victims – they had to be part of socially despised closed groups: prisoners, homosexuals, and so on. The CIA needed socially despised closed groups. (p. 143)

In *The Childlike Life of the Black Tarantula by The Black Tarantula*, fear of controlling agencies and lobotomisation is presented at a more microcosmic, private, familial level:

> I'm forced to wait; I'm forced to enter the worst of my childhood nightmares, the world of lobotomy: the person or people I depend on will stick their fingers into my brain, take away my brain, my driving will-power, I'll have nothing left, I won't be able to manage for myself. In the midst of this level anxiety, I'm constantly at rest. (p. 53)

The paradox of being at rest in the midst of anxiety is another distinctly postmodern trope – the oxymoronic twist, often seen in Acker's work. The threat of lobotomy is so great that, as one of the multiple I's in *Tarantula* states, 'I think I would rather die than submit become a robot let them lobotomize me' (p. 61).

A potential antidote to the constant threat of lobotomisation is escape into a purely sexual, sensual realm. Desire and madness are elaborately interwoven in Acker's texts. In *The Childlike Life of the Black Tarantula by The Black Tarantula*, pure physical sexual desire displaces rationality and selfhood – it is utterly consuming. Furthermore, it forms a hallucinatory realm of its own which is preferable to any social reality. The I's in the text desire to be part of a world of pure sensation, rather than a social or mental world. The displacing sensation of orgasm has hallucinatory qualities:

> I have no idea what comes from inside and what comes from outside; I descend into the mental and physical blackness. I see a frame [...] My eyelids are sewn to the skin below my eyes. I'm an opening in the earth, moving and crying through the rain [...]
>
> [...] I'm both liquid and solid. I'm completely pleasure [...] I sense textures of everything against textures; I'm completely part of and aware of the object world. I don't exist. My nerves so quiver, quiver burning, up and down the secret inflamed passages of my skin, the nerves tensing my muscles so that my blood zooms to the edge of my body, swells and inflames me, and unable to burst, I begin to come. (1973, p. 60)

The displacing orgasm does not always protect against negative emotions – the multiplicity of desiring I's in *Tarantula* suffer a range of disturbing paranoias, for example.

Yet the descent into insanity – even if undertaken in defiance of lobotomising reality – is nihilistic, and proves unsuccessful in Acker's eyes. Her rousing message, through the character of Abhor, against both agencies of control and the descent into madness, provides a more optimistic way forward in *Empire of the Senseless* – 'Let our madness turn from insanity into anger' (p. 169). This may be the message of much postmodern fiction – particularly that written by women. Certainly in Acker's case anger is often the most productive *and* protective emotion against a patriarchal, societally induced madness.

Postmodern novels utilise madness thematically, metaphorically, textually, and literally for two purposes. Firstly, to organise and explain individual existence in an otherwise chaotic, confusing, unknowable, unmappable, un-understandable world. And secondly, to depathologise and demythologise something which has baffled for centuries – madness – and which is now not only an individual phenomenon but, as explored by postmodern theorists, a cultural condition.

7
Literature and Clinical Education

> I sit there pondering while you tell me your thoughts, and with
> my grunts and sighs, my occasional interruptions, I guide you
> toward what I believe to be the true core and substance of your
> problem. It is not a scientific endeavour. No, I feel my way into
> your experience with an intuition based on little more than a
> few years of practice, and reading, and focused introspection;
> in other words, there is much of art in what I do. (McGrath,
> 2008, p. 5)

This passage comes from Patrick McGrath's recent novel *Trauma*, and it
seems appropriate to begin our concluding chapter with a quote from
a fictional psychiatrist (Charlie Weir) who is willing to confess that the
processes of psychiatry involve much 'art' – a view that goes against
the increasingly dominant, biomedical models of madness. We take
issue with the bluff Dr Nash in *Stanley and the Women*, Kingsley Amis'
1984 novel, who describes madness as an 'artistic desert. Nothing of
any general interest can be said about it' (p. 185). Nash continues: 'A
fellow wants to put some madness into his novel because it is strange
and frightening and quite popular. But if he bothers to go into the reality he finds it's largely unsuitable, an unsuitable topic for his purposes'
(p. 185). Throughout this book, we have suggested that madness literature in fact has much of value, both for the literary world and for clinicians, and additionally for carers and people who experience madness
themselves.

Fiction focusing on madness emphasises the need to look at the
individual rather than the collective, to look outside the confines of
biomedicine in order to fully appreciate the wide range of human experience that is (somewhat arbitrarily) demarcated as madness. Psychiatric

clinical practice is developing the idea that exploring and working *within* the subjective experience of madness may be more beneficial to suffering individuals. Geekie and Read write: 'it seems to us that much of the scientific literature and research in this area has tried to develop theories of madness that pay little heed to subjective experience' (2009, p. 21). Their position, on the other hand,

> [...] is that any understanding of madness which overlooks subjective experience will inevitably provide an incomplete and, ultimately, inadequate conceptualization of the experience. This is, we believe, true of much human experience, but particularly true of madness given that it is the individual's subjective experience (such as hearing a voice, or having a 'delusional' belief) that is at the heart of how we define madness when we use terms such as psychosis and schizophrenia. To try to understand madness without recognizing, acknowledging and incorporating the subjective aspects of the experience into our understandings is an impossible task, doomed to failure. (p. 21)

Allan Beveridge suggests that with their innate focus on the individual and the human, 'techniques involved in understanding and analysing a novel can be applied to the understanding of patient discourse. One can become more sensitive to the nuances and subtexts of a patient's communication' (2009, p. 5). From a literary perspective, Robert de Beaugrande suggests 'we can empathize through literature with values we do not endorse in life, without becoming – as simple-minded moralists assert – "immoral" persons. This multiplicity enables art to reveal many versions of life and our ability to understand them frees us from the inevitable limitations of any one version' (1994, p. 27). This is, of course, not a new proposition. Writer and novelist E. M. Forster wrote in 1927 that, through fiction, writers give us 'a reality of a kind we can never get in daily life', continuing:

> We cannot understand each other except in a rough and ready way; we cannot reveal ourselves, even when we want to; what we call intimacy is only a makeshift; perfect knowledge is an illusion. But in the novel we can know people perfectly, and, apart from the general pleasure of reading, we can find here a compensation for their dimness in life. In this direction fiction is truer than history, because it goes beyond the evidence, and each of us knows from his own experience that there is something beyond the evidence, and even if the novelist has not got it correctly, well – he has tried. (p. 44)

Of course, the novelist can make any mistake with his or her portrayal that he wants under the disguise of creativity – the psychiatric clinician does not have this luxury. Their errors in judgement
or portrayal of individuals can have catastrophic effects in terms of
diagnosis or stigma, and they also sometimes make life-and-death
judgements. On a basic level, reading literature enables us to step into
another person's shoes, to begin to develop an empathic and ethical understanding of reactions, responses, behaviours, individuality,
and relationships. Literature, at the very least, can enhance our understanding of the multifarious nature of human lives. And, importantly,
literature provides a way of experiencing situations, lives, behaviours,
and reactions that does not have the same consequences as real-life
explorations.

Literature, in particular fiction and autobiography, is beginning to
find a place in both medical education and the expansion of clinical
knowledge via the development of the medical humanities, which has
now reached the status of an established or 'mature' discipline (Ahlzen,
2007). As with any new discourse or educational development, there
are those who suggest that the medical humanities – in particular,
the use of literature in clinical education – is progressive and potentially beneficial (Charon et al., 1995; Crawford and Baker, 2009; Evans,
2003; Louis-Courvoisier and Wenger, 2005; Oyebode, 2009a, 2009b,
2009c), though there are those who are wary of the benefits of the
medical humanities (Stempsey, 1999). Beveridge (2003) provides an
excellent summary of both sides of this argument, expanding upon
this in his 2009 chapter. In this later work, he summarises the use of
literature in education as coming from two sides – the 'additive' and
the 'integrative'. The *additive* approach 'sees the arts as adding to an
existing bio-medical knowledge base, so that, for example, we might
start from the traditional categories of psychiatric disease and seek out
literary accounts that illustrate these conditions', while the *integrative*
approach 'attempts to refocus the whole of medicine to an understanding of what it is to be fully human' (2009, p. 8). Throughout this book,
like Beveridge, we have suggested that literary studies can draw medical professionals towards this integration, in addition to the simpler
achievement of adding literature to existing clinical knowledge. We
drew attention in Chapter 2 to the suggestion that the essence of being
human is the ability to experience psychological disruption and madness. Given that psychiatry and literature *both* focus on the processes
and experiences of being human, it seems reasonable that literature
can help to redirect psychiatry towards a human perspective rather

than, or at least in addition to, searching for universal clinical absolutes. As Oyebode suggests:

> What literature can do (autobiographical narrative is particularly good at this) is to express the patient's distress and subjective, but no less real, understanding of this distress in the language of everyday life. In other words, the psychiatrist can have access to the sheer humanity of the experience in other than technical language. In this way we as psychiatrists can deepen our own understanding of the nature of these conditions and acquire a more felicitous language both to engage our patients with and to assimilate the subjective reality of their conditions. Like every other skill, our moral imagination, that is, our empathy, needs to be exercised and tested and literature provides a safe way of doing this. (2009c, p. viii)

In addition to furthering the clinician's interpersonal, empathic, and interpretational skills, literature can teach clinical staff about the very practices and processes they are engaged in on a discoursal and institutional level.

We have explored in Chapter 3 how abuse can occur when one group of individuals is given power and dominance over another. But the more 'everyday' representation of clinicians can be equally educational. A brief look at the representation of psychiatrists in fiction will therefore conclude our book – a look that differs from the postmodern, satirical portrayal of doctors that we referred to in Chapter 6. As Janet Frame indicates, individuals who encounter psychiatry tend also to encounter a variety of different styles of interaction:

> The trait for which Dr Steward became noted, therefore, was his understanding. There were doctors who 'got things done' and doctors who cut short whatever you were trying to say to them and doctors who spoke to you in a loud voice as if you couldn't hear properly and doctors who asked you strange questions but only Dr Steward dared to admit that he felt 'exactly the same way' as you felt. (1961, p. 181).

Perhaps this notion of *connectivity* is missing from psychiatric practice – that missing element that leads so many protagonists of novels to be at least dissatisfied with the 'care' they receive, and at worst irreparably damaged by it. Like Oyebode (2009c, p. viii), we assert that human connectivity and interaction can be reflected upon by clinicians via the non-damaging medium of fiction.

There are also novels that examine the difficulties psychiatric clinicians may face with their *own* mental health. Two of Samuel Shem's novels, for example – *The House of God* (1978) and *Mount Misery* (1997) – examine the training of doctors in the USA and semi-humorously portray the various pressures that medical students and newly qualified doctors can encounter during this stressful and difficult time. Another particularly noteworthy example is Alistair Campbell's first foray into literature, *All In The Mind* (2008). The hero of this book is a psychiatrist, Professor Martin Sturrock, who rates his own depression at six on a scale of one to ten:

> [...] but he didn't let anyone know, which ran counter to the guidelines for psychiatrists who feel they may have their own psychological issues. He knew the guidelines better than most, having updated them personally four years ago, but he could see no point, for himself or the department, in drawing attention to his own shifting moods. Instead, he tried to manage them himself. And seeing David helped. (pp. 10–11)

David is a patient suffering from depression treated by Sturrock. The two develop a strangely codependent relationship, in which Sturrock uses David to mitigate his own low mood:

> Secretly, though, Sturrock knew that as well as treating David, he used him to deal with his own depression. In his behaviour and his words, David articulated a lot of what he himself was forced to suppress. [...] He could just about bear to admit to a general feeling of being beleaguered. He could not bear to admit all the reasons though.
> It was one of the great ironies of his life that he urged his patients, and friends in his own circle, to be open about their own feelings and experiences, yet remained so closed about his own. (pp. 34–35)

In novels and in real life, psychiatrists are encouraged to ask for help if they feel they need it – indeed, they have a professional responsibility to do so (Royal College of Psychiatrists, 2009). However, issues of stigma, professional reputation and licencing, and shame at being unable to 'heal thyself', all lead to doctors being *less* likely to seek treatment (Center et al., 2003). In Campbell's novel, Sturrock does not ask for help, having 'always resisted doing what he knew he should. It was partly the fear of damaging his own reputation inside the profession, or within the politics of the hospital. There was also a little arrogance in there, a belief he could analyse himself better than others could' (p. 35). Notably, despite treating a patient who is a prostitute, Sturrock compulsively visits brothels on his journey home after clinical sessions: he is a damaged individual, as damaged as the patients he treats. Sturrock's isolation ultimately leads to his tragic demise. We know that Campbell's novel reflects an acute problem – doctors are a professional population with one of the highest risks for completed suicide (Schernhammer, 2005; Schernhammer and Colditz, 2004). Literary representations such as Campbell's may help to deal with the taboo of doctors seeking help, so that it will be less like professional suicide, and more like an ordinary human response.

There is often a gulf represented in fiction between the psychiatrist's ability to help their patient, and their ability to help themselves. Dr McBride, the unhappily married psychiatrist in Salley Vickers's 2006 novel *The Other Side of You*, reflects: 'The understanding I brought so readily to my work failed me in my private life, and failure tends to bring indifference or at best a defensive incuriosity in its train' (p. 101). In his feigned invulnerability and blurring of professional and personal boundaries, Campbell's Professor Sturrock resembles the psychiatrist in Patrick McGrath's *Trauma*:

> Desire accompanied by the almost imperceptible answering cry from somewhere in my own psyche: yes, my darling, I will help you. It is the narcissism of a psychiatrist, or of this psychiatrist, at least, to play the indispensible figure of succor and healing. This is how I appeared to my patients. But it seemed I'd made the same implicit promise to my lover. (McGrath, 2008, p. 95).

Patients also – rightly or wrongly – perceive elements of narcissism in their psychiatrists: Darien, in *The Good Patient*, suspects her good psychiatrist of self-aggrandisement at her expense:

> How dare Dr Lindholm drag this out of me? I wonder what sort of prize it represents, if she will mount it on her wall alongside a dozen other such trophies – another credential, another example of her superior emotional strength – or if she would simply dump it in the trash once I'm out of the door, today or some day soon. My pain, her satisfaction, that's the true currency of our relationship, but Oh, Dayton, isn't it true that I did that to you, too? Unbalanced, that was the written rule: you good, me bad. (p. 312)

Yet far from being narcissistic, highly successful or manipulative people, many of the psychiatrists in these novels are desperately lonely, struggling to maintain personal relationships, a work-home balance, and the tenuous boundary between humanity and professionalism. And loneliness is seen as a shameful personal failing, according to the psychiatrist in *The Other Side of You*: 'I'm not sure why there is something shaming about having no one to confide in, but in my view a good deal of aberrant behaviour stems from unbearable isolation and the socially unacceptable sense of being quite alone' (p. 51). Sebastian Barry's Dr Grene, Clare Dudman's Dr Hoffman, Campbell's Professor Sturrock, and McGrath's Charley Weir all retreat from intimacy into their professional work.

Patient Roseanne describes Dr Grene in *The Secret Scripture* as being 'like an angel' (p. 99), but he is wary of his own dedication to his patients. He fears that after he retires he will be lost, unneeded, and bereft. He reproaches himself for his 'habit of feeling fatherly towards my patients', aware that his length of service can 'deaden the impulses and instincts of other souls working in this sector' yet 'jealous of the safety, the happiness, if slightly despairing, of the progress of my patients' (p. 44). Dr Grene has insight into the personal psychological gains he receives from providing care, and has none of the professional arrogance of some of the psychiatrists we have discussed in this book. On the contrary, he shares with Dr Hoffman, the superintendent of the Frankfurt asylum in *98 Reasons for Being*, the fear that 'sometimes his role in this place seems so futile' (Dudman, 2004, pp. 142–143). Dr Grene is painfully aware of his limitations: 'So often my patients seem to me like a crowd of ewes pouring down a hill towards a cliff edge. What I need to be is a shepherd that knows all the whistles. I know none of them' (Barry, 2008, p. 46). Dr Hoffman also reproaches himself for failing his patients: '[...] and afterwards, it always seems to me that there must have been something, if only I could think of it, if only I'd been there' (Dudman, 2004, p. 313). Both Grene and Hoffman appear to struggle with their very human limitations, believing that an integral part of their role should be to save all their patients, to know all the 'whistles' and signs, to mend even the most broken of souls. Failure to do so is seen as a personal failing rather than professional reality.

These novels reveal how, in the relationship between the psychiatrist and the patient, there is constant tension between empathy, which includes the sharing of grief and sorrow, and boundary violation in the form of undue self-revelation. The somaticist Dr Hoffman, who believes that the roots of insanity lie in an organic disease of the brain, decides to try Heinroth's moral talking cure with his mute patient, Hannah. He talks somewhat inappropriately about his own failures and unhappiness, yet this seems to provoke her first tentative vocalisations. Dr Grene, mourning his estranged wife, writes in his journal: 'How difficult it is to live. I'd almost say all my world *is* at an end. How often I must have listened blithely and with professional distance to some poor soul tortured by depression, a sickness that might have had its origin in just such a catastrophe as has hit me' (Barry, 2008, p. 114). Here we see him reflecting with regret on the boundary he has maintained very professionally. But we ask, is Dr Grene exploiting Roseanne when he later takes refuge in her presence, or – like Professor Sturrock finding solace in the fortitude of his depressed patient David – is he in fact demonstrating his humanity in seeking the company of others?

Both Dr Hoffman and Professor Sturrock unethically have their favourite patients. For Dr Hoffman it is protagonist Hannah, and he 'feels a small feel of pleasure at the thought of seeing her again. He turns to his diary and enters her name, the last session of the day as a treat for himself' (p. 143). But eventually he becomes besotted with his 'pet case', leading to him 'skipping over the rest simply in order to get to her', while neglecting his other patients (p. 197). One of them starves to death in the asylum while he is preoccupied with Hannah, and he consequently tells her that he will have to terminate their regular talking sessions. Ironically, this announcement is cathartic as it provokes the mute patient to talk fluently for the first time about the appalling experiences which provoked her breakdown (p. 212).

These alienated psychiatrists find it easier to speak with a stranger – and that stranger is often their patient. In *The Secret Scripture*, Roseanne is mutually sustained by Dr Grene: 'Dr Grene feels himself washed up on this terrible shore of the asylum, if he feels in anyway yesterday's man, as the saying goes, for me he is tomorrow and tomorrow' (p. 99). Psychiatrists might learn from these novels about both the processes of transference and counter-transference, as presented in Vickers's *The Other Side of You*: 'I can't pretend to have liked all my patients, but those I did like tended to be the ones I found I was able to help most. I could never decide whether it was gratitude at having some positive effect on their lives which made me like them, or if liking made some significant therapeutic difference' (p. 52). Yet 'like' or 'dislike' are among the very human emotions that clinical staff are expected to disregard, espousing rather the ethically correct but humanly difficult values of unconditional therapeutic optimism and respect.

Psychiatrists have access to clear guidelines about professional boundary violations in publications by the General Medical Council (2006) and the Royal College of Psychiatrists (2009). These cover sexual and financial exploitation, but there is insufficient discussion of the clinician's potential emotional dependence on their patients, and the possible reversal of therapeutic roles. The novels described in this book also accurately depict the sense of pessimistic therapeutic impotence that can contribute to the psychiatrist's sense of alienation. Clinically this is referred to as 'burnout', which can include emotional depletion, loss of empathy, irritability, and even callousness. We may see the psychiatrists depicted in novels as purely fictional – but we can indeed find real-life parallels in the kind of experiences described.

Psychiatrist Simon Dein bravely describes his own reaction to a referral letter about a young single mother, living on benefits in poor accommodation in Deptford, a socioeconomically deprived area of south-east London, who has taken an overdose of medication. Her children are in care and she misuses alcohol and drugs. She was abused by her own parents and is now victimised by her boyfriend. He writes, 'Where do I begin? Do I look at her mood, her sexual abuse or her social problems? She needs mothering, money and love, none of which I can provide. I realise that the reason that I am irritable is because I feel impotent in these circumstances' (Dein and Lipsedge, 1998, p. 144). Simon Dein's story is powerful because it reads more like a novel than a textbook. As Samuel Johnson wrote in 1750, fiction conveys 'the knowledge of vice and virtue with more efficacy than axioms and definitions', and this is certainly true in the fiction we have examined, by contrast with psychiatric clinical writing.

One highly respected psychiatrist and teacher, F. Kräupl-Taylor, deliberately invoked the patient's sympathy in his 'prokalectic therapy' (1969). Kräupl-Taylor's neurotic or hysterical patients would be confronted with the psychiatrist's sense of failure, which was probably only partially contrived. He describes his technique as 'admission of therapeutic failure', and comments:

> It is often surprising to see the effect on a patient of the therapist's regretful and resigned statement: 'I am afraid my treatment has failed', or 'I am afraid you have been unable to respond to my treatment'. Before the statement, the patient may have been engaged in a pessimistic recital of complaint after complaint. The therapist's statement halts this recital and turns the patient into an optimist who

tries to comfort his doctor by a hopeful enumeration of all sorts of improvement. (pp. 411–412)

This kind of practice tests the boundaries of the General Medical Council, or the guidelines of the Royal College of Psychiatrists, but was surprisingly effective for patients according to anecdotal reports from Dr M. Lipsedge, co-author of this text.

Just as there will always be good and bad clinicians, the question of what constitutes a 'good' or a 'bad' representation of madness in fiction is repeatedly raised, though we do not profess to have a definitive answer. Not only for psychiatrists and psychiatric clinicians, but for the reading public as a whole, literature has, to a certain degree, an ethical responsibility in imparting information and knowledge about the experience of madness. Authors may well be – or at least should be – acutely aware of this responsibility, as Patrick McGrath suggests:

> People must be educated about mental illness and cease to despise or demonise those who suffer it. In this regard, novelists and psychiatrists have much in common. Both attempt to make sense of human experience, particularly when that experience is at its most disordered. To explain such disorder, and strip it of its threat and horror, is to hasten the acceptance of those with mental illness in the community. The novel, I believe, can be a powerful tool for promoting such understanding. (McGrath, 2002, 143)

This does not necessarily require that fiction or autobiography be clinically accurate in a strict diagnostic or symptomological manner. It does however suggest that, at the very least, literature should not further stigmatise those suffering from mental illness.

The question of what constitutes a 'good' representation of madness in fiction is one that the authors of this book have asked themselves repeatedly during the development of our international Madness and Literature Network (MLN) (www.madnessandliterature.org). The MLN is part of the development of Health Humanities at the University of Nottingham in the UK, and convenes the first International Health Humanities Conference in August 2010. The use of the term *Health Humanities* – much like our use of *madness* rather than *mental illness* – represents our belief that *medical humanities* can be inherently unidisciplinary. Health Humanities includes the majority of allied health professionals, service users, carers, and self-carers, who share our interest in applying knowledge from the humanities to their professional lives and/or their experiences of well-being and illness. With this book we hope to have provided clinicians and non-clinicians with contemporary literary examples of the diversity of lived experiences of madness; and we hope to have promoted the use of literature in clinical education by showing how madness is constructed and framed within literary fictions.

Notes

1. The following discussion developed from a conversation with Professor Robert Eaglestone at the second Madness and Literature Network Seminar, University of Nottingham, 1 May 2009, and CB is indebted to his insights.
2. This analysis develops out of PC's earlier monograph *Politics in History in William Golding: The World Turned Upside Down* (Columbia and London: University of Missouri Press, 2002).
3. This chapter features much of the work that CB is currently doing as part of her PhD thesis at Royal Holloway, University of London.

Bibliography

Acker, K. (1991) 'Devoured by Myths: An Interview with Sylvère Lotringer' in K. Acker (1991) *Hannibal Lecter, My Father* (New York: Semiotext(e)).

—— (1988) *Empire of the Senseless* (London: Picador).

—— (1980) *I Dreamt I Was a Nymphomaniac: Imagining* in K. Acker (1992) *Portrait of an Eye* (New York: Grove Press, 1998).

—— (1968) 'Politics' in K. Acker (1991) *Hannibal Lecter, My Father* (New York: Semiotext(e)).

—— (1973) *The Childlike Life of the Black Tarantula by Black Tarantula* in K. Acker (1992) *Portrait of an Eye* (New York: Grove Press, 1998).

—— (1997) 'William Burroughs's Realism' in K. Acker *Bodies of Work* (London: Serpents Tail).

Adorno, T. W. (1955) *Prismen. Kulturkritik und Gesellschaft* (Berlin, Frankfurt a.M.: Suhrkamp).

Adshead, G. (2001) 'Murmurs of Discontent: Treatment and Treatability of Personality Disorder', *Advances in Psychiatric Treatment*, 7, 407–416.

Ahlzen, R. (2007) 'Scientific Contribution: Medical Humanities – Arts and Humanistic Science', *Medicine, Health Care and Philosophy*, 10, 385–393.

Alexander, F. G. and Selesnick, S. T. (1967) *The History of Psychiatry: An Evaluation of Psychiatric Thought and Practice from Prehistoric Times to the Present* (London: George Allen and Unwin).

Allan, C. (2006) *Poppy Shakespeare* (London: Bloomsbury, 2007).

—— (2006) 'Poppy Shakespeare', date accessed 24 December 2009 http://www.clareallan.co.uk/default.asp?sec=2andsec2=1andsec3=2

Allen, P. G. (1990) 'Special Problems in Teaching Leslie Marmon Silko's *Ceremony*', *American Indian Quarterly*, 14, 379–386.

Allen, W. M. (1938) 'Paul Lawrence Dunbar: A Study in Genius', *Psychoanalytical Review*, 25, 53–82.

Alvarez, A. (2005) 'The Myth of the Artist' in C. Saunders and J. Macnaughton (eds) *Madness and Creativity in Literature and Culture* (London: Palgrave).

American Psychiatric Association (2000) *Diagnostic and Statistical Manual of Mental Disorders* 4th edn Text Revised (Washington DC: American Psychiatric Association).

Amis, K. (1984) *Stanley and the Women* (London: Vintage, 2004).

Andreasen, N. C. (1987) 'Creativity and Mental Illness: Prevalence Rates in Writers and Their First-Degree Relatives', *American Journal of Psychiatry*, 144, 1288–1292.

Appignanesi, L. (2008) *Mad, Bad and Sad: A History of Women and the Mind Doctors from 1800 to the Present* (London: Virago).

Apple, M. W. and Buras, K. L. (eds) (2006) *The Subaltern Speak: Curriculum, Power, and Educational Struggles* (New York: Routledge).

Appleyard, B. (1989) *The Pleasures of Peace: Art and Imagination in Postwar Britain* (London: Faber).

Archer, M. (1996) *Culture and Agency: The Place of Culture in Social Theory* (Cambridge: Cambridge University Press).

Aronowitz, S. (2006) 'Subaltern in Paradise: Knowledge Production in the Corporate Academy' in M. W. Apple and K. L. Buras (eds) (2006) *The Subaltern Speak: Curriculum, Power, and Educational Struggles* (New York: Routledge).

Ashcroft B., Griffiths G. and Tiffin H. (eds) (1997) *The Postcolonial Studies Reader* (New York and London: Routledge).

Askey, R., Holmshaw, J., Gamble, C. and Gray, R. (2009) 'What Do Carers of People with Psychosis Need from Mental Health Services? Exploring the Views of Carers, Service Users and Professionals', *Journal of Family Therapy*, 31, 310–331.

Auster, P. (1987) *The New York Trilogy* (London: Faber and Faber, 1992).

Bains, J. (2005) 'Race, Culture and Psychiatry: A History of Transcultural Psychiatry', *History of Psychiatry*, 16:2, 139–154.

Baker, C. (2007) 'An Interview with Paul Sayer', unpublished manuscript. The University of Nottingham, Nottingham.

Baker, C., and Crawford, P. (2010) 'Spatial Psychosis in Postmodern Fiction', unpublished manuscript under review with *Contemporary Literature*.

Baker, C., Crawford, P., Brown, B. J., Lipsedge, M. and Carter, R. (2008) 'On The Borderline? Borderline Personality Disorder and Deliberate Self Harm in Literature', *Social Alternatives*, 27:4, 22–27.

Baldick, C. (1990) *Oxford Concise Dictionary of Literary Terms* (Oxford: Oxford University Press, 1996).

Baldwin, J. (1949) 'Everybody's Protest Novel', *Partisan Review*, 16, 578–585.

Ballard, J. G. (1996) *Cocaine Nights* (London: Flamingo, 1997).

—— (1974) *Concrete Island* (London: Vintage, 1994).

—— (1973) *Crash* (London: Vintage, 1995).

—— (1975) *High Rise* (London: Flamingo, 2003).

—— (2006) *Kingdom Come* (London: Harper Perennial, 2007).

—— (2003) *Millennium People* (London: Harper Perennial, 2004).

—— (2000) *Super-Cannes* (London: Flamingo, 2001).

—— (1993) *The Atrocity Exhibition* (London: Flamingo, 2001).

Barham, P. (1992) *Closing the Asylum: The Mental Patient in Modern Society* (Harmondsworth: Penguin).

Barham, P. and Hayward, R. (1991) *From the Mental Patient to the Person* (London: Routledge).

Barker, P. (1998) 'Creativity and Psychic Distress in Artists, Writers and Scientists: Implications for Emergent Models of Psychiatric Nursing Practice', *Journal of Psychiatric and Mental Health Nursing*, 5, 109–117.

Barker, Pat. (1991) *Regeneration* (London: Penguin, 1992).

—— (1993) *The Eye in the Door* (London: Penguin, 1994).

—— (1995) *The Ghost Road* (London: Penguin, 1996).

Barry, S. (2008) *The Secret Scripture* (London: Faber and Faber).

Bartlett, P. and Wright, D. (eds) (1999) *The History of Care in the Community 1750–2000* (London and New Brunswick, NJ: Athlone Press).

Bass, A. (2008) *Side Effects* (Chapel Hill NC: Algonquin Press).

Bateson, G. (1972) *Steps to an Ecology of Mind: Collected Essays in Anthropology, Psychiatry, Evolution, and Epistemology* (Chicago: University Of Chicago Press).

Bateson, G., Jackson, D. D., Haley, J. and Weakland, J. (1956) 'Toward a Theory of Schizophrenia', *Behavioral Science*, 1, 251–264.

Baudrillard, J. (1983) *Simulations* (New York: Semiotext(e)).

Bavidge, M. (1989) *Mad or Bad?* (Bristol: Bristol Classical Press).

Becker, G. (1978) *The Mad Genius Controversy* (London and Beverley Hills: Sage).

Bentall, R. P. (2003) *Madness Explained: Psychosis and Human Nature* (London: Penguin, 2004).

Berlin, M. (ed.) (2008) *Poets on Prozac: Mental Illness, Treatment and the Creative Process* (Baltimore: Johns Hopkins University Press).

Berrios, G. E. (1996) *History of Mental Symptoms* (Cambridge: Cambridge University Press).

Berrios, G. E. and Porter, R. (eds) (1995) *A History of Clinical Psychiatry: The Origin and History of Psychiatric Disorders* (London: Athlone).

Bertens, H. (1995) *The Idea of the Postmodern: A History* (London: Routledge).

Beveridge, A. (2003) 'Should Psychiatrists Read Fiction?', *British Journal of Psychiatry*, 182, 385–387.

—— (2009) 'The Benefits of Reading Literature' in F. Oyebode (ed.) *Mindreadings: Literature and Psychiatry* (London: Royal College of Psychiatry).

Bex, T., Burke, M. and Stockwell, P. (eds) (2000) *Contextualized Stylistics* (Amsterdam: Rodopi).

Bhabha H. K. (1994) *The Location of Culture* (London and New York: Routledge)

Bhugra, D. (2008) 'Transcultural Psychiatry', *Medicine*, 36:8, 402–404.

Bhaya Nair, R. (2003) *Narrative Gravity* (London: Routledge).

Bigler, W. (1998) *Figures of Madness in Saul Bellow's Longer Fiction* (Bern: Peter Lang).

Biles, J. I. (1970) *Talk: Conversations with William Golding* (New York, Harcourt Brace Jovanovich).

Boylan, C. (1999) *Beloved Stranger* (London: Abacus, 2000).

Boyle, M. (1996) ' "Schizophrenia" Re-Evaluated' in T. Heller, J. Reynolds, R. Gomm, R. Muston and S. Pattison (eds) (1996) *Mental Health Matters: A Reader* (Basingstoke: Palgrave Macmillan).

Boyle, T. C. (1998) *Riven Rock* (London: Penguin, 1999).

Bracken, P. and Thomas, P. (2005) *Postpsychiatry: Mental Health in a Postmodern World* (Oxford: Oxford University Press).

Bradbury, M. (1975) *The History Man* (London: Secker and Warburg)

Bragg, M. (2009) *Remember Me* (London: Sceptre).

Broer, L. R. (1994) 'Images of the Shaman in the Works of Kurt Vonnegut' in B. Rieger (ed.) *Dionysus in Literature: Essays on Literary Madness* (Bowling Green: Bowling Green University Popular Press).

Brown, B. J. and Crawford, P. (2006) 'Personality Disorder in Uk Mental Health Care: Language, Legitimation and the Psychodynamics of Surveillance' in R. Iedema (ed.) *Hospital Communication and Clinical Interaction: Investigating the Organization of Health Care* (London: Palgrave).

Brown, C. (1965) *Manchild in the Promised Land* (New York: Signet Books).

Brown-Guillory, E. (1996) *Women of Color: Mother-Daughter Relationships in 20th Century Literature* (Austin: University of Texas Press).

Buckman, A. R. (1995) 'The Body as a Site of Colonization: Alice Walker's "Possessing the Secret of Joy" ', *Journal of American Culture*, 18:2, 89–93.

Burgess, A. (1962) *A Clockwork Orange* (London: Penguin, 1972).

Burke, A. (1984) 'Racism and Psychological Disturbance among West Indians in Britain', *International Journal of Social Psychiatry*, 30, 50–68.

Burroughs, W. S. (1953) *Junky* (London: Penguin, 1977).

—— (1959) *Naked Lunch* (London: Flamingo, 1993).

—— (1964) *Nova Express* (New York: Grove Press, 1992).

—— (1961) *The Soft Machine* (London: Flamingo, 2001).

—— (1962) *The Ticket That Exploded* (London: Flamingo, 2001).

—— (1969) *The Yage Letters* (San Francisco: City Light Books, 1975).

Byrd, M. (1974) *Visits to Bedlam: Madness and Literature in the Eighteenth Century* (Columbia: University of South Carolina Press).

Callaghan, P. (2008) 'Artaud's Madness: The Absence of Work' in A. Morgan (ed.) *Being Human: Reflections on Mental Distress in Society* (Ross-on-Wye: PCCS Books).

Camfield, G. (1997) *Necessary Madness: The Humor of Domesticity in Nineteenth-Century American Literature* (New York and Oxford: Oxford University Press).

Campbell, A. (2008) *All in the Mind* (London: Arrow, 2009).

Carey, L. (2004) *Love in the Asylum* (New York: Perennial, 2005).

Carter, R. (2004) *Language and Creativity: The Art of Common Talk* (London: Routledge).

Center, C., Davis, M., Detre, T., Ford, D. E., Hansbrough, W., Hendin, H., Laszlo, J. Litts, D. A., Mann, J., Mansky, P. A., Michels, R., Miles, S. H., Proujansky, R., Reynolds, C .F. and Morton M. Silverman, M. M. (2003) 'Confronting Depression and Suicide in Physicians: A Consensus Statement', *Journal of The American Medical Association*, 289:23, 3161–3166.

Césaire, A. (1972) *Discourse on Colonialism* Trans. J. Pinkham (New York: Monthly Review Press).

Chadwick, P. K. (2009) *Schizophrenia: The Positive Perspective* 2nd edn (London: Routledge).

Charon, R., Banks, J. T., Connelly, J. E., Hawkins, A.H., Hunter, K. M., Jones, A. H., Lancaster, T., Hart, R. and Gardener S. (1995) 'Literature and Medicine: Contributions to Clinical Practice', *Annals of Internal Medicine*, 122, 599–606.

Cheng, Y.-J. (1999) *Heralds of the Postmodern: Madness and Fiction in Conrad, Woolf, and Lessing Studies in Literary Criticism and Theory* (New York: Peter Lang).

Cochrane, R. and Sashidharan, S. P. (1995) *Mental Health and Ethnic Minorities: A Review of the Literature and Implications for Services* (Birmingham: University of Birmingham and Northern Birmingham Mental Health Trust).

Cockburn, A. and St Clair, J. (2004) *Imperial Crusades: Iraq, Afghanistan, and Yugoslavia* (New York: Verso).

Colley, A. C. (1983) *Tennyson and Madness* (Athens, Ga.: University of Georgia Press).

Conrad, J. (1899) *Heart of Darkness* (London: Penguin, 2007).

Crawford, P. (2002) *Nothing Purple, Nothing Black* (Lewes: The Book Guild).

—— (2002) *Politics in History in William Golding: The World Turned Upside Down* (Columbia and London: University of Missouri Press).

Crawford, P. and Baker, C. (2009) 'Literature and Madness: A Survey of Fiction for Students and Professionals', *Journal of Medical Humanities*, 30, 237–251.

Crawford, P., Brown, B. J., Tischler, V., Mooney-Smith, L. and Baker, C. (2010) 'Health Humanities: The Future of Medical Humanities', unpublished manuscript under review with *Mental Health Review*.

Crompton, D. (1985) *A View from the Spire: William Golding's Later Novels.* Edited and Completed by J. Briggs (Oxford: Blackwell).

Dalal, F. (1988) 'The Racism of Jung', *Race and Class*, 29:3, 1–22.

Dalrymple, T. (1995) *So Little Done: The Testament of a Serial Killer* (London: Andre Deutsch).

Dawson, J. (1985) *The Ha-Ha* (London: Virago).

Day, E. and Smith, I. (2009) 'Literary and Biographical Perspectives on Substance Use' in F. Oyebode (ed.) *Mindreadings: Literature and Psychiatry* (London: Royal College of Psychiatry).

de Beaugrande, Robert (1994) 'Literary Theories and the Concept of Madness' in B. Rieger (ed.) *Dionysus in Literature: Essays on Literary Madness* (Bowling Green: Bowling Green University Popular Press).

Dein, S. and Lipsedge, M. (1998) 'Negotiating Across Culture, Race and Religion in the Inner City' in S. Okpaku (ed.) *Clinical Methods in Transcultural Psychiatry* (Washington: American Psychiatric Press).

Delgado, J. M. R. (1969) *Physical Control of the Mind: Toward a Psychocivilized Society* (New York: Harper and Row).

Department of Health (2003) *Inside outside: Improving Mental Health Services for Black and Minority Ethnic Communities in England* (London: Nimhe).

DePorte, M. V. (1974) *Nightmares and Hobby Horses: Swift, Sterne, and Augustan Ideas of Madness* (San Marino: Huntington Library).

Dick, B. F. (1987) *William Golding* Revised edn (Boston: Twayne)

Dick, P. K. (1977) *A Scanner Darkly* (London: Millennium/Gollancz, 1999).

Digby, A. (1985) *Madness, Morality and Medicine: A Study of the York Retreat, 1796–1914* (Cambridge: Cambridge University Press).

Diski, J. (1990) *Then Again* (London: Vintage, 1991).

Dozier, E. P. (1983) *The Pueblo Indians of North America* (Prospect Heights, IL: Waveland Press).

Du Bois, W. E. B. (1903) *The Souls of Black Folk* (Chicago: A. C. McClurg and Co.).

Dudman, C. (2004) *98 Reasons for Being* (London: Hodder and Stoughton, 2004).

Duggan, L. (2000) *Sapphic Slashers: Sex, Violence, and American Modernity* (Durham: Duke University Press).

Duncker, P. (1996) *Hallucinating Foucault* (London: Picador, 1997).

Dykes, M. and McGhie, A. (1976) 'A Comparative Study of Attentional Strategies in Schizophrenic and Highly Creative Normal Subjects', *British Journal of Psychiatry*, 128, 50–56.

Eagleton, T. (1987) 'Awakening from Modernity', *Times Literary Supplement*, 20 February, 194.

—— (1996) *The Illusions of Postmodernism* (Oxford: Blackwell).

Edel, L. (1959) *Literary Biography* (Garden City, NY: Anchor/Doubleday).

Ellestrom, L. (2002) *Divine Madness: On Interpreting Literature, Music, and the Visual Arts Ironically* (Lewisburg, PA.: Bucknell University Press).

Ellison, R. (1952) *Invisible Man* (New York: Random House).

Emmott, C. (2002) ' "Split Selves" in Fiction and Medical "Life Stories": Cognitive Linguistic Theory and Narrative Practice' in E. Semino and J. Culpeper (eds) *Cognitive Stylistics: Language and Cognition in Text Analysis* (Amsterdam: John Benjamins).

Eugenides, J. (1993) *The Virgin Suicides* (London: Abacus, 2001).

Evans, M. (2003) 'Roles for Literature in Medical Education', *Advances in Psychiatric Treatment*, 9, 380–386.

Everett, P. L. (2001) *Erasure* (London: Faber and Faber, 2006).

Eysenck, H. J. (1993) 'Creativity and Personality: Suggestions for a Theory', *Psychological Inquiry*, 4, 147–178.

Fanon, F. (1961) *Les Damnés de la Terre (The Wretched of the Earth)* (Paris: Francoise Maspero).

—— (1952) *Peau Noire, Masques Blancs (Black Skin, White Masks)* (Paris: Edition de Seuil).

—— (1964) *Towards the African Revolution* Trans. F. Maspero. (New York: Grove Press).

Faulks, S. (2005) *Human Traces* (London: Vintage, 2006).

Feder, L. (1980) *Madness in Literature* (Guildford: Princeton University Press).

Fee, D. (ed.) (2000) *Pathology and the Postmodern: Mental Illness as Discourse and Experience* (London: Sage).

Felman, S. (1985) *Writing and Madness: (literature/philosophy/psychoanalysis)* Trans. M. N. Evans (California: Stanford University Press, 2003).

Fernando, S. (2005) 'Multicultural Mental Health Services: Projects for Minority Ethnic Communities in England', *Transcultural Psychiatry*, 42:3, 420–436.

Forster, E. M. (1927) *Aspects of the Novel and Related Writings* (London: Edward Arnold, 1974).

Foucault, M. (1965) *Madness and Civilization: A History of Insanity in the Age of Reason* Trans. R. Howard (New York: Random House).

Foulds, A. (2009) *The Quickening Maze* (London: Jonathan Cape).

Fowles, J. (1963) *The Collector* (London: Vintage, 1998).

Frame, J. (1961) *Faces in the Water* (London: The Women's Press, 1996).

Friedman, E. G. (1989) 'A Conversation with Kathy Acker', *A Review of Contemporary Fiction*, 9:3, date accessed 26 December 2009, http://www.dalke-yarchive.com/catalog/show_comment/216

Frosh, S. (1991) *Identity Crisis: Modernity, Psychoanalysis and the Self* (Basingstoke: Macmillan).

Furedi, F. (2004) *Therapy Culture: Cultivating Vulnerability in an Uncertain Age* (London: Routledge).

Furst, L. R. (2002) *Idioms of Distress: Psychosomatic Disorders in Medical and Imaginative Literature* (Albany: State University of New York Press).

Gale, P. (2007) *Notes from an Exhibition* (London: Harper Perennial, 2008).

—— (2007a) 'The Comforts of Fiction' in P. Gale *Notes From An Exhibition, P. S. appendix* (London: Harper Perennial, 2008.)

Gandhi, L. (1998) *Postcolonial Theory: A Critical Introduction* (New York: Columbia University Press).

Garton, S. (2009) 'Seeking Refuge: Why Asylum Facilities Might Still be Relevant for Mental Health Care Services Today', *Health and History*, 11:1, 25–45.

Geekie, J. and Read, J. (2009) *Making Sense of Madness: Contesting the Meaning of Schizophrenia* (East Sussex: Routledge).

General Medical Council. (2006) *Good Medical Practice*, date accessed 31 December 2009, http://www.gmc-uk.org/guidance/good_medical_practice.asp

George, O. (2001) 'Alice Walker's Africa: Globalization and the Province of Fiction', *Comparative Literature*, 53:4, 354–372.

Giddens, A. (1990) *The Consequences of Modernity* (Cambridge: Polity Press).

Gilbert, S. M. and Gubar, S. (1979) *The Madwoman in the Attic: The Woman Writer and the Nineteenth-Century Literary Imagination* (New Haven, Conn. and London: Yale University Press, 2000).

Glazer, E. (2009) 'Rephrasing the Madness and Creativity Debate: What Is the Nature of the Creativity Construct?', *Personality and Individual Differences*, 46, 755–764.

Gleyzer, R., Felthous, A. R. and Holzer, C. E. (2002) 'Animal Cruelty and Psychiatric Disorders', *The Journal of the American Academy of Psychiatry and the Law*, 30, 257–265.

Goffman, E. (1961) *Asylums* (London: Penguin, 1991).

Golding, W. (1982) *A Moving Target* (London: Faber and Faber).

—— (1980) *Darkness Visible* (London: Faber and Faber).

—— (1970) *The Hot Gates and Other Occasional Pieces* (London: Faber and Faber).

—— (1985) *The Paper Men* (London: Faber and Faber).

Gooch, S. (1980) *The Double Helix of the Mind* (New York: Harper Collins).

Gramsci, A. (1971) *Selections from the Prison Notebooks* (London: Lawrence and Wishart).

Grasi, E. and Lorch, M. (1986) *Folly and Insanity in Renaissance Literature* (New York: State University of New York).

Gray, B., Robinson, C. A., Seddon, D. and Roberts, A. (2009) 'An Emotive Subject: Insights from Social, Voluntary and Healthcare Professionals into the Feelings of Family Carers for People with Mental Health Problems', *Health and Social Care in the Community*, 17:2, 125–132.

Grob, G. (1994) *The Mad Among Us: A History of the Care of America's Mentally Ill* (New York: The Free Press).

Guba, E. G. and Lincoln, Y. S. (1994) 'Competing Paradigms in Qualitative Research' in Denzin, N. K. and Lincoln, Y. S. (eds) *Handbook of Qualitative Research* (Thousand Oaks, CA: Sage).

Haffenden, J. (1985) *Novelists in Interview* (London: Methuen).

Hall, S. (1992). 'New Ethnicities' in J. Donald and A. Ratansi (eds) *'Race' Culture and Difference* (London: Sage).

Hare, R. D. (1993) *Without Conscience: The Chilling World of Psychopaths Among Us* (New York: The Guildford Press, 1999).

Harper, S. (2003) *Insanity, Individuals and Society in Late-Medieval English Literature: The Subject of Madness* (Lewiston, N.Y. and Lampeter: Edwin Mellen Press).

Harris, G. (2009) 'Drug Makers Are Advocacy Group's Biggest Donors', *New York Times*, date accessed 21 October 2009, http://www.nytimes.com/2009/10/22/health/22nami.html?_r=3

Healy, D. (1997) *The Antidepressant Era* (Cambridge, Mass.: Harvard University Press).

Heller, J. (1961) *Catch-22* (London: Vintage, 1994).

Henderson, D. J. (1994) 'Commentary on Women's Voices in Nineteenth Century Medical Discourse: A Step Towards Deconstructing Science', *Awhonn's Women's Health Nursing Scan*, 8, 22.

Hershkowitz, D. (1998) *The Madness of Epic: Reading Insanity from Homer to Statius* (Oxford: Clarendon Press).

Hickling, F. W. (2002) 'The Political Misuse of Psychiatry: An African-Caribbean Perspective', *The Journal of the American Academy of Psychiatry and the Law*, 30, 112–119.

Hill, S. (1972) *The Bird of Night* (London: Penguin, 1981).

Hinsie, J. and Campbell, R. (1970) *Psychiatric Dictionary* 4th edn (New York: Oxford University Press).

Holloway, K. F. G. (1990) 'Revision and (Re)membrance: A Theory of Literary Structures in Literature by African American Women Writers', *Black American Literature Forum*, 24:4, 617–631.

hooks, b. (1990) 'Postmodern Blackness' in b. hooks. *Yearning: Race, Gender, and Cultural Politics* (Boston, MA: South End Press).

Horgan, J. (2005). 'The Forgotten Era of Brain Chips', *Scientific American*, 93:4, 66–73.

Hountondji, P. J. (1983) *African Philosophy: Myth and Reality* Trans. H. Evans and J. Ree. (Bloomington: Indiana University Press).

Howitt, D. and Owusu-Bempah, J. (1994) *The Racism of Psychology: Time for Change* (New York: Prentice Hall).

Ignatieff, M. (1992) *Scar Tissue* (London: Vintage).

Ingram, A. (1991) *The Madhouse of Language: Writing and Reading Madness in the Eighteenth Century* (London: Routledge).

Jahner, E. A. (1994) 'Leslie Marmon Silko' in A. Wiget (ed.) *Dictionary of Native American Literature* (New York: Garland).

Jameson, F. (1991) *Postmodernism or, the Cultural Logic of Late Capitalism* (London: Verso, 1992).

Jamison, Kay Redfield. (1995) *An Unquiet Mind: A Memoir of Moods and Madness* (London: Picador, 1996).

—— (1993) *Touched With Fire: Manic-depressive Illness and the Artistic Temperament* (New York: Free Press, 1994).

—— (1989) 'Mood Disorders and Patterns of Creativity in British Writers and Artists', *British Journal of Psychiatry*, 52, 125–134.

Jarvis, B. (1998) *Postmodern Cartographies: The Geographical Imagination in Contemporary American Culture* (New York: St Martin's Press).

Jaspers, K. (1963) *General Psychopathology* 7th edn, Trans. J. Hoenig and W. Hamilton (Manchester: Manchester University Press).

Jenkins, A. (1981) 'The Cambridge Debate, Continued', *Times Literary Supplement*, 30 January, 112.

Johnson, S. (1750) *The Rambler* 4, 31 March.

Jung, C. G. (1985) *The Practice of Psychotherapy: Essays on the Psychology of the Transference and Other Subjects* Trans. R. F. C. Hull (New Jersey: Princeton University Press).

Juno, A. and Vale, V. (1984) 'Interview by A. Juno and Vale' in V. Vale and A. Juno (eds) *RE/Search 8/9: J. G. Ballard* (San Francisco: V/Search Publications).

Kandell, J. (2001) 'Richard E. Schultes: Trailblazing Authority on Hallucinogenic Plants', *New York Times*, 13 April 2001, C11.

Kanneh, K. (1995) 'Feminism and the Colonial Body' in W. Ashcroft, G. Griffiths and H. Tiffin (eds) *The Post-Colonial Studies Reader* (New York: Routledge).

Katzenbach, John (2004) *The Madman's Tale* (London: Corgi, 2005).

Kean, D. (2009) 'I Just Don't Want to Go There. Interview with Melvyn Bragg', *The Independent on Sunday*, 22 February 2009, 22–23.

Keating, F. (2007) 'African and Caribbean Men and Mental Health: A Race Equality Foundation Briefing Paper', *Better Health Briefing no. 5* (London: Race Equality Foundation).

Keitel, E. (1989) *Reading Psychosis* Trans. A. Ball (Oxford: Blackwell).

Kermode, F. and Golding, W. (1959) 'The Meaning of it All', *Books and Bookmen*, October, 9–10.

Kesey, K. (1962) *One Flew Over The Cuckoo's Nest* (London: Penguin, 2005).

Kleinman, A. M. (1977) 'Depression, Somatization and the "New Cross-Cultural Psychiatry"', *Social Science and Medicine*, 11, 3–10.

Koolish, L. (2001) '"To be Loved and Cry Shame": A Psychological Reading of Toni Morrison's *Beloved*', *MELUS* (Multi Ethnic Literature of the United States), 26:4, 169–195.

Kramer, P. D. (1994) *Listening to Prozac* (London: Fourth Estate).

Kräupl-Taylor, F. (1969) 'Prokalectic Therapies. Derived from Psychoanalytic Technique', *British Journal of Psychiatry*, 115, 407–419.

Laing, R. D. (1960) *The Divided Self: An Existential Study in Sanity and Madness* (London: Penguin, 1990).

Laing, R. D. and Esterson, A. (1964) *Sanity, Madness and the Family* (Harmondsworth: Penguin Books).

Lamb, W. (ed.) (2003) *Couldn't Keep It to Myself: Wally Lamb and the Women of York Correctional Institute* (London: Harper Collins, 2004).

—— (1998) *I Know This Much Is True* (London: Harper Collins, 2000).

—— (2008) *The Hour I First Believed* (London: Harper, 2009).

Lane, C. (2007) *Shyness: How Normal Behaviour Became a Sickness* (New Haven and London: Yale University Press).

Lange, R. J. G. (1998) *Gender Identity and Madness in the Nineteenth-Century Novel* (Lewiston, N.J. and Lampeter: Edwin Mellen Press).

Lessing, D. (1971) *Briefing for a Descent into Hell* (London: Flamingo).

—— (1962) *The Golden Notebook* (London: Flamingo, 1993).

Lewis, G. and Appleby, L. (1988) 'Personality Disorder: the Patients Psychiatrists Dislike', *British Journal of Psychiatry*, 153, 44–49.

Lewis, G., Croft-Jefferys, C. and David, A. (1990) 'Are British Psychiatrists Racist?' *British Journal of Psychiatry*, 157, 410–415.

Lincoln, K. (1983) *Native American Renaissance* (Berkeley and Los Angeles: University of California Press).

Lindauer, M. S. (1994) 'Are Creative Writers Mad? An Empirical Perspective' in B. Rieger (ed.) *Dionysus in Literature: Essays on Literary Madness* (Bowling Green: Bowling Green University Popular Press).

Lipsedge, M. (1994) 'Dangerous Stereotypes', *Journal of Forensic Psychiatry & Psychology*, 5:1, 14–19.

Littlewood, R. and Lipsedge, M. (1982) *Aliens and Alienists: Ethnic Minorities and Psychiatry* (Harmondsworth: Penguin).

Lodge, David (1975) *Changing Places* (London: Secker and Warburg).

—— (2002) *Consciousness and the Novel* (London: Secker and Warburg).

—— (1984) *Small World* (London: Secker and Warburg).

—— (1977) *The Modes of Modern Writing: Metaphor, Metonymy, and the Typology of Modern Literature* (London: Arnold).

Logan, P. M. (1997) *Nerves and Narratives: A Cultural History of Hysteria in Nineteenth-Century British Prose* (Berkeley, Calif. and London: University of California Press).

Louis-Courvoisier, M. and Wenger, A. (2005) 'How to Make the Most of History and Literature in the Teaching of Medical Humanities: the Experience of the University of Geneva', *Medical Humanities*, 31, 51–54.

Lupack, B. T. (1994) 'Inmates Running the Asylum: The Institution in Contemporary American Fiction' in B. Rieger (ed.) *Dionysus in Literature: Essays on Literary Madness* (Bowling Green: Bowling Green University Popular Press).

—— (1995) *Insanity as Redemption in Contemporary American Fiction: Inmates Running the Asylum* (Gainesville: University Press of Florida).

Lyotard, J.-F. (1984) *The Postmodern Condition: A Report on Knowledge* Trans. G. Bennington and B. Massumi (Manchester: Manchester University Press).

Macdonald J. M. (1963) 'The Threat to Kill', *American Journal of Psychiatry*, 120, 125–130.

Mackenzie, H. (1771) *The Man of Feeling* (Oxford: Oxford University Press, 2009).

MacLennan, G. (1992) *Lucid Interval: Subjective Writing and Madness in History* (Leicester and London: Leicester University Press).

Martin, M. (1987) *Mad Women in Romantic Writing* (Brighton: Harvester).

Mason-John, V. (ed.) (1995) *Talking Black* (London: Cassell).

McCarron, K. (1995) *The Coincidence of Opposites: William Golding's Later Fiction* (Sheffield: Sheffield Academic Press).

McCarthy, P. (1990) *'The Twisted Mind': Madness in Herman Melville's Fiction* (Iowa City: University of Iowa Press).

McEwan, I. (1997) *Enduring Love* (London: Vintage, 1998).

McGee, P. and Johnson, M. (2004) 'Editors' Introduction', *Diversity in Health and Social Care*, 1, 1–4.

McGovern, D. and Cope, R. (1987) 'The Compulsory Detention of Males from Different Ethnic Minorities, with Special Reference to Offender Patients', *British Journal of Psychiatry*, 150, 505–512.

McGrath, P. (1996) *Asylum* (London: Penguin, 1997).

—— (2002) 'Problem of Drawing from Psychiatry for a Fiction Writer', *Psychiatric Bulletin*, 26, 140–143.

—— (1990) *Spider* (London: Penguin, 2002).

—— (2008) *Trauma* (London: Bloomsbury, 2009).

Mead, M. (1959) 'Mental Health in the World Perspective' in M. K. Opler (ed.) *Culture and Mental Health: Cross-cultural Studies* (New York: Macmillan Company).

Melley, T. (2000) *Empire of Conspiracy: The Culture of Paranoia in Postmodern America* (New York: Cornell University Press).

Menicucci, G. M. (2005) 'Sexual Torture, Rendering, Practices, Manuals', *ISIM Review*, 16, 18–19.

Menya, D. (1993) Bookshelf: 'Possessing the Secret of Joy' by Alice Walker, *The Lancet*, 341: 423

Metzger, C. R. (1989) *F. Scott Fitzgerald's Psychiatric Novel: Nicole's Case, Dick's Case* (New York: Lang).

Micale, M. and Porter, R. (eds) (1994) *Discovering the History of Psychiatry* (New York and Oxford: Oxford University Press).

Miller, K. (1985) *Doubles: Studies in Literary History* (Oxford: Oxford University Press).

Mohanty, C. T. (1996) 'Under Western Eyes: Feminist Scholarship and Colonial Discourses' in P. Mongia (ed.) *Contemporary Postcolonial Theory: A Reader* (New York: Arnold).

Montsho, Q. (1995) 'Behind Locked Doors' in V. Mason-John (ed.) *Talking Black* (London: Cassell).

Moore Campbell, B. (2005) *72 Hour Hold* (New York: Anchor Books, 2006).

Morgan, A. (ed.) (2008) *Being Human: Reflections on Mental Distress in Society* (Ross-on-Wye: PCCS Books).

Morrison, T. (1987) *Beloved* (New York: Alfred A. Knopf).

—— (1977) *Song of Solomon*. New York: Alfred A. Knopf.

—— (1990) 'Unspeakable Things Unspoken: The Afro-American Presence in American Literature' in H. Bloom (ed.) *Modern Critical Views: Toni Morrison* (New York: Chelsea).

Mosher, L. R. and Hendrix, V. (2004) *Soteria: Through Madness to Deliverance* (Philadelphia: Xlibris).

Motion, A. (2009) 'The Asylum in the Forest', *The Guardian*, 2 May, 10.

Motz, A. (2001) *The Psychology of Female Violence: Crimes Against the Body* (East Sussex: Brunner-Routledge).

National Institute for Mental Health in England. (2003) *Personality Disorder: No Longer a Diagnosis of Exclusion* (London: Department of Health).

Oandasan, W. (1997) 'A Familiar Love Component of Love in Ceremony' in W. Fleck (ed.) *Critical Perspectives on Native American Fiction* (Pueblo, CO: Passeggiata Press).

O'Connor, J. (1997) *Dramatizing Dementia: Madness in the Plays of Tennessee Williams* (Bowling Green, OH: Bowling Green State University Popular Press).

O'Donnell, Patrick (2000) *Latent Destinies: Cultural Paranoia and Contemporary U.S. Narrative* (Durham: Duke University Press).

O'Reilly, T., Dunbar, R. and Bentall, R. P. (2001) 'Schizotypy and Creativity: an Evolutionary Connection?' *Personality and Individual Differences*, 31, 1067–1078.

Orlando, V. (2003) *Of Suffocated Hearts and Tortured Souls: Seeking Subjecthood Through Madness in Francophone Women's Writing of Africa and the Caribbean* (Oxford: Lanham).

Owens, L. (1994) *Other Destinies: Understanding the American Indian Novel* (Norman, OK: University of Oklahoma Press).

Oyebode, F. (2009a) 'Autobiographical Narrative and Psychiatry' in F. Oyebode (ed.) *Mindreadings: Literature and Psychiatry* (London: Royal College of Psychiatry).

—— (2009b) 'Fictional Narrative in Psychiatry' in F. Oyebode (ed.) *Mindreadings: Literature and Psychiatry* (London: Royal College of Psychiatry).

—— (ed.) (2009c) *Mindreadings: Literature and Psychiatry* (London: Royal College of Psychiatry).

Oyewumi, O. (2001) 'Alice in Motherland: Reading Alice Walker on Africa and Screening the Color "Black"', *Jenda: A Journal of Culture and African Women's Studies*, 1:2, date accessed 22 July 2009, http://www.jendajournal.com/vol1.2/oyewumi.html

Parker, I., Georgaca, E., Harper, D., Mclaughlin, T. and Stowell-Smith, M. (1995) *Deconstructing Psychopathology* (London: Sage).

Perkins Gilman, C. (1892) *The Yellow Wallpaper* (New York: Dover, 1997).

Piercy, M. (1976) *Woman on the Edge of Time* (London: Women's Press, 2000).

Pickering, G. (1974) *Creative Malady* (London: George Allen and Unwin).

Plath, S. (1963) *The Bell Jar* (New York: Bantam).

Platizky, R. (1989) *A Blueprint of His Dissent: Madness and Method in Tennyson's Poetry* (Lewisburg, PA.: Bucknell University Press).

Pope, R. (2005) *Creativity: Theory, History, Practice* (London: Routledge).

Porter, R. (1991) *The Faber Book of Madness* (London: Faber and Faber).

—— (2002) *Madness: A brief history* (Oxford: Oxford University Press).

Post, F. (1996) 'Verbal Creativity, Depression and Alcoholism. An Investigation of One Hundred American and British Writers', *British Journal of Psychiatry*, 168, 545–555.

Pratt, W. (1996) *Singing the Chaos: Madness and Wisdom in Modern Poetry* (Columbia: University of Missouri Press).

Pynchon, T. (1965) *The Crying of Lot 49* (London: Vintage, 2000).

Quayson, A. (2000) *Postcolonialism. Theory, Practice or Process?* (Cambridge: Polity Press).

Quirk, A. and Lelliott, P. (2001) 'What Do We Know about Life on Acute Psychiatric Wards in the Uk? A Review of the Research Evidence', *Social Science & Medicine*, 53, 1565–1574.

Rack, P. (1982) *Race, Culture and Mental Disorder* (London: Tavistock Publications).

Racine, L. (2009) 'Applying Antonio Gramsci's philosophy to postcolonial feminist social and political activism in nursing', *Nursing Philosophy*, 10, 180–190.

Ramsay, R. (1990) 'Community Care or Community Neglect?', *British Journal of Psychiatry*, 14:4, 232–233.

Reed, P. B. (1974) *Nebuchadnezzar's Children: Conventions of Madness in Middle English Literature* (New Haven and London: Yale University Press).

Reid, G. J. (2002) *A Re-Examination of Tragedy and Madness in Eight Selected Plays from the Greeks to the 20th Century* (Lewiston, N.Y. and Lampter: Edwin Mellen Press).

Revell, G. (1984) 'Interview by Graeme Revell' in Vale, V. and Juno, A. (eds) *RE/Search 8/9: J. G. Ballard* (San Francisco: V/Search Publications).

Ricciardi, M. (1982) *African Saga* (London: Collins).

Rice, N. M. (2004) 'Ceremonies That Defeat Despair: "Things Which Don't Shift and Grow Are Dead Things": A Reading of Leslie Marmon Silko's *Ceremony*', date accessed 13 June 2006, http://www.womenwriters.net/summer04/reviews/silko.html

Richards, R., Kinney, D., Lundy, I. and Benet, M. (1998) 'Creativity in Manic-Depressives, Cyclothymes, and Their Normal First-Degree Relatives', *Journal of Abnormal Psychology*, 97, 281–288.

Rider Haggard, H. (1887) *She: A History of Adventure* (Oxford: Oxford World Classics, 2008).

Rieger, B. M. (1994a) 'Introduction. Dionysus in Literature: Essays on Literary Madness' in B. Rieger (ed.) *Dionysus in Literature: Essays on Literary Madness* (Bowling Green: Bowling Green University Popular Press).

—— (1994b) 'The Class Flew Over the Cuckoo's Nest: A Theme Course on "Madness in Literature"' in B. Rieger (ed.) *Dionysus in Literature: Essays on Literary Madness* (Bowling Green: Bowling Green University Popular Press).

Rohrer, G. (2005) *Mental Health in Literature: Literary lunacy and lucidity* (Chicago: Lyceum Books Inc).

Roszak, T. (1971) *The Making of a Counter-Culture: Reflections on the Technocratic Society and Its Youthful Opposition* (London: Faber and Faber).

Roth, M. and Kroll, J. (1986) *The Reality of Mental Illness* (Cambridge: Cambridge University Press).

Rothenberg, A. (1994) *Creativity and Madness: New Findings and Old Stereotypes* (Baltimore and London: The Johns Hopkins University Press).

Rothman, D. (1970) *The Discovery of the Asylum* (Boston: Little, Brown).

Royal College of Psychiatrists. (2007) *Bipolar Disorder*, date accessed 12/12/09, http://www.rcpsych.ac.uk/mentalhealthinfo/problems/bipolardisorder/bipolardisorder.aspx

—— (2009) *Good Psychiatric Practice* 3rd edn, date accessed 31 December 2009, http://www.rcspsych.ac.uk/files/pdfversion/CR154.pdf

Rubens, B. (1969) *The Elected Member* (London: Abacus, 2009).

Sacks, O. (1984) *A Leg to Stand On* (London: Duckworth).

Said, E. (1979) *Orientalism* (New York: Vintage).

Salkeld, D. (1993) *Madness and Drama in the Age of Shakespeare* (Manchester: Manchester University Press).

Sass, L. A. (1992) *Madness and Modernism: Insanity in the Light of Modern Art, Literature, and Thought* (Cambridge, Mass. and London: Harvard University Press).

Saunders, C. and Macnaughton, J. (2005) *Madness and Creativity in Literature and Culture* (London, Palgrave).

Sayer, P. (1988) *The Comforts of Madness* (London: Sceptre 1992).

Schernhammer, E. (2005) 'Taking Their Own Lives: The High Rate of Physician Suicide', *New England Journal of Medicine*, 352:24, 2473–2476.

Schernhammer, E. and Colditz, G. A. (2004) 'Suicide Rates Among Physicians: A Quantitative and Gender Assessment (Meta-Analysis)', *American Journal of Psychiatry*, 161, 2295–2302.

Schildkraut J. J. and Otero A. (1996) *Depression and the Spiritual in Modern Art: Homage to Miró* (Chichester: John Wiley and Sons).

Schultes, R. E. and Von Reis, S. (1995) *Ethnobotany: Evolution of a Discipline* (New York: Dioscorides Press).

Scull, A. (1984) *Decarceration: Community Treatment and the Deviant: A Radical View* (New York: Prentice Hall).

—— (1979) *Museums of Madness: The Social Organization of Insanity in Nineteenth-Century England* (New York: St Martin's Press).

—— (1991) 'Psychiatry and Social Control in the Nineteenth and Twentieth Centuries', *History of Psychiatry*, 2, 149–169.

—— (1999) 'Rethinking the History of Asylumdom' in J. Melling and B. Forsyth (eds) *Insanity, Institutions and Society, 1800–1914: A Social History of Madness in Comparative Perspective* (London: Routledge).

—— (1989) *Social Order/Mental Disorder: Anglo-American Psychiatry in Historical Perspective* (Berkeley: University of California Press).

—— (2006) *The Insanity of Place/The Place of Insanity: Essays on the History of Psychiatry* (London: Routledge).

Self, W. (2004) *Dr Mukti and Other Tales of Woe* (London: Bloomsbury).

Semino, E. and Culpeper, J. (2002) *Cognitive Stylistics: Language and Cognition in Text Analysis* (Amsterdam: John Benjamins).

Senaha, E. (1996) *Sex, Drugs and Madness in Poetry from William Blake to Christina Rossetti: Women's Pain, Women's Pleasure* (Lewiston, N.J. and Lampeter: Mellen University Press).

Shem, Samuel. (1997) *Mount Misery* (New York: Ballantine Books, 1998).
—— (1978) *The House of God* (London: Black Swan Books, 1985).
Shepherd, B. (2001) *A War of Nerves: Soldiers and Psychiatrists 1914–1994* (London: Cape).
Shorter, E. (1997) *A History of Psychiatry: From the Era of the Asylum to the Age of Prozac* (New York: Wiley).
—— (1992) *From Paralysis to Fatigue: A History of Psychosomatic Illness in the Modern Era* (New York: Free Press).
Showalter, E. (1997) *Hystories* (London: Picador, 1998).
—— (1987) *The Female Malady: Women, Madness and English Culture 1830–1980* (London: Virago Press).
Silko, L. M. (1977) *Ceremony* (New York: Viking).
Simpson, P. (ed.) (1993) *Language, Ideology and Point of View* (London: Routledge).
Sims, A. (2003) *Symptoms in the Mind: An Introduction to Descriptive Psychopathology* (Philadelphia: Elsevier Science).
Slim, I. (1969) *Pimp: The Story of My Life* (Los Angeles: Holloway House).
Small, H. (1996) *Love's Madness: Medicine, the Novel, and Female Insanity, 1800–1865* (Oxford: Clarendon Press).
Smith, J. (1992) 'Book Review: Genitally Does It: Possessing the Secret of Joy by Alice Walker', *The Independent Sunday Review*, 18 October 1992, 38.
Spivak, G. C. (1988) 'Can the Subaltern Speak?' in C. Nelson and L. Grossberg (eds) *Marxism and the Interpretation of Culture* (Urbana and Chicago: University of Illinois Press).
Stempsey, W. E. (1999) 'The Quarantine of Philosophy in Medical Education: Why Teaching the Humanities May Not Produce Humane Physicians', *Medicine, Health Care and Philosophy*, 2, 3–9.
Storey, E. (1986) *A Right to Song: The Life of John Clare* (London: Methuen).
Styron, W. (1990) *Darkness Visible* (London: Vintage Classics, 2001).
Sullivan, P. (1998) 'Progress or Neglect? Reviewing the Impact of Care in the Community for the Severely Mentally Ill', *Critical Social Policy*, 18:55, 193–213.
Szasz, T. (1974) *The Myth Of Mental Illness* (New York: Perennial, 2003).
Taguba, A. M. (2004) *Article 15–6 Investigation of the 800th Military Police Brigade* (Fort McPherson, GA: Department of the Army).
Thiher, A. (1999) *Revels in Madness: Insanity in Medicine and Literature* (Ann Arbor: University of Michigan Press).
Timpanaro, S. (1976) *The Freudian Slip: Psychoanalysis and Textual Criticism* (London: New Left Books).
Trotter, D. (2001) *Paranoid Modernism: Literary Experiment, Psychosis, and the Professionalization of English Society* (Oxford: Oxford University Press).
Ussher J. (1991) *Women's Madness: Misogyny or Mental Illness?* (London: Harvester Wheatsheaf).
Vickers, S. (2006) *The Other Side of You* (London: Harper Perennial, 2007).
Vonnegut, K. (1969) *Slaughterhouse-Five* (New York: Dell, 1991).
Walker, A. (1992) *Possessing the Secret of Joy* (London: Vintage, 1993).
Waterfield Duisberg, K. (2003) *The Good Patient* (New York: St Martin's Press).
Waugh, P. (2005) 'Creative Writers and Psychopathology: The Cultural Consolations of "the Wound and the Bow" Thesis' in C. Saunders and J. Macnaughton (eds) *Madness and Creativity in Literature and Culture* (London: Palgrave).

Welshman, J. (2007) *Community Care in Perspective: Care, Control and Citizenship* (London: Palgrave Macmillan).

Whitaker, R. (2003) *Mad in America: Bad Science, Bad Medicine and the Enduring Mistreatment of the Mentally Ill* (New York: Perseus Books).

White, A. (1954) *Beyond the Glass* (London: Virago, 2006).

Widdowson, P. (1982) 'Introduction: The Crisis in English Studies' in P. Widdowson (ed.) *Re-Reading English* (London: Methuen).

Wiesenthal, C. (1997) *Figuring Madness in Nineteenth-Century Fiction* (Basingstoke: Macmillan).

Williams, R. (1984a) 'Cambridge English, Past and Present' in R. Williams (ed.) *Writing in Society* (New York: Verson).

—— (1984b) 'Crisis in English Studies' in R. Williams (ed.) *Writing in Society* (New York: Verson).

Wilson, A. (1952) *Hemlock and After* (London: Secker and Warburg).

Wilson, C. E. (2005) *Race and Racism in Literature* (Westport CT: Greenwood Publishing Group).

Wilson, T. P. (1994) *Navajo: Walking in Beauty* (San Francisco: Chronicle Books).

Wittkower, E. D. and Fried, J. (1958) 'Some Problems in Transcultural Psychiatry', *International Journal of Social Psychiatry*, 3:4, 245–252.

World Health Organisation (2008) *Eliminating Female Genital Mutilation: An Interagency Statement* (Geneva: WHO Press).

—— (1992) *The ICD-10 Classification of Mental and Behavioural Disorders* (Geneva: WHO Publications).

Wright, R. (1940) *Native Son* (New York: Harper).

—— (1957) *White Man Listen!* (New York: Doubleday).

Zola, I. K. (1972) 'Medicine as an Institution of Social Control', *Sociological Review*, 20, 487–504.

Film and Theatre

One Flew over the Cuckoo's Nest (Garrick Theatre, 2004 and 2006).

One Flew over the Cuckoo's Nest (Dir. Milos Forman, 1975).

Index

absolute terror, 39–43
abuses of power by psychiatric staff, 78–86
Acker, K.
　The Childlike Life of the Black Tarantula by the Black Tarantula, 27, 168, 169, 181–2
　Empire of the Senseless, 169–70, 181–2
　I Dreamt I Was a Nymphomaniac: Imagining, 168, 169
　Politics, 170–1
　postmodern madness and, 14, 159, 165–6, 168–71
　'William Burroughs's Realism', 166
additive approach to using literature in clinical education, 186
Adorno, T. W., 160
Adshead, G., 10, 56
African American dialect, 100–1
African American literature, 12, 99–109, 114–29
African Saga (Ricciardi), 118
Ahlzen, R., 186
Alexander, F. G., 62
alienated psychiatrists, 188–94
Allan, C., 6, 61
　Poppy Shakespeare, 11, 13, 88–91, 97–8, 132, 142, 148–9, 157
Allen, P. G., 113
Allen, W. M., 101
All in the Mind (Campbell), 188–92
Alvarez, A., 132
Alzheimer's disease, 126–7
American Psychiatric Association, 56
　DSM-4TR, 4, 6–7, 9
Amis, K.
　Stanley and the Women, 59, 184
Andreasen, N. C., 130
anti-psychiatry movements, 7, 86, 164
antisocial personality disorder (ASPD), 55, 56
Appignanesi, L., 8, 15, 56, 62

Apple, M. W., 108
Appleby, L., 10, 56
Appleyard, B., 155
Archer, M., 120
Aristotle, 131
Aronowitz, S., 108
'Artaud's Madness: The Absence of Work' (Callaghan), 22–3
Ashcroft, B., 107
Askey, R., 59
ASPD (antisocial personality disorder), 55, 56
Asylum (McGrath), 26
asylums
　abuses of power in, 78–86
　closure of, 86–90
　history of psychiatry and, 62–74
　as total institutions, 74–8
Asylums (Goffman), 10–11, 61, 76–8, 80, 82, 88, 90, 180
The Atrocity Exhibition (Ballard), 166
Auster, P., 14, 160
　The New York Trilogy, 165, 170, 174–5, 176
autobiography, 32, 146–8, 169–71, 186–7, 193
　See also The Bell Jar; Junky; An Unquiet Mind: A Memoir of Moods and Madness
Ayahuasca (*Banisteriopsis Caapi*), 43–4

'badness' in fiction, 52–9
'bad' representations of madness in fiction, 193
Bains, J., 102
Baker, C., 16, 36, 58, 131, 163, 174–5, 177, 186
Baldick, C., 14
Baldwin, J., 121
Ballard, J. G., 6
　The Atrocity Exhibition, 166
　Cocaine Nights, 47, 175
　Concrete Island, 175

Ballard, J. G. – *continued*
  Crash, 175
  High Rise, 46, 47, 175–6
  Kingdom Come, 46–7, 175
  Millennium People, 47, 175
  postmodern fiction and, 14, 160
  Super-Cannes, 47, 175
Banisteriopsis Caapi (Ayahuasca),
    43–4
Barham, P., 71, 86
Barker, P., 130
Barker, Pat
  Regeneration, 10, 61, 68–70
Barry, S., 6
  The Secret Scripture, 10, 61, 71–4, 77,
    78–9, 84–5, 86, 93, 190–1
Bartlett, P., 71, 86
Bateson, G., 94
battle fatigue, 109
  See also post-traumatic stress
    disorder
Baudrillard, J.
  notion of 'schizophrenic vertigo',
    14, 163, 171
Bavidge, M., 52
Becker, G., 130
The Bell Jar (Plath), 13, 85, 96, 130,
    132, 139–41, 157
Beloved (Morrison), 12–13, 121,
    122–5, 128–9
Beloved Stranger (Boylan), 38–9, 59
Bentall, R. P., 27, 31, 39, 130
  *Madness Explained: Psychosis and
    Human Nature*, 21–2
Berlin, M., 132
Berrios, G. E., 62
Bertens, H., 161
Beveridge, A., 185, 186
Bex, T., 8
Beyond the Glass (White), 6, 11, 28,
    62, 93–6
Bhabha, H. K., 108
Bhaya Nair, R., 8
Bhugra, D., 103
Bigler, W., 8
Biles, J. I., 155
biology *vs.* psychology, 64
bipolar affective disorder (BPAD),
    38–9, 85–6, 104, 142–6, 151–3

The Bird of Night (Hill), 13, 130, 133,
    143, 149, 151–5, 158
Black American literature, *See* African
    American literature
*Black Skin, White Masks (Peau Noir,
    Masques Blancs)* (Fanon), 100
borderline personality disorder (BPD),
    56–9
Boylan, C.
  Beloved Stranger, 38–9, 59
Boyle, M., 30–1
Boyle, T. C.
  Riven Rock, 10, 61, 65–8, 71, 131
BPAD (bipolar affective disorder),
    38–9, 85–6, 104, 142–6, 151–3
BPD (borderline personality disorder),
    56–9
Bracken, P., 164
Bradbury, M.
  The History Man, 149, 155
Bragg, M.
  Remember Me, 13, 132–3, 142,
    146–8, 157–8
Briefing for a Descent into Hell
    (Lessing), 9, 25, 28, 32–5, 37
Broer, L. R., 50–1
'The Broken Word' (Foulds), 139
Brown, B., 10
Brown, C.
  Manchild in the Promised Land, 101
Brown-Guillory, E., 117
Buckman, A. R., 117
Buras, K. L., 108
Burgess, A.
  A Clockwork Orange, 82, 165
Burke, A., 11, 102
Burke, M., 8
burnout, psychiatrist, 192
Burroughs, W. S.
  Acker on, 166
  cut-up/fold-in technique, 4, 27–8,
    159–60, 165–8
  drug addiction and, 43–6, 172–3
  intermingling of autobiography
    and fiction, 170
  Junky, 44
  Naked Lunch, 44–5, 166–8, 172–3,
    179–80
  Nova Express, 166, 167–8, 172–3

Burroughs, W. S. – *continued*
  psychotic texts and, 4, 165–8
  The Soft Machine, 166, 167–8, 172–3
  The Ticket That Exploded, 166,
    167–8, 172–3
  The Yage Letters, 43–4
Byrd, M., 8

Callaghan, P.
  'Artaud's Madness: The Absence of
    Work', 22–3
Cambridge English debate, 149–50
Camfield, G., 8
Campbell, A.
  All in the Mind, 188–92
Campbell, R., 11, 102
'Can the Subaltern Speak?' (Spivak), 108
Carey, L.
  Love in the Asylum, 6, 85–6, 97, 143
Carter, R., 131
Catch-22 (Heller), 70
celebratory madness, 22, 39, 43–8
Center, C., 188
Ceremony (Silko), 12, 108–14, 120–1
Césaire, A., 3
Chadwick, P. K.
  *Schizophrenia: The Positive
    Perspective*, 4, 31, 50
Changing Places (Lodge), 149
Charon, R., 111, 114, 186
Cheng, Y.-J., 8
*The Childlike Life of the Black Tarantula
  by the Black Tarantula* (Acker), 27,
  168, 169, 181–2
chronology of diagnostics, 67–8
Clare, J., 131–2, 137–9, 157
climacteric, 73
clinical education and literature,
  15–16, 184–94
A Clockwork Orange (Burgess), 82, 165
Cocaine Nights (Ballard), 47, 175
Cochrane, R., 10, 11–12, 102
Cockburn, A., 180
coherence of madness fictions, 15,
  26–8
Colditz, G. A., 189
Colin MacCabe affair, 149–50
The Collector (Fowles), 10, 92
Colley, A. C., 8

'The Comforts of Fiction' (Gale), 146
The Comforts of Madness (Sayer), 11,
  28, 32–3, 35–8, 39, 61, 79–80, 131
community-based care, 65, 86–90
Concrete Island (Ballard), 175
connectivity, 186
Conrad, J.
  Heart of Darkness, 118
Consciousness and the Novel (Lodge), 16
consolation fictions, 13, 132, 141–9,
  157–8
content of madness, 9, 30–9
continuum model of madness, 21–3,
  39–52
Cooper, D., 86, 164
Cope, R., 11, 102
Craig-Smith, G., 146
Crash (Ballard), 175
Crawford, P., 10, 15, 16, 36, 163,
  174–5, 177, 186
  Nothing Purple, Nothing Black, 9,
    40–1, 43, 52, 87
creativity and madness in fiction,
  13–14, 130–58
  consolation fictions, 13, 132, 141–9,
    157–8
  fragmentation, 12–13, 15, 96–7,
    132–42, 157, 159–74
  furor scribendi, 13, 133, 149–57, 158
criminal justice system, 10, 74–8, 92
critics, literary, 13, 133, 149–57, 158
Croft-Jefferys, C., 11–12, 102
Crompton, D., 154, 156
The Crying of Lot 49 (Pynchon), 6,
  172, 176–8, 180–1
cultural postmodernism, 14–15
cut-up/fold-in technique, 4, 27–8,
  159–60, 165–8

Dalal, F., 12, 118
Dalrymple, T. (A. Daniels)
  *So Little Done: The Testament of a
    Serial Killer*, 9, 53–6, 59
*Les Damnés de la Terre (The Wretched of
  the Earth)* (Fanon), 100
dangerous to self or others, 10, 65–6,
  73, 87–8, 92–3
Daniels, A., *See* Dalrymple, T.
Darkness Visible (Golding), 154

Darkness Visible (Styron), 140
David, A., 11–12, 102
Dawson, J.
    The Ha-Ha, 96
Day, E., 131
day-care facilities, 61, 88–91
De Beaugrande, R., 28–9, 49, 185
decarceration, 86–90
de Clerambault's syndrome
    (erotomania), 92, 150
decolonisation, 100
Dein, S., 192
Delgado, J. M. R., 83
delusions, 30–1, 32, 36–9, 73, 135–9,
    148–9, 165, 177, 185
dementia praecox, 65
    See also schizophrenia
Department of Health, 102
DePorte, M. V., 8
depression, 45, 71, 80, 140–4, 188,
    191
Derrida, J., 24, 163
descriptive psychopathology, 32
deviant behaviour, 1, 52–9, 175–6
*Diagnostic and Statistical Manual of
    Mental Disorders* (DSM-4TR),
    4, 6–7, 9
diagnostics, chronology of, 67–8
dialect, African American, 100–1
Dick, B. F., 155
Dick, P. K., 14
    A Scanner Darkly, 160, 173–4, 178–9
diegesis (telling)/diegetic texts, 27, 28
Digby, A., 62
Diski, J., 130
    Then Again, 13, 132–3, 135–7
dissociation, 12, 124–5, 128
diversity, ethnicity and madness in
    fiction, 11–13, 99–129
    in African American literature,
        99–109, 114–29
    fantasy, paranormal and science
        fiction, 121–5
    in Hispanic literature, 12, 121–2
    and identity, 126–7
    in Native American literature,
        109–14
    in post-colonial literature, 107–9,
        114–21

Diversity in Health and Social Care
    (McGee and Johnson), 99
*The Divided Self: An Existential Study
    in Sanity and Madness* (Laing),
    153–4, 174–5
double-consciousness, 101
Dozier, E. P., 112–13
Dr Mukti and Other Tales of Woe (Self),
    180
drug addiction, 168, 172–4, 181
drug-induced madness, 42–6
DSM-4TR (*Diagnostic and Statistical
    Manual of Mental Disorders*), 4,
    6–7, 9
Du Bois, W. E. B., 101
Dudman, C.
    98 Reasons for Being, 70–1, 84–5,
        190–1
Duggan, L., 8
Dunbar, P. L., 101, 126
Dunbar, R., 130
Duncker, P.
    Hallucinating Foucault, 13, 133,
        149–52, 154, 155
Dykes, M., 130

Eagleton, T., 160–1
eccentricity, 130
eclecticism, 65
economics, 83–4, 88, 108, 162
ECT (Electro Convulsive Therapy),
    80–2, 85, 101, 143
Edel, L., 130
The Elected Member (Rubens), 41–3
elective insanity, 47
Electro Convulsive Therapy (ECT),
    80–2, 85, 101, 143
*Eliminating Female Genital Mutilation:
    An Interagency Statement* (WHO),
    120
Ellestrom, L., 7
Ellison, R., 126
    Invisible Man, 101
Emmott, C., 8
empathic psychiatric care, 16, 84–6
Empire of the Senseless (Acker), 169–70,
    181–2
Enduring Love (McEwan), 10, 92, 150
English literature syllabus, 149–50

Erasure (Everett), 59, 126–9
erotomania (de Clerambault's syndrome), 92, 150
Esterson, A., 125
ethnicity and madness in fiction, *See* diversity, ethnicity and madness in fiction
Eugenides, J.
    The Virgin Suicides, 93
Evans, M., 186
Everett, P.
    Erasure, 59, 126–9
evil in fiction, 45, 52–9
experimental cures for madness, 82–6
extradiegetic texts, 28

Faces in the Water (Frame), 80–1, 187
familial expectations of women, 93–6
Fanon, F., 3–4
    Black Skin, White Masks (Peau Noir, Masques Blancs), 100
    Les Damnés de la Terre (The Wretched of the Earth), 100
fantasy, 121–5
Faulks, S., 67–8
    Human Traces, 10, 61, 62–5, 70, 71
Feder, L.
    Madness in Literature, 7, 20–1, 32–3, 39
Fee, D., 163
feigning madness, 70, 74–8
Felman, S., 7, 18–19, 23–4, 164
Felthous, A. R., 55
female genital mutilation, 109, 115–21
female sexuality, 70–3, 93
Fernando, S., 100
force-feeding, 65, 79
Forster, E. M., 185
Foucault, M., 22, 24, 62, 150, 163
Foulds, A.
    'The Broken Word', 139
    The Quickening Maze, 13, 132, 137–9, 141, 157
Fowles, J., 137
    The Collector, 10, 92
fragmentation, 12–13, 15, 96–7, 132–42, 157, 159–74

Frame, J.
    Faces in the Water, 80–1, 187
Fried, J., 102
Friedman, E. G., 169
Fromm-Reichmann, F., 24
Frosh, S., 6
Furedi, F., 131
furor scribendi, 13, 133, 149–57, 158
Furst, L. R., 8

Gale, P., 130
    'The Comforts of Fiction', 146
    Notes from an Exhibition, 13, 132, 142–6, 157
Gandhi, L., 107
Garton, S., 62
Geekie, J., 3, 9, 19, 31, 43, 185
gender and madness, 11, 15, 57, 93–6, 182
gendered diagnostics, 70–3
General Medical Council, 192–3
genetic heritage, 142, 145–6
George, O., 118, 119
Giddens, A., 14–15
Gilbert, S. M., 8, 15
Ginsberg, A., 43–4
Glazer, E., 132
Gleyzer, R., 55
Goffman, E.
    Asylums, 10–11, 61, 76–8, 80, 82, 88, 90, 180
The Golden Notebook (Lessing), 13, 24, 132, 133–5, 141
Golding, W.
    Darkness Visible, 154
    'Gradus ad Parnassum', 156
    The Paper Men, 13, 133, 149, 153–8
Gooch, S., 130
good mental health, defined, 11, 102
The Good Patient (Waterfield Duisberg), 57–9, 93, 189
'good' representations of madness in fiction, 193
'Gradus ad Parnassum' (Golding), 156
Gramsci, A., 11, 108
Grasi, E., 7–8
Gray, B., 59
Green, H.
    I Never Promised You a Rose Garden, 24

Griffiths, G., 107
Grob, G., 62
Guba, E. G., 107
Gubar, S., 8, 15
guilt, 59–60, 65–7, 146–7, 181

Haffenden, J., 155
The Ha-Ha (Dawson), 96
Hall, S., 100
Hallucinating Foucault (Duncker), 13, 133, 149–52, 154, 155
hallucinations, 30–1, 32, 40, 42–3, 52, 165, 168, 172–3, 182
hallucinogens, 39, 43–5
Hare, R. D., 55
Harper, S., 7–8
Hayward, R., 86
health humanities, 15, 193–4
Healy, D., 7
Heart of Darkness (Conrad), 118
Heller, J.
  Catch-22, 70
Hemlock and After (Wilson), 135
Henderson, D. J., 73
Hendrix, V., 48
Hershkowitz, D., 7
High Rise (Ballard), 46, 47, 175–6
Hill, S., 130
  The Bird of Night, 13, 133, 143, 149, 151–5, 158
Hinsie, J., 11, 102
Hispanic literature, 12, 121–2
The History Man (Bradbury), 149, 155
history of psychiatry, 62–74
holistic methods of care, 86
Holloway, K. F. G., 124
Holzer, C. E., 55
homoeroticism, 151
hooks, b., 107
Horgan, J., 83
Hountondji, P. J., 119, 120–1
The Hour I First Believed (Lamb), 60
The House of God (Shem), 188
Howitt, D., 12, 118
Human Traces (Faulks), 10, 61, 62–5, 70, 71
hyperreflexivity, 160
hysteria, 56, 69

The ICD-10 Classification of Mental and Behavioural Disorders (WHO), 4, 6–7, 9
I Dreamt I Was a Nymphomaniac: Imagining (Acker), 168, 169
Ignatieff, M.
  Scar Tissue, 59
I Know This Much Is True (Lamb), 59–60, 79, 91–3
illegal drug use, 160, 172
incoherence of madness fictions, 26–8, 165–8
individual reality, 18–19, 28–30
I Never Promised You a Rose Garden (Green), 24
Ingram, A., 8
inner transformations, 32–8
institutions in fiction, *See* power and institutions in fiction
integrative approach to using literature in clinical education, 186
International Health Humanities Conference, 193
intradiegetic narration, 28
Invisible Man (Ellison), 101

Jahner, E. A., 113
Jameson, F., 162–3, 174
Jamison, K. R., 130, 132, 142–3
  An Unquiet Mind: A Memoir of Moods and Madness, 85–6
Jarvis, B.
  Postmodern Cartographies: The Geographical Imagination in Contemporary American Culture, 176
Jaspers, K., 19–20, 27–8, 30, 43
Jenkins, A., 149–50
Johnson, M.
  Diversity in Health and Social Care, 99
Johnson, S., 192
judicial system, 10, 74–8, 92
Jung, C. G., 12, 116, 118
Junky (Burroughs), 44
Juno, A., 46, 175

Kandell, J., 44
Kanneh, K., 119

Katzenbach, J.
  The Madman's Tale, 10, 92
Kean, D., 146–7
Keating, F., 102
Keitel, E., 8
  imitative psychopathography, 24
  literary psychopathography, 24
  pathographies, 25
  psychopathographies, 24–6, 164
  Reading Psychosis, 24–6, 164–5, 167
  theoretical psychopathography, 24
Kermode, F., 156
Kesey, K.
  One Flew Over the Cuckoo's Nest,
    3, 11, 61, 74–8, 81–2,
    97–8, 122
Kingdom Come (Ballard), 46–7, 175
Kleinman, A. M., 103
Koolish, L., 125
Kraepelin, E., 39
Kramer, P. D., 7
Kräupl-Taylor, F., 192–3
Kroll, J., 7

Laing, R. D., 54, 86, 125, 164
  *The Divided Self: An Existential Study
    in Sanity and Madness*, 153–4,
    174–5
Lamb, W.
  The Hour I First Believed, 60
  I Know This Much Is True, 59–60,
    79, 91–3
Lane, C., 7
Lange, R. J. G., 8
Lelliott, P., 180
Lessing, D.
  Briefing for a Descent into Hell, 9, 25,
    28, 32–5, 37
  The Golden Notebook, 13, 24, 132,
    133–5, 141
Lewis, G., 10, 11–12, 56, 102
Lincoln, K., 109
Lincoln, Y. S., 107
Lindauer, M. S., 130
Lipsedge, M., 10, 11–12, 102,
    192–3
literary critics, 13, 133, 149–57, 158
literary madness, *See* madness in
  fiction; madness in literature

literature of duality, 154
Littlewood, R., 10, 11–12, 102
lobotomy, 80–1, 181–2
Lodge, D., 154
  Changing Places, 149
  Consciousness and the Novel, 16
  Small World, 149
Logan, P. M., 8
Lorch, M., 7–8
Lotringer, S., 166, 170, 171
Louis-Courvoisier, M., 186
Love in the Asylum (Carey), 6, 85–6,
    97, 143
loving small, 124
Lupack, B. T., 1–2, 29, 50, 61, 74,
    81–2
Lyotard, J.-F.
  *The Postmodern Condition: A Report
    on Knowledge*, 161–2

Macdonald, J. M., 55
Mackenzie, H.
  Man of Feeling, 83
MacLennan, G., 7
Macnaughton, J.
  *Madness and Creativity in Literature
    and Culture*, 130, 132
mad doctors, 64–5, 180–2
mad genius, 13, 131–2
The Madman's Tale (Katzenbach),
    10, 92
madness
  content of, 9, 30–9
  lay perspective of, 22
  literary, *See* madness in fiction;
    madness in literature
  medical, 22–3
  sociopolitical, 29
  of writing, *See furor scribendi*
*Madness and Creativity in Literature
  and Culture* (Saunders and
  Macnaughton), 130, 132
Madness and Literature Network
  (MLN), 193
*Madness and Modernism: Insanity in the
  Light of Modern Art, Literature, and
  Thought* (Sass), 160
*Madness Explained: Psychosis and
  Human Nature* (Bentall), 21–2

madness in fiction
  as absolute terror, 39–43
  antisocial personality disorder
    (ASPD), 55, 56
  'bad' representations in, 193
  celebratory, 22, 39, 43–8
  coherence of madness fictions, 15,
    26–8
  continuum model of, 21–3, 39–52
  drug-induced, 42–6
  experimental cures for, 82–6
  feigning, 70, 74–8
  functions of, 5–6
  gender and, 11, 15, 57, 70–3,
    93–6, 182
  'good' representations in, 193
  incoherence of madness fictions,
    26–8, 165–8
  individual reality, 18–19, 28–30
  power over judicial system, 74–8
  as preferable alternative to reality,
    47–9, 52, 82–3
  science fiction and, 49–52,
    121–5, 179
  thematising, 39–52
  See also clinical education and
    literature; creativity and madness
    in fiction; diversity, ethnicity and
    madness in fiction; mental states;
    postmodern madness
madness in literature, 19–28
Madness in Literature (Feder), 7, 20–1,
  32–3, 39
madness of writing, *See furor
  scribendi*
mad *vs.* bad in fiction, 52–9
*The Making of a Counter Culture:
  Reflections on the Technocratic
  Society and Its Youthful Opposition*
  (Roszak), 154
male rape, 79
male violence against women,
  119–20
Manchild in the Promised Land
  (Brown), 101
Maniacs in the Fourth Dimension
  (Trout), 51–2
Man of Feeling (Mackenzie), 83
Martin, M., 8

masculine expectations of women,
  93–6
Maupin, R. L., *See* Slim, I.
McCarron, K., 155–7
McCarthy, P., 8
McEwan, I., 4
  Enduring Love, 10, 92, 150
McGee, P.
  *Diversity in Health and Social
    Care*, 99
McGhie, A., 130
McGovern, D., 11, 102
McGrath, P., 10
  Asylum, 26
  on authors' responsibility for
    educating about mental
    illness, 193
  Spider, 9, 26, 28, 29–30, 40, 43,
    52, 87
  Trauma, 26, 184, 189–90
Mead, M., 102–3
medical madness, 22–3
medication, 12, 82–9, 143, 157
melancholia, 71
  See also depression
Melley, T., 32, 165, 176
menarche, 73
Menicucci, G. M., 180
menstruation, 73
mental illness, *See topics related to
  madness*
mental states, 18–60
  impact of madness on others,
    59–60
  madness in literature, 19–28
  mad *vs.* bad in fiction, 52–9
  symptomatology, 28–39
  thematising madness, 39–52
Menya, D., 120
Metzger, C. R., 8
Micale, M., 62
Millennium People (Ballard), 47, 175
Miller, K., 154
mimesis (showing)/mimetic texts,
  27–8
MLN (Madness and Literature
  Network), 193
Mohanty, C. T., 119–20
Montsho, Q., 11, 102

Moore Campbell, B.
 72 Hour Hold, 11, 12, 60, 61, 87–8,
  91, 103–7
Morgan, A., 19–20
Morrison, T., 99
 Beloved, 12–13, 121, 122–5, 128–9
 Song of Solomon, 124
 'Unspeakable Things
  Unspoken', 129
Mosher, L. R., 48
Motion, A., 139
Motz, A., 57
Mount Misery (Shem), 188
mutism, 39, 68–9, 75–8, 191

Naked Lunch (Burroughs), 44–5,
 166–8, 172–3, 179–80
National Institute for Mental Health
 in England, 9–10
Native American literature, 109–14
Native Son (Wright), 101, 126, 127
negative symptoms of psychosis, 165
neologisms, 165
neurodegenerative loss, 128
neurosis, 27, 52, 68–70
*Newsletter of Transcultural Research
 in Mental Health Problems*
 (Wittkower), 102–3
The New York Trilogy (Auster), 165,
 170, 174–5, 176
98 Reasons for Being (Dudman), 70–1,
 84–5, 190–1
Notes from an Exhibition (Gale), 13,
 132, 142–6, 157
Nothing Purple, Nothing Black
 (Crawford), 9, 40–1, 43, 52, 87
Nova Express (Burroughs), 166, 167–8,
 172–3
nymphomania, 70–2

Oandasan, W., 112
O'Connor, J., 8
O'Donnell, P., 32, 159, 165, 176
One Flew Over the Cuckoo's Nest
 (Kesey), 3, 11, 61, 74–8, 81–2,
 97–8, 122
O'Reilly, T., 130
Orlando, V., 8
Otero, A., 130

otherness, 21, 53
The Other Side of You (Vickers), 189–91
Owens, L., 113
Owusu-Bempah, J., 12, 118
Oyebode, F., 8, 16, 19, 26–7, 30, 31–2,
 186, 187
Oyewumi, O., 119

The Paper Men (Golding), 13, 133, 149,
 153–8
paranoia, 32, 36–42, 56, 159, 165,
 176–83
paranormal, 121–5
Parker, I., 163
patriarchal expectations of women,
 93–6
*Peau Noir, Masques Blancs (Black Skin,
 White Masks)* (Fanon), 100
Perkins Gilman, C.
 The Yellow Wallpaper, 97
personal rather than institutional
 history of psychiatry, 71–4
pharmaceuticals, *See* medication
physical violence, 78–9
Pickering, G., 130
Piercy, Marge
 Woman on the Edge of Time, 9,
  12–13, 28, 47–9, 52, 74, 78–9,
  82–4, 91, 96, 121–2, 128
Pimp: The Story of My Life (Slim), 101
Plath, S., 130
 The Bell Jar, 13, 85, 96, 132,
  139–41, 157
Platizky, R., 8
plurisignant, 124
Politics (Acker), 170–1
Pope, R., 131
Poppy Shakespeare (Allan), 11, 13,
 88–91, 97–8, 132, 142, 148–9, 157
Porter, R., 7, 62, 83
Possessing the Secret of Joy (Walker), 12,
 108–9, 114–21
post-colonial literature, 107–9, 114–21
*Postmodern Cartographies: The
 Geographical Imagination in
 Contemporary American Culture*
 (Jarvis), 176
*The Postmodern Condition: A Report on
 Knowledge* (Lyotard), 161–2

postmodernism, 2, 14–15, 133, 160–1
postmodern madness, 14–15, 159–83
   defined and located, 160–5
   paranoia and, 176–83
   psychotic texts, 4–5, 27–8, 165–8
   selfhood and subjectivity, 168–76
postmodern perspective of
   madness, 22
postpsychiatry, 164
post-traumatic stress disorder, 12, 60,
   68–70, 109–14, 125
power and institutions in fiction,
   9–10, 16, 61–98
   as agency of social control, 9–10,
      62–74, 179–82
   closure of asylums, 86–90
   history of psychiatry, 62–74
   multiple power systems, 90–6
   psychiatric abuses of power, 78–86
   total institutions, 74–8
Pratt, W., 8
pregnancy, 73
Prestonia Amazonica (Yage), 43–4
prokalectic therapy, 192–3
protest novels, 12, 121
Prozac, 7
psychiatric abuses of power, 78–86
psychiatrists
   abusive, 78–86
   alienated, 188–94
   alliance of, 102–3
   burnout of, 192
   as characters, 46–7, 52, 68–72,
      84–6, 105
   clinical education through
      literature and, 184, 187
   disdain for, 53–4, 55–6
   in postmodern fiction, 180–93
   symptomatology and, 30
   unreliable narrators and, 23, 28,
      29–30
   as writers, 27
psychiatry
   as agency of social control, 9–10,
      62–74, 179–82
   bias towards ethnic minorities in,
      101–2
   Burroughs and, 45–6
   goals of, 39

history of, 62–74
media and, 52–3, 92
positive developments in, 93
postmodernism and, 160, 162–4
satire on, 45, 55–6
symptomatology and, 28–39
transcultural, 102–3
psychology, 19–21, 45, 52, 64, 164
psychopathology, 21, 26–7
See also madness in fiction
psychosis, 21–2, 24–35, 42–7, 52–3,
   93, 95–6, 164–8, 170–3
psychosurgery, 80–4, 181–2
psychotic texts, 4–5, 27–8, 165–8
Pynchon, T., 6, 14, 160
   The Crying of Lot 49, 6, 172, 176–8,
      180–1

Quayson, A., 107
The Quickening Maze (Foulds), 13, 132,
   137–9, 141, 157
Quirk, A., 180

race, *See* diversity, ethnicity and
   madness in fiction
Racine, L., 107
Rack, P., 11–12, 102
rage for writing, *See furor scribendi*
Ramsay, R., 86–7
rape, 78–9
Read, J., 3, 9, 19, 31, 43, 185
Reading Psychosis (Keitel), 24–5,
   164–5, 167
Reed, P. B., 7–8
Regeneration (Barker), 10, 61, 68–70
Reid, G. J., 8
Remember Me (Bragg), 13, 132–3, 142,
   146–8, 157–8
resettlement in community, 86–90
respectful psychiatric care, 84–6
Revell, G., 47, 175
Ricciardi, M.
   African Saga, 118
Rice, N. M., 113
Richards, R., 130
Rider Haggard, H., 118
Rieger, B. M., 1, 7, 20–3
Riven Rock (Boyle), 10, 61, 65–8,
   71, 131

Rohrer, G., 8
Roszak, T.
    *The Making of a Counter Culture:
    Reflections on the Technocratic
    Society and Its Youthful Opposition,*
    154
Roth, M., 7
Rothenberg, A., 131
Rothman, D., 62
Royal College of Psychiatrists, 142,
    188, 192–3
Rubens, B.
    The Elected Member, 41–3

Sacks, O., 130
sadness, *See* neurosis
Said, E., 107
Salkeld, D., 7–8
Sashidharan, S. P., 10, 11–12, 102
Sass, L. A., 8
    *Madness and Modernism: Insanity in
    the Light of Modern Art, Literature,
    and Thought,* 160
Saunders, C.
    *Madness and Creativity in Literature
    and Culture,* 130, 132
Sayer, P.
    The Comforts of Madness, 11,
    28, 32–3, 35–8, 39, 61,
    79–80, 131
A Scanner Darkly (Dick), 160, 173–4,
    178–9
Scar Tissue (Ignatieff), 59
Schernhammer, E., 189
Schildkraut, J. J., 130
schizophrenia, 3–4, 43–4, 59, 65–7,
    153–4, 160–3, 169–70, 174–5
Schizophrenia: The Positive Perspective
    (Chadwick), 4, 31, 50
schizophrenic vertigo, 14, 163, 171
Schultes, R. E., 44
science fiction, 49–52, 121–5, 179
Scull, A., 62, 86
The Secret Scripture (Barry), 10, 61,
    71–4, 77, 78–9, 84–5, 86, 93,
    190–1
Selesnick, S. T., 62
Self, W.
    Dr Mukti and Other Tales of Woe, 180

self-harm, 56–8, 87–8, 92–3, 117,
    140–1
selfhood and subjectivity, 168–76
Senaha, E., 8
72 Hour Hold (Moore Campbell), 11,
    12, 60, 61, 87–8, 91, 103–7
sexology, 65
Sexton, A., 140, 142
sexuality, 70–3, 93
shame, 72, 147–8, 188
shell shock, 68–9, 109
    See also post-traumatic stress
    disorder
Shem, S.
    The House of God, 188
    Mount Misery, 188
Shepherd, B., 69
Shorter, E., 62
Showalter, E., 8, 15, 56, 69, 73
showing (mimesis), 27–8
Silko, L. M.
    Ceremony, 12, 108–14, 120–1
Simpson, P., 8
Sims, A., 32
Slaughterhouse-Five (Vonnegut), 6, 9,
    49–52
slavery, 12, 122–5
Slim, I. (R. L. Maupin)
    Pimp: The Story of My Life, 101
Small, H., 8
Small World (Lodge), 149
Smith, I., 131
Smith, J., 119
societal expectations of women,
    93–6
sociopolitical madness, 29
The Soft Machine (Burroughs), 166,
    167–8, 172–3
*So Little Done: The Testament of a Serial
    Killer* (Dalrymple), 9, 53–6, 59
Song of Solomon (Morrison), 124
Spider (McGrath), 9, 26, 28, 29–30, 40,
    43, 52, 87
Spivak, G. C.
    'Can the Subaltern Speak?', 108
Stanley and the Women (Amis),
    59, 184
St Clair, J., 180
Stempsey, W. E., 16, 186

stigma, 53, 63, 91–2, 188
Stockwell, P., 8
Storey, E., 131–2
storytelling/story-creating, 73–4
Styron, W., 130
    Darkness Visible, 140
subalterns, 108, 129
subjectivity and selfhood, 168–76
suicide, 92–3, 140–1, 146–7, 189
Sullivan, P., 86–7
Super-Cannes (Ballard), 47, 175
supernatural perspective of
    madness, 22
supportive psychiatric care, 84–6
symptomatology, 28–39
Szasz, T., 4, 86, 164

Taguba, A. M., 180
talking therapy, 84–6
telling (diegesis), 27, 28
terror, absolute, 39–43
thematising madness, 39–52
Then Again (Diski), 13, 132–3, 135–7
Thiher, A., 7
'thingification', 3
Thomas, P., 164
The Ticket That Exploded (Burroughs),
    166, 167–8, 172–3
Tiffin, H., 107
Timpanaro, S., 6
transcultural psychiatry, 102–3
trauma, 51–2, 72–3, 160, 178
    See also post-traumatic stress
    disorder
Trauma (McGrath), 26, 184, 189–90
Trotter, D., 8
Trout, K.
    Maniacs in the Fourth Dimension, 51–2

*An Unquiet Mind: A Memoir of Moods
    and Madness* (Jamison), 85–6
unreliable narrator, 23, 28, 29–30
'Unspeakable Things Unspoken'
    (Morrison), 129
un-understandability, 27–8
urban black experience in US, 101
Ussher, J., 73

Vale, V., 46, 175

Vickers, S.
    The Other Side of You, 189–91
The Virgin Suicides (Eugenides), 93
voluntary insanity, 47
Vonnegut, K., 6
    Slaughterhouse-Five, 6, 9, 49–52
Von Reis, S., 44

Walker, A.
    Possessing the Secret of Joy, 12, 108–9,
    114–21
warfare, 109–14
war neurosis, 68–70
    See also post-traumatic stress
    disorder
Waterfield Duisberg, K., 6
    The Good Patient, 57–9, 93, 189
Waugh, P., 132
welfare system, UK, 91
Welshman, J., 86–7
Wenger, A., 186
White, A.
    Beyond the Glass, 6, 11, 28, 62,
    93–6
White Man Listen! (Wright), 100
WHO (World Health Organisation)
    *Eliminating Female Genital
    Mutilation: An Interagency
    Statement*, 120
    *The ICD-10 Classification of Mental
    and Behavioural Disorders*, 4, 6–7,
    9
Widdowson, P., 149–50
Wiesenthal, C., 8
'William Burroughs's Realism'
    (Acker), 166
Williams, R., 149–50
Wilson, A.
    Hemlock and After, 135
Wilson, C. E., 111
Wilson, T. P., 113
Wittkower, E.
    *Newsletter of Transcultural Research
    in Mental Health Problems*, 102–3
Woman on the Edge of Time (Piercy),
    9, 12–13, 28, 47–9, 52, 74, 78–9,
    82–4, 91, 96, 121–2, 128
women
    expectations of, 93–6

women – *continued*
  genital mutilation and, 109,
    115–21
  madness and, 71–4, 93–6
  male violence against, 119–20
  sexuality and, 70–3, 93
women's movement, 65, 67
World Health Organisation (WHO)
  *Eliminating Female Genital
    Mutilation: An Interagency
    Statement*, 120
  *The ICD-10 Classification of Mental
    and Behavioural Disorders*, 4, 6–7, 9

The Wretched of the Earth (*Les Damnés
    de la Terre*) (Fanon), 100
Wright, D., 71, 86
Wright, R., 121
  Native Son, 101, 126, 127
  White Man Listen!, 100

Yage (*Prestonia Amazonica*), 43–4
The Yage Letters (Burroughs), 43–4
The Yellow Wallpaper (Perkins
    Gilman), 97

Zola, I. K., 9